Never Forget the Bridge that Crossed You Over

Never Forget the Bridge that Crossed You Over

Adriene Pickett

Copyright © 2002 by Adriene Pickett

Library of Congress Number:		2002095617
ISBN :	Hardcover	1-4010-8103-7
	Softcover	1-4010-8102-9

All rights reserved. No part of this book may be reproduced or transmitted in any form or by any means, electronic or mechanical, including photocopying, recording, or by any information storage and retrieval system, without permission in writing from the copyright owner.

This is a work of fiction. Names, characters, places and incidents either are the product of the author's imagination or are used fictitiously, and any resemblance to any actual persons, living or dead, events, or locales is entirely coincidental.

This book was printed in the United States of America.

To order additional copies of this book, contact:
Xlibris Corporation
1-888-795-4274
www.Xlibris.com
Orders@Xlibris.com
16966-PICK

ACKNOWLEDGEMENTS

I give endless thanks to my mother, Addie Marie Pickett, brother, Darryl, and sisters, Terri and Cheryl for their love, encouragement and support.

I want to thank my dear friends Shirley Martinez, Kecia Carkhum and Naa-Momo Ashie. You have been extremely encouraging and supportive.

I'd like to thank my cousin Willis James Brown. Your kindness and guidance have helped me tremendously over the years.

A special thanks to Richard Quatrone, my creative writing teacher at Passaic High School. It was your poetry class that put me on this writing path.

A big thanks goes to my editor Karl Monger. Thanks for your keen eye and candid suggestions.

The spirit of this story belongs to my grandparents, parents, aunts, uncles, cousins and siblings. Love you all.

In loving memory of my father,
Jerry D. Pickett

PART ONE

CHAPTER 1

Three of the Walker sisters were abducted at the end of summer in 1964.

The air was still hot and sticky. Fourteen-year-old Solomon spent most of his time at Lake Hope ogling the water hyacinths and occasionally diving into the lukewarm water. Swimming was the surest relief from the brutal heat.

It was a typical scorching August afternoon in Mission, Georgia when Ivory Walker returned home from the hospital and ordered her eldest child, Solomon, to go get his three younger sisters. "Bring them back home," she said, "and don't forget to stop by Mr. Cloverfield's store to get them a slice of watermelon."

Solomon smiled and shook his head. His baby sisters loved the sweet goodness of watermelon, made all the better by a dash of salt. He never disappointed his mother or his sisters.

After leaping off the porch and starting on his way, Solomon didn't mind the sun beating down on his back, and the moist air that soaked his shirt, and even the tight shoes that caused his feet to ache, all because his sisters were coming home. It had been more than two months since he last saw them, and that was way too long for him.

More than two months ago, his mother was diagnosed with breast cancer. Solomon's schoolteacher, Miss Smith suggested that his four-year-old sisters, Magnolia, Hyacinth, and Rose be placed in the care of her friends until Ivory recuperated.

* * *

On the side of the dirt road stood a large maple tree that blocked the view of the other homes. For years it had served as a resting place and a source of shade for Solomon and his siblings.

Solomon jumped and snatched a leaf from the tree. He slid his fingers across it and pressed it flat. Then he brought the leaf to his nose. The scent was fresh, the way it was supposed to be—nice and simple. Instead of discarding the leaf he decided to keep it in his pocket for good luck.

Before continuing, he glanced back at his house and smiled. Everything was normal—from his mother's fastidious garden to the meandering peach tree in the backyard and the ragged outhouse to one side. Everything would be complete now that his baby sisters were coming home.

The house itself was a shotgun shack, tucked back in the woods. Made of wood, it was held up by large concrete cinder blocks at each corner. The shutters banged raucously against the outer sides on windy days. The slanted front door squeaked—a sound that over time became accepted by the Walker family as a normal part of things.

On the walls hung a few paintings. Ivory tried to make her home attractive with what little she earned working two jobs as a housekeeper for the Cloverfields and a seamstress at Ethel's Tailor Shop.

Solomon's father had made the wobbling kitchen table when Solomon was a child. According to Ivory it wobbled even then. She maintained her late husband deliberately made it that way. He knew she would argue with him over it. The fact was, he loved to watch her fuss.

The house was wired for electricity right before his father died. The children enjoyed doing homework and helping their mother with chores at night after the quality of light had improved and kerosene lamps became a thing of the past.

Ivory brought home useless items the Cloverfield family had thrown away. There were always fresh bouquets of flowers from Ivory's garden throughout the house. The lingering floral scent of their home made up for the things it lacked.

Ivory's true passion was the natural world. Aside from her children, gardening was the most important thing in her life. It brought out the best in her. Her conversations were always enlightening, but after gardening they conveyed a sense of calm wisdom. She tended to smile and laugh more, even when her children were defiant. After gardening, she wasn't as critical of the kitchen table. It put her in control. When she gazed at the sun, she saw it as serene, not fiery. And when the clouds gathered above, it no longer meant rainfall; instead it signaled a chance for her to congregate and have personal closeness with her children and friends.

Everything their home possessed brought life to it. From the second-hand furniture to their every thought and physical movement. Everything was infused with meaning.

A painting of a bouquet of flowers hung on the door. His mother's sister had painted it as a wedding gift. The small pink vase held an assortment of beautiful flowers that spilled over the bulbous container. White daisies with yellow disks, common sunflowers, heart-formed violets of a lovely blue, and trumpet-shaped wild potato vines beautified the ordinary vase.

Solomon appreciated the time his Aunt Ruby had taken. She had thickened the paint of the flower heads, making them radiant. The colors were so well blended they looked animated. Solomon felt certain she had intentionally broken off a flower from its stem and placed it on the bottom of the painting, where it lay next to the vase, enhancing its realism. Aunt Ruby's message seemed to be that no matter how beautiful life may seem all things will ultimately wither.

His mother hung the painting in its place before Solomon was born. She said it was real pretty years ago. Solomon Senior said it was meant to be there. The brilliant colors were warm and made him happy. They reminded him of glory. He was happy with who he was and what he had. And that is why he left it up, even after the cheerful colors had faded. It was a welcoming symbol. And the Walker family certainly had their share of visitors.

* * *

Hard times set in after his father died in 1959. Because Solomon Senior had been the breadwinner and sole provider they all had to pitch in and work. Luxuries became a thing of the past; a piece of fat back was fundamental to their survival.

There were two small rooms and a small kitchen. Amazingly, Solomon's entire family managed to live in it. Ivory and the children shared one room. At one time, the second room was the children's bedroom and play area, but when Ivory's boyfriend and the father of his three younger sisters, Bill, moved in, it was strictly used for his junk and belongings.

Solomon Senior wasn't even in the ground when William Chicago Wright appeared in the Walkers' lives. Bill, as most people called him, had been waiting for someone like Ivory his entire life—someone who would take care of him. He counted the days and finally met the lonely woman who fell in love with him and showered him with love and affection—the very things Ivory needed most.

Solomon was convinced Bill had his eye on his mother for quite some time. During the funeral service, Miss Parker, an elderly woman who was a beloved family friend and was like a grandmother to Solomon and his siblings, began consoling him, rubbing his back and fanning his face with an accordion-shaped paper fan. When Solomon turned around to see the young child kicking the back of his chair, he caught his first glimpse of Bill.

Uninvited, Bill sat in the back of the room unconcerned with the sad faces and painful cries. He was calm, a bit too calm for Solomon's taste. It was clear something was wrong with him. His pokerfaced expression never changed during the entire funeral service. Looking at him sent an eerie chill down Solomon's spine.

When Solomon glanced at him again, Bill shook his head and acknowledged him. Bill smiled, showing every last crooked tooth in his mouth. He gave the impression he was doing a good deed just by being there, but Solomon knew the happy face was as phony as the skin-tight brown suit and shimmering yellow tie. The sight of him disgusted Solomon.

Solomon was baffled as to why this strange man who was of no relation was sitting on the family side. Bill stood out like a green tomato with his high yellow skin tone, cinnamon hair, and unsightly freckles. His eyes were sinful green. He was short and thin and had the frame of a young boy. He was a sight for sore eyes.

From that day on, Bill carefully observed Ivory, studying her behavior and her speech, even correcting her when he felt it was appropriate. He befriended her family, acquaintances, and friends and made a special effort to analyze Solomon, who was her right hand and now the man of the house. If he could manage Solomon, he'd be a shoe-in. Life for Bill would be a piece of cake.

Bill followed Ivory to the market and to work, and sent her flowers and cheap gifts. He gave all the classic signs of being in love with her. She needed a companion and he came into her life at the perfect time.

One afternoon following church service, Bill walked over to Ivory. He rubbed his nose before speaking. "Hello, Ivory. How are you this afternoon?"

Goose bumps spread on her arms. She was a zealous admirer. "Just fine, Bill. And yourself?" she said, massaging her arms.

"I'm feeling good," he said. His tongue slowly slid across his lips. "Reverend Dean gave a good sermon today."

Ivory smiled.

"He impressed me a great deal," said Bill. "I think I will join the church."

Ivory looked up at him cross-eyed, as if she didn't understand the word "impressed."

"It's been a long time since I've been in church," he said. "But after hearing Reverend Dean's oration—" He raised his eyebrows and took in a deep breath. "He encouraged me this morning. His words just took me off my seat. I couldn't stay still."

"Yeah, he do that all the time," Ivory said in her typical unschooled manner. "I really like him too."

She stared at Bill's freckles and smiled. "The congregation is like family. They real good to everybody."

Bill grinned. "Yes, I can see that. They're quite a family unit."

Solomon stopped attending church soon thereafter because it was too painful watching Bill seduce his mother. Bill hounded her, grinning with his stained teeth. The word around town was that Solomon Senior was a hard workingman and had some money stashed away at home. But the story was farfetched.

Solomon felt betrayed. How could his mother be with another man? How could she let someone like Bill inside their home? Then one day, Miss Parker explained things to him. She said, spitting snuff into a tin can, "Solomin, yo mama is like any person out there. She human and she need a friend too." She raised her eyebrows. "If you know what I mean."

She grabbed Solomon's hand. He pursed his lips. Her words only enraged him more. "Besides, you chil'rens need a man around the house."

Solomon started to say something but she quickly interrupted. "You chil'rens need a daddy. That's what I mean, Solomin. You all will have a daddy now!"

It took some time, but Miss Parker finally convinced Solomon to see things as she saw them. Her words of wisdom were always soothing. He walked into her home feeling betrayed and left with a complete understanding of his mother's emotions. He would soon have to reconcile his feelings in order to put up with Bill's presence.

Miss Parker pushed the old can aside, her eyebrows rising emphatically again as she stared at him from an angle. She wiped away some snuff from her face with her apron. "I know he ain't nothin' like Senior, but he can be a good person if you give him a chance." She pointed her finger at him. "He's gonna take good care of you chil'rens. You wait and see."

With that, Ivory let herself fall in love again. There was a humorous side to Bill that reminded her of her late husband. He had a rare way of brightening both her laugh and her smile.

There was also a dark side to Bill that was nothing like Solomon Senior. Bill loved to be around white folks—the kind that allowed black folks in their lives momentarily; either because black folks cooked for them, cleaned for them, took care of their children, or were plain subservient to them.

Bill was uncomfortable being around most black folks, who he considered largely ignorant people. He believed white people respected him and treated him more like their own because his skin was extremely light—nearly white but not quite.

He once told Ivory that his grandfather was white, as if that had any impact on his racial background. Any fool knew that white folks believed only one thing: if a person had even one drop of black blood in him, he was black. His bragging did not impress Ivory or Solomon.

Bill rarely worked to provide for the family. Yet Ivory continued to love and protect him. She learned to live comfortably with what she had because she believed she would never find anyone like her late husband again.

The only decent quality Bill possessed was that he was kind to the children. He never beat them, but that didn't stop Solomon from disliking him. His mother deserved to be treated like a queen—the way his father had treated her.

Bill was in heaven living in the house. He had a roof over his head, food in his stomach, and a woman who catered to his every need.

* * *

Space had grown scarce when Solomon's three younger sisters were born. Yet Bill wouldn't allow his mother to clean the second room and make additional space for the growing family. "Bill's junk," as Solomon often referred to it, was his prized possession. No one could disturb it. His belongings were too precious to be in the same room with Ivory's furniture and personal things. His junk needed to be segregated in its own storage room. This was Bill's view anyway.

Neither Bill nor Ivory ever knew it, but Solomon and his friends Jefferson and Augustus Booker, who were twins, had gone through Bill's things one afternoon. What they found had surprised them. Inside one of the large trunks were nude photographs of white women in explicit poses—caressing their genitalia, and several pieces of gold jewelry, such as a watch without a wristband, and a massive ring that Bill had gotten from an ex-girlfriend. There was an inscription on the inner circle that read, *Happy Birthday Bill—Love, Mary Anne.*

Bill could have pawned the jewelry or sold it for food when Solomon's family had needed it.

There were historical books about World War I and II. There were old photographs of Bill's family that featured graceful handwritten notes describing his family members by names and the places they had visited.

And there were the love letters—from a woman named Agnes Hartley who he loved and wanted to marry. One of the letters revealed how Agnes' father found out about their relationship and along with a group of rednecks, tried to hunt Bill down. Bill fled Atlanta and ended up in Mission.

* * *

So two adults and six children found a way to live in a single room. Ivory put up a partition of stained, lime-colored curtains that separated the children's area from the adults.

It was cramped space. Most times, Solomon and his nine-year-old brother, Nathaniel slept on the floor while his twelve-year-old sister, Lily shared a bed with the girls.

Solomon and his siblings often played outside because of the limited indoor space. They enjoyed playing with their neighbors—the Booker family on the left side of their house and the Jamison family on the right. All three houses were old and tattered—probably built at the same time.

The Jamison's had eleven children and lived, commonly enough, in a pint-size house. Most families were sharecroppers who earned very little and couldn't afford spacious living quarters.

Although the Booker family didn't have any children, Mr. and Mrs. Booker were raising their twin nephews, who were Solomon's age. Mrs. Booker's sister abandoned them when they were infants.

Life was rough. They were three families struggling to get through each day and holding on to each other for support. Each other was all they had.

Solomon's family had been more fortunate, especially when his father was alive. He was a good man. He was good to his many friends, never disappointed anyone, and folks trusted him. He would give the shirt off his back to someone who needed it. So they always had friends who looked after them and helped them through demanding times.

Ivory and her late husband made a habit of sharing their food with neighbors and friends even when money was tight. On a day Solomon had earned fifty cents for picking cotton and was chewing over whether or not to share it, his father told him, "If you're good to your friends, Junior, one day they will be good to you. Especially, when you're in need."

Whenever the Walkers received they in turn would give. That was their master plan, their purpose in life. After reading an article in the newspaper about the treatment of some black teenagers at a convenience store in Mississippi, Solomon Senior angrily held up the paper, glanced at Solomon wide-eyed, and said, "Kindness never hurt anyone, Junior."

It certainly never hurt his parents.

The Jamison family handled more than its fair share of misfortune. When Ivory made scrumptious biscuits on Sundays, her family ate them with fruit preserves or syrup. The Jamisons weren't nearly so lucky. They ate their biscuits with lard. Ivory gave them jars of preserves and syrup whenever possible.

The act of sharing formed the backbone of the Walker family, although Miss Parker took exception. "That's why you don't have nothin'," she said to Ivory one Sunday afternoon. "Cause you give it all away!"

It was also difficult for Mr. Jamison to keep a job. He wasn't lazy like Bill, and there was no doubt that he was a hardworking man, but it was liquor that held him back.

White folks didn't tolerate black folks arriving to work intoxicated and disobedient. At his worst, he was an abusive alcoholic who beat his wife and children.

Often—usually on payday—he frittered his money on gambling and blamed it on Mrs. Jamison. One day at work, his boss questioned him about a machine that was inoperable. Mr. Jamison pursed his lips, slammed his hand against the countertop, and harshly cursed his boss. "Hell if I know!" he shouted. "You the boss! You should know what's wrong with yo machines!"

Solomon Senior did his best to give him advice, but Mr. Jamison's mind was already set. Pig-headedness controlled him and liquor consumed him, wearing down his better self.

Solomon Senior's advice went in one of Mr. Jamison's ear and out the other. Mr. Jamison lost his job that day. He didn't pay attention to Solomon Senior's suggestions and apparently wasn't concerned about his family's well being and future. This unfortunate penchant would lead the Jamison family to hell and back many times.

CHAPTER 2

As Solomon walked on, he saw Fannie Mae sitting in a swing chair on the porch. Fannie Mae was his mother's best friend. She seemed sad and appeared to have been crying.

Solomon stood behind the broken fence holding onto the shabby pole. He said, "Hey, Fannie Mae."

"Hey, Junior," she answered. "Where you going?"

He leaned forward, bending the already collapsed fence, and yelled, "To get my sisters!"

"Um, is that right," she said softly.

"Yeah, Mama wants them home. She's all better now."

Solomon could sense Fannie Mae's uneasiness. "I was going to see Ivory this afternoon but I was waiting for Carter," she said.

Solomon sensed something was wrong. He opened the gate and quickly walked up the steps. "You never waited for Carter before just to see Mama," he said with concern.

"I know, but—" Fannie Mae nervously uttered.

Solomon saw her shivering. He moved close and sat beside her. "Is something wrong, Fannie Mae?" he said.

She didn't respond immediately. She turned her head toward him, stared into his eyes, and swallowed hard. "Junior," she forced herself to say, "Pearl Lee said she was by Miss Smith's house the other day and nobody was there with her."

"What are you saying, Fannie Mae?"

She shrugged and went on, "Pearl Lee said Miss Smith didn't know nothing about the girls. Said they ain't been staying there with her."

"What?" he said disbelievingly. "Are you sure, Fannie Mae?" Fannie Mae whacked the bottom of his leg. "Is my name Fannie Mae and am I your mama's best friend?" she yelled.

Solomon nodded. "Yes, ma'am."

"Then that's what she said to me, Junior!"

Solomon could see her chest shudder when she exhaled.

"I was so scared and nervous—I walked down to Mr. Cloverfield's store and called Carter at work." Her voice trembled as she spoke.

"But . . . maybe . . . Pearl Lee drunk some moonshine today. You know how she is," Solomon said.

Fannie Mae rolled her eyes and waved her hand. "You know Pearl Lee ain't touch none of that stuff since she accidentally shot off her husband's foot."

"Well . . . the Pearl Lee I know . . ."

Fannie Mae interrupted, "And the Pearl Lee I know don't lie. Not even when she drunk. That woman got a good heart."

Solomon lowered his head and scraped his fingernail into the wooden chair.

"You of all people should know that, Junior."

"But what she said doesn't make any sense."

"I know that. That's why I'm waiting for Carter."

Solomon turned away from her and stared at the road in confusion. He knew Fannie Mae would never make up a bogus tale. Something wasn't right and Pearl Lee must have gotten the story wrong.

Fannie Mae began scratching her arms, then her legs. "I can't keep still, Junior. I'm waiting for Carter to go with me down to see Ivory." She shook her head. "Something ain't right, Junior. I can feel it in my bones. Something ain't right at all."

"Well, I can't wait for Carter! I'm going over to Miss Smith's house to see for myself!"

"Naw, you wait for Carter," she insisted.

"Fannie Mae, I can't! I have to go now! They're my sisters!"

Solomon took off running. Fannie Mae got up and ran after him. "Junior, we should wait for Carter!"

Solomon raced by a maple tree. He considered its simplicity and hoped that when he arrived at Miss Smith's home, things would be the same way: familiar and trouble-free.

In fact, the day had started out simply: Solomon should have been at the field engrossed in a rousing game of baseball, or at the movie house with his siblings watching a funny film, or even taking a walk to his favorite resting spot, Lake Hope.

Instead, he and Fannie Mae found themselves in a race to save his three younger sisters from some very evil people.

CHAPTER 3

Nothing could keep Solomon from looking back. He had to get to Miss Smith's house. More than two months earlier he had promised his sisters he would bring them back home, and he was going to make good on his promise.

Solomon ran as fast as he could. He moved swiftly through the backwoods as if time was running out—as though the world were about to end. His chest heaved and his heartbeat quickened with every step. The force of his effort pained him.

Fannie Mae trailed behind, willing herself to speed up. She tried to lift her long legs higher and move quickly, but she didn't have it in her. She kept pace with Solomon but lagged behind, gasping for air. She could have caught up to him or even beaten him had she been ten years younger, but years of working in the fields and carrying heavy loads of cotton had compromised her knees and weakened her legs. She tried to keep up but he was too fast for her. She pleaded for him to slow down but Solomon simply ignored her and made straight for Miss Smith's house.

Fannie Mae was a tall slender woman with short straight hair that was neatly trimmed at the edges. Folks who didn't know her often mistook her for a man because she always wore pants, oversized shirts, and blazers. But once she took off those heavy garments and sported a T-shirt or a form fitting dress that accentuated her voluptuous figure, there could be no doubt as to her sex.

Solomon kept running. He knew the moment Miss Smith suggested that his three sisters be placed into her friend's custody it was a bad idea. He knew it then and he knew it now.

Now, months after the infamous meeting with Miss Smith and his mother, and just barely a hundred feet from her house, a bad feeling spread through him. He was nearing the moment of truth.

Solomon ran. He stumbled over a rock and fell face down. He tried to stand but his unsteady legs weren't ready. He fell again, this time hard. He wanted to reach out to break the fall but his body hit the ground anyway.

He clutched a handful of dirt and moaned in pain. He looked up at the sky and beheld the glare of an ominous sun that seemed to prevent him from going further and discovering the truth.

He lay helpless on the ground struggling to roll over. With his back against the hot earth, he placed his palm on his chest in an attempt to calm down. He took several deeps breaths and slowly exhaled.

Solomon crawled inch by inch, tearing his already scruffy jeans. He pulled his white T-shirt up to his face to wipe off the sweat. He was determined to get to the house.

Slowly raising his head, he caught sight of the house. It was a modest ice-tea-colored home sitting on two acres of land. It wasn't like most of the other homes in the area, which were little more than shacks.

Miss Smith's younger brother had recently built the house. Solomon admired the beautifully decorated white window frames and wraparound porch, so much so that he promised his mother he would build her one just like it. He loved the porch, sometimes sitting in Miss Smith's rocking chair for hours, mesmerized by the swaying pecan trees and brilliantly blue violets.

Solomon turned away from the sizzling sun, determined to look again at the house—the one place that would haunt him for the rest of his life.

Tears trickled down his face. Once the salty wetness grazed his lips, he tried to stand but was unable, paralyzed by fear.

As the dirt sifted between his fingers, his heartbeat picked up again. He suddenly felt sick, as if a thousand knives pierced his flesh, gradually ripping his soul apart. He closed his eyes and prayed. "God, help me. Please."

Suddenly Fannie Mae's shadow fell over him as she reached out her hand. He took hold and she pulled him to his feet. He looked at her firmly and was determined to stand again. "Thank you."

Fannie Mae smiled. "Let's go now."

Soon they headed straight down the short path that led to Miss Smith's home. The distance seemed endless, as if the road were extending as they moved closer.

Miss Smith was standing on the porch—all three hundred and fifty pounds of her—without a care in the world. She must have known they were coming—the devil always knows.

She wore a slight grin as they approached her—Solomon's father called it a crooked grin—but her expression changed and she looked troubled. Solomon and Fannie Mae quickly approached, both of them nervous and hoping that their worst fears had not come true.

Solomon stared solemnly at Miss Smith. His intention was clear and he hoped she'd grasp the seriousness of the situation. She looked startled, feigning the jumpiness and pretending not to notice his sober state. Then her fat hands began to tremble and she spoke slowly. "Solomon, I have some . . ." She hesitated, raising her hand to her mouth and gently coughing. After clearing her throat, she said, " . . . disturbing news to tell you."

Solomon's hands flew up to his chest as if to ward off an emotional blow. He had known better to trust anyone other than family.

"What is it, Miss Smith?" he said. "What's happened to my sisters?"

"The girls are gone, Solomon. They—"

He broke in, shaking his head. "What do you mean they're gone?" Angry and frightened, he spread his legs wide to keep them from shaking. Then he kneeled down and started to breathe heavily.

"Those people I told you about, Solomon, well . . ." she stammered. Her hands fell away from her large hips and went up in the air. "They just upped and took the girls. I don't know where they could be." She lowered her head and turned away from Solomon and Fannie Mae toward the end of the porch wearing a scarcely perceptible grin.

When Miss Smith heard Fannie Mae yell out her name, she glanced up and turned to them. "I practically looked all over Georgia for them, Solomon." She spoke mechanically, as though from a script. "That's why I haven't been to the hospital the past few days to see your mother."

Solomon's face grew hot and his heart raced. He'd expected something to be wrong, but never in his wildest dreams did he expect this. He was distraught, panting and pacing the floor of the porch, inching his way toward Miss Smith. He wanted to hurt her. *How could my sisters have disappeared? Why would her friends do this? This can't be happening.*

He stood in front of Miss Smith and stared at her chubby face, which was wet from perspiration. Their eyes locked, unmoving. She was scared now and breathing heavily.

Fannie Mae observed them both and thought that at any moment Miss Smith was going to collapse from heart failure. The woman always perspired easily, no matter what she was doing.

Miss Smith's face turned pale. She didn't know what Solomon's next move would be—so she eased herself back a few paces. When Fannie Mae saw Solomon curl his fingers into a fist, she jumped between them. "No, Junior!" she screamed.

He closed his eyes trying very hard to hold back the anger and keep his hand at his side. Fannie Mae whispered into his ear, "Junior, getting upset will only make things worst." She moved closer, talking quietly. "And hitting her would be wrong. Your mama and daddy raised you better then that!"

Solomon sucked in the hot air in deep breaths. He knew Fannie Mae was right. He needed to control his temper if he wanted some answers. So he turned toward Miss Smith again and calmly asked,

"Weren't those people friends of yours? Friends you went to school with? Friends you trusted?"

"No," she said, shaking her head. "Oh, no. No no no, Solomon, those were people I had met recently. I told you that. Remember?"

"Naw, Miss Smith. I don't remember you telling me that. You must have left that part out."

He knew she was lying. She had told his mother and him that those people were her good friends, dear friends. Suddenly his fist rose to Miss Smith's cheek and she quickly raised her hands to protect herself. "Don't hit me, Solomon!" she screamed. "Please!"

Fannie Mae shouted, "Junior, don't do it!"

Tears jetted down his face and he shouted, "Miss Smith, you told Mama and me those were your friends! You lied to us! You lied to Mama and you knew she was sick! You knew she would do anything you suggested!"

Miss Smith was speechless. Solomon waited for an answer. When she didn't respond, Solomon, who was two inches taller than her, came close—so close that her perspiration dampened his shirt. He felt her coldness, her wickedness. It sent chills down his spine.

Solomon pointed his finger at her forehead. "You said they would help us out until Mama got well! That's what you said all right!"

Although Miss Smith was very big, she knew full well the implications of Solomon's young strength. She was terrified. Her massive body shook as she stood next to him. "Solomon, you must be mistaken," she said. She glanced down at the cracked floor. "Anyway, we have got to try and find them. I know they're somewhere in Georgia."

"You know they're somewhere in Georgia," Solomon repeated.

Solomon grabbed her hair that she kept neatly twisted in a bun, pulling the bun apart and her face close to his. She was shaking. Miss Smith knew he had every right to hurt her. She carefully grabbed his other hand while Fannie Mae held onto to the one that was grappling with her hair.

As soon as he felt Fannie Mae's hand, he eased his grip on Miss Smith's hair. Then Miss Smith smirked again, apparently thinking she had gotten away with something. As soon as the smile tapered off, Solomon slapped her—hard. "You son of a bitch, Miss Smith! You must think I'm a fool or something. Don't you?"

Sobbing, she patted at her face. She was shocked heart at what he'd done. "You . . . hit me! How could you? I don't know what you're talking about, Solomon."

Solomon reached for her hair again and shouted, "I'll do it again if you don't tell me where my sisters are!"

"I told you: I don't know! Those people took them! Why are you so mad at me! I didn't do anything wrong! They did!"

Fannie Mae pulled Solomon by his shirt, in the process tearing it. As she dragged him away from Miss Smith, his sneakers scratched the wooden floor, leaving skid marks. "Junior, she ain't gonna give us no more information."

Solomon fell to the floor and cried. "But she knows more. I know she does."

Fannie Mae kneeled down next to him. She grabbed his chin, pinching it, and whispered in his ear, "Look at her, Junior. You think she's gonna admit to something like this? Look at her good, Junior. She's a smart lady and she knows better."

Fannie Mae picked him up. "Come on, let's go wait for Carter. Then we can go get Sheriff Thomas."

Solomon clenched his teeth and jumped up. He patted down his clothes, shaking off the dirt. He turned toward Miss Smith, wanting to ask her why. Why did she have to hurt his family? But his lips could not form the words.

Solomon gazed into Miss Smith's eyes and realized that the person he had befriended and trusted had shattered his life.

He turned away from Miss Smith and slowly walked down the steps. She carefully watched his every move—her eyes darting between him and the rope he kicked to one side when Fannie Mae pulled him away from her.

Solomon took his time in an effort to ensure she felt afraid. He wanted her to know that at any moment he could turn around and strangle her with the piece of twine that lay on the porch. He saw the cord too.

He looked up at the pale blue sky and exhaled when he reached the bottom of the steps. He knew his life would never be the same, as surely as he knew this news would destroy his mother, tearing into her soul with its sadness.

When Solomon started to look back again, Fannie Mae said, "No . . . don't. She's the one that has to answer to God one day."

He and Fannie Mae then headed toward the path that would lead them home.

CHAPTER 4

Despite their troubled life, none of the members of this hardworking family could have ever envisioned such a tragedy. The Walkers lived in an imaginary world believing all they needed to survive was each other. Love would keep them together, faith would sustain them, and hope would lead them out of poverty.

They believed God would call forth better days, put more food on the table, and fill their pockets with money. But God hadn't warned them about Miss Smith.

Solomon was six years old when his father told him not to trust anyone but family. His father had offered this advice after Solomon became convinced that his classmate Tate Hawkins had stolen the dollar he earned picking cotton. Solomon was devastated because he had considered Tate his friend.

Solomon sat on the porch steps while his father clipped his hair with a pair of scissors. His glassy eyes looked up at his father, when he tapped his shoulder with the scissors. "Junior, never trust anyone you don't know and always go with your first instinct."

Solomon turned away from him not to avoid the lesson but because he was hurt and gripped by the pain of betrayal.

"Never overestimate anyone because nobody is who you think they are," his father said.

When Solomon didn't respond, his father smacked him with

the back of his hand. "You hear me, boy?"

Solomon simply nodded like the child that he was.

"Never forget the bridge that crossed you over, Junior. Always be there for your family because they are the only ones who'd always have your back."

Solomon considered his father's critical statement as he and Fannie Mae returned home. It was the most difficult walk of his life. He and Fannie Mae remained silent——dead silent—both of them sadly ruminating over what had just transpired. His sisters were gone and no one knew where they were.

How was he going to break the terrible news to his mother and siblings? No adolescent should ever have to experience so much heartache and suffering, but Solomon had seen it all. He was learning first hand what it was like to lose someone you love suddenly and tragically.

He and Fannie Mae decided to leave a note outside her door for Carter, instructing him to come to Ivory's house right away. Solomon couldn't wait any longer; he had to tell his mother at once.

They took the shortcut home—the route leading to the hill. He and the children always took this way home. It was a rough course but quick. When he was a child his father also took this route home, and Solomon always complained about the rigorous walk. "Nothing in life comes to you easy," his father said. "So stop complaining and keep on marching forward."

And that in turn is what Solomon would say to the other children when they fussed over the hike.

He paused when he and Fannie Mae reached the top of the hill, then he took a moment to reflect on his life's purpose. *Why had he been put on this earth? Was it to forever witness pain? Would he ever see better days?*

Fannie Mae turned to him and saw the sadness in his eyes— the same sadness that had nearly ruined his life just five years earlier. "We got to go and tell Ivory, Junior," she said with urgency.

When he did not respond, she squeezed his shoulder. "You aw right?"

Solomon couldn't speak or move. He refused to take another step, paralyzed by the realization that he didn't want to be the bearer of bad news. He remembered what had happened the last time. He knew more bad luck would certainly kill his mother with grief. *Could her heart take another blow? Could she survive another disastrous incident?*

He looked up at Fannie Mae with puffy red eyes. He softly said, "You go on. I'll be there soon."

Fannie Mae started to walk forward when he yelled, "Please, don't tell Mama nothing until I get there!"

She smiled, and went back to him to caress the side of his face. "I'll wait for you, Junior. I promise."

His lips were quivering, "Thank you. I just need some time to myself. Just a little more time, that's all."

Fannie Mae continued down the hillside toward Solomon's house. Lily and Nathaniel suspended their catch ball when they saw her heading down the slope. They watched her slowly trek down the bumpy hill trying not to fall.

"Why she moving so slow?" said Nathaniel.

"I don't know, Nate," Lily responded sharply. She hated when Nathaniel asked simple questions. "What I want to know is, where are Junior and the girls?"

Nathaniel picked up the ball and dribbled it. "Maybe he took them to the store to buy them candy or something."

"Maybe," Lily said as she snatched the ball away from him.

Lily was concerned. Mature for a twelve-year-old, she acted more like an adult, emulating her mother's maternal qualities.

Fannie Mae was all smiles when she reached them. Although she ached with stomach spasms and her legs felt like buckling, she maintained her phony, pain-defying grin.

"Hey, Aunt Fannie Mae," Lily said.

"Hey, babies." She rushed over to them and gave them each a big hug.

"Where's Junior?" Lily and Nathaniel said in unison.

Fannie Mae turned and glanced at the hill. Solomon was nowhere in sight. Suddenly her eyes became glassy and a teardrop rolled down her face as she turned away from the bright sunlight. She quickly wiped her face. "He'll be here soon."

"He'll be here?" Lily said. She was puzzled. Her hands went up in the air. "And what about my sisters?"

When Fannie Mae grabbed her hands Lily could feel her shivering. "You're shaking, Auntie. What's wrong?"

"Nothing," she said.

"You promise it's just nothing?" Lily begged.

"Now, Lily . . . you know I ain't go'n promise you nothing."

Fannie Mae chuckled nervously and said, "Let's just wait for Junior." She tried to change the subject. "Hey, what your Mama got cooking in there?"

"Fried chicken," Nathaniel said giggling. "John Henry and Miles stole two chickens from Mr. Amos' farm and gave one to Mama."

"You bet not ever do nothing like that if you know what's good for you!" Fannie Mae voiced, placing her hands on her hips and shaking her head. "That was wrong. All Mr. Amos done for that family. But since Ivory cooked it . . . good . . . 'cause I'm hungry."

Fannie Mae could always make the children laugh with her refreshing capacity for silliness. Yet Lily merely eyed her mother's best friend with a firm stare. She never gave in to anything and she definitely didn't buy her story. Lily was as headstrong and persistent as a bull.

"That girl knows she got her daddy's ways," Carter had said to Fannie Mae on one occasion. "Nobody can make her budge."

This time, however, Fannie Mae got her way. Perhaps Lily simply couldn't handle any bad news just yet. Perhaps she wanted the fried chicken as much as Fannie Mae did. Or perhaps she was just being respectful and decided not to inquire again—something she had learned from both of her parents.

Lily held onto Fannie Mae's hand, gripping it tightly. They walked inside the house.

CHAPTER 5

As Solomon stood on the hilltop, the weight of panic burdened his shoulders like a mound of bricks. He staggered a few steps, then he tried to collect his thoughts and calm himself down. He took in deep breaths and slowly let them out.

Day turned into night. Solomon had been sitting on the top of the hill for hours. Before Bill, his mother's illness, and his sister's separation, he thought he knew everything. After all, it was his father, his idol, and the bravest man he had ever known who had been his teacher.

His father taught him how to be a man, how to care for his family, and how to survive in a sometimes sinful world. He showed him the difference between right and wrong, good and bad, love and hate, honesty and deceit.

Solomon sat on the bluff and recalled something his mother told him. He remembered the story about his grandmother and how she could foretell the future. Folks in their part of town claimed people like her had a second sight. Solomon thought it silly to think about folks who could foretell the future. Why should he believe in foretelling when he'd never witnessed it for himself? All he seemed to know was hard times.

Everyone went to Mamie Youngblood for answers, including Clare Lennox—a young newlywed who had bore a child by another man.

"Keep dat baby way from yo husband. If you know what's good for ya," Mamie said after rolling a tobacco leaf and stuffing it in her pipe. After taking a few puffs, she pulled the pipe out of her mouth and sucked in her jaws.

Clare's eyes were swollen and red. "Why, Miss Mamie?"

"Why you come here fo?" Mamie asked with a stern look. "You know dat man is evil. Like a snake he is."

"A snake," Clare spit out.

"Yes, like a snake, I tell you. He'a watch you and when you make the wrong move, turn the wrong way, he gonna dig his teeth in you."

"But where am I gonna go, Miss Mamie? Where can I take my baby?" Clare whispered, holding the light-skinned, blue-eyed baby in her arms.

"Far away from here. You hear me? Far away."

Clare caught the first train out of Mission that afternoon. Her husband Jimmy was run out of Ed's Tavern later that day because he had consumed too much liquor. He was drunk as a skunk and out of money.

Jimmy was fuming with disgust when he left the bar and headed for his car. He got in and sprung back on the seat. When he slammed the door and reached down to start the car, he realized he had lost the keys somewhere between the bar and his car. So he spun around and grabbed his shotgun from the back seat. He stepped out of the car, kicked the door shut, and staggered a few feet. He coughed up saliva and spewed it out on the ground. He took a deep breath and slowly moved forward.

He was going home to set his wife straight and fix the problem. Everyone in town had been telling him "that his wife was making a fool of him and that no man in his right mind would let it go on."

Jimmy headed home mumbling and cursing the entire way. "I'm gonna kill 'em both," he said. "She gonna pay for making me look like a jackass."

Jimmy was a housekeeper at the Virgoan Heights Hotel on

the Adriatic peninsula. Well-to-do white folks went there to eat dinner, but mainly they went to let loose at the Zodiac ballroom.

Jimmy was dressed in his uniform—brown trousers and a brown shirt. The shirt bore a beige inscription of his first name and the name of the hotel.

When he got home he kicked opened the door and stormed in the house. But once inside he moved covertly as a burglar. He swung his head from side to side looking for them and held his rifle with his finger on the trigger. He was ready to kill.

Suddenly Jimmy saw something move in the back room. "Come out, bitch," he yelled. "I know you in there."

Then something sped by him and he sprayed his rifle at random, firing shots into the back room. Jimmy ran inside the room and stopped dead in his tracks. Lying on the floor in a pool of blood and squealing in pain was his black German Shepherd.

Mamie Youngblood was always right. She knew when the sun would come out, and when it would rain, hail, or sleet. She knew who would die and who would live in any given year. She knew if you were sick or in good health. She knew whether you were lying or not. She could foresee it all.

But even after the stories he'd heard about his grandmother and after that day at the market five months earlier, when he'd met a strange old man, Solomon still wouldn't have believed anyone if they had told him what would soon take place in his life.

The old man explained something to him that he would never forget. At first Solomon didn't notice the old man as he stood talking to his schoolmate, Emma Joe Jenkins. But when her bag fell to the ground, Solomon rushed to pick it up, and that's when he saw the well-polished leather shoes. Solomon had never seen a black man wearing a brand new pair of shoes before.

When he slowly looked up, the old man winked at him. Solomon thought he was a sissy. His Uncle Eugene had warned him about men like that. The old man smiled, showing off his healthy-looking pearly white teeth. He quickly walked over toward Solomon and Emma Joe.

They carefully watched him, checking him out from head to

toe. He was dressed in a freshly cleaned and pressed blue striped suit. Emma Joe's eyes widened as this man, who smelled as if he wore a woman's fragrance, came close to Solomon and grabbed his hand. Solomon jerked his hand away and tucked it in his pocket. But the old man was persistent and tugged at his arm.

Then he leaned over and whispered in Solomon's ear. "A real man never fears the night because it is the night that gives him strength. It is the night that provides freedom."

Emma Joe snatched her bag from Solomon, said good-bye, and walked away, wanting nothing to do with their goings-on.

Solomon thoroughly looked the old man over again. The aged eyes glared at him in a strange yet inviting way—as if they were moving him.

At five-six, the old man had a neatly trimmed goatee and long, straight silver hair. He had a thin, feminine face and walked with his head high and a wide smile beaming pride. The old man motioned his hands in the manner of young girls, casually waving them in the air. Then he awkwardly moved his slender body close to Solomon. His breath smelled of liquor.

Solomon backed away, not out of fear, but because he heard his mother call his name. She was ready to head home. When he turned his head toward her, the old man—who greeted folks with a simple *Good evening* and who boasted that he was once a professor at the Tuskegee Institute—grabbed Solomon's arm firmly. He wanted Solomon's attention.

"Don't worry about me, son," he said, giggling. "I'm not drunk." Then he came close and shook his head. He tried very hard to sound serious. "I won't hurt you."

The old man winked, reassuring Solomon that he was indeed sober. Solomon thought otherwise but was too startled to react. He continued to look down at the old man's small hand and the tight grip it had on him. He prayed he would let go, but the old man simply stared him in the eye again and said in a soft, low tone, "Son, the night can never singe the flesh of a familial bond. The cord can only be destroyed under the sun."

"Flesh . . . cord . . . sun . . ." Solomon mumbled. *What is this man talking about?*

Solomon smiled—it was a nervous smile—as he tried to comprehend the old man's words. He wanted to know why the old man was holding him with such force and priding himself on the information he just shared.

Still the old man studied Solomon with a straight face, wondering if he had gotten through to him. He held onto Solomon's arm with all his energy. For such a petite man he was very strong, much stronger than Solomon. And Solomon was a hefty teenager. The old man's refined appearance concealed his uncanny strength.

The old man pressed his lips against Solomon's sweaty face and said in an almost robotic tone, "Sometimes the one you think you love, and the one you know you can trust, is the one person that will break you into a thousand pieces, leaving you on that sizzling road for the vultures."

Solomon was puzzled. His heart raced and his breathing intensified. Now he was simply frightened of the man. He slowly turned his head away from the old man's lips. The old man's body trembled like someone who had done something good—something brave.

Solomon wanted to jerk his arm free but he felt as though he owed the old man something—approval maybe. He stayed still and listened to him babble on.

When the old man finally released his arm, Solomon considered running toward his mother, but the old man whispered in his ear, "Sometimes what you cannot see won't hurt you. It's what you can see that poses the danger."

Solomon glanced up and met his gaze. The old man eyes were the color of dark cherries as if they had been bleeding. They weren't sad eyes but were the eyes of a man who knew about pain all too well. They were eyes of a man who wanted to help a young boy. Those bloodstained eyes seemed to warn Solomon to watch out for the people around him. The people he trusted. The people he loved.

The old man somehow had lifted some of Solomon's burden, passing some important knowledge to him. As he walked away, he gazed up at the light blue sky, nodded his head, and grinned. "He knows now," he said. "I can go home."

So on that warm evening as Solomon sat on the hill looking down at his home, he thought about the old man's words. He wondered who had sent him. Was it God? Was it his father?

He sat cross-legged and stared at the sky, unafraid of the darkness because he understood its greatness and that it would never hurt him. Then he observed the bright stars and couldn't help thinking about the old man and his prophecy.

CHAPTER 6

Solomon entered the house hours later and took his time closing the door. His eyes were red and swollen, and tearstains tracked down his face. Ivory knew something was wrong. She put her fork down and immediately rose from her chair. "What's wrong, Junior?" she said.

Solomon said nothing.

"And where my babies at?"

Solomon approached his mother and held her hand as he spoke slowly. "Mama, please sit down."

"For what?" she said, yanking his hand away.

"Just sit, Mama. Please."

Ivory sat down but didn't take her eyes off of Solomon. The room was deathly silent. Everyone stared at him, waiting for an answer. Solomon gasped and then breathed out fast.

"Fannie Mae and I went over to Miss Smith's house and she said the girls are gone," he said.

"What?" Lily and Nathaniel shouted as one.

Ivory's eyes widened. "Where they at then?"

"Gone?" Lily mumbled. Solomon was growing annoyed with her—the same way she became when Nathaniel asked her silly questions.

"She said those friends of hers—" He paused and stared at

Fannie Mae, who nodded, signaling him to carry on. "She said those friends of hers took the girls."

"Well . . . let's go get 'em!" Ivory yelled.

"It's not that easy, Mama," Solomon insisted.

Fannie Mae began to rub Ivory's back.

"Why ain't it that easy?" Ivory said, looking at his glazed eyes.

"They're gone, Mama. Those people done run off with the girls."

"Junior, I ain't got time for games!" shouted Ivory, who rose with determination. "Where my babies?" she demanded then headed toward the front door. "Is they outside?"

"Naw . . . Mama. They're not outside. They're gone." Solomon began to cry.

"Who would want to take my babies?" Ivory said innocently.

"Miss Smith and her friends obviously wanted them," Solomon said.

"Why?" Lily screamed.

"I don't know why, Lily!" he yelled back.

"Where she said they gone, Junior?" Ivory inquired.

"She didn't say."

"Why?" Lily screamed again.

"Lily . . . if you ask me that again . . ." Solomon shouted then knocked over the plate that was on the table. He ran to the window, crouched down, and sobbed.

Suddenly the door flew open and there stood Carter. "I heard what happened," he blurted. "I saw Pearl Lee and she told me."

"Pearl Lee know," Ivory said.

Carter looked at Fannie Mae. "Yeah, Pearl Lee said she saw Miss Smith the other day and she acted like she ain't know nothing about the girls."

Ivory glanced from Fannie Mae to Carter to Solomon. She didn't know whether to scream or run out the door again so she simply pulled her apron up to her face and cried. Fannie Mae held her tight.

"My babies are gone! Those people took my babies!" Ivory screamed. She pushed Fannie Mae away, reached over the counter, and grabbed her handbag. "Come on . . . we got to go and find my babies!"

"Where, Ivory? Where we gonna go?" Fannie Mae said. "We don't know where they at."

"Sheriff Thomas on his way over here," said Carter.

"Pearl Lee and her son, Jacob, went over and got him."

It all seemed like a bad dream. Ivory's entire world had crumbled in an instant. She felt faint and collapsed to the floor. Carter and Fannie Mae quickly grabbed hold of her and carried her into the bedroom, placing her on the bed. Ivory wailed and clutched the pearly white sheets with all her might.

Solomon tried to comfort her, smoothing back her thick hair and wiping away the tears as they fell, but he knew that offered little real relief. He knew the pain would live in her heart forever.

Ivory screamed with abandon: she screamed for her baby girls, she screamed out of anger, she screamed because she was weak and couldn't make that woman pay for what she had done to her family, and she screamed because that was all she could do.

Solomon had seen his mother this sad only once before and never thought he would see such despondency from her again.

"She betrayed me," Ivory cried. "Why? I treated her like family." She pointed her finger at the bedroom door and yelled, "I brought her in my house and she ate my food at my kitchen table!"

Then she looked her eldest son in the eye and softly asked in a distracted tone. "How we get here, Junior?" She patted her chest and said, "What I do that was so wrong that put us in this predicament?"

Solomon shrugged his shoulders. What could he possibly say that would ease her mind, stop the tears, and heal her broken heart? Nothing. Nothing could make it right. Nothing could bring his sisters back home. Nothing could make her smile again.

On that supremely hopeless day, Solomon was transformed into a person gripped by anger. A basic mistrust in other people took root of him. His heart grew numb—as hardened as that of Miss Smith. Since that day, he would be haunted by guilt.

The sheriff's department learned that Miss Smith was paid a

handsome fee for the girls. She knew exactly what she was doing and had profited from the Walker family's weakness. Solomon and his mother trusted her and she had betrayed them—all for the sake of money. It was becoming increasingly clear Miss Smith and the people she worked for had orchestrated the abduction.

During the investigation, Solomon would also learn that Miss Smith began teaching at their school about two years ago. No one knew much about her except that she was friendly, and liked to engage in conversation and eat a lot. She appeared to care for the children. She also seemed educated and even taught her students subjects other teachers knew nothing about.

Folks in town, mainly the women, wondered why she didn't have a man, but Ivory often defended her. "That ain't none of yo bizzness. Besides, a man ain't nothing but trouble."

Miss Smith was no mystery—she was an ordinary schoolteacher that people simply knew little about.

By the time the news spread, Miss Smith had skipped town. The Walker family never saw or heard from her again. Eventually, people stop talking about what happened. Talk was cheap and they knew the gossip accomplished little besides hurting Ivory and her family.

Whenever the opportunity arose, Solomon and his family would take the train to different counties in Georgia in search of his sisters. They knocked on doors, visited churches, and talked with hundreds of people. They did whatever they could to unearth any information about the girls.

Soon they became involved in an organization that assisted families in locating missing loved ones. The staff claimed the girls could be anywhere in the United States, if not anywhere in the world.

Teary-eyed and exhausted, Ivory spoke softly to the young white woman sitting behind the desk taking notes. "My heart will never be right till I see 'em again." She buried her head in her bosom.

The stress of searching drained them mentally, but it ended soon enough months later. The pursuit was fruitless and it became financially impossible to continue. Before long, Solomon and his family lost all hope of ever finding the girls.

The township ultimately found a replacement for Miss Smith and another school term soon passed. It was a demanding year for Solomon, Lily, and Nathaniel—struggling to continue to live life without their baby sisters. They struggled to maintain their strength and self-love, and the ordeal would prove a learning experience that few knew.

On a raining evening, Solomon and his mother sat on the porch. Ivory observed the overcast sky. "Junior," she said, "maybe this was His plan. I know one day we will all be together soon." She grabbed his hand. "There's a reason for everything and for that, we must believe in Him. He will guide us and keep my babies safe. They know we love 'em, Junior. They know we want 'em back."

Even God cannot change the past and Solomon knew that things were out of his control after what had occurred. No one could not turn back time. What was done was done.

The only thing left to do was pray that one day he would be met with opportunities to find what he had lost. He knew that to accomplish this he had to go forward and make something of his life, and avoid becoming embittered or letting the past destroy him.

A large part of his life had been abducted on that summer day. In the wake of the agonizing incident, Solomon steadily followed his instincts and never overestimated anyone. Most importantly, he never again abandoned his family.

In his heart of hearts Solomon believed his sisters would return home. His willpower, coupled with the inspiration that one day his entire family would come together again, allowed him to move forward and live his life to the fullest.

CHAPTER 7

The next morning Ivory and Solomon sat on the swing chair, swaying slowly back and forth in the cool breeze. Wordlessly they reflected on what had occurred.

Ivory rubbed his hand and kissed the palm of it. She smiled, got up, and walked into the house to fix breakfast.

Solomon stayed outside and stared at the trees—the only things that made him feel decent again, like a human being.

A car with a rattling engine passed by, its lights on. Solomon placed his fingers on his brow and began to massage it. A headache was coming on. Then he heard the front door open. The tragic event of five years ago replayed itself before his eyes.

His father was leaving for Lake Hope and had given him some words of warning. The unforgettable phrase came back to him as clear as the sound of the chime that hung on the porch and the sky-scraping maple tree in the front yard.

In a split second, the past came to him like the cast of characters in a picture show. This time everything was unrehearsed. And for some reason, Solomon always thought of the incident whenever something bad happened or was going to happen.

"If anything should ever happen to me, Junior," said his father as he walked toward the front door, "you make sure you take care of your mother and the two youngins."

His father's exact words would stick to Solomon's soul like a postage stamp, bound to become part of him just like the rich ebony complexion, wide eyes, and high cheekbones he inherited from his Cherokee ancestors—the parts of his body that looked specially created by God.

That phrase was as much a part of him as his full lips and nappy hair he hated combing and his long arms and legs that allowed him to walk great distances without ever breaking down—the solid arms and legs that made him seem much older than he really was.

His father's parting words never varied, even on that hot July afternoon in 1959 as he headed for Lake Hope to swim. His calculated words would establish the direction Solomon's life would soon take.

Solomon remembered that day well. It started out as a typical Saturday afternoon with he, Lily, and Nathaniel playing inside their tiny home and helping their mother with chores.

As the day turned into night and there was no word from his father, Solomon found himself standing helpless in front of the kitchen window, staring at the darkness. He replayed that faithful expression in his mind the entire time.

The kitchen was small. Four people barely fit in it because the large table took up most of the space. Yet that is where Solomon stood for the past four hours, breathing heavily with his eyes fixed on the bleak road that led to Lake Hope.

Had his father returned home promptly, Solomon would still have been in front of the window studying the night. He'd pretend to be in an imaginary world where he was a powerful black knight slaying dragons and twenty-foot monsters. He'd pretend to be in a world where he fought evil men and gave riches to the poor in a crusade for equality and independence.

Sometimes he was a regular kid in his fantasies, running and playing with his brother and sister on acres of green countryside. He'd picture himself walking out of a well-built good-looking home with a wraparound porch and indoor bathroom—a far cry from the shack he lived in and the foul-smelling outhouse with worms squirming at the bottom of the hole.

He'd envision a town where everyone lived in harmony. He called it "Paradise."

His vision grew blurry after a few hours. He thought he saw something moving behind the bushes and quickly pushed his head forward hoping to catch a glimpse of whatever went there. Looking carefully, he noticed it was Mr. Jamison. He smiled and waved to Mr. Jamison who waved back. After Mr. Jamison stepped inside his home, Solomon banged his head on the window ledge. He was scared and worried.

The kitchen was stifling and all he could do was suck in the sticky air and wait. It was a very hot and humid evening in Mission. It was so hot that if you gave in to the evening's seductive charm, it could literally bake you.

Most folks just sat still at night fanning their faces and bodies with paper fans. They splashed water on themselves from time to time and let their spirit take control by breathing in the sticky air. Some folks didn't leave their doors open at night for fear of the Klan or some lunatic lurking in the darkness.

The only relief for Solomon and his family came from the delicate humid breeze that flowed in through the house's four tiny windows.

Solomon raised his right arm and wiped away the sweat that ran down his face. He bit down on his lip and lowered his head. He wanted to cry—cry for his father's absence. *Where are you, Daddy? You should be home by now.*

Ivory, who was also agonizing from the scorching heat and her husband's absence, saw the discomfort on her son's face and handed him a cool wet cloth. He thanked her and pressed the fresh fabric against his sweaty face, holding it there for a moment. He gasped. The feeling felt good but would have been wonderful if only his father were home.

Ivory was a tall, attractive-woman with a medium built, a chestnut complexion, light brown eyes, and long thick black hair. According to Solomon's father, she once had a curvaceous physique, but it was her eyes he noticed first. They had charmed him.

Ivory began to stretch her housecoat to free the heat from her body, but this caused the fabric to cling further to her already damp frame. As she walked around the tiny kitchen, her waxy feet lifting from the wood floor sounded like the peeling of a corncob.

Solomon extended his head and neck over the ledge again searching for the trail that led to the main road. Maybe his father was coming soon. Yet after several hours of watching and waiting, no one appeared. His heart raced as fear took over and began to suffocate him. He breathed heavily to release the pain tangled inside.

His large eyes slowly moved from side to side carefully examining every figure, home, tree, even the squirrels that were inching their way between the bushes. When he noticed the sound of the night's soft cry and several lightening bugs moving on air, his nostrils expanded taking in more of the sizzling heat.

He was upset and forced himself to breathe in and out again. He needed some strength to keep himself from screaming. He wanted to climb on top of the highest mountain and let the entire world feel his anguish. There clearly was something wrong. His father was always on time.

Hours passed and Solomon's eyes remained glued to the path. He continued to play the phrase over in his head like a broken record. Although his father had expressed it so matter-of-factly, Solomon never realized how crucial those words were until now.

Solomon didn't want to believe the unthinkable—that the worst had possibly happened. Yet deep down he knew something was terribly wrong.

To calm himself down, he lifted his head and strained to breathe. Letting out a mouthful of air, he accidentally banged his head against the windowpane. It was then that he succumbed to the inescapable conclusion that his father was gone forever.

Solomon's heart picked up speed, feeling fit to burst out of his chest. He squeezed shut his eyes and firmly pressed his hand against his chest to ease the pain.

Solomon slowly shook his head as he stood in front of the damaged window. He promised himself then and there that despite his destiny, he would always be there for his family. He would never abandon them. Never.

With tears streaming down her face, Ivory stood behind her eldest child, covered him with both arms, and rocked him back and forth while he cried. She too felt the night's bitterness and knew the end somehow had come for her husband.

The entire evening Ivory walked on tiptoe and was afraid to make any noise for fear of interrupting Solomon's concentration. Her body filled with nervous energy. The force was so contagious it spread to Lily who also had cold feet. To calm herself, she grabbed a bible from the shelf and quickly flipped through the pages reading in silent several Psalms.

It was now eleven o'clock in the evening and from time to time, she'd sneak a quick look out of the window with a flickering hope that someone would knock on the door bearing good news. It had been eleven hours since she last saw her husband. He'd sworn when he left at noon as he had done a hundred times before that he'd be gone for just a few hours. *He lied,* she pondered, nervously giggling to herself. *Sho'nuff, he lied to me today.*

Eleven hours later, her memory was still fresh, centering on the way he smiled and stared at her. She remembered his big brown eyes and the way they sparkled. She remembered how they gave her all the love and warmth a woman needed to get through the day, even those most difficult of days.

The pain on her face was as evident as the perspiration. It stood out as clear as the fluorescence picture of flowers hanging on the cracked wall. She struggled to rationalize his absence. Maybe he went to visit friends or stopped and helped someone who had car trouble—he enjoyed repairing cars. Maybe he was at church chatting with Reverend Dean.

Those ideas spun around in her head to such a degree it gave her a headache. Her face suddenly sunk in her breasts, then she immediately raised her head and stared at Solomon with such sadness. Earlier that week she'd confided to Fannie Mae that she had a strange notion her worst fears might soon be realized.

"You just tired of the way things is. That's why you thinking like that," Fannie Mae said and then sort of giggled.

"Naw," Ivory said nodding, "I keep dreamin' about it, Fannie Mae," she declared, staring into her eyes.

Ivory began to sob and then mumbled, "Please God, shake these bad feelings from me. Please."

Solomon continued to stare into the night, trusting that his father would come soon. His head jerked toward the right, and for a second Ivory and Lily thought he saw someone, but he hadn't. Then he began to wildly pace the floor. For the first time in his life, Solomon was afraid—afraid of living life without his hero.

Lily walked the floor at a leisurely pace, shuffling around like a zombie. The gradual marching eventually drew out the anxiety inside her. Nathaniel continued playing with his toys. The stifling tension in the room couldn't sway his attention away from the fun he was having.

Suddenly an automobile made its way down the trail. When it reached the house, the loud clattering sound of the running motor moved everyone's attention toward the window.

It was a dilapidated reddish brown truck. The driver parked it a few feet away from the run-down set of steps. The brilliant headlights beamed through the curtains, illuminating the inside. Solomon raised his arm above his face, shielding his eyes from the intensity. Ivory and Lily jumped up in excitement.

In spite of the powerful glow, Nathaniel continued to toss the small soldiers in the air. He was unconcerned with the beat-up truck, its noisy engine and blazing lights.

When Ivory noticed the flaming lights, she looked at Solomon and Lily in horror, as if the truck might be driven by Satan himself. She wanted to speak but couldn't as fear gripped her spirit. The force caused her to fall on the floor gasping for air. Lily dashed to her rescue. When she reached her mother, she firmly hugged her and shouted, "Everything will be all right, Mama! It will!"

Ivory nodded and motioned her hand that she was okay. But the truth was she was as frightened as her children. Her head dropped on Lily's chest and she felt as though she had lived this night before: the night those evil men came for her sixteen-year-old half-brother, Luther, and lynched him just for helping a white woman pick up her groceries. Deep inside her heart, she knew those evil people had finally succeeded in destroying the love of her life.

Lily caressed her mother's hair and looked into her gloomy eyes. She whispered, "It has got to be Daddy, Mama."

Before Ivory could respond, Nathaniel, who was by the table listening in on the commotion, accidentally knocked over a cup of milk. The oozing liquid spread over the table and splattered onto the floor. Yet no one rushed to clean up the mess because their attention was still on those blazing lights.

Fear glued Ivory to Lily, both of them trembling as though the weather were freezing. They gradually helped each other up and headed toward the window.

At first, Ivory had cold feet and was too frightened to go near the window. She cautiously drew closer to the table that was just a few feet away.

When Solomon turned to his mother, he seemed spooked, too—his father told him this might happen.

"Too many hateful folks roam Georgia, Junior," his father sternly said once he learned of the lynching of a black man in the neighboring town. "I can't fight them all, but I'll try my best to. Even if I have to die doing so."

His father reached over and tapped Solomon's shoulder. "That man could have been me, son."

Nathaniel shrugged and laughed, finding amusement in the pandemonium. He knew it couldn't have been a big deal because no one bothered wiping up the milk. He just turned back to the toys and began playing again.

Ivory rushed her words. "Who that, Junior? Is it yo Daddy?"

"I don't know, Mama. I can't see anybody. It looks like Uncle Eugene's truck, but . . . I can't tell if it is."

Solomon continued to look out the window, praying the truck was his uncle's and that his father was inside too. Then the truck's door flew open and a large foot hung down, nearly touching the ground. The shabby shoe looked familiar. Uncle Eugene owned a pair similar to the one hanging, but it was dark and the lights blocked Solomon's view.

"I think it's . . ." mumbled Solomon.

"Who is it, boy? Is it Senior?" Ivory impatiently said as she toyed with a dishtowel she'd grabbed off the countertop. She quickly wiped the milk off the table and floor—an excuse to get her mind off the inevitable. She then nervously stared at the window.

"Naw, Mama," Solomon said. "It's not Daddy."

Solomon knew his father's large frame. Yet the person he saw sitting in the truck wasn't his father. He continued to examine the figure when the man stepped down from the truck, slammed the door and slowly moved away from it.

Solomon's eyes widened with joy when the person approached the steps. A huge smile was plastered across his face. It was his uncle. But the happy face disappeared when no one got out of the passenger's side.

Solomon stormed toward the door, but when he reached it he found he was too scared to open it. He ran back to the window and peered out again. He took a hard look at his Uncle Eugene, who looked as though he was staggering and confused. The man was clearly weakened. His face was dead—as dead as the night before him.

Uncle Eugene somberly looked up at Solomon and then slowly climbed the stairs. Each step was a struggle, as though his legs were giving out. Ivory's heart thumped with each heavy step.

Uncle Eugene's nose and eyes were watery. He reached into his pocket and pulled out a handkerchief. He wiped his face and paused for a moment. Then he began to wipe the beads of sweat that formed on his forehead with the back of his hand. He slowly looked up at Solomon again.

Solomon's body gradually shifted and he faced his mother. His heart throbbed and his breathing quickened.

"What is it, Junior? Tell me for God sake," Ivory begged.

Solomon was speechless as the strength of his uncle's presence drew near. Soon there came an intense knock at the door. Bang!

Bang! The force of the knock shook, the worn door. The deafening rattle caused Nathaniel to stop playing. His head jerked to the side and he turned his attention to the door.

Ivory stood by the wood stove holding the dishtowel in one hand. "Open it, Junior!" she yelled, throwing the dishtowel at him. "What you standing there for?"

Solomon cautiously grabbed hold of the warm doorknob. He bit down on his lip, a bad habit that his father reprimanded him for. "Please God, let everything be okay," he whispered.

When Solomon twisted the doorknob, the squeaky door unlocked and there stood Uncle Eugene trembling. Solomon's eyes widened. Uncle Eugene's uneasy body inched back a bit. He lost his balance and was out of control. He tumbled backward, his hands moving frantically in the air. Boom! Boom! Boom! He tumbled down the steps and hit the ground.

Solomon wanted to help his uncle but his body was numb with terror. All he could do was watch him fall. Solomon squeezed shut his eyes and then opened them, hoping his uncle had not been hurt by the fall.

Uncle Eugene struggled to stand. He held firmly onto the railing while his legs shook. It was clear to Solomon that his uncle was troubled.

"Uncle Eugene!" Solomon shouted. "Where's Daddy?"

Uncle Eugene stood frozen in his tracks, looked Solomon in the eye, and ignored him. Standing at the bottom of the staircase, he sniffled and then said, "Where's your mother, Junior?"

Solomon turned toward his mother and pointed to her. "In here," he said. "Where's Daddy?"

His uncle continued to ignore him. Uncle Eugene marched up the steps past Solomon. This time he was strong-minded because he had to get to Ivory. When he walked forward, his unsteady hand gripped Solomon's shoulder. The weight of his hand was unbearable. Solomon gritted his teeth and moaned. Solomon looked at his uncle's face and read the anguish there.

"Where Senior, Eugene?" Ivory said, sobbing. "It been hours since he left."

Uncle Eugene walked toward Ivory. Her eyes were swollen and caked with dried tears. She moved close to him but quickly stepped back when he stretched his hand to her.

Uncle Eugene stood before her. Ivory stared at his thin yet towering frame and began to cry. He grabbed her, firmly holding her body close to his. They sobbed. The force of her trembling made him cry even more.

Then Ivory's fragile body slid from his arms like melting butter. When her body finally slumped over, he grabbed hold of her and held her with all the energy left in him.

"Naw . . . Naw . . . don't tell me!" she cried. "Please . . . Lord no! Ah . . . no . . ."

"Senior is dead, Ivory," Uncle Eugene cried. His chest heaved violently. He stared at the ceiling before continuing in a mild tone. "We found his body in the lake."

Solomon let out a painful sigh. He jolted the back of his head against the wall. He tried to act grown up and composed just like his father taught him. "Don't you ever cry in front of nobody, Junior!" his father said. "Especially not in front of any white folks!"

Solomon sucked in the sour air and turned toward Nathaniel expecting some kind of response—perhaps comfort. He wanted to be cradled too. He wanted to be told that it was okay to cry, it was okay to shout, it was okay to let loose and run and kick and curse because that's all he wanted to do.

Nathaniel simply shrugged his shoulders and stared at Lily, who ran into the arms of her mother.

Ivory and Lily both let loose a loud and painful cry that broke through their walls and spread into the homes of their neighbors.

CHAPTER 8

Mr. and Mrs. Jamison were in bed when they heard the screams. Mr. Jamison didn't waste a second. He grabbed his trousers and yanked them on, nearly losing his balance in the process.

Once dressed, he dashed to the front door and gripped the fragile doorknob there and ripped it out of its socket. He sped out of the house, missing a chance to witness his wife's panicky reaction.

He cleared four wide steps and leaped above two bulky bushes to get across the yard to the Walkers' home. As soon as she caught her breath Mrs. Jamison stumbled behind her speed demon husband. The Bookers also heard the horrific screams and were rushing there.

Mr. Jamison slammed opened the door, punching a neat, medium-sized hole in the process.

Nathaniel jumped and hid in a corner. Solomon patted his head and whispered, "It's all right, Nate."

Solomon began to shut the door when he noticed Mrs. Jamison and the Bookers heading his way. He waited until they were all inside and then closed the door behind them.

Out of breath, Mr. Jamison yelled, "What the hell happened?" He glanced over at Ivory. "What's wrong, Ivory? Please, tell me."

Ivory was still sobbing. She looked at her daughter and then at

Mr. Jamison. "Senior is dead," she said softly.

"He's dead!" Mr. Jamison said, flustered. "How?"

He raised his hands and spread them in the air.

Still dazed, Solomon simply stared at the overwrought adults. Uncle Eugene was silent, and present only in body. He was beyond words; when he suddenly tried to mumble something, only drool spilled out.

"Will somebody tell me how?" Mr. Jamison demanded, as if any answer to that question could lessen his madness. Deep in his heart, he knew how.

Uncle Eugene's body slumped over the kitchen table, and Mr. Jamison and Mr. Booker ran over to catch him. They pulled a chair away from the table and sat him down. Uncle Eugene's eyes were dark and somber. His face was dry and brittle as though it were ready to break into a thousand pieces of sadness. Long hours of searching for his older brother had aged him. The ordeal had been pure torture.

He looked around the room. "He drowned," he said to no one in particular, the words flowing out of his mouth with ease.

"Drowned!" shouted Mr. Jamison. "Naw," he said, shaking his head, "Senior was a good swimmer."

"A damn good swimmer!" remarked Mr. Booker.

Looking up at the men again, Uncle Eugene mumbled, "Nothing ... was ... wrong ... with ... him."

He took a deep breath and carried on. "Me ... Carter ... Harvey and Clay pulled him out the lake." He stared at Solomon and began to cry. "Took us ... hours ... to find him." He sniffled again and wiped his nose and then stared at the two men. "Like I say ... nothing was wrong with him. He wasn't lynched."

"How you know?" Ivory said, wiping her damp face with her apron.

"Cause ... I saw his body. That's how I know."

"And where is his body?" Mr. Booker shouted.

"In my truck," said Uncle Eugene. He turned his head toward the window and noticed that his lights were still on. His large hand covered his face. He felt miserable. He cuffed his hands and lowered his head into them, wailing like a child. "My brother is gone. Just like that . . . he's gone."

A sudden, ear-piercing sound brought everyone to attention. Solomon had swung the door open and run outside. There he met John Henry and Miles Jamison, who stood silent as statues at the back of Uncle Eugene's beaten-up truck, looking at Mr. Walker's body.

The first thing Solomon saw was his father's long muscular legs, which were stone still. His initial reaction was to touch them but he pulled his hand back. He turned toward John Henry and Miles. "Look at my Daddy!" he cried.

He turned back toward the body and stared at it. He caressed the lifeless legs that were cold and stiff. He rubbed them hard, as though to warm the body. Then he climbed atop the corpse and began to shake it. "Wake up, Daddy! Wake up!" he cried. "Please wake up!"

John Henry threw himself on top of Solomon, pulling him away. "There's nothing you can do, Junior!" he yelled, "Let him be. He's gone!"

Miles began to cry. "Leave him lone, John Henry! Mr. Walker is dead and that ain't right!" Shaking his head. "It ain't right! Just ain't right."

Before long all eleven children and the two Booker children had gathered around the truck, standing like ghosts. Most of them prayed, bidding a final goodbye to the man they knew well—a dear family friend who was always around to lend a helping hand.

Seeing Mr. Walker's dead body devastated the children. Solomon stared at them. His eyes turned glassy. He never thought he would ever be without his father.

Later Mr. Booker held a kerosene lamp in his hand and walked outside. Mrs. Jamison and Mrs. Booker held Ivory by both arms and helped her out of the house and toward the truck. Using the lamp, he guided the women to the vehicle. When he shone the light on her husband's numb body, Ivory collapsed. "Lord, no! Tell me that's not Senior! Lord, tell me . . ."

Lily went to her father and gently trailed her tiny finger across the back of his cold foot. He loved that feeling when he was alive. It made him laugh with joy when she often did that. But now there was no response. She stroked his foot again, wanting him to get up and say, "Girl . . . stop that . . . you know I'm ticklish!"

After the second try and still no reaction, Lily turned and ran into her mother's arms again.

Nathaniel stood by the door and witnessing the entire distressing scene. He refused to go near the truck because he wanted to remember his father the way he last saw him, alive and well, joyfully playing with him. He also had no wish for bad dreams at night.

"What we go'n do with the body, Eugene?" Mr. Booker said softly, almost whispering. He didn't want to upset Ivory any more than she was.

"I'm gonna leave him here and put him in the storage room," Uncle Eugene said fretfully.

"He should be all right for a couple of hours," Mr. Booker whispered.

"Good, 'cause Johnny Albright, the undertaker, will be here by daybreak to get him ready for the funeral."

"Aw right, then," hissed Mr. Booker. "We'll put him in the storage room."

But Solomon had second thoughts. He stepped forward and shook his head. "No!" he shouted. "Bring him in the house where he belongs."

The men looked at each other and then at Ivory, who nodded. They struggled with Mr. Walker's body and carried it into the house and to Ivory's bedroom, carefully placing it on the bed. Solomon followed. He passed his mother and sister, and reached down and hugged them. Then he kissed his mother's cheek and whispered, "Daddy's gone home now, Mama. He's okay because he's with Big Daddy, Big Ma, and the rest of the family."

Ivory put his hand to her cheek for a brief second and then let it go. "I know, baby," she uttered. "He gonna be okay now."

Solomon walked into the large room and watched the men

closely as they positioned his father's heavy body on the bed near the window facing his mother's garden.

When the men walked away, Solomon stood before his father and rubbed his hand across his face. He kneeled down and just stared at him. Before him lay the man he so loved and admired. He raised his father's stiff hand, holding it tightly, and said, "I promise you, Daddy, I'll never leave Mama and the children. I'm going to take good care of them, just the way you did." He winked his eye. "You'll see. I'm going to be the man you always wanted me to be."

He pulled a dusty golden-brown sheet over his father's body up to the neck. "Big Daddy is going to be happy to see you, huh," he whispered. "Tell him I said hey." Then he giggled. "Tell him I miss him." Solomon started to cry. "I'll miss you too, Daddy." He leaned forward and kissed his father's cheek. "Goodbye, Daddy."

He slowly stood and walked toward the door, then glanced back at his father, who appeared to be sleeping peacefully. His expression was angelic and his dark skin glistened. His father looked as handsome as he did on his wedding day—it brought a smile to Solomon's face when he glanced at an old photograph of his parents resting on a corroded dresser. Solomon turned and walked toward the half-opened door.

* * *

The funeral was held on Monday. It was a warm afternoon and every black family in Mission was present. The men cleared out the furniture in the bedroom, which was used as the viewing room. Mr. Walker's body lay in a plain pine box. The entire afternoon, folks filed in and out to view the body. They stood around and sat outside the house fanning their faces with newspapers and gossiped about what had happened.

Once the gossip waned and after several hours of viewing, Reverend Dean agreed it was time to take the body to the cemetery. Once Lily heard the announcement, she rushed inside the house and headed in the direction of the coffin.

She tripped over a piece of wood and fell face down on the floor, then quickly stood and, ladylike, brushed the dust off her black ruffled dress and headed toward her father to say goodbye.

She considered what her father might have said if he had seen her stumble on the floor, and had to smile at the thought. "See? That's what happens when you're always in a rush," he'd have said. "Next time, take your time, girl."

Johnny Albright and his assistant had positioned the coffin on a large, cloth-draped brass stand. Lily, too tiny for a good view, pulled out a small stepladder from the closet and walked up the three steps. She leaned over the pine box and began to straighten her father's black-and-white tie and his black jacket, something she did every Sunday. She kissed his stiff cheek and whispered, "Bye, Daddy. I love you."

Uncle Eugene and Reverend Dean walked into the room and stared at each other, both recalling the drowning, both wondering what really happened, and both angry with themselves for living with threats and hate crimes and incidents like this while most black folks looked the other way. Yet this time, they both wanted revenge. Their hands shook as they placed the lid over the box before leaving the room.

The pallbearers—Solomon, the Booker twins, and three of the Jamison brothers—carried the coffin without faltering to the glossy black hearse that Johnny Albright had polished himself and parked directly in front of the house. He often bragged that he wanted black folks "to be put away well—just like them white folk."

"On the count of three," Solomon said, "let's pick it up and put it in the car." They glanced at one another once they had a good grip on the coffin. "One . . . two . . . three . . ."

They carefully raised the heavy casket and slid it into the automobile.

Ivory and Lily hopped into the front seat of Uncle Eugene's truck. Ivory swallowed the hot air and then slowly released it. Life wasn't supposed to be this way. She wasn't ready to be a widow and bury the father of her children. Not yet. She wanted to believe she could say goodbye and live life without him, but she knew it was going to be difficult. *My life never go'n be the same. God . . . tell me why this had to happen?*

"Ivory, you aw right?" Uncle Eugene said, looking at her unblemished face.

"I'm fine," she said softly. She looked at Lily and put her arms around her. Then she glanced at Uncle Eugene reassuringly. "Don't worry about me, Eugene. I'll be aw right. What about yourself?" she said.

He shrugged. "I'm managing . . . I guess." Ivory smiled and turned her head toward the road.

Solomon, Nathaniel, the other pallbearers, and all those who had attended the service stood behind the hearse. Solomon clutched Nathaniel's miniature hand. "You think you can walk to the cemetery?" he said. "You know it's a half-mile away."

Nathaniel fixed his eyes on his older brother and nodded. "Umm-hmm," he said.

"You sure? You know, you can ride with Mama and Lily if you want."

Nathaniel whispered, "I want to walk with you, Junior." He smiled. "I can walk it. I walked with you and Daddy all the time, 'member? It's not long."

"Okay," said Solomon.

The truck moved forward, inching its way toward the road. Solomon and Nathaniel held hands, leading the procession to Hope Baptist Church Cemetery.

* * *

At the burial service, Ivory and her children sat in front of the large interment opening on some shabby wood chairs and stared at the pine box in a daze. She thought of how nice the chairs were and looked at Johnny Albright with disgust. She rolled her eyes. "Probably stole them from somebody," she whispered. "Hypocrite."

Reverend Dean asked everyone to stand, and then recited Psalm 23. "The Lord is my shepherd, I shall not want," he said in a loud and distinctive voice.

Ivory always found his voice charming. At fifty-three, he looked forty, with handsome good looks, an athletic built, and a smooth voice that made the female church members smile when he touched their hands, said hello, or looked at them. Ivory didn't smile because she was infatuated with him; she smiled because she had such high esteem for the man.

Reverend Dean paused and stared at Ivory, who was visibly distraught. What could he say or do to ease her pain? He closed his eyes and said, "He maketh me to lie down in green pastures. He leadeth me beside the still waters."

Soon Ivory could hear everyone's voice. Each person's voice stood out as subtly distinct. She heard Fannie Mae's high alto pitch, Miss Jamison's husky timber, and Miss Parker's crackling chant.

"He restoreth my soul," Reverend Dean shouted. "He leadeth me in the paths of righteousness. For His names' sake."

Suddenly Lily's voice grew louder than the rest as she held her mother's hand. "Yea, though I walk through the valley of the shadow of death, I will fear no evil. For You are with me. Your rod and Your staff, they comfort me."

During the closing of the burial service, Ivory and her children walked up to the large hole and threw in a handful of flowers. Solomon stood there for a moment looking down at the coffin. *I can't believe you're gone.*

He stooped down and leaned forward, then grabbed a handful of dirt and slowly let go of it. He spoke in a hushed tone. "Goodbye, Daddy. I'll see you in heaven one day."

Nathaniel bent down next to his brother. "Is they gonna keep Daddy down there forever?"

"Yeah," Solomon said. "He'll be okay."

"You sure, Junior?"

"Yeah, I'm sure."

"But how he gonna breathe?" Nathaniel said.

A slight smile lit Solomon's face as he pulled his brother close to him. "Daddy's in heaven now. He doesn't need to breathe because God will be breathing for him." He caressed the top of his younger brother's head. Nathaniel nodded.

Solomon turned to his mother, who had overheard the conversation and who wore a big smile.

As they stood by the breach in the soil, Ivory looked at Solomon and whispered, "You the man of the house now, Junior." He nodded.

He knew this the moment his uncle had walked into their home that dreadful evening.

CHAPTER 9

Everyone headed back to the house to eat. They sat in the yard, lounging around, laughing and joking with one another. It was just like old times except for the absence of Solomon's father.

Still upset about his father's death and the circumstances surrounding it, Solomon paced the yard and soon found his way up the road. He needed to get away from all the chitchat. His father hated gossip: "All black folks know how to do is talk about nothing. When there's something to really talk about, they act like they're dumb or something."

Walking down the road, Solomon heard noises coming from behind some bushes. He squinted and shaded his eyes with his hand to get a clear view of the person there. He noticed a white face far-off. "Who's there?" he yelled.

It was Buford Cloverfield who had come to pay his respects. Buford was one of the two white people Mr. Walker had really liked. "He the second white person I know with some sense," his father commented about Buford. Judge Booth was the first.

Solomon darted toward him. When he finally reached him, he gasped and then uttered, "Hey there, Buford."

Buford's pink face was moist and glowed like it was lit from within. He was quiet and fidgeted with his shirt, turning his head to the side like he were afraid someone might be listening in on them.

Seventeen-year-old Buford was wearing khaki pants and a ruby-tinted shirt. He seemed hesitant to approach and simply stood by a tree scratching his head. He noticed Solomon eyeing his shirt. "Mama sent my Sunday clothes off to Miss Hedda for washing," he said.

Solomon, who behaved much older than his youthful nine years, snapped, "Buford, I ain't stun your shirt. I was looking at you. You look like you scared or something."

"Naw," he giggled, "I came to pay my respects, that's all."

"Then why you all the way out here?" Solomon said. "Come on back by the house and join everybody."

Buford dreaded this moment. The last thing he wanted to do was go near a group of angry and bitter black folks. Still, he returned with Solomon and greeted everyone. "Hey there, Reverend Dean. Good evening, Miss Parker. How you doing, Fannie Mae?"

He sat next to Solomon and observed everyone's reaction. They all wanted someone to blame and he was a perfect scapegoat. "What he doing here?" Miss Parker said, shaking her head.

"I don't know but he got some nerves," Fannie Mae voiced. "Son of a bitch."

"They make me sick," Carter shouted. "His own folk probably had something to do with it."

"Um-hmm," Miss Parker said. "They most likely did."

Buford ignored all the accusations—he had no choice being outnumbered, and stood no chance of defending himself under such unfriendly circumstances. He knew evil lay hidden in the flesh of his people, and that included his own family, but what could he do? He simply had a different heart than the rest.

"Solomon, I'm really sorry about your daddy," Buford whispered into Solomon's ear. "He was a good man." He wiped the perspiration from his forehead. "I'm gonna miss him. He taught me everything I know about cars." Buford chuckled and brushed his shoulder against Solomon's.

Solomon was too angry to smile. "Do you know what happened, Buford?"

Buford shrugged, feigning ignorance, then looked down at

the ground. "Naw," he said shamefully, "all's I know is your daddy went down to the lake for a swim. I know he stopped by Miss Parker's house for something to eat beforehand." He drew a breath, then blew it out looking at Solomon sideways. "He most likely caught a cramp and drowned."

"Yeah, that's what they all say, Buford," Solomon replied staring into his blood-shot eyes.

Mr. Booker, who had been behind them eavesdropping, approached them with his hands in his pockets. "Did them white folks send you down here to make sure we don't start no trouble?" he said.

Buford glanced up. "Mr. Booker, you know how much Mr. Walker meant to me. Shoo, he was more of a daddy to me than my own." He looked at Solomon and gave the impression that he was sincere. "You of all people should know that, Solomon. I came here to pay my respects."

"I know one thing for sure," Mr. Booker shouted, pointing his finger at Buford. "You gon back and tell 'em, we'll find out what happened. And when we do—"

"Booker!" yelled Mrs. Booker. "Now ain't the time, specially not in front of the chil'rens."

Buford was relieved for the momentary reprieve. He turned his head away and continued eating a piece of fried chicken. Solomon watched his every move and sensed he was holding back information but also realized that now wasn't the time to probe. His mother and family members were in pain.

Solomon shifted his head away from the blistering sun and in the direction of his uncle's truck to stare at his father's last ride. He banged his hand against the side of the chair. *God is my witness . . . I will find out what happened to my father. If it takes me the rest of my life, I will find out what happened.*

Buford sat next to Solomon looking like a cat on a hot tin roof. When he glanced at Solomon he was met by Solomon's gaze, and it was not by chance. Solomon knew wrong when he saw it. And he knew the truth would not elude him for long.

Buford's face and arms were covered in sweat and his blond

hair was wetly plastered to his head. Solomon felt sorry for this blue-eyed teenager who didn't fit in with the blacks or the whites no matter how much he tried. Still, white folks accepted and tolerated him only because he was one of their own.

Solomon studied Buford as never before. Buford's chunky body sunk in the chair. He leaned back, rocking the chair up and down. When he saw Solomon looking at him, he slowly lowered the chair to the ground. And just when the chair touched down, he squeezed the plastic cup in his hand, dimpling it. He raised the cup to his mouth uneasily and started to take a sip of the sweet iced tea. But when he saw Mr. Booker staring at him with real hatred, his hand began to tremble and he nearly dropped the cup.

All eyes were on him. They hated him for being what he was—white. Goosebumps soon spread over his body. He turned back around, faced Solomon, took another swig of iced tea, and smiled.

Solomon smiled back. *Look at his guilt-ridden face. I know he knows what happened. Oh, don't worry Buford, I will uncover the truth someday.*

The sun slowly descended into the horizon, and the grieving crowd scattered back to their burdensome lives in the fresh darkness. The scene was all too common for Solomon but he'd never accept it. He knew a better life awaited him someplace in this world.

Solomon and Buford made small talk and, before long, laughter filled the air as the two of them swapped stories of Mr. Walker. Buford laughed with such intensity tears trickled down his face.

Solomon stared at him. *Were they real tears?*

Suspicion kept Solomon's eyes glued to Buford's. He learned from his father that by watching a person carefully you could see through him. That bad manners were only skin-deep. Eventually, a person's true colors would surface. Solomon waited for the liar before him to show his true colors.

He continued to stare Buford in the eye. *One day you will tell me. One day.*

CHAPTER 10

The year following his father's death was a trying time for Solomon and his family. Ivory continued to clean house for the Cloverfield's and worked as a seamstress at Ethel's Tailor Shop.

The shop catered to all the upper crust folks in Mission and surrounding towns. It specialized in wedding gowns, dresses, and tailored suits for men. The work wasn't steady but it allowed Ivory to feed her children.

Once Bill arrived on the scene, things got worst; food and money was in short supply. He was of no help to the family. Food and goods became more expensive because there was now an additional adult to feed and clothe.

Bill could eat a lot for a little man. Fannie Mae thought he ate out of boredom. "Lazy folks do that, just to be doing it. He see it, he gonna eat it," she said to Solomon.

The house had to be heated all day because Bill rarely worked and was always at home.

Ivory took home scraps from the Cloverfield's, something she never had to do when her husband provided for the family. Frustrated with the way things were going for her best friend and her family, Fannie Mae finally spoke her peace. "That good for nothing sapsucker just eat up everything. He'll bleed you dry if you let him."

She looked at Ivory who was folding a shirt. "Ivory, people

only do to you what you allow."

But Ivory, a good-hearted person, just put the shirt in a storage bin and nodded. "Fannie Mae, he not that bad. Things will get better. They have to."

But things got decidedly worse once the girls were born. They were a blessing to the family, but their demands sank the family into a state of total poverty. Solomon knew what the Jamison kids did was wrong but he tagged along with them anyway. It was his last resort, too. He began stealing food from farms in order to feed his family. He wasn't proud of it, but he'd had little choice.

* * *

The girls were born on Christmas day in 1960. God sent the Walker family three precious angels. It was a Sunday. The air was incredibly warm for a winter day and the sky was a brilliant blue, full of promise. God blessed them with a beautiful and flawless delivery process, taking Solomon, Lily, and Nathaniel's breath away.

In giving birth to triplets Ivory gave her three older children the perfect Christmas gift that year.

The scant rain that fell that morning disappeared as soon as it touched the ground. The day was emotionally charged. All were panicked and elated at the same time. Solomon was overjoyed, and anxious for the delivery.

In fact, everyone in Mission was excited because they knew something special was going to happen that Christmas. Ivory's stomach was huge. She was beyond performing most tasks, even such basics as bathing herself. She couldn't even reach below or around herself. So Lily bathed her each night. Ivory felt big and clumsy, and for good reason. All she wanted to do was eat, sleep, and drink soda pop.

That morning, Solomon heard his mother sounding frantic. "Bill, they comin'. Go get Miss Parker!"

In a matter of minutes, Miss Parker rushed into their house with what seemed like half of Mission, all of them carrying blankets and rags.

Midwifery was the norm because most families lived far from town and few of them had vehicles. Fannie Mae and Carter owned the only car, and Solomon's father had left behind a tattered truck. It needed some patching up, but every time Ivory earned enough to fix it, Bill found an excuse to spend the money. With no way to get around town, they walked most places.

Ivory was in terrible agony. She wailed scream upon scream, nearly bursting her lungs. No one knew for sure how many babies she was carrying, but they all knew it was more than one.

Solomon stood nervously by his mother's bedside and witnessed the entire scene.

"Push, Ivry! Damn it, push, girl!" yelled Miss Parker. She peered into Ivory's bloody vagina. "I see the head. It comin'!" A woman named Hattie patted Ivory's forehead with a damp cloth. She wore a dirty rag around her head that she kept fiddling with. "You aw right, Ivry?"

"No," Ivory cried. "It hurt! Lord, it hurt!"

"Okay, now, here we go again," Miss Parker said with a gasp. She shook her head and then puffed out air. There was more sweat on her face than on Ivory's. "Okay now, push, girl! Push!" she yelled.

A woman missing several front teeth—Mary Joe—held Ivory's hand and yelled, "Okay, Ivry, push!"

Ivory struggled to raise herself up. She grabbed onto the sides of the mattress, closed her eyes, bit down on her lip, and pushed hard with her stomach muscles.

Solomon thought his mother was going to die lying there in pain.

"Here come one!" Miss Parker screamed with joy.

The tiny head oozed out, shiny with hair. And when Ivory pushed again, the baby's entire body gushed out onto the blood-soaked bed.

"It's a girl, Ivry," Miss Parker shouted as she whacked the baby's buttocks. Then she turned to Ivory, smacking her lips. "Who this be?"

Ivory looked at Solomon and then glanced furtively at the

women. "Mag . . . Magnolia."

"Okay, this here Nolia," said Miss Parker, quickly passing her to the bucktoothed woman.

Ivory looked up and cried, "Let me see her."

"Naw, we gots work to do, Ivry," Miss Parker said. She looked inside Ivory's canal again. "The other one comin'! Let's go to work y'all."

"It sho' comin' too," yelled Hattie. She strained her eyes to get a good look and saw the baby's head.

Lily and Nathaniel's eyes were transfixed behind the curtain. When the other baby came out, they giggled at each other and then ran outside to tell their friends.

"This one a girl too, Ivry. Look like you got yo'self two girls here today."

And before Miss Parker could ask, Ivory sternly said, "That one Rose."

"Um-hmm," said Miss Parker, passing Rose on to Solomon. "This here yo sister, Rose. Now, go and give her to Mary Joe, boy."

Solomon looked down at Rose, wiped her moist face with a cloth, and kissed her. He giggled because it was all real, too real. His hands trembled as he handed her over to Mary Joe.

Magnolia and Rose whined well after Miss Parker spanked them. Miss Parker wiped her sweaty face with her apron. She was exhausted. She leaned down and examined Ivory's genitalia again, then she glanced at Hattie, pressed her eyes down a bit, and stared at the bandanna tied around her head. "You sho look silly with that rag on yo head, girl."

Hattie laughed. "Shoo, it's hot in here."

Suddenly Miss Parker took a swig of the stuffy air and quickly blew it out. She placed her hands on her hips. "Mary Joe?" she said calmly.

"Ma'am?" Mary Joe said, her eyes the size of golf balls.

Miss Parker wiped her forehead. "You not gonna believe this."

"What you say, Miss Parker?"

"Another one in there."

"Lord, have mercy!" Hattie screamed.

Ivory's head fell back on the bed. "Three babies!" she cried.

"I don't believe it!" Solomon shouted. "I don't believe it!"

"Believe it, 'cause it the truth!" said Miss Parker. "You go'n have to push again, Ivry! Come on now, push, girl!"

Clutching the pillow, Ivory bit down on her lip again and strained. "Lord, please! Why you doing this to me?" she screamed.

Once the body appeared, the baby immediately began wailing, robbing Miss Parker of her bottom-whacking duty.

Miss Parker held the baby in her arms and wiped the blood from its forehead. She smiled and glanced at Ivory. "Another girl, Ivry. Lord have mercy, you got three girls here," Miss Parker said, pulling her blouse up to her nose and wiping off the wetness.

"That one is Hyacinth," Ivory announced proudly.

* * *

It had been a long night and the women were all thankful the babies had been delivered into the world safe and sound.

Later that evening, Solomon crept over to his mother's side and donned the biggest grin.

"What you laughing for?" Ivory said. "That was the hardest thing I ever did in my life. I ain't never brought three babies into this world the same time before."

"I'm so happy," he said.

Miss Parker grabbed a shoe. "You so happy then, why don't you help us womens and get on out of here!"

The thought of three grown women running around like chickens without a head made Solomon howl.

"Oh, you still think it's funny, huh?" Miss Parker said. She threatened to throw a shoe at him but he ran toward the curtain and slid it across halfway. He turned back at the girls and saw them sleeping in shoeboxes that had been placed on a small stand near the curtain. Their eyes were half closed and smiles lit their faces.

Solomon stood over his little angels, mesmerized. It was the most beautiful sight he'd ever seen. He muttered, "Look what God brought us."

Miss Parker and her team grew impatient with him and soon chased him out of the room. "Boy, don't you know yo mama needs her rest!" yelled Hattie.

Reluctant to leave, he turned back toward his mother and blew a kiss. Ivory smiled. Then he walked away, but not before turning back and looking at the girls once more.

Solomon vaguely remembered Lily and Nathaniel's birth. This occasion was beyond description. It was the most wonderful thing he'd known in his life. He was now the oldest brother of triplets. A feeling of peace and utter completeness rushed through him. To say he was delighted would be an understatement. His family was intact again and the part that had been missing for a year was now replaced with three little babies.

* * *

Solomon and Lily were so happy they prepared breakfast for their mother the next morning. There was still plenty of meat left that he and the Jamison boys had stolen from Mr. Summers, who owned a farm a mile away. Solomon went into the storage room and grabbed a slab of bacon. He and Lily cooked his mother's favorite meal: bacon, grits, and eggs.

Ivory craved bacon during those difficult eight months, and there were times she couldn't have it because she couldn't afford to buy it. So he and Lily fried a heap of bacon, simmered some buttered grits, and scrambled eggs on the wood stove.

Bill missed the girls' births. He sped out of the house just as soon as Miss Parker and her team arrived, alleging the sight of blood sickened him. But he made sure to come home the next morning for breakfast; he knew the meat was in the storage room.

Solomon knew his nonappearance was just another lame excuse for him to spend time with his so-called white friends. He also knew he didn't love his mother or her children, didn't in fact care if she died right there on the bed giving birth to his daughters.

Bill was a coward. He disregarded the girls' wailing that morning. Instead of tending to them, he simply asked Lily to cook him four eggs, sunny-side up. He claimed they were flavorless when scrambled or fried. Lily rolled her eyes at the ignorant man and prepared his eggs separately. The sight of those soupy eggs dribbling down the side of his mouth disgusted them, making them all nauseous.

Solomon trailed behind Lily, who carried a tray of food into Ivory's room because she was still tender and couldn't get out of bed. When Ivory sat up, her face blanched, the soreness was that apparent. She began slowly to chew on a piece of bacon while Lily fluffed her pillow. Ivory looked at Lily sideways. "You fried the bacon too hard, baby."

"Sorry, Mama."

Solomon sat at the foot of the bed and played with his mother's curved toes and the cleaned sheets that Miss Parker put on after the delivery. "Mama, how did you come up with those names?" he said.

"Why? Don't you like 'em?"

"Yeah, I do. As a matter of fact, I really like them. I just wondered, that's all."

Ivory smiled bashfully and remembered the vow she'd made to her late husband that any females born into their family would be named after nature's finest flowers and trees because she so loved the natural world.

Ivory chose Magnolia for the Southern Magnolia tree. With their sweet smell and large, oval leaves, their creamy flowers, it's been said that magnolias were the ancestors of all other flowering plants.

Ivory loved roses because of their arching form and wing-like petals, their bright hips and attractive fragrance.

She decided on Hyacinth because of the awesome water hyacinths down by the lake that floated on leafstalks. Their leaves were sometimes round, sometimes kidney-shaped, and the flowers were purple with a yellow eye on the upper center petal. Ivory adored those water hyacinths. Their heart-shaped petals intrigued her.

 She taught her children about wild flowers, plants, and trees. She wasn't an educated or articulate person like her late husband, and she definitely wasn't a dedicated reader. But she'd often challenge herself and attempt to read anything that was related to vegetation and nature.

CHAPTER 11

Four years later . . .

Bill acted strange for months. He had never been much of a talker, but these days found him totally silent. He paced their small home, mumbling and cursing to himself. Ivory could tell he was angry with someone but she couldn't tell with whom. She simply left him alone since obviously he wasn't going to share his thoughts with her.

Solomon didn't know what was wrong with him either and didn't care. Bill was the strangest man he had ever known. He spent much of his time alone. He and Ivory rarely spoke. When they did communicate, it was because of a quarrel over money or work.

The girls were now four years old. Bill had barely noticed them growing up. Solomon dreamed of the day he would wake up and find this shiftless man gone from their lives, but he was cautious because every instinct he had told him dreams didn't come true. So the best solution for him was simply to ignore Bill.

It was a cool, crisp spring morning. Solomon left the other children at home and went to Lake Hope. The fresh air and quiet scenery would do him good. He sat at the edge of the lake staring at the calm water. All was in harmony. Even the trees and flowers seemed utterly content as they kept an eye on him.

He stared at the sprawl of Lake Hope, so named by Reverend Dean's grandfather, the founder of the church that stood at its shore. He had chosen "Hope" to convey the lake's broad shape, calm waters, flowered border, and how the pecan and maple trees sheltered it, ensuring harborage.

Reverend Dean claimed God had positioned the lake in a such a way that when the sun beamed down on it, it illuminated the water, delivering folks, lifting their spirits, and giving them strength to hold on and live life to its fullest. The view was widely regarded as heaven on earth.

Solomon gazed mesmerized and wondered if it would ever be possible to leave Mission. A sudden smile lit his face and he glanced at the clear sky. He knew it was possible. There had to be a way out.

He stared at the lake again. A bird flapped its wings and flew past him, and he looked up into the bluish sky again. He whispered, "What's it like up there, Daddy? Are you happy?"

He remembered his father and the times they'd spent at the lake. He remembered the time he asked his father about heaven. His father proclaimed heaven was a place for everyone, a paradise for the dead and the living. Solomon chuckled as he tossed a rock into the sparkling water. Those were good days—like the incredible lake before him, they were simple truths in a world that seemed to have a shortage of them.

He thought back nine years, to when he and his father sat by their favorite rock his father had named, Sweet Betsy—"sweet" because she felt so good when you leaned your back against her and "Betsy" after his childhood girlfriend.

They often came to the lake and talked for hours on end. Solomon treasured the memories of his father's storytelling—stories that made his faith stronger, particularly when good days turned bad and the road to success seemed endless. As he sat at the edge of the lake daydreaming, he remembered his history as his father explained it to him. His father always managed to connect his life story to heaven—the special place that would one day bring him deliverance. Recalling the stories of his family's past always dispelled unhappiness and uplifted him with sustaining confidence. They gave him the courage to persevere. And that is what he promised to do at his father's funeral: go on with his life and make every moment count.

"Heaven," Solomon uttered as he covered his eyes from the blinding sun. "Oh, sweet heaven."

Solomon's first introduction to this special place was as a five-year-old conversing with his father at Lake Hope. On one joyous occasion, he tagged along with his father to the lake after an exhausting day picking cotton. It was a warm summer evening and they lounged around on the lake's border sipping soda.

His father placed a knitted blanket he carried with him in front of Sweet Betsy and relaxed, allowing the peaceful sound of the night to soothe his aching body.

While taking in the nightfall's summer breeze, Solomon noticed his father's large eyes fixed on the shimmering sky.

Solomon had been a curious kid. Harsh or sudden responses from his father never deterred him. He was thrilled to have the opportunity to absorb his father's wisdom. It was a privilege and he never allowed fear to hinder his desire to learn more.

The two of them shared an uncommon bond—like a precious jewel, genuine and everlasting. Unfortunately, Solomon's peers didn't recognize their fathers' greatness or even appreciate their fathers as human beings. It was hard to witness because these were courageous and hardworking men. They were fathers who faithlessly tolerated narrow-mindedness and humiliation because of the absolute threat of violence against them. They were sons who sacrificed their lives so that their children would not endure suffering. They were brothers who fought oppression before it destroyed their souls. They were brave human beings who lived life with dignity.

Solomon's heart broke as he watched his friends underestimate these honorable role models. Yet despite this, he felt blessed and truly cherished the relationship he had with his father.

Gazing into his father's unwavering eyes, he gently tapped his shoulder and his father flinched. "Daddy, what are you thinking about?" Solomon said softly.

His father turned his head, the richness of his ebony complexion still visible in the night. Obvious contentment spread across his face. He calmly shook his head and displayed a simple smile. "Nothing's on my mind, son," his father said, steering his head skyward again. "I'm just looking past those stars up there."

When his father moved his muscular arm, the veins wiggled like worms. He aimed his index finger toward heaven. His large, dry, bruised hand remained immovable above Solomon, who couldn't help but stare at his father's fingers, which were swollen and blistered. Lacerations covered his hand. His fingers were eaten away by years of grueling work in the scorching cotton fields.

His father picked cotton in the blistering heat until his fingers swelled, tore, and bled. He loaded bales of cotton onto wagons from sunrise to sunset until he was stone-blind from the fiery sun and his back failed him. He earned just about enough money to feed and support his family. Yet he worked seven days a week picking cotton, vegetables, and doing handiwork around town to provide for his family.

His father pointed to the sky and uttered, "You see, Junior, way up there?"

Solomon was tongue-tied. "Naw, Daddy," he stammered, irritated because he couldn't see what his father saw. He strained his eyes toward the glittering sky and uttered, "I can't see it, Daddy. What's up there?"

"Our paradise, Junior," his father said, beaming again. "That's what's up there."

Solomon was puzzled. He shrugged and frowned, unable to see his paradise. *Where was it?* he thought.

His father grinned, showing all his white teeth. "Beyond those stars is a heaven for all of us, son."

Solomon's jaw dropped with high hopes and his heart thumped. Soon moisture began to slowly trickle down his lips and he immediately envisioned his paradise—the paradise he so often thought about looking out of the kitchen window.

His father laughed, knowing what Solomon was thinking. He shook his head and grinned again. Feeling a bit silly, Solomon stared at his father. "Isn't heaven for dead peoples, Daddy?"

"Naw, son. That's a place for the dead and the living," said his father, taking an intense swig of the fizzing soda. After swallowing hard, he said, "People like you and me."

Solomon aimed his finger at his tiny chest and then at his father. "Me and you."

"Yep, son. You and me."

His father's tongue slowly swirled around his full lips, erasing the foam that lined them. He gulped a mouthful of the soda, this time emptying the bottle, and aimed the tip of the bottle downward and into his mouth so that the peanuts that settled at the bottom of the bottle would spill out. He grinned, chewing the nuts.

His father wiped his mouth with the back of his hand and said, "Whenever you need comfort or strength, Junior, look past those stars and ask God for it. Tell him your troubles and He will guide you in the right direction."

A huge crease crossed Solomon's face. He had never dreamed there was another way to talk to God outside of church. All the shouting, yelling, and dancing that went on in church could intimidate him. At times, he felt smothered. He used every excuse not to attend. "My stomach hurts. My legs hurt and I can't walk. I don't want to go today."

When the excuses worked he made home his church where he was at ease with himself and comfortably talked to the Lord. "God, bless Mama and Daddy. God, bless Lily. God, please bless little Nathaniel because he cries a lot," he would say.

When the excuses were hopeless he was forced to attend church with his family feeling deeply insecure. Now there was a place where he could divulge his thoughts and emotions in private at any time.

Resting next to his father, Solomon nodded, not in disbelief but in full confidence that, ultimately, this special place would bring him and the people he loved joy.

He glanced at his father and smiled. He was absolutely thrilled. Once his father saw the satisfaction in his eyes, he chuckled softly. Then he rubbed his son's back and commented, "When you need a friend to talk too, talk to God, Junior. He's up there waiting for you." His father smiled again and winked. He was pleased he had lifted his son's spirits that evening.

Later that evening, his father's massive hands poked around inside his pouch trying to find another soda. After unearthing the bottle, he twisted the cap off and took another satisfying swig. "Ahh, that was so good," he cheerfully said.

Since that warm evening, Solomon fully understood that heaven was for everyone, not just the dead. It would be his refuge, a sacred refuge where God would provide direction, support, and love.

His father also believed that if you walked the path God created for you, your life would always be intact. No mistakes or failures could touch that completeness because God was the only entity that could get the best of you. "That means you'll be fearless, Junior," his father said.

Solomon knew that if he followed God's plan, he'd have the determination to be someone. He often would close his eyes and imagine being in paradise when his spirit submerged into loneliness and confusion, like it had done the night of his father's death and the day Bill came into their lives.

At night, he'd climb on top of Mr. Cloverfield's store and gaze at the vivid stars and the silver sky. The firmament fascinated him, carefully capturing and restoring his soul. He would ask God for instruction and inspiration. Time and again, God cleansed his soul of despair, encouraging him to confront the distractions and move on with his life.

Spending time at Lake Hope that afternoon boosted Solomon's spirits. He needed that. He headed back home rejuvenated.

CHAPTER 12

The girls' spotted Solomon coming down the hill and raced toward him. "Junior! Junior!" they yelled.

Magnolia came to a sudden stop with one leg perched. She placed her hand on the leg. "Where you been?" Her heavy breathing slowed and she tried to regain her composure. "We been waiting a long time for you, Junior."

Rose and Hyacinth stopped halfway and caught their breath too. Rose shouted, "I missed you!"

Solomon smiled and rushed toward them. He kneeled down and grabbed and kissed them. "I wasn't gone long," he said.

Hyacinth jerked her thumb out of her mouth. "Next time, can we go with you?"

Grinning, he replied, "All right, next time."

The girls were identical but everyone could tell them apart because they each possessed special traits. A large, light-colored birthmark stained the left side of Hyacinth's face. Ivory called it the mark of God.

Magnolia talked a lot like her mother and older sister Lily. Although they had different fathers, Magnolia reminded Solomon of his father in many ways. She was strong-minded and extremely bright.

Rose walked with a limp. She fell into a deep well in the back yard and injured her leg when she was two years old.

Solomon remembered that day well. Bill was caring for the girls one afternoon, and instead of watching them, like a responsible parent, he had his back turned away from the girls and was writing a letter to his lover. Solomon found the letter on the ground days later.

It all happened so fast. One minute Rose was picking peaches off the ground and the next everyone heard her scream. The horrible sound still bellowed in Solomon's mind.

Solomon was incensed; he could have killed Bill. All the neighbors helped with the rescue. Miles Jamison dashed to get Buford, who was at the home of his mistress, Annie Ingram.

The scene grew chaotic. People gathered, trying to help, yet not one person there was experienced with such an emergency. Solomon wanted to ease Rose's fear, which was clear in her voice.

Bending down on his knees, he yelled to her, "Rose, we'll get you out of here. Don't cry baby, it'll be over real soon. I promise. Okay?"

"O . . . k . . . kay, Jun . . . yer," she cried.

Everyone grew uneasy. The circumstances were frightening. Meanwhile Bill stood around like a child who had done something bad. His hands trembled and he felt ashamed. He glanced sheepishly at Solomon and Miles, and felt as helpless as they did. All he could do was fiddle with his fingers while the young boys and their parents tried to rescue his daughter. His eyes scrolled from side to side and his miniature head sunk as he watched them fight for her life.

Mr. Jamison, Buford, and Solomon tied together several pieces of heavy twine to form a lengthy rope. Mr. Jamison tugged firmly on the last piece of twine, a look of desperation on his face. It showed in every bulging vein and every pebble of moisture. He knew that if they didn't hurry, Rose might die.

Then he and Solomon inserted the long cord into the tiny opening and begged Rose to grab hold of it. When she did, they slowly hoisted her to the surface. The crowd let out a sigh of relief when her tiny head emerged from the small hole. She had both hands folded over her chest. Ivory almost fainted.

The entire ordeal took hours, and in spite of their diligent efforts Rose's right leg was severely wounded when it brushed against the harsh gravel. Dr. Benson secured her leg with bandages, trying to relieve the pain. He used herbs and redressed the wound every day. He even performed massage therapy but his efforts failed. Nothing helped. Not even prayer.

Since then Rose staggered often and cried occasionally, but the Walker family simply thanked God she didn't die from the fall.

Despite their dissimilarities, the girls bore Ivory's facial features: beautiful mahogany complexion and lovely brown eyes. Everyone in town knew they were her daughters.

* * *

Solomon let the girls jump rope and he walked up the steps. Upon reaching the front door, he noticed it was cracked open. He heard his mother's weak voice. She seemed worried. He took a quick look inside and saw grief written all over her face—the same way it looked the day his father died.

He slowly opened the door and was shocked. His mother was chasing Bill around the room and visibly upset. Ivory never was good with words but she tried her best to articulate her feelings. She was agitated and began to cry. Soon she started to choke on her words. "Bill, where you goin'?"

He didn't respond and continued stuffing clothes into a suitcase. Ivory raced toward him and threw the suitcase on the floor. "When you comin' back?" she demanded, out of breath. She mingled her trembling hands through her hair and stormed around the room. Bill simply laughed. She stared him in the eye. "Bill," she yelled, "you just cain't walk away from yo family!"

Ivory's medium frame slumped to the floor and her hands grabbed one of his legs. He boldly kicked her off of him. She begged him to stay. "Bill, how we gonna live? You cain't leave us. We need you. Please Bill, don't go."

Bill snatched up the suitcase that belonged to Solomon's father, tossed it on the bed, and continued to pack his belongings with a grin, ignoring her.

He continued grinning until she screamed. It was a nervous scream—a plea for someone to walk right into the bedroom and stop this pitiful man.

Then he stopped packing because he knew she wouldn't shut up. Suddenly he turned toward her. "We just goin' to have to work a little harder 'round here, Ivry," he said mockingly.

He walked over to her and jabbed his finger in her face. "Member, I only have three chil'rens. Dem other three not mine. Dey yours. Solomin old enough to work. Y'all do just fine without me."

When he slammed the suitcase shut, the noise made her jump and grab her belly. She felt sick.

Bill drew in and released a deep breath as though some horrible load had been lifted off his shoulders. He turned to Ivory again, still grinning. It was all amusing to him.

Solomon stood by the door listening in on the commotion. He never thought someone could have gotten satisfaction from toying with another person's feelings this way. His father always told him that a person like Bill was half-grown and uncivil.

Bill paused and then gazed around the room, making sure he hadn't left behind any of his useless possessions. He faced Ivory again. "I'm not coming back, Ivory. I'm going out west to live with my brother."

Solomon heard the old suitcase covering constrict when Bill clutched it as though it were his own. "There's nothing here for me in Mission," Bill shouted, heading for the kitchen. "Not a got damn thing!"

"Hush yo mouth," Ivory yelled. "You should be a shame of yo'self, cursing in my home!"

She looked away from him and toward the window. Tears rolled down her spotless face. She started to speak but then shook her head and raised her hands to him. During the past four years she had seen and heard enough. If he wanted to leave then that was his choice. She had never done him wrong. All she ever did was love him. She had been good to him, better than any woman he had ever been with.

She mumbled, "Bill, just remember that I loved you and I never meant to cause you no pain."

Bill's adolescent face turned apple red as if her honesty embarrassed him. He stood there shameless like he'd always done in the past—just like the day he first met her at her husband's funeral, and just like the day he ran out on her after she gave him twenty dollars to fix the truck that had been sitting in the back yard for years, and just like the day he bragged to Buford that she was just comfort meat and he loved only himself.

Ivory finally realized that Solomon's assessment of Bill had been correct. He was less than a man. He was pure trash. Nevertheless, Bill ignored her. He grabbed the suitcase and walked toward the door, bobbing all the way. A glass of sweet iced tea sat on the kitchen table. Solomon couldn't believe his eyes when Bill picked up the glass and gulped down the contents like it was his last drink.

After downing the iced tea, he slid the back of his hand across his wide silly mouth and put the cup back on the table. Solomon heard him whisper, "I should have done this a long time ago."

He passed Solomon by just like it was yesterday. He didn't dare look at him. Solomon smelled his rotten breath as he swung the front door open. Bill proudly stared ahead and walked down the broken steps.

He headed toward the trail that led to the hill. There wasn't an ounce of compassion in his heart. He wasn't even man enough to say goodbye to his daughters, who were playing in the yard. They stopped playing as soon as he passed them. Hyacinth giggled when she saw the hole in his shoe.

Then Magnolia yelled, "Bye, Daddy!"

Rose shouted, waving her hand, "See you later, alligator!"

Ivory and Solomon stood on the porch holding each other and watched the sun beam down on his red soul. Ivory was deeply hurt but Solomon was pleased to be finally rid of the man.

Then Ivory fell to her knees and sobbed. Solomon reached

down and rocked her, trying to console her. He glanced up for a second and noticed Bill slowing. For a moment, it seemed as though he was swaying, as if with pride. It was pathetic.

Solomon looked down at his mother and held her in his arms. He wanted to go back inside but his mother's hands were stuck to his. She wiped her eyes with her apron and stared at Bill's retreating shadow.

Her tears stopped when Bill reached the top of the hill. Oddly, he paused and his body began to turn toward them. Ivory's eyes gleamed. But then Bill's body turned around and his back faced them once again. Soon his immoral reflection disappeared and they never saw William Chicago Wright again. Solomon and his family needed their dignity back. It was time they were a real family again.

"Thank God he didn't have a change of mind," Solomon muttered.

Ivory heard Solomon's smart remark. She looked away from him and pressed her fingers hard against her forehead. Her pain was so strong she knew she could never love another man again.

Once again, they found themselves alone. Solomon knew they would persevere. He knew they were strong and that nothing prevented them from succeeding.

That night while the kids were asleep, Ivory sat on her bed weeping. Solomon always considered his mother a brave woman, but there were times when her heart could only take so much.

Ivory sluggishly kneeled down and prayed. She asked God to bring Bill back. She told God that she was sorry. And she wanted to know what had she done wrong.

Solomon crept up behind her and gently tapped her shoulder. She spun her head, looking spooked. For a split second she thought it was God answering her prayers.

Solomon sat on his heels next to her. "God will look after us, Mama." He rubbed his hand on the bible that was lying on the bed. "We're too strong to give up and we're too strong to lose hope. And God only knows, we're too strong to place blame on ourselves."

Her tears flowed. Ivory loved Bill dearly and could not fathom how it was he had abandoned them. She felt like a battered ship winding through troubled waters. Solomon gently pressed his thumb against her face and wiped away the tears.

She stared at her son, gripping his shoulders. "Junior, how could he do what he did? You think he was in his right mind?"

"Mama, sometimes people aren't kind. When you don't have love in your heart, you have no love for others."

He held her hand and hugged her.

"You right, Junior," she said. "We got to be strong if we going to survive." She smiled. "The Man above will look after us. If we have each other, everything will be fine."

* * *

The next morning Ivory awakened bright and early and cooked grits for breakfast. The girls loved it with plenty of butter.

Normally she had high spirits and always conversed with her children. They looked forward to their morning conversations with her because they were always refreshing and rewarding. Ivory heightened their curiosity, forever challenging them. She made her children use their good judgment. There was never a dull moment in the Walker home, especially at the kitchen table.

Yet this morning, she was quiet and reserved, shifting around as though the life had been sucked out of her. Solomon volunteered to serve breakfast but she insisted that she could manage. He knew she was hiding her emotions, and he also knew she didn't want the kids to see her so unsettled.

Ivory fought back the tears. Solomon could feel her pain and sense of betrayal. A feeling of worthlessness clutched her soul. She wanted to scream and let the world know she was suffering, but instead, she continued serving breakfast and forced herself to answer the children's frequent questions.

Hyacinth leaped out of the chair and raced toward her. She kissed and touched her mother's unblemished face. "Mama, what are we doing today? Can we go down to Pa Pa's farm?"

"If he come for you," Ivory said, "you can go."

Pa Pa was Mr. Williams and a family friend. He and his wife lived on a farm in Perry. He didn't own the farm, just lived and worked on it.

Mr. Williams enjoyed the children's company and cherished their visits. The girls so enjoyed playing with the animals and helping him tend to the farm. It was Mr. Williams who nicknamed Lily "Teacher" because she taught him how to read and write.

Mrs. Williams made the best ice cream for miles around. Every time the children came over she'd make cherry vanilla ice cream, their favorite.

On Saturday mornings, Mr. Williams came to Mission to sell fruits and vegetables. By late afternoon, his last stop was their home. He'd often take the kids to the farm and drop them back home in the evening. Solomon usually stayed behind to help his mother with housework and errands.

On that particular morning, Ivory sent them all to the Williams' farm. She had decided to go to town and find more work. They would need more money now that Bill was gone. He had taken most of the money that she had saved in the cookie jar with him. Solomon would have to leave school if she didn't find more work. Ivory wouldn't have it.

CHAPTER 13

The porch light was on when Mr. Williams dropped the children off that evening. As his truck approached the house, Solomon noticed his mother sitting in the rocking chair. She looked sad and more than likely was thinking of Bill. Solomon knew it would take some time to get him out of her head. For better or for worse, time was all she had.

Solomon jumped off of Mr. Williams' truck and saw his mother rocking languidly back and forth. She half-smiled at the sight of her children. She knew her children were on their best behavior at the farm because she taught them well.

The children thanked Mr. Williams, the girls giving him a lively hug and kiss. "Bye, Pa Pa," said Magnolia, pinching his rusty cheek.

Blowing a kiss to him, Rose uttered, "We love you!"

Then Hyacinth pointed her finger at him. "I'll be mad if you don't come for us next time, Pa Pa."

Solomon was shocked by her sharp remark and spanked her buttock. "You know better than that, Hyacinth. Say you're sorry."

"Sorry, Pa Pa. But, please . . . don't forget. Okay!" she said apologetically.

Mr. Williams let out a heavy rough laugh and replied, "You know I won't forget my grandbabies. I'll be back here same time next weekend."

He waved goodbye, hopped into his truck, and sped away—the tires leaving deep imprints in the dirt road. The girls ran after the truck until they were weak from fatigue.

"Girls, don't go too far! Come back now!" shouted Ivory.

So they ran back toward the house. Rose yelled to the others, "Don't mess up the marks!"

"I'm not!" said Hyacinth.

They were all out of breath yet completely challenged when they reached the house. For Solomon, the tire marks were a steady reminder of the way out of Mission.

The kids settled inside while Solomon sat with his mother. They listened to the pleasing sound of night. Ivory was happy to hear that the kids had milked the cows, fed the pigs, and helped Mrs. Williams with her vegetable garden. She was relieved they had a wonderful time in spite of the ugliness that had occurred the day before.

"Seems like you all had a good time today, huh, Junior?" she said.

Solomon eased up next to his mother on the rocking chair. "We sure did, Mama. Can't wait until next weekend."

He banged his knuckle on the wood. "You know, Mama . . ." said Solomon, "the kids didn't mention Bill at all. They didn't even ask where he was. Isn't that something?"

She looked at him sideways and then at the ground. Her eyelids flickered. His remark had hit home and her hands began to tremble. Solomon carried on because he felt it was important that she understand his feelings. "I really think we're better off without him, Mama."

Ivory turned away. He was breaking her heart all over again and he had no idea he was doing it. After all, he was just fourteen.

"He didn't do us any good when he was here, and he's surely not doing us any good now that he's gone," he preached on.

Tickled by his words, her hands flew back. She chuckled and said, "That's the honest truth, Junior."

Solomon knew her heart ached but he felt it was time to release the pain and go forward if they were going to survive. He knew laughter would ease her suffering, making her wiser and stronger and keeping them focused.

Ivory told Solomon that the work at Ethel's Tailor Shop was getting slow and that she might have to find another family to clean for. She would clean the Cloverfield's home during the day, work at the shop during the evening, and clean the other family's home on the weekends.

Solomon knew his mother was going to work herself to death so he suggested that he take on a full-time job. She told him not to worry and to concentrate on the upcoming school year that was going to start on Monday. She believed their trials and tribulations were a test.

"The Man above know what He doing, Junior. He guiding me. I know it." She patted her chest. "I feel it in my heart."

Ivory believed God was watching over them. She would hold on to that faith for the rest of her life.

* * *

It was seven in the morning and the heat of the sun spilling through Solomon's window dissolved all of his concerns about life and family.

He was thrilled it was the first day of school. While eating his hot grits, he and Lily discussed their class assignments, both of them wondering what their teacher, Miss Smith, had up her sleeve for them that day.

Nathaniel was learning advanced arithmetic. Solomon and Lily were studying algebra. Solomon's passion was for math and science. He told his mother he was going to be a scientist someday. Discovery excited him. He intentionally took things apart and put them back together, never making a single mistake.

The girls were awake and curious as usual. Solomon promised he would bring them a sweet treat after school if they were good. They swore they would be good but he knew the girls: there was never a dull moment in their home thanks to them. They weren't mischievous, simply hard to keep up with at times.

Lily asked Ivory who would care for the girls while they were in school. Ivory leaned over her, poured herself a glass of milk, and replied, "Miss Parker, of course."

"But, isn't Miss Parker sick, Mama?"

Ivory filled Nathaniel's cup too. "No, she doing better these days. Said she didn't mind at all."

It was a two-mile trek to school. Solomon and Nathaniel didn't mine it but Lily hated the hike, even to the point she'd pretend to be sick just so she could stay home. This tendency in fact had caused her to be demoted one year. Yet through her love of reading and desire to learn, Lily advanced quickly the following year.

Solomon and Lily excelled in school, as had their father. He was an intelligent man. Most folks thought he had gone to a university but he hadn't. He simply read lots of books.

It was important to him that his children had a good education. He made sure they read and told them how difficult it was for him to earn an education in the south. He and his siblings couldn't attend school because they had to work in the cotton fields to support the rest of the family. He had worked in the fields ever since he was four years old.

His parents had had very little education too. They too quit school to help feed their family. And education had been forbidden to Solomon's great grandparents because there simply were no schools available to them. They didn't know how to read or write. Back then blacks caught teaching others to read and write were lynched.

Solomon once asked his father why white children attend different schools than black children. His father rolled his eyes while sucking on a fish bone and said, "You want to know what, Junior?"

Solomon repeated the question slowly.

His father shook his head and sighed. "This is how it is, son." He threw the bone in a trashcan, pushed his thumb in his mouth, and pulled it out again.

"White folks know what they're doing to us," he said. "You go to an all-black school so they can keep you in your place. They know most of us don't know anything and they know that we don't have a lot of teachers to teach our kids. Not all of them, but some of them don't ever want us to succeed, Junior."

He gave Solomon a cruel stare. "You with me? You understand now?"

Solomon shook his head and said softly, "Yeah."

"They make us lose our respect for ourselves, until we don't know who we are anymore—until we are unable to trust anyone, not even our own kind, Junior. They put fear in us and that is how they get power. They try to control us."

His father looked hard at him again and said, "You satisfied with that answer?"

"Yeah."

Solomon's father demanded they attend school and made sure they stuck to their studies.

Solomon, Lily, and Nathaniel went to the same all-black school. One teacher taught the entire class of thirty children ages five through fourteen.

Most of the school's teachers were young and only taught for a year or two. Some of them studied at small colleges; most just had a high school education.

The white owner of Mr. Williams' farm loved to read. His wife threw away many old books, claiming there were constantly too many in her house. She offered the books to Mr. Williams but he'd refused every time, even though he knew that "Teacher" and Solomon loved to read. A poor reader, Mr. Williams felt that no one else should have a chance to read books if he couldn't.

So when Mr. Williams frequented the big house to drop off the profits, he usually would have the children in his truck. Lily and Solomon would sneak around back and sift through the trash, searching for the next great novel. They would slip any books into their bags and hide them in the back seat. Their secret was never exposed.

Mr. Williams described the owner's house as an immaculate mansion saturated with books, art, and antiques. He never knew that Mrs. Williams told Lily and Solomon about the discarded books.

"Junior, you know dat man got mo books din anybody I know." He said while scratching his balding head. "What a man need with all dem books?"

Snapping some green beans, Solomon replied, "There's nothing wrong with reading, Mr. Williams. Shoo, Daddy loved to read and so do we."

"Yo daddy ain't no how to read. He just tell you dat." Mr. Williams said with a laugh. "Black folk can't read."

It was useless arguing with Mr. Williams because he believed what he believed. Solomon couldn't fathom why he'd refuse to take the books when Lily was teaching him how to read, as if he were determined not to learn.

When Solomon told Fannie Mae about Mr. Williams, she said, "Ignorant folks are just ignorant folks."

Ivory told Solomon that Mr. Williams once owned the farm. Years ago, the present owner deceived Mr. Williams. Apparently Mr. Williams borrowed some money from the owner and when he couldn't repay the loan on time, the owner insisted that Mr. Williams sign a contract that supposedly confirmed the outstanding amount including interest. But the paper in fact transferred ownership of the farm to the present owner. Mr. Williams' illiteracy prevented him from deciphering exactly what he was signing.

Mr. Williams suddenly blinked his eye. "Junior, you smarter din yo daddy." He chewed on a green bean. "You know what black folk be. Black folk got no bizzness readin' all dat stuff in the paper and books no way. What dey gon do with it. Nothin'!"

Solomon lost some respect for Mr. Williams that afternoon. He couldn't believe what he thought of his father. His father was no fool. He was just as smart as the next white person. He was an intelligent man, despite what Mr. Williams said.

"Yeah, Mr. Williams, I guess you're right. We don't have no business reading or writing," said Solomon.

Mr. Williams' thick scruffy eyebrows arched. "Ain't dat right."

"Yeah," said Solomon, "what would we do with it anyway? Shoo, where could we go? Up north to some big college?"

"See, Junior. I know you was smarter din yo daddy."

Solomon's father had taught him that knowledge was the only way out of Mission. It was the key to his future. "Learn all you can, son," he said. "There's nothing wrong with being smart."

CHAPTER 14

The first day of school started out fine for Solomon. He was excited about learning new things and being with his friends. But things began to change by late afternoon when Miss Smith said something to him that made him uncomfortable.

Miss Smith was a pleasant woman. She had taken a liking to the Walker children because they were so close and had what no one in Mission had—triplet sisters. Ivory often invited her over for supper on Sundays.

She was a tall, heavy set, light-skinned woman who loved to eat. Everyday she brought to school cakes, cookies and candy. When she'd go over to Solomon's house, she'd also take something with her. It might be a baked ham, fried chicken, potato salad, or collard greens. Usually she'd bring her delicious caramel cake.

Her massive weight shook the classroom floor when she strolled over in Solomon's direction, practically out of breath. "Daydreaming, Solomon Walker," she remarked, aiming a piece of chalk at him. "One day, I'm going to reach inside that mind of yours and . . ."

Solomon immediately rose to attention. "Sorry, ma'am. What was the question again?"

"I asked if you were daydreaming?"

"Yeah, I was. I'm sorry, ma'am," he said feeling embarrassed.

"About what, Solomon?"

"I was thinking about everything, ma'am. My life. School."

Some students quit playing around. Then the classroom grew quiet and all eyes were fixed on him. Now everyone, especially Lily and Nathaniel, wanted to know what worried him. He turned toward the window, suddenly feeling self-conscious.

Miss Smith had observed him daydreaming again. Something he'd been doing since last year. He had much on his mind. He was worried that because of the lack of resources and money, he and his family would not be able to carry on.

So after school, Miss Smith called him to the front of the class, demanding to know everything.

"I guess I'm just anxious to get back into my studies and finish this school year," he said.

Miss Smith glanced up at him with an ugly grin and said something he would never forget. "Solomon, never be too anxious of what is to come, just thank God for what has come."

Solomon smiled. Her words puzzled him. He scratched the back of his head and pursed his lips. "Okay, ma'am. I'll do that."

He turned and walked away. But when his feet leaned against the door and his ashy hand touched the knob, she yelled, "Solomon!"

"Ma'am."

"Remember, always hold on to today because tomorrow is not promised."

This left him baffled. *What did she mean? Never mind. She probably had a lot on her mind too.*

He turned back to her and half-smiled. "Thank you, Miss Smith. I'll see you tomorrow morning."

She grinned, the same way Bill had when he left. Afterward she reached into her bag and took out a flattened slice of sweet potato pie. A bitter chill crept up his spine and his ears began to buzz. He released a deep breath and headed out the classroom.

When he started walking home with Lily and Nathaniel, his stomach began to ache. He dashed behind a tree, dropped his books to the ground, and slouched to his knees and vomited. It was like all of his energy spewing out of his body. *Did she do this to me?*

Miss Smith was responsible. She was no longer the happy-go-lucky, generous, chunky, sweet teacher. Now she was wicked.

Lily and Nathaniel laughed at him, but Solomon ignored them and wiped the residue from his mouth.

Like clockwork they stopped by Miss Parker's house to get the girls. They were waiting outside when they arrived.

"Good afternoon, Miss Parker," they said in unison.

The girls were combing Miss Parker's hair. "Hey, chil'rens. It's a fine day, itn't?" she said.

"It sure is. Just beautiful," Lily replied.

"I sure hope you all gonna stay a while. I like yo company," she said, spitting snuff into a can. "Don't run off so fast now!"

Still weak, Solomon staggered over to her and sat down on the steps. "Okay, Miss Parker, we'll stay here for a few minutes. But only for a few minutes."

She laughed while chewing on snuff. "That's fine with me." Slowly she reached down and whispered into Solomon's ear, "Solomin, Ivry told me 'bout Bill."

"Yeah, I figured she would, Miss Parker."

She motioned her left hand upward and told the girls to stop combing her hair. Bending over again, she said, "How you feeling?"

Solomon shrugged. "I'm okay, I guess."

His stomach was still boiling. He grabbed on to the porch railing and said, "I just want things to go well for all of us. I'm worried about Mama, though. But I know she'll pull through this."

Glancing at Miss Parker, he added in a serious tone, "She worked so hard and gave so much to him." He moaned with pain. "Ahh . . ."

"You okay, Solomin?"

"Yeah, ate something that didn't agree with my stomach, that's all. Anyway, she trusted him and he took advantage of her kindness. You know what I mean, Miss Parker?"

Tapping his shoulder, she said, "I know. But believes me, things will go well for y'all. They will." She shook her head. "I just don't understand it. He go and take off and go out west. What's out there but dry land and no water. I tell you, that's what out there."

Solomon laughed.

"You know what, Solomin?" Miss Parker said.

"What's that, Miss Parker?"

"He gonna fall flat on his face like he always do and be back begging."

Solomon shook his head and said, "No, Miss Parker. I know he's gone for good. I hope and pray he doesn't come back for Mama's sake. Shoo, for our sake too." Squeezing the railing, he went on, "I'm not saying that he didn't help us at all, but what little he did do for us wasn't much. He was more of a problem than a solution."

"You know that's right. Preach, boy!"

Solomon couldn't avoid grinning. Then he stared at her and said, "He was a stranger, Miss Parker. He wasn't family."

"Preach it now!"

"Family don't do this to one another. I don't believe he loved the girls either. He was in love with himself. You know what I mean?"

"I know what you mean! I know!"

Solomon paused. Then he stood up and looked at her wild mane. Miss Parker's eyes widened.

"I know in my heart that nothing but good will come out of this. I have to believe that," he said, banging his hand on the railing.

"I do."

"I know if we follow God's plan," he said as he stood, "and believe me, He has a plan for us, Miss Parker."

"Yes, He do, Solomin!" she yelled, clapping her crumpling hands.

"Everything will be all right."

She smiled and absorbed all that he said. "Go on with yo bad self!"

"And for those like Bill," Solomon went on to say, "God won't judge or punish them. Instead He will change their hearts one day. I tell you, one day, Miss Parker."

Grinning, she replied, "Um-hmm, you right now! Boy, you right!" She placed the can aside. "But you know what, Solomin? Your mama is good folk and y'all good chil'rens. I know nothing but good will come out of this." She laughed. "She the daughter I never had and y'all the grandchil'rens I always wanted." Waving a paper fan back and forth, she added, "We all will make it!"

It was getting late and the girls were restless. "Well, Miss Parker, it's time to go," he said. "You have a good evening and we'll be back tomorrow."

The girls yelled, "We be back tomorrow, Granny."

Rose yelled, "I'm gonna bring some bows for your hair, Granny. It's a mess!"

"Okay, I be waiting for 'em."

* * *

On pleasant days, after getting the girls from Miss Parker, Solomon and the children usually trekked down to Lake Hope to play kick ball, swim, or just relax and talk.

They'd raced to Lake Hope drained from the sweltering heat and humidity. The sparkling blue water was captivating, unmoving. They would stand around the lake mesmerized. A feeling of tranquility would sweep through their bodies.

The lake's fragrance was in its way as good as Ivory's biscuits, and the sense it imparted was that of the end of a strenuous worked day, a feeling of contentment. It was a beautiful sensation, like the beginning of sundown, the sound of wind whispering through trees at night, the feeling of cool water grazing your sun-baked skin.

While at the lake, Solomon would grab hold of Rose's hand, who held onto Magnolia, who held Hyacinth's hand, who held Nathaniel's hand, until they were linked together like one spirit, staring in awe at God's creation.

So that afternoon, Solomon led them there. He told them the stories his father had told him. The girls were infatuated with the stories.

Standing on the lake's edge, Solomon extended his hand toward the sky and showed them their paradise. He said proudly, as it was expressed to him years earlier, "Beyond those stars is a heaven for all of us."

He looked down at Rose and then uttered, "Whenever you need someone to talk to," and pointed back up again, "look past those stars and ask God for it. He will help you and guide you in the right direction."

The girls smiled. "Heaven is for everyone," he said, "not just for dead people."

"How can we get there, Junior?" said Rose.

"By praying."

"Just pray, that's all?"

"Yep. If you pray, God will take you there."

"What does it look like, Junior?" Magnolia said.

"It's beautiful. Just beautiful."

Soon Lily, who knew the story too, spoke up, "It's a place that has big mountains, the bluest oceans, and grass is everywhere."

"For real?" yelled Hyacinth.

"For real!" Nathaniel said. "Everything is nice, especially the homes and people." He glanced at Solomon and winked his eye.

"I want to go right now, then!" demanded Rose.

They all laughed.

"Never be afraid to come here," Solomon said. "Because there's always someone here watching over you."

Lily and Nathaniel looked at him and smiled.

"God is," said Rose.

"That's right, baby," Solomon remarked. "God is here."

CHAPTER 15

They hiked another mile home. Ivory usually returned home around six in the evening. Solomon, Lily, and Nathaniel got the girls cleaned up, completed their homework, and started supper.

Solomon heard his mother chatting with Fannie Mae outside. Fannie Mae worked for a family that lived near Ethel's Tailor Shop and gave Ivory a ride home everyday.

When Solomon peeked out the window, his mother stepped out of Fannie Mae's car and waved goodbye. "Thanks for the ride, Fannie Mae. See you tomorrow."

Fannie Mae's car sped off.

"Hey, Mama!" the girls yelled with arms opened wide, awaiting a hug.

"Give me a kiss," insisted Rose.

"I love you," Hyacinth shouted.

"Okay, okay, let me put my bag down first," Ivory declared. She placed her purse on the kitchen table and hugged and kissed them.

Solomon walked toward her. "Hey, Mama."

"Hey, Junior. Is everything okay?"

"Everything is just fine, Mama. We made some smothered chicken and rice."

"Chicken, huh," she said. "Last time I looked, we didn't have no chicken."

"A little birdie dropped it by," Nathaniel said.

"Oh, is that right?"

"Um-Hmm."

"He did!" Rose said.

Ivory quietly laughed, then looked at Solomon sideways. "You know I ain't raise no thieves."

"I know, Mama, but we got to eat."

She rolled her eyes. "Whatever you say, Junior."

They were starving and had been waiting impatiently for her arrival. Solomon enjoyed making supper ranking it right up there with his appreciation of math and science. He'd learned how to cook by watching his mother, Fannie Mae, and Miss Parker. He kept the house tidy too. His father had also been a good cook and housekeeper.

It wasn't a burden helping his mother nurture the girls and take care of the house because he really enjoyed it. Caring for six children was rough. His mother needed rest after working two jobs and also relished those quiet moments.

Even though he was busy as well, Solomon stayed involved in sports and hung out with his friends. When he wasn't working at the store, he enjoyed playing with his neighbors. They would go down to an open lot not far from home and play basketball, which was Solomon's favorite sport. Whenever they had money, the older kids gambled it on the games. Eventually they would give the money back to each other, knowing that they needed it for food or other basic necessity.

Jefferson and Augustus Booker, the twins, were really good basketball players but not as good as Solomon. Nevertheless, they eventually landed on the same team and always won.

John Henry, Miles, and Lucas Jamison were always on the same team too. John Henry was sixteen, ebony complexioned, and tall and muscular, like Solomon's father. Solomon envied his fitness but knew one day he would be as tall and broad as he.

John Henry would try to intimidate the other players with his boisterous mouth but was always unsuccessful. Once Solomon made him mad when he laughed at John Henry's losing team. John Henry's eyebrows crumpled and he shut his mouth tight. Then he growled like an animal. At that, Solomon laughed louder because John Henry looked like a fool.

John Henry bit down on his massive lip and headed straight toward Solomon with hungry speed. Jefferson and Augustus pointed their fingers at Solomon and yelled, "Junior, look out!"

Solomon turned toward the twins and it took a second to notice their fingers pointing in John Henry's direction. When he turned back around and faced John Henry he was suddenly slammed hard to the ground. He didn't have a chance to react.

John Henry expected Solomon to cry and run home to his mother. But instead, Solomon looked around and grabbed a large piece of wood. He ran toward John Henry like a madman and struck him powerfully across the face. John Henry was knocked to the ground. Solomon hit him again when he looked up. There was absolute silence.

Blood squirted out of a massive wound on the side of John Henry's face. Solomon didn't want to hit him again because it wasn't fair and the game was over.

From then on, Solomon never had any problems with John Henry. The neighborhood kids nicknamed John Henry, Dog Man. Most people in town tolerated Dog Man's foul mouth and threats, but not Solomon. He stood his ground and never wavered.

Miles was the same age as Solomon and the twins. He was the spitting image of his older brother. Miles had a loud mouth like Dog Man and was also tall and husky. He too tried in vain to frighten the rest of the gang. He was the better player of the three brothers and preferred to play on Solomon's team, but Jefferson and Augustus were reluctant to play with him because his demeanor was unbearable as well.

Lucas was thirteen and a serious bookworm. He had the biggest crush on Lily. Solomon made sure it stayed a crush and nothing more. The young boys were as dishonest and low as the grown men in Mission. The things they had done or wanted to do would have made Solomon's father roll over in his grave if he knew Solomon had befriended them.

United they had the strength to move a mountain, but no one among them had the courage to try. So they remained in Mission, idle if not downright submissive.

In reality no one had the courage to leave, to achieve the self-respect and sense of accomplishment they deserved. God forbid anyone did. Where would they go? What would they do? And that is exactly what worried most folks in Mission. They didn't hide their feelings about it either, making other folks uncomfortable and apprehensive about accomplishing their goals and living like a human being, if that was at all possible.

In spite of their parents' unwillingness and lack of confidence to migrate north to improve their livelihood, they and most of the children labored day in and day out to put food on the table. They were skilled and hardworking people, tough as leather.

Yet bad luck and those endless obstacles never got the best of Solomon's parents. His mother never worried because she believed one day her family would overcome the hardships. One day, a finer day awaited them all.

Solomon admired his mother's rock-hard resolve, her focus in life, her profound love for her family and friends, and her everlasting belief in God.

She was a stronger person than he was. Fourteen years old was considered adulthood then. Yet he hadn't developed the kind of bravery, concentration, and unbending disposition his mother possessed.

Getting an education was the last thing on the minds of Solomon's friends. But as much as he loved school he wanted to work full-time and do more for his family. He prayed his school years to be over.

Before Bill left Solomon couldn't wait for the next school year to begin. He would start high school in the fall. There was a time when he looked forward to high school because there would be real science laboratories there. He could study biology, chemistry, and physics. He vowed to take all of the science classes. Meeting new friends excited him. Maybe he would have a chance to meet teachers who had traveled across country or abroad and spoke different languages. Maybe he would meet teachers who wouldn't get the best of him and make him sick to his stomach like Miss Smith did.

CHAPTER 16

The last week of school finally arrived, and the children were thrilled. It hadn't been an easy school year for Solomon. This would also be the last time he would attend school with his siblings.

Miss Smith approached him on the last day of school. He feared hearing those same words she said to him on the first day of class. They had made him ill, which was sad because he liked her otherwise.

Miss Smith wobbled over to him wearing a twisted smile. "Still anxious, Solomon?"

Solomon closed his eyes briefly and thought, *Not again.*

"Ma'am, I'm just glad I did well this year," he said smiling. "Looking forward to a fun summer."

She grinned scornfully fanning her face with a pamphlet. "And you know it's going to be a hot one, too."

They both let out a phony laugh. *That wasn't too bad,* he thought.

Miss Smith let the school out early, telling the students to be good and stay out of trouble. But Solomon felt her presence behind him as he packed his bag. Her breathing was heavy. She spoke again with concern in her voice. "Solomon."

"Yes, ma'am."

"Tell your mother hey. I'll come and see her real soon." He

sighed with relief.

* * *

Later, they stopped by Mr. Cloverfield's store for some candy. While he was there Solomon fired up the nerve and asked him if he could work during the summer. Mr. Cloverfield's watery gray eyes were saturated with tiny red veins. They widened when he saw Solomon coming toward him. Suddenly his bulky eyelashes scrunched up. He was cold and wicked.

Mr. Cloverfield acted like an angry, pampered child. He puckered his dry ashy lips, then stared at Solomon for what seemed like several minutes and said, "Yes."

Solomon couldn't believe he said yes. He asked him when could he start and Mr. Cloverfield answered in a harsh tone, "Boy, ain't this the last day of school?"

"Yes, sir."

His aged hands trembled as he lifted a cigar from its case and gently tasted the tip. Smacking his lips, he said, "You sho' not like them other niggra chil'ren that don't want to do nothing but sit round here and make trouble."

Inserting the tip into his mouth, he said, "Come back on Monday." When he jerked the cigar out of his mouth and pointed it at Solomon, his saliva grazed Solomon's face. Solomon quickly wiped the spit off of his cheek.

Then Mr. Cloverfield warned, "And you better be on time, boy. Or else!"

There were times when Solomon pitied Mr. Cloverfield. He often prayed for him because it made no sense for a person to be so cruel and so full of hate. Yet that's all he had known of most white people all his life. They treated animals better than they treated black folks.

Bill often misbehaved when he was around them. He'd embarrass Ivory and her children, making white folks believe they depended on him. Yet Solomon's father let them know that he would not tolerate their wicked ways. He let them know he was just as smart as they were.

As a child, Solomon said to his father, "Daddy, why white folks so evil? Why they have to control and kill us black folk? Why do they act like we are stupid and talk down to us? Why do they spit in our faces sometimes?"

His father chuckled. His son was too inquisitive. Yet he knew there were some things he ought to know in order to survive in this mad world.

He caressed his son's head and said, "And they do this in God's name too."

Shocked by his father's answer, Solomon remarked, "God's name! I don't know a God like that."

His father sat up straight and fixed his eyes on his son. "Neither do I, but apparently they do!"

Solomon's father and Carter drilled in his head the stories about their family. Carter's parents were killed in a fire and Solomon's grandmother cared for him. He didn't have any siblings and was very close to Solomon's family.

Solomon remembered well one story about his grandfather Elijah Walker, a robust and brave man. He was a black Cherokee. He was over six feet tall, dark skinned, and had a keen nose. He wore his straight hair in a ponytail. Elijah made corn liquor deep in the woods. When word got out that he was making liquor, some rednecks tried to waylay him.

Many times they'd fly a small plane around the area where he'd set up shop. And when his grandfather saw the plane, he would hurriedly pack up his belongings, move to a new place, and set up shop anew.

White folks didn't want any of the black folks to have a piece of the action. Elijah made liquor for himself and his friends but would sell it to white folks.

On one occasion, Uncle Eugene and Carter were out in the woods late one evening making corn liquor when some men waylaid them. They put up a hell of a fight. Carter got away and quickly made his way home to get help. Poor Uncle Eugene was left behind in the scuffle.

Carter frantically opened the Walker's door with news of what had happened. Elijah, Solomon Senior, and the rest of the siblings loaded up their guns and swiftly returned to the woods. When Solomon Senior spotted the first white man, he put his huge dark hands around his neck, almost squeezing the life out of him, and said in a deep penetrating voice, "Where's my brother?"

The pasty faced man trembled so and urinated in his pants. Scared and speechless, the man pointed to the bushes. Solomon Senior screamed for his brother. "Eugene! Eugene, you there?"

A faint voice could be heard. "Yeah, Solomon, I'm here back in these woods."

Uncle Eugene told them that once he escaped from the madmen, he hid in the woods. He was outnumbered and hoped they would go away, but they didn't.

Solomon's family was powerful and courageous. They didn't take intimidation from anyone. Solomon Senior said what he meant and he meant what he said. Most white folks knew this about him and he had few problems with them. However, Solomon did witness one incident.

His father and Carter loved to fish, and in the summertime they would head down to the fishpond just about every weekend. Solomon Senior usually took the children along but not this time. That day, Solomon Senior used some of Carter's fishing equipment and left his own on the front porch.

Solomon and his family were eating supper when several teenage boys came by and stole his father's fishing poles. Solomon and his mother ran outside and tried to stop them but the youths were too fast. The teenagers called them every hateful name imaginable, even threatened them.

The shortest of the group, who was very pale and freckle faced, said to Ivory, after spitting at her, "If you bring yo nigga ass any closer, I'll shoot your got damn head off."

Hours later Solomon Senior returned. When he saw his wife and children standing outside the house irately conversing, he knew something was wrong. Just when he noticed his fishing poles were missing, Solomon told him about the culprits.

His father picked up his gun and walked toward town, Solomon and Lily followed close behind. Ivory begged her husband not to go but he ignored her plea. He was going to get his fishing poles back.

One of the teenager's fathers named Mitchell met him in the middle of the road. Mitchell's moist crimson-colored face was evident a half mile away. His hands trembled as he handed Solomon Senior the fishing poles. He nervously said, "Solomin, here yo poles. My boys was just playin' around."

Mitchell scratched his neck. "They was just . . . just having fun, that's all." Mitchell forced a smile. "I knew you would be back for 'em!"

Everyone in town knew about the Walker family. They weren't weak. No one could bully them. When other children told Solomon things that had been done to them and their families, Solomon couldn't comprehend it because his family experienced no such foolishness. The Walkers stood their ground and never moved once.

Eventually Solomon's family moved throughout the south. Uncle Eugene married a nice woman named Sarah and moved to Atlanta after Solomon Senior died. He was devastated by his older brother's death and frequently visited after the funeral, but stopped when Bill moved in. Still, he would send Ivory money from time to time.

CHAPTER 17

Solomon told his mother the good news when she arrived home; Miss Smith sent the children home early and she'd promise to stop by and visit. He also told her about working at the store for the summer.

Ivory was happy for him. She knew he wanted to do more.

Lily said out of the blue, "I wished school lasted all year round."

Patting the back of her head, Ivory said, "Lily, you chil'rens need a break. That's what summer is for. Time to have fun."

She leaned Lily's head against her bosom and kissed her forehead. "You can learn when you're having fun too."

Lily smiled.

"It gives you more time to spend with yo family," Ivory explained.

Nathaniel said in disbelief, "Are you crazy? School year round! I don't know what I would do." He threw a cookie at Lily. "I like school but I don't like it that much!"

The girls gathered around, asking when would they be able to attend school.

"In two and a half months!" Lily said, giving Magnolia a sip of her milk. "Yep, in a little more than two months, you'll all be in school, learning everything I taught you."

"ABC's and 123's," Magnolia said.

"Yes, all of that stuff," Lily said.

Hyacinth placed her hands on her hips, rocked from side to side, and said, "Are you sure? Only two more months?"

Jumping up and down, Rose screamed, "I can't wait!" Then she collected herself and said, "Do you think Miss Smith can handle us?"

Solomon laughed and jokingly replied, "If Miss Parker can keep up with you three, and so can Miss Smith!"

The girls chuckled.

Later that evening, Ivory sat at the kitchen table motionless, troubled by something. She moved her head from side to side slowly and meditated.

Solomon tried to read her mind. He thought if he made a sound she would move, so he shifted a glass around on the table. Despite his efforts, her mind drifted farther away. It was sad watching her withdraw from the world, withdraw from him. She sat there possessed by sheer calmness.

Solomon grew restless and was unwilling to permit sorrow back into their home. So he voiced the inevitable question. "Mama, what's on your mind?"

She jumped and without lifting her head up, softly uttered, "Everything."

Ivory took on the world. She carried a heavy load and something was always on her mind.

"I been sick."

He looked surprised. His mother never got sick. She was always so strong and full of life. "Sick, Mama?" he said.

She placed her hands on the side of her face and began to rub it. "Yeah, and I don't know if doing all this work be enough for us."

She forced herself up then quickly sat down again. She was weak and began to breathe in and out. It caused her pain. Soon she let out a desperate moan. Her head dropped and her eyes were fixed on the wood floor. She didn't cry this time when she muttered, "I miss Bill, too. Wonder what he doing right about now."

Before Solomon could utter a word, she whispered, "I know

you don't understand. You see the picture better when you're older, Junior."

Ivory leaned her head back and sucked on her lips in such a way it seemed as if she were praying. She closed her eyes and faced the ceiling. "No matter how much a person hurt you," she placed her hand on her chest, "deep down there's a part of them that's good and you never forget that, Junior."

Solomon did not answer. He refused to. His concern was her health, not her feelings.

"Mama, what's wrong with you?" he said. "You said you're not feeling well. Something must be wrong."

She was quiet. Solomon slid closer to her and touched her arm. "What's hurting you?"

"My whole body ache, Junior. I feel like some truck done run ova me."

"Maybe . . . you're tire, working two jobs and all. You've been working a lot, Mama. Too much."

Her eyes stared into his and her face quivered. She said, "Junior, I work hard my whole life. Birth six chil'ren including three at one time, and I never felt this way before."

She tightened her fists and shut her eyes again. He felt her pain. His mother was suffering.

"Something must be wrong with me. I hurt all ova," she said.

Soon a gust of energy took over his heart and he hastily said, "Mama, I have decided to stay on at the store year round, if it's possible."

Ivory was heartbroken. She struggled to move closer to him, and when she did, she touched his hand. "Junior, you mean . . . you gonna miss school?"

"Mama, it's the best thing to do right now."

She was sobbing. "But it's not the right thing to do."

"Mama, you . . . you just said you're not feeling well. And . . . we may not have enough money to get by. If . . . if . . . I can stay on a little longer at the store, I know we can make it."

He stood and began to pace the room. Then he inched over toward the window, sneaking a quick look out. He stared at the hill and said, "Mama, you really need to rest. You've been working so hard. The kids miss you. I miss you." He clenched his hand. "I'll skip one year of school. That's all. It won't take any time to catch up."

That evening Ivory made her son promise her that he would forego only one year. And he made her promise that she would visit Dr. Benson the next day while she was in town.

The next morning Ivory was up early delegating a list of chores for her three eldest children. Clean, cook, and take care of the girls—the usual stuff.

All of the kids were dear to Solomon but Rose had his heart. He felt an incredible feeling of attachment for her ever since she injured her leg. Rose lacked what most kids took for granted—self-esteem. It was Solomon who taught her about self-love and courage. He helped her run again. He taught her to reach higher and never give up in life. He also taught her the difference between physical pain and injustice.

Solomon was the protective older brother because he had to be. She was disabled and someone needed to be there for her, particularly when the other kids ridiculed her and called her names like cripple or half-legged Rose.

Late that afternoon he took the girls and some of the other kids to an open field to play kick ball. When Hyacinth kicked the ball Magnolia ran as fast as she could to second base. Solomon pretended like he couldn't catch the ball when it was Rose's turn, giving her time to run to first base. It was a struggle to run, but she did well. She bit down on her lip, and her head and arms swung wildly. She was determined to get to the base as her arms stretched outward like an eagle. Finally, she staggered to home base, worn yet ecstatic.

It was important that Rose understand she could excel in whatever she applied herself to. That she knew that, despite her disability, she was strong mentally.

Later Rose and Solomon sat on the swing chair, swaying to a cozy rhythm. She giggled a lot but suddenly her mood turned serious. She shook her head and pondered. Then she turned to Solomon. "Junior, when is Daddy coming home?"

This startled him because it was the first time any of them ever had mentioned Bill's name. At first Solomon was speechless. He didn't want to lie to her and he didn't want to hurt her either. In her eyes, Bill was everything. He was her daddy.

He inhaled the sweet air and exhaled. He said softly, "Baby, I don't think he's coming home any time soon."

Her chubby face frowned. "You mean he left us, gone for good?"

Solomon picked her up and sat her on his lap. "I don't know, Rose," he said. "Bill had a lot on his mind and he needed to get away and figure out what he wants to do."

"Did he love us, Junior?"

Kissing her forehead, he said, "Rose . . . he . . . he . . . yes, he loved you but he had to go away and take care of business."

Solomon hated lying to his baby sister. Bill loved no one except himself. He probably loved those shallow folks he worked around more than he loved Ivory and his daughters.

Bill always tried to emulate them. He wanted to believe he was white but in spite of his fancy talk and fair complexion, he was still a nigger in their eyes.

In the south, most white folks hated black people. Carter persistently reminded Bill of the fact, yet he never listened. It was as if Bill had been born in another world and didn't understand what was going on around him in this one. Bill was always in their faces—laughing, telling them the Walkers' business, and warning them about other black folks whom despised them.

Years ago, Bill worked for a white doctor in Atlanta and had an affair with his youngest daughter, Agnes. Bill had a big ego and liked to remind Ivory about his fairy tale love story. He recited this story many times like it was some kind of badge of honor, and every time he recounted the story Solomon wanted to spit in his face.

"She was beautiful, innocent, and pure," Bill said smiling.

Ivory simply chuckled, pretending to brush it off. She knew

Bill was an ignorant man trying to be someone he could never be. Solomon cut his eyes at Bill.

"Miss Agnes was elegant, had the eyes of an angel and looked like a fashion model or Hollywood actress," he bragged.

Ivory began to mess around with her torn and stained housedress, feeling self-conscious. Solomon had enough of Bill's impolite behavior. "If she was all what you say, why are you here and not with her?"

Bill grabbed his jacket, put it on and stormed out of the house. He wasn't bold enough to punish Solomon.

This attractive white woman with her long flowing blond hair, petite waist, and seductive blue eyes had practically swept Bill off his feet. She also took him across country, disguising him as her servant. She taught and showed him things he had never seen before.

After his fling with Miss Agnes, he became convinced he was white and considered himself better than most black folks. For a while, Bill didn't want to be around his own people. He told Buford their uneducated ways appalled him.

Before he left Mission, Bill asked his white friend Vernon, a person he worshipped and would die for, for a loan to start his own business.

"A what?" Vernon said, sniffling.

Vernon thought Bill had gone crazy. He even asked Bill if he was sick.

"No, I'm not sick. I'm alright," Bill said fidgeting with some keys, "remember that store I told you about—the one off Hawkinsville Road—the one I want to buy."

"Naw, I don't remember," Vernon said shaking his head, "I don't recall that conversation."

Vernon gulped down a glass of cold ice water, looked at a picture of his overweight wife on the wall, and laughed in Bill's face. "Boy, I'll give my money to an orangutan before I'd give it to a nigger."

Bill chuckled and said, "Umm-hmm."

"What you say? Vernon asked.

"Nothing," Bill said as he tightly gripped the keys in his hand. "I'll find a way to get it."

"Yeah, you do just that," Vernon voiced.

Tugging on Solomon's shirt, Rose voiced, "You hear me, Junior. You love me. You won't ever leave me, right?"

Solomon leaned down and held her firmly. "Never! I'll never leave my babies," he said.

"Never, Junior."

Solomon's heart raced and his breathing grew heavy. "Never, Rose!" He held her by both arms, stared straight into her eyes, and said, "Rose, always remember that Mama and I try to do the best we can for all of you."

She smiled but Solomon sensed she didn't quite understand, so he shook her little body, causing her to cry.

"We brought you into this world because we loved you and wanted you," he said, then placed her head on his shoulders. "Rose, always remember that. Promise me you'll never forget what I just said."

Her head slowly raised and she wiped away the tears. She jumped off his lap and positioned her hands on her hips, a sarcastic grin on her face. "Okay, Junior. I promise."

Then she spread her hands wide and returned a hug. "I love you this much, Junior."

She giggled and ran toward the other children.

CHAPTER 18

Fannie Mae's car pulled up in front of their home that evening. It was clear Ivory had an exhausting workday by the way she stepped out of the car limply. As expected, the girls ran to her. "Mama, you're home!"

They escorted her inside. Ivory was weak and did not have the strength to place her bag on the table—it slid off her shoulder and onto the floor. She closed her eyes, slowly breathing in the night's soothing air and struggled to release it.

Shambling toward the table, she said in misery, "Is the house cleaned?" Then she looked at the stove. "Supper ready?"

"Yeah!" The girls said jubilantly. They jerked on her purse, hoping it contained candy. She usually brought home something sweet for them.

Ivory said apologetically, "Sorry, babies. I didn't bring anything today. Maybe tomorrow." She fell on to the chair. "Now, go and get ready for supper."

Ivory barely touched her food. She covered her forehead with her hands and lowered her head. She shut her eyes. "I'm so hot," she said.

Solomon jumped up. "Mama, are you all right?" He ran to the sink and dipped a washcloth into the water and put the cool rag on his mother's forehead.

Her body and hands shivered like those of an old woman. Something terrible was wrong but he stayed calm until the kids went to bed.

Afterward he asked her what was troubling her. She started to cry and then she told him. Solomon wanted to die. It was as though his heart had stopped beating and the world didn't exist anymore.

Dr. Benson found a lump in Ivory's breast and suspected she had breast cancer. He said more tests were needed in order to confirm his suspicion and that Ivory required admission into the hospital in Macon.

Painful tears rolled down his eyes and his head suddenly throbbed. He held his breath for a moment and pleaded with God. *Why my mother?*

Ivory didn't know what to do. She knew she couldn't afford the medical tests.

Solomon urged, "Mama, you have to go into the hospital. There's no ifs or buts about it." He held her hand. "Promise me you'll go. You need to get well."

She swallowed hard and nodded.

"I'm going to start work on Monday and I'll ask Mr. Cloverfield to put me on around the clock permanently," he said.

Ivory forced a smile. She wasn't happy about that because she really wanted him to finish school.

Solomon knew Mr. Cloverfield needed the help and he knew he was a dedicated and strong worker.

"We'll have the money for the hospital and for everything else. Promise me you won't worry. Worrying will only drain you."

She nodded again.

He reached for her hand and held it tight. He prayed. "Dear Lord, please help Mama through this difficult time. Keep her safe and keep her mind clear. Please keep her body strong, so she can fight this. Lead her in the right direction, Lord. Heal and bless her. Amen."

"Amen," Ivory uttered.

* * *

Saturday morning seemed like it would never come. The entire evening, Solomon scuffled in his sleep wishing the night would end. It seemed like eternity in coming.

It was five-thirty when he threw on some shabby pants and a long-sleeve shirt and hurried to Miss Parker's house.

Once he arrived, he banged on her door for several minutes before she answered.

"Who there?"

Breathless, he said, "Solomon, Miss Parker. It's Junior."

She opened the door cautiously. Her frizzled hair stuck out and her wide eyes fixed on him for a moment. She looked afraid.

Folks' first impression of Miss Parker usually wasn't kind. She had a frightful, evil looking appearance. If you didn't know her well, you would have been afraid to look at her the wrong way for fear she would cut your throat.

She was of medium height and build and walked with a cane. Jet-black hair coated her head. Ivory said she treated it with dye and always did a poor job of it, resulting in a gruesome looking scalp.

Miss Parker suffered from rheumatoid arthritis and her hands curved into ball shapes. They were practically deformed. Massive lumps covered her skinny legs and some were on top of her hands. Making matters worse, she had a deep charcoal complexion and wrinkles stretched across her face. She rarely smiled unless she knew you well.

Solomon moved his body forward so she could get a clear shot of him. "Miss Parker, it's me, Solomon Walker."

Suddenly she said, "Oh, Solomin, it's you all right. Everything okay?"

"Miss Parker, Mama needs your help," he said. He glanced at the porch ceiling and began to sob. "Dr. Benson thinks Mama has cancer."

Miss Parker's hands topped her face. "Oh, Lord! Oh, Lord have mercy!" She quickly unlatched the door lock and opened the door. "Solomin, come inside while I put on some clothes."

She hastily dressed while Solomon stood lifeless in the kitchen. He felt as though he had succumbed to nothing. His best friend and the only woman he'd ever loved was in poor health. He felt confused and hurt. He wanted to shout but merely slammed his fist into the wall and cried.

"Solomin, you okay?" she said, reaching out for him.

He placed his sore hand in hers and sobbed like a baby. After a few minutes, he collected his thoughts and reassured himself that everything would be fine now that Miss Parker knew. "I'm okay now, Miss Parker."

She smiled. "Now then, let's go. Ivry needs me."

"Okay, ma'am."

It was daybreak as they walked back home hand in hand. Ivory had awakened as soon as she heard the two of them whispering in the kitchen. She stepped out of bed and stared at them, shocked to see Miss Parker standing there so early in the morning.

Miss Parker reached for Ivory's hand. "Sweet baby, you all right?"

When Ivory did not answer, she caressed her hair and said, "Don't worry, Miss Parker is here. Don't you worry 'bout nothing. I'll stay here and everything will be alright."

Ivory collapsed into Miss Parker's arms like a helpless child and sobbed, "I don't want to die."

"You not going to die, Ivry."

"I'm not afraid to die but . . . I'm just not ready to go now. My babies need me."

"I know they do. Nothing gonna happen to you, Ivry," Miss Parker said, wiping Ivory's tears with her crinkled finger. "Nothing gonna happen. Be strong now, you gonna get through this."

While Miss Parker and Ivory talked, Solomon prepared breakfast for the kids even though his mind was filled with despairing thoughts.

It wasn't long before he began to think of his father, Mr. Positive. "Negativity is not going to get you any where, Junior. Think about the good things. Be positive," his father said to him one day at the fishpond while struggling to teach Solomon how to fish. Solomon thought he would never learn, but his father never gave in to hopelessness. He was eternally optimistic. That's how they persevered. Solomon had to believe in his mother. He had to be confident if they were going to survive this ordeal.

Like clockwork, Mr. Williams arrived on time. Solomon stayed home. There was much to discuss and his mother needed him. Now would be her chance to rest.

Miss Parker told them she had saved quite a bit of money during the past twenty years. They would now have the money to pay for the medical exams.

Miss Parker said she would inform Reverend Dean about Ivory's condition and the congregation could take up a collection on Sunday. She would also keep the kids while Solomon was at work. Before Miss Parker left, they all prayed again.

Monday morning finally arrived. The day Solomon had looked forward to all year would turn into the worst day of his life.

Fannie Mae picked up Ivory and drove her to the hospital. On the way there, they dropped the kids off at Miss Parker's. Solomon walked to work because he knew the fresh morning air would ease his mind.

Fannie Mae stayed with Ivory at the hospital. She would send someone to the store to get Solomon if there was any news.

Pretending to be excited about working that day, Solomon joyfully said, "Good morning, Mr. Cloverfield."

"Mornin', Solomin," he said, glancing at his watch. "Glad to see you on time today." He coughed—it was a hoarse cough. "There's plenty of work to be done round here."

Then he stared at Solomon, studying him. "You sure you up for the challenge?"

Solomon thought, *Apparently Mr. Cloverfield believes I never worked a hard day in my life before. After all, I only started picking cotton when I was four years old.*

Solomon wanted to tell that evil, charred lip, bad-tempered man that he didn't know what a challenge was.

Silently cursing Mr. Cloverfield, Solomon said, "I'm as ready as I'll always be."

Mr. Cloverfield laughed.

During his lunch break, Solomon asked him if he could work there on a full-time basis the entire year. At first Mr. Cloverfield immediately said no, claiming he didn't need any help and that Buford was capable of helping him. But Solomon knew it was only a matter of time before he changed his mind because Buford couldn't care less about the store, the movie house, the café, or anything associated with his family's name. He never told Solomon why. Solomon believed it was simply because Buford was different. He had a kind spirit.

Buford's only concern was hot and lustful black women. When Solomon was a young boy, he caught Buford in the bushes with his pants down, hollering like he was getting the crap beat out of him. Most of the white folks didn't know about his secret, but all the black folks did. He was always in Solomon's neck of the woods, visiting Annie Ingram, who had eight kids. The last five were his.

Annie swore Buford loved her and no one could tell her any different. She walked around town with a perennial pop belly. He'd come around her home and bring her kids food and candy from the store. Sometimes he would give her money. Still she was dirt poor and struggling like the rest. Although she considered herself high and mighty, her attitude was not as bad as Bill's.

Buford sure knew how to knock up women. Word had it that he had fathered about twenty children and didn't financially support any of them. He hardly ever worked.

Buford's only form of employment was loving a race he knew would one day get him in serious trouble if not killed. He wasn't like his father and did not possess the same sinister traits. Mr. Cloverfield was a racist and murderer. It was no secret he was the Grand Wizard of the Ku Klux Klan.

Buford's older brother, Morgan, oversaw the movie house and his brother-in-law, Chester, managed the café.

Before Solomon left for the day, Mr. Cloverfield eased up next to him. He whispered in his ear, "You know, Solomin, I been thinking it over. It would be better if I had an extra person on hand permanent."

Solomon had fully expected the sudden change of heart, so it came as no surprise. He was just amazed that Mr. Cloverfield didn't have a wisecrack or racist remark to add.

The workday finally came to an end. Solomon quickly finished unpacking the last box of fruits. When he picked up the empty box to break it down, he saw a familiar face standing outside the store. It was Miss Smith, and her presence gave him a bad feeling.

He threw the box on the floor and quivered as though gripped with cold. He mumbled, "Please God, don't take Mama away from us."

He rushed toward the front and approached the entrance. Miss Smith smiled.

"Miss Smith, how are you?" he said nervously.

"Oh, I'm fine, Solomon. How are you?"

He shrugged his shoulders. "Things could be better, I guess." Solomon wiped his sweaty face with his smock. "I guess you heard about Mama."

She moved closer to him. "Yes, Solomon. I heard at church that your mother wasn't feeling well."

Solomon slowly untied his smock and gently swung it over his shoulders. He could feel her breath when she came forward. It was strong. Suddenly her bulky hands grazed his face. "Solomon, I went to the hospital today. And—"

"How's she doing? Is it cancer, Miss Smith?"

He watched her gaze descend to the ground.

"Unfortunately, Solomon, it is." She stroked his arm, trying to comfort him. "Your mother has breast cancer."

Solomon stood shivering, trying to get his mind around the words. He fell back against the wall, banging his head on the window. Suddenly he sloped and fell to his knees. "No! Not Mama!"

Miss Smith reached inside her purse and handed him a handkerchief. She walked over to him, helped him stand, and held him in her arms. Everyone in the store ran outside and watched him sobbing.

He was breathing hard while she helped him to her car. He could feel the high temperature whiz through his body as he sat on the hot vinyl seat. All he could do was close his eyes and envision his mother lying in a hospital bed, powerless and scared.

He slowly said, "Miss Smith . . . can you . . . take . . . me . . . to the hospital?"

He glanced at her and saw tears trickle down her cheeks.

"Of course, Solomon," she said.

CHAPTER 19

Solomon confronted the tall ashen-colored hospital building when Miss Smith turned the corner onto Main Street.

A hedge of shrubs and eye-catching flowers encircled the structure. Solomon knew his mother must have appreciated the scene from her window.

He dreaded going inside, afraid of seeing his mother so powerless. Once Miss Smith pulled into the parking lot, he knew he would have to set foot in it.

But he grew self-assured once he set foot in the building. He didn't want his mother to see him afraid. Ivory lay in the hospital bed when he entered her room. Fannie Mae was sitting on a chair and Carter was standing near the window.

The bed's side rails were up. Ivory looked caged. She was depressed and sad. Her face had water stains and she held a handkerchief in one of her hands. She stared out of the window looking confused.

Solomon approached her. He leaned over the railing and kissed her cheek. His mother felt hot to the touch. He placed his hand on her head and asked her if she was running a fever.

"No," she said.

He turned to Fannie Mae and she simply shrugged. Fannie Mae whispered, "She aw right. Just nervous, that's all."

Solomon turned back to his mother. He saw her fear. Ivory

pushed the weight of her body up and tried to sit up straight. She looked at Solomon and said, "They want to take my breast." She sobbed. "Cut it off and give me ray-dee-aa-shun."

Solomon fought back the tears and gripped his mother's hand. She lifted up her head. "What is that, Junior? Ray-dee-aa-shun?"

Solomon turned toward Fannie Mae. Tears soon fell. He wiped his eyes and said, "It's medication, Mama. Medicine that will get rid of the cancer."

Dr. Benson told Ivory that she required a lengthy hospital stay. She was frightened and concerned about her children's welfare.

Ivory told Solomon she wished her mother were alive because she would know what to do. They had been inseparable. Her mother died the year Nathaniel was born.

Solomon reassured his mother that the medicine would cure her. And soon she would be able to go home. He learned about radiation from the science books at the library.

"Junior, I don't know how long that be," she said. "Miss Parker can't keep the kids forever. And . . . you have to work."

"Mama, everything will be all right, just concentrate on getting well. Okay?"

"I guess I ain't got no other choice, huh."

"No other choice," he said, giggling.

Later, Ivory instructed Solomon to go home and pick up the kids from Miss Parker. She asked him to tell them that she was not feeling well and the doctor put her into the hospital for a few days. She insisted that he bring them by the next evening, and begged him to get a good night's sleep.

Ivory's surgery was set for the following day. Solomon kissed his mother's cheek again and told her that he loved her. He begged her to be strong and asked that she contact him at the store if she needed him.

Miss Smith dropped him off at Miss Parker's house and he told her the news. Miss Parker said she would accompany them to the hospital the next evening.

When they arrived home, the girls raced inside the house

searching for Ivory. "Mama, we home," they yelled.

"Where you at?" Magnolia said.

Hyacinth walked into her mother's bedroom and then spun around when she found no one there to greet her. She threw her hands in the air and said, "She's not there."

Solomon sat them down and told them that Ivory was not well and that the doctor had admitted her into the hospital.

"Mama needs to have an operation. Do you know what that means?" he said to the girls.

When they nodded their heads, he explained. He rubbed his hands on his thighs, took in a deep breath, and blew it out. "The doctors will open a part of Mama up and take what's bad out. Then they will give her medicine to make her feel better."

"What part?" Hyacinth said.

Rose jumped on his lap and gripped his shirt. "Will it hurt?" Gripping his shirt again, she said. "Will Mama cry, Junior?"

"No. No. It's not going to hurt. She'll be sleeping when it happens."

"You promise?" said Magnolia.

Smiling, he answered, "I promise." He kissed Magnolia's forehead. "We can visit her tomorrow after I get off of work. Okay?"

After dinner, Solomon and Lily took out some games to play. They needed to get their attention off of their Mama.

When they retreated to bed after playing for hours, Solomon went by the window and stared out. He had to be strong although he felt like breaking down. He shut his eyes and prayed. "Dear Lord, protect Mama. Give her the strength and the power to recover. Save her, Lord. We love her. Please, don't take her away from us."

The next morning, Lily whispered to him, "Junior, is Mama going to die?"

"No, Lily!" he shouted, slamming his hands on the table. "Mama is sick. I know she's going to get better."

"I didn't mean to make you mad," she said crying. "I'm worried about her too, you know."

"I'm sorry, Lily. I just don't want to hear that word. Ever!"

"It may happen."

"It will not."

Lily quickly picked up some dishes and walked toward the washbasin. She turned around and stared at him. Her expression was unchanged. "Junior, I prayed for Mama last night," she said.

"So did I, Lily."

Suddenly as if possessed, she threw a fork at him. "I want to see her now, Solomon!"

Solomon caught the fork with his hand. He stood and yelled, "Lily, what's wrong with you!"

"I'm sorry. It's just that—"

"You know I have to work today. Somebody has to work now that Mama is in the hospital. I promise, you'll see her this evening. I promise."

She leaned over and clutched her stomach.

"Lily! Are you all right? Please don't get sick on me too."

"I'm okay. I just can't stop thinking about it," she said. "I don't know what I will do if Mama dies."

He hugged her. "She's not going to die," he said. "I promise you, she'll get better."

* * *

Smoking an old cigar from the day before, one leg leaning on a crate, Mr. Cloverfield commented, "You act like you in some kind of rush, boy!"

"No sir, I'm just thinking. That's all."

When he approached Solomon, his speckled face gleamed and sweat poured down like a powerful waterfall.

"Thinking! Thinking about what?" he yelled, spitting on the floor. "You ain't got no bizzness thinking while you're working for me!"

Solomon stepped back a few paces before the spit whipped across his face. "Sir, I was only thinking about this job."

He spoke looking at Mr. Cloverfield from the corner of his eye. "I really like it and I just want to learn everything."

Mr. Cloverfield's body came up and he took his foot off of the crate. "Well, you ain't gonna learn nothin' if you keep throwing them boxes like that."

He pointed his blotched pudgy finger at him. "Take your time, boy! That's how you learn!"

Solomon smiled and pretended to agree with him. "Yes, sir. You're right, Mr. Cloverfield."

Solomon hated being there but he needed the money and he had no other choice. He really wanted to be with his mother, protecting her.

"Dear God, please rescue me," he said.

It was five in the evening and time to go home. Solomon uttered his daily slogan: "Have a good evening, Mr. Cloverfield. I'll see you tomorrow morning."

Walking toward the front entrance, he muttered, "Thank you, Lord, for letting time pass so quickly."

Solomon glanced through the window and noticed Miss Smith sitting in her car. He ran in the back, tore off his smock, and placed it on the shelf then jetted outside.

His mind raced with thoughts while he sat in her hot car. He wanted to ask a lot of questions, but he didn't. He could not utter one word. His heart beat fast while he fumbled with his fingers. So they both sat in the car and watched people passing by.

He meditated during the ride to Miss Parker's house. *Maybe God's testing Mama and us. This is a sign to make us work harder. Yes . . . He's challenging us. He wants us to be stronger.*

Then he wondered, *Why would He give Mama cancer? Who can live up to that test?*

Miss Parker had a feeling they were coming soon because she and the kids were all standing outside, fresh and spotless, looking fit for church service.

The kids jumped right into the car as soon as it pulled up to the house. They rode to the hospital in silence; even the girls were quiet, which was rare. Maybe they were all thinking the same thing or maybe they needed some solitude.

The silence ended when they entered the hospital. They took

the elevator to the second floor and the girls raced to Ivory's room.

Ivory was sitting up in bed and smiling like old times. The girls raced to her. Lily stood back for a moment. Then she walked up to Ivory and gave her a big hug and kiss. Nathaniel stood back by the door.

"Where did they open you up, Mama?" said Magnolia.

"How you know about that, girl?"

"Junior told us," Rose said, pulling on Ivory's arm.

"Show me the boo-boo, Mama?" Hyacinth said.

Lily's tears poured out when Ivory pointed her finger to her breast area.

"You sure it didn't hurt?" Hyacinth said.

"I'm sure."

"So, you got a boo-boo, huh, Mama," said Rose.

Lily leaned her head on her mother's shoulder. Ivory patted her head and said, "Yeah, it's a small one though."

Ivory wiped away Lily's tears and pleaded with them not to worry. "I'll be up and out of this place soon," she muttered.

Forcing a smile, she said, "I love y'all. Y'all mean the world to me."

Lily kissed her hand and cried.

"You can come see me in a few weeks, okay?" said Ivory.

Rose and Magnolia sucked on their thumbs. Then they nodded.

"Promise Mama y'all won't give granny any hard times."

"We promise," the girls said.

Nathaniel, who was the quiet one, remained in the background. Solomon shoved him forward but he refused to go toward the bed. He felt like that four-year-old child all over again. Reluctantly, he inched his way toward his mother's bed.

"Come here, baby," she said.

He came closer. When he reached the bed, his head sunk in her chest.

"Nate, watch out!" Solomon yelled.

Nathaniel eyed his mother's breast. He couldn't move.

"Be careful," Solomon said.

"It's aw right," Ivory said, rubbing the back of Nathaniel's head. "It's aw right."

Later, Miss Smith took the kids to the commissary, giving Solomon and Ivory time to talk with Miss Parker.

Miss Parker said to Ivory, as she fluffed her pillow. "You feeling aw right, Ivry? You look like you cold."

"I am."

As soon as the first nurse entered the room, Miss Parker yelled at her, "Do something, she ain't right. She hurting."

The nurse said, "Ma'am we're doing the best we can. We've given her pain medication."

Miss Parker rolled her eyes. "Obviously, it ain't enough."

The nurse gritted her teeth. "The pain should go away soon. There's no need to yell, ma'am."

The nurse walked away. Ivory joked about losing her breast. "What man gonna want me now," she said. It was the only way she could hide her pain.

"You hush now!" Miss Parker said. "Ain't nothin' wrong with that. Besides, you always be beautiful in my eyes."

Dr. Benson and a specialist entered the room. Ivory asked that Solomon stay because she didn't quite understand the medical terminology.

The short, gray-haired oncologist named Dr. Grover said, "You're mother's cancer was contained."

"What you mean by that?" Miss Parker said.

"It did not spread to other parts of her body."

"The dam thing can move around! Oh, my Lord!" shouted Miss Parker.

"Her prognosis looks very good," said Dr. Benson.

"Oh yeah," Ivory softly said, gazing out of the window.

Dr. Benson continued, "Ivory, you're going to heal. Everything will be fine. Soon, you'll be home with your children."

The doctors said that Ivory would undergo radiation therapy and that the treatments would make her ill. She would probably lose her hair at some point.

When Ivory heard that, she lifted her hand up to her head and gently combed her fingers through her lustrous thick hair. She bit her lip and fought off the tears. The thought of her losing her hair sent a bitter chill down Solomon's spine. Then Dr. Grover stressed that Ivory would need to remain in the hospital.

"How long?" Solomon said.

Dr. Grover glanced at him while he scribbled on a notepad. "A while, son."

They prayed before they left for the night, Miss Parker taking the lead. Then everyone left the room. Solomon stayed behind.

Ivory confided in him. "Junior, I'm so scared."

He hugged her. Ivory was no longer afraid of the radiation or the possibility of losing her hair. She was scared for her children. How would they survive without her?

Solomon told her to concentrate on recovering and to let him worry about their life at home.

CHAPTER 20

After undergoing several cycles of radiation, Ivory was fatigued, nauseated, and in extreme discomfort. When Solomon entered her room one Saturday afternoon, she lay helpless in the bed.

The nurse told him that she had just received a cycle of radiation that morning and it was just taking effect. Solomon was too scared to ask how or where it was administered. The truth might make him sick to his stomach.

He stayed with his mother all night. He tried to feed her but she refused, unable to keep anything down. She could only manage a sip of juice.

The next evening, Miss Smith picked him up from the store and they headed straight to the hospital. Ivory was suffering.

Solomon's blood boiled and his face flushed with angry frustration. He had never seen his mother so sick, even when she gave birth to the girls. He wanted God to stop her misery.

"Let it be me!" he screamed.

Ivory cried in Miss Smith's arms and soberly said, "I want to die. Lord, please take me away from all this pain."

For the first time in the ordeal, things looked hopeless. Solomon felt defenseless and so wept constantly because it was all he could do.

Kneeling down next to his mother, he said, "No, Mama. Don't

say that. I know it hurts but the pain will soon go away." He sobbed. "Mama, please be strong. I'm here. I'll always be here." He stroked her face. "I'll never leave your side."

The more she screamed, the more he cried, his head resting on the bed. Miss Smith called for the nurse and she immediately entered the room. "This is normal," the nurse said. "These are the side effects."

The nurses didn't show much sympathy toward his mother. They always had quick responses but no solutions. Solomon wanted to wrap his hands around the thin nurse's scrawny neck so she would know what it was like to suffer too. But then he just looked at her sideways as if what she said made any difference; as if what she said would make his mother better.

The nurse thought her words were comforting but they were not. The only consolation Ivory needed was a miracle. The nurse left the room when she heard a buzzer ringing. A few minutes later, she returned with some pills. The medicine calmed Ivory and she soon fell asleep.

Several weeks had passed. Ivory was still a patient in the hospital, and she underwent many changes, including losing most of her hair and a lot of weight.

The entire ordeal took a toll on everyone. Solomon was restless and couldn't concentrate at work. He would stay overnight with his mother on the weekends.

Miss Parker had taken ill, so Lily became the sole caretaker for the girls. The children were worried and missed Ivory terribly. Solomon hated being away from them but Ivory needed him more. Some church members tried to help by making supper for them but the bills continued to mount. The money he made at the store barely made a difference.

One afternoon Solomon received a call from his mother at the store. She said she had something important to tell him. When he visited her that evening, Ivory told him that she had been discussing their financial problems with Miss Smith, who offered to help.

Miss Smith hinted that a few of her friends were willing to

take care of the girls until Ivory recovered. Lily and Nathaniel were old enough to take care of themselves.

These friends did not have children. Miss Smith had known them for years. She had grown up with them. She convinced Ivory that her friends were happy to lend a hand until she was well enough to leave the hospital.

There was one detail that troubled Solomon. The girls would be split up. Miss Smith said that neither of her friends could take care of all of the girls at once.

"No way!" he said, throwing the urinal pan across the room. "No way in hell will I ever leave my babies!" He squeezed Ivory's hand. "Besides, everything isn't so bad, Mama. You know that."

Ivory insisted that he wasn't seeing the whole picture and begged him to reconsider. They argued throughout most of the night. Solomon could not believe what he was hearing. He was angry and thought for sure his mother had gone crazy.

Miss Smith knew they were close. *Why would she want to separate us?* he thought.

Miss Smith acted as if Ivory was going to die, which had Solomon questioning her motives. *Why would she want us to do this? Will this really benefit us?*

He left the room and walked down the corridor to vent. He stood by the window and whispered, "Daddy, please talk to me. Tell me what to do."

There was no sign of his father. After a few minutes of waiting and hoping, Solomon walked back into the room.

He overheard his mother talking to Miss Smith. Apparently Ivory met one of her friends a year before and assured Solomon that this friend was very nice. She reminded her of Fannie Mae.

Miss Smith jogged Solomon's memory that Miss Parker had not been feeling well too and that everyone in town had done all they could to help them financially.

It was past midnight when Ivory and Miss Smith convinced him. Miss Smith promised them the arrangement would be temporary.

Solomon mumbled to himself, "Solomon C. Walker, Jr., are

you crazy? Go back into that room and tell them no. Tell her you've changed your mind."

Then he remembered his mother's heartbreaking expression from the other day and how she now seemed so confident. She believed she was doing the right thing. Ivory needed his trust.

Solomon soon let go of the issue. He and Ivory prayed that God would take care of the girls, then he and Miss Smith went home.

On the ride back home Miss Smith assured him they were doing the right thing. "Solomon, your mother needs some peace of mind," she said as she pulled a candy bar out of her purse and began to unwrap it. Chewing on it, she turned her head sideways and looked at him. "That's why she's not getting any better."

She crumbled the candy wrapper and threw it in the ashtray. "Your mother is worrying too much, Solomon." She winked at him. "Leave everything in my hands. Trust me, everything will be fine."

Solomon stepped out of the car and waved goodbye to her. He sat on the porch for a few minutes and wondered, *How am I going to break the news to the girls? How can I do this to my family? Lord, please help me.*

He slowly opened the door and there they were, playing and having fun.

"Junior! Junior, you're home," yelled Magnolia.

Nathaniel jumped out of the chair. "How's Mama feeling?"

"Is she coming home soon?" Lily said.

"Did you tell her we love her?" Hyacinth added.

Then Rose ran up to him. He leaned forward to grab her. "Yes, I told her you all love and miss her so much." His eyes began to water. "I told her that we want her home soon."

Rose kissed his face. "Why you crying, Junior?"

"It's just sweat, that's all."

"Yes, sir, you crying."

Lily interrupted. "Is the medicine working?"

"Yeah, it's just working a little slow. Taking its time."

Lily said, "Mr. and Mrs. Williams came by and brought supper."

"Guess what, Junior?" Rose said.

"What?"

"Granny Williams brought some cherry vanilla ice cream and it was good!"

"We saved some for you," screamed Magnolia.

Solomon asked them to gather around the table. He was nervous, wiping the non-stop flow of sweat from his brow. His mind wanted to forget about it all, but his heart knew they had to know what was going to happen to them.

He mumbled to himself, "Stay focused and be strong for them."

Once composed, he began. "Mama is not getting better fast enough. So, there's going to be some changes around here for a short while."

Solomon couldn't bring himself to look in their eyes.

"What kind of changes?" said Lily.

"Mama needs to spend more time in the hospital and . . . the girls . . . they will spend some time with friends of Miss Smith."

Lily and Nathaniel dropped their mouths open. They were in complete shock. Solomon fiddled with his shirt and tore off a button.

He went on, "Lily, you and Nathaniel will stay here until Mama gets out of the hospital."

Lily and Nathaniel were dumbfounded. They looked at him like he was insane. The look in the girls' eyes broke Solomon's heart. Initially they seemed at peace with the decision but then they wanted to cry. But somehow they stayed composed.

Sadly, Rose said, "Are you coming too, Junior?"

Tears streamed down his face, soaking his shirt. "No, I can't, baby. I need to stay behind and take care of the house." Hyacinth walked up to him and wiped his eyes with her tiny fingers. He held her.

He said, "There's a lot to be done around here. I need to focus on taking care of our business."

Solomon began to cry. "It'll all work out for the best. I promise. It'll . . . only be for a short while!"

"How short is a short while, Junior?" said Lily.

"A few weeks—just a few weeks, Lily. We'll be together before school begins. I promise."

The girls said in unison, "You promise?"

"Yes. I promise."

With a curious expression, Magnolia said, "Will you come to see us, Junior?"

"I will only be able to see you on the weekends." He took a deep breath. "Hopefully, if I can get a ride up there."

Smacking his shoulder with her notebook, Lily screamed, "Where's up there, Solomon?"

He spoke nervously. "Magnolia will stay in Atlanta." Breathing heavy again. "Hyacinth will stay in Savannah." Then he paused and lowered his head, starting to cry again. Spit foamed in his mouth. "And . . . Rose will stay in Columbia."

"Savannia! Where is that?" Rose said.

"It's right here in Georgia."

"I don't like this!" Lily shouted again. She got up from the chair and shook her head. "Three different places." Pointing her finger at him. "Why? This doesn't make any kind of sense, Solomon."

She began nervously twisting her braids. "Are you sure Mama agreed to this, Solomon? I don't think she would. Why are the girls being separated?" Sobbing, she said, "We can stay with Mr. and Mrs. Williams' or Miss Parker. Shoo, we can stay with—"

"Listen! Listen!" said Solomon. "Before you ask any more questions, remember, this will only be temporary. Just for a few weeks."

She wailed and buried her head in his chest. Solomon looked around at the girls. "You will have fun. Three weeks will be here and gone in no time."

Before the girls left, Solomon took them back to the hospital to visit Ivory. She could barely talk, but managed to force a slight smile. The girls embraced her and began to cry. They were terrified.

Ivory slowly began to speak. "I . . . love you." She tried to raise her hand. "Be good for Mama. It'll be aw right, okay?"

The girls stood stone still. Their tears stopped flowing and they moved closer to her bedside to hear her voice clearly.

"We'll be good, Mama," cried Magnolia.

Solomon hoisted Rose up to Ivory's face. She grabbed her mother's hand and leaned forward clutching her gown. She said, "I love you, Mama." Rose kissed her forehead.

Struggling to pull her body forward, Ivory strained and said, "I love you too, baby."

A tearful Hyacinth said, "Mama, do we have to go?"

Ivory nodded. Solomon asked them to give her a final kiss because it was past their bedtime and they had to go home.

Tears flowed freely from Ivory's eyes. This must have been the saddest day of her life. It was heartbreaking seeing her children confused and scared. The feeling was more painful than the illness itself.

Years later Ivory told Solomon that she had seen it all. Nothing surprised her and nothing could break her, but that day surely broke her soul. The thought of her children being placed in the hands of strangers frightened her profoundly. She told him that from that moment on she knew she had to recover. It was a fight for her life—a fight for her children. She prayed, asking God to give her the strength to live.

CHAPTER 21

It was late. Solomon sat on a bench in the hospital's outdoor dining area. The air was cold and the night was dim. He came there in search of answers.

He looked at the twinkling stars and said to himself, "What's wrong with me? Why am I feeling this way? Things were supposed to get better."

Then he rubbed his nose with his index fingers and glanced back up at the sky. "Daddy... God... somebody... please talk to me."

Solomon's life felt like a failure. His family relied on his strength and guidance. Yet on that cool night, he was helpless, weak, alone—just like the night he saw his father's listless body in the back of his uncle's truck. He knew he could not protect his family anymore, could no longer be the leader they needed. They would have to go on without him.

The night was dull and unfeeling contrary to his thoughts. He could no longer hide his feelings and act grown up. He was like a time bomb ticking down.

Solomon believed he'd failed helping his family brave poverty. He was afraid none of them would ever leave Mission.

He had succumbed to society's perception that he'd never be as good as the next white kid. He would live the life of a shallow man—a man without goals and a future, a man free of good luck.

That was all that was left for him. He wanted to join his father in heaven.

The past months had been trying for Solomon. He felt overwhelmed by the adversities that dictated his life. He had been forced to work like an adult and attend a school with limited educational resources. The disadvantages overpowered him to the point that death seemed like the only way out.

After his visit at the hospital, an unthinkable incident transpired. The course of his life was lost to Solomon, who knew only one thing: he had to get home.

Miss Smith dropped him off halfway and he made the rest of the journey on foot. Lily and Nathaniel were staying overnight with her because they were upset and needed consoling.

Solomon thoughtlessly plodded through the country. The way was second nature—he could have walked the roads blindfolded. This did little to stave off the sense of unease as he walked. He felt stalked by fate, judged and laughed at. He believed the world's ways had foretold his death and he was ready to give in to the cruel hand he'd been dealt.

His head swam with disconcerting emotions. Suddenly he stopped in his tracks. He squeezed shut his eyes and prayed for an escape. Then a bizarre, unrecognizable voice flew around him. The voice echoed, "Every . . . thing . . . is . . . out . . . of . . . your . . . control . . . Solomon."

Solomon stood frozen, scared, wondering what was this voice and why it was speaking to him.

He tried to fight off the fear by blocking out the voice from his mind, but as the pitch magnified, his body trembled. Solomon looked around, trying to see whom it was that was speaking to him. His body moved to the left, and then to the right, and finally he turned full around.

The land was unmoving. Only the buzzing in his ears lingered. His head turned to each side as he tried to catch sight of the invisible speaker. The calmness drove him mad. Soon, the suspicion began to annoy him and he screamed, "Who are you! Whoever you are, please go away!"

In his state of confusion, Solomon thought he saw the trees beginning to sway and saw leaves and rocks fly above him, blinding him. He fell to the ground and began to breathe heavily, inhaling and exhaling the foul air. He coughed to clear his throat. When he tried to shield his eyes from the litter, the voice grew louder and louder. In a wicked pitch it said, "There's nothing you can do, Solomon! You have done all you can!"

For all his effort, Solomon found himself alone. The voice spoke again, this time harshly: "Come with me and be at ease!"

Everything was blurred and Solomon couldn't make out a thing. His heart jumped to a powerful rhythm and his stomach grew unsettled. He felt dizzy and held his hand to his stomach. His guts rumbled and the contents inside spilled out and over him. He grew weak at the knees and twisted over onto the ground.

Solomon's frail body lay inert while he stared at the puke. He turned his head in disgust and slowly wiped the residue from his mouth. He struggled to get back on his feet and keep his balance. Once he stood up, he couldn't move. He didn't know what to do next.

The voice returned just when he thought it was over. This time its sound was mild-spoken but offensive. "Listen to me, Solomon. Listen very carefully," the voice said, seducing him. "The best thing you can do for your family is to go away."

The voice laughed and then became impatient when Solomon didn't respond. Confusion and fear silenced him.

"Damn it, Solomon! Why don't you die now? It's the only smart thing to do!"

Solomon placed his trembling hands up to his ears, squeezing them tight. "Stop! Please . . . leave!"

"You called for me, remember!"

"No! No! I didn't!" Solomon cried.

The voice gently said, "Solomon, I'm here to set you free."

"No, I . . . I . . . prayed for God. I prayed for—"

"You know what to do!"

Aching tears rolled down Solomon's face and he begged, "Please, go away! My family needs me!"

The mighty wind subsided and the voice vanished. Solomon wasn't relieved because he knew the voice was still out there. And instantly, the voice returned in a boisterous tone, "Your family needs a miracle right now! Something you are unable to give them!"

Now the faces of his mother and siblings flashed in front of him. He fell hard on his knees and prayed, "God, please help me!"

"Solomon, go home and do it! God can't help you now!" Solomon didn't have the strength to resist the voice's proposition; by now, his mind was drained. Whoever it was, it was right. What else could he do for them? "Miracle" was simply just another empty term.

It was unlike Solomon to lose hope, but he did. He remembered his mother's somber voice that afternoon at his father's funeral: "You the man of the house now, Junior."

Yet he wasn't the man his father was. He wasn't strong. After all, his best solution was to die, although it wouldn't be fair to his family.

He'd given in to the controlling spirit's lethal advice and decided to escape the misery that awaited him and his family. He rushed home ready to end his pain.

He burst through the door and dashed inside the house, heading toward the kitchen area. Resting on a small metal cabinet was a large bottle of his mother's pain medication.

His heartbeat quickened as his hand touched the plastic bottle—the means to heaven. "Yes, this will do the job."

He shook the bottle to view the contents and was pleased to find it almost full. "Yes, this is more than enough."

He tossed the bottle into his pouch and reached over the counter, grabbed a pitcher of water, and poured a cupful. He pushed aside the stained lime-colored curtains and walked into the bedroom.

Everything seemed to happen in slow motion. After taking the bottle out of the bag, he threw the bag on the window ledge and placed the cup on the nightstand. Solomon gulped a half bottle of the medication and followed it with the lukewarm water.

Within seconds, the humming of his heart relaxed and the

birds and the gusty trees grew soundless as well. He struggled to pick up the bottle again a few seconds later. When he did, he emptied the remaining pills into his mouth and swallowed hard without a drink. A bitter taste lingered in his mouth for hours.

He glanced at the watch Carter had given to him the day after they found his father's body. He said it was resting on top of Sweet Betsy. The time was 1:48.

Solomon cherished the watch. It fit his wrist perfectly. The rim was sparkling silver and it was engraved with a rectangular design. The wristband was ebony and made of sturdy leather. The numbers were large. His father liked them that way because his vision had deteriorated over the years.

Judge Booth gave it to his father as a wedding gift. His father and Uncle Eugene did handy work for the judge. On a wintry day in December, Judge Booth gave Solomon's father what he thought was good advice. "Solomon," the Judge said sternly, "You know it's not good taste to walk down the aisle without a timepiece."

Judge Booth was determined that his father hear his proposal when he took a powerful whiff of a Cuban cigar and continued: "An honest individual like yourself must have a watch on his wedding day."

Solomon's father didn't want to offend the judge. He hesitated, taking a moment to consider his reply. After some consideration, he asserted, "I don't need to wear a watch on my wedding day, Judge Booth."

The judge yanked the cigar away from his mouth, wanting to flick it and remove the ashes, but when he glanced at the bulky cigar he realized the ashes had already fallen on the floor. He nodded then placed the cigar back into his mouth and spoke in fragments. "You . . . you're . . . going to . . . tell me . . . that . . . you . . . don't . . . care . . . to know . . . the time . . . on your wedding day, Solomon!"

Solomon's father howled with amusement at the Judge's comment. He'd wear a watch on his wedding day if he could afford one. And that was exactly what he told the judge. It was obvious the judge didn't appreciate his father's response judging from the uncharacteristic growl. His breathing hastened and he stared down at the book he was reading, pretending not to have been offended.

His left eyebrow arched diabolically and fixed on Solomon's father. The judge gently pulled the slippery cigar from his wet lips and slowly stirred his tongue around the inside of his mouth and seemed to be smiling.

There would not be another discussion about a timekeeper from Judge Booth from that day forward. Two weeks had passed. The day before his parents were married the judge gave that fine watch and twenty dollars to his father.

The judge said rubbing the crystal on a khaki cloth, "I really appreciate your hard work, Solomon." He handed the watch and money to his father. "I thought you might like this."

His father relished the watch but never revealed his feelings to the judge. It wasn't his pride that prevented him from telling the judge how much he cherished the watch, it was that he didn't ask for the watch and in fact didn't even need one. He had gone without one for practically a year. What was vital was keeping food on the table and a roof over his family's head.

The steady clicking sound of his father's watch remained faithfully in his heart as a reminder of his father's living days. It is a testament to his father's hard work.

* * *

Solomon had awakened in a puddle of vomit hours later. His head throbbed and the scorching sun beaming directly through the window warmed his limp body.

He lifted his hands to shield his stinging eyes from the burning sun. He struggled to fully open them despite being still weak from the overdose.

He opened his eyes and reached over the nightstand to grab a broken glass that Lily used to look at herself each morning.

His eyes were puffy, cobwebbed by bloody streaks. He felt his organs twinge and began to choke on the sour air. He suddenly felt confined and needed a breath of fresh air. He tried to rise but couldn't. He fell back hitting his head on the semi-hard bed padding that jabbed into his skin.

Solomon started to touch his face and body, taking stock. He stroked his legs little by little. *Am I still living?*

His aching head rolled over to the side, feeling like it had been hit by a ton of bricks. As he lay in bed thinking about what he had done, different emotions visited him—uneasiness, doubt, even gladness.

He was alive and wanted to celebrate. That happy feeling was bittersweet because he'd gone through with a terrible plan and failed. He glanced at the ceiling feeling half-dead and half-alive, the whole time knowing that God had saved him.

He managed to turn his head to the left and soon his eyes found a dirty washcloth on the nightstand. He gazed at the oak nightstand. His father had made it for his mother.

He began to treasure his surroundings. The nightstand that he saw every day for the past six years was real. He took in a mouthful of the stale air. He grinned, appreciating the moment.

While reaching over the nightstand to pick up the rag, he knocked over his book pouch that was on the window ledge. The noise caused his body to shift and he nearly tipped over the bed. He caught himself and held onto the edge. He kicked his left leg out and then his right leg. He tried to collect his strength by breathing in and then out again. Slowly he edged his way up as he held onto the bedpost.

Finally he stood but immediately stumbled over the book pouch, falling face first onto the wood floor. He was too weak to scream for help. It wouldn't matter if he did because he was alone.

Solomon struggled to rise again. This time he held firmly onto the delicate bedpost. He scaled over the book pouch and placed his hands on the window ledge. He remained there for a few seconds. "Hold on," he whispered as his eyes pounded. "You've come this far by faith."

Solomon found himself ambling toward the front door knocking over everything in his path. He barely opened the door when the cool fresh scent of air gushed in, caressing his face. It soothed him and calmed his panicky heart. His face was etched with a smile. He had escaped death.

Standing at the door, he allowed the serene air to graze his face. It relaxed him. Soon he was walking through the farmed land. He ended up on the roof of Mr. Cloverfield's store. He came there to look past the stars and feel God's presence. He could still feel those sinful thoughts flaring in his mind. He yearned for God's support in confronting the evil spirit that was trying to pollute his brain.

Solomon dropped to his knees and lowered his head in prayer. He glanced up at the sky and begged. He begged for a savior. He begged for his life. *Maybe this time, God will hear me*, he thought. *With His help, I know I can fight these demons.*

He forced shut his eyes and prayed again. He heard noises coming from behind him. His eyes snapped open and got wide as golf balls. He quickly moved from side to side, searching for the enemy. The familiar wicked voice sounded off again, soaking through his body and causing it to tremble.

He had gone to the top of the roof to confess his sins, to tell God what an awful thing he'd done. But now, he realized this thing was still after him.

The voice began to harass him, penetrating his broken body. His head revolved to the voice's direction and large goose bumps covered his body.

"Go ahead and jump! Jump, damn it!" the voice yelled.

"Is it that same voice from this afternoon?" Solomon said to himself.

Now it became clear to him. He understood what the sound was. It had to be the devil. His presence was potent and controlling. His father once told him that misery loves company. "Be your own leader, Junior. Make your own decisions. Don't let anybody tell you what to do."

Solomon had begun to feel confident and strong, but the voice came along and dominated his short-lived bravery. It was unafraid of the shiny stars and the mellow night Solomon looked up to as heaven.

Solomon could hear the voice babbling. Its breath was filled with rage. It teased him, insisting that he go ahead with his plan. Solomon grew tired of the harassment and shouted, "Go away! I didn't ask you to come here!"

The evil voice laughed.

"Leave me alone! I'm not going to do it again!" Solomon yelled. He awkwardly swung his fists at the invisible speaker. It was useless talking to the voice.

Instead of surrendering to death, Solomon sat on the roof and prayed to God. He didn't want to die. He desperately wanted to live his life like any other kid. He wanted to excel in school, marry, and have children. And unlike his father, he wanted to grow old enough to witness the things that would change one day.

"Lord, help me," he begged with tears flowing down his face. "Please give me strength."

The Solomon of old had been able to combat anything and anyone, even the most crooked bully. Yet on that evening, he was powerless, too frightened to shove the devil off the roof. Bad luck had consumed him, broken his spirit. His life was in total disarray and all he needed was guidance. He wanted to return home to his family.

"Get off this roof and go home, Solomon!" he yelled at himself. "You have a family waiting for you!"

Bound by the love of God and family, Solomon chose to fight for his life. He inhaled, then exhaled and turned toward the invisible thing. He stared it in the eye. He wanted it to take a good look at the person it had tried to destroy. It was important that it recognize the spark of hope left in his eyes. There was light at the end of the tunnel and for Solomon that meant hope and change. Things could only get better if he tried to improve them.

Solomon began to laugh, chuckling at the very thought of its pitiful sound and shameless energy. He stooped on his knees and lowered his head. This time, he challenged himself to reach inside his soul and recognize that his life was significant.

Despite his constant pleas, the night remained dead and unsympathetic to his prayers. Somehow the sinful spirit had stained the essence of the night. The stillness created a sharp tingling sensation in Solomon's ears. His anxiety level intensified. His nose started to run and mucus smeared his face.

The cold night startled Solomon because he had never witnessed it so heartless and distant before. God usually corresponded with a twinkling of a star, a delicate raindrop, or a peaceful breeze. The view of the sky had always been clear and heavenly.

Though, somehow, only the devil held company with him, uninvited company. It skillfully composed him, numbing his spirit. Solomon ran to the edge of the roof and gasped for air. He tried to brave the evil spirit but it was too powerful. The voice began to seduce him, compelling him back into the darkness. It clutched at his soul like a sprinter's grip on a baton. Once again the voice set out to produce sinful thoughts in his mind.

Solomon's mental state began to wither and he was filled with a desire to jump. But instead he protected his ears with his hands and refused to surrender. *If only I could just focus on the good things life has to offer*, he thought.

"Concentrate!" he cried. "Believe in the stars! Believe in heaven! Ignore him!"

Soon Solomon's head turned to the right and struggled to glance at the sky. His eyes widened when he looked at the blurred heavens and the tiny dark stars moving forward. Silence, fear, and temptation jammed into his chest. His heart pounded with increased frequency. "Look for God," he muttered.

He continued to stare at what seemed like the integration of heaven and hell. There was no sign of God, and it was as though hopelessness commanded his brain to the point of consumption. The powerful feeling whirled around in his head like a raging tornado invading the powerless. He didn't know whether to scream so God could save him or dive onto the cold red dirt that beckoned his pathetic soul.

Like an ill-fated dream, this unfriendly world began to revolve around him. It was because of this unkind place that he thought of ending his life. He sat on the frigid roof and asked God for relief from the pain and bad luck that seemed to be smothering him.

The world moved before him in slow motion. Bitter tears streamed down his face and his body was soaked in perspiration.

As he looked to the left, he saw the dilapidated shack he lived in and the old outhouse alongside. And when he looked straight ahead, he witnessed the Jamisons' children stealing food. He turned toward the right and saw five spineless white men throwing rocks and spitting on two young black girls walking home from school. Then he lowered his head and glanced below and noticed Bill's trademark footprints on the dirt road.

He saw a sudden flickering gleam of blue, then white, green, and yellow. Then he noticed Mrs. Jamison and Mrs. Booker leading his mother out of his house. Soon a flash of bright red beamed in front of him and he felt his mother's anguish as she stared at his father's dead body.

The weather grew cold and hail fell from the sky. He shouted, waving both hands in the air, "Yes!"

His body hardened but soon the freezing feeling dwindled to a tingling sensation. He felt sedated, and rejoiced with laughter. *It's Him*, he thought. *God is listening.*

Solomon glanced at his drenched wrists. He lowered his head. Then he swirled his tongue around and out, touching the wetness. His lips quivered. He realized the feeling was not strange at all. It was all too familiar. Soon he smelled the organic aroma of the Williams' farm. He sampled the sweetness of Lake Hope. He could see the richness of his mother's laugh. He remembered the sincerity of his father's wisdom. And in his hands he fondled the blazing vitality God awarded him—resilience.

The moisture tasted good. He smiled and welcomed the pleasant feeling. He was sure this was God's message—the sign he had long awaited. It was a signal to endure the pain and never give in to despair. A signal to fight insensitive nights like the one before him.

"God is good," he mumbled.

On that discouraging night God restored Solomon's belief in himself. Solomon had resisted death and was a stronger person for it. He would never hand his existence over to anyone. Only God could take it away. It was important that he live, for there, awaiting him at home, were other dazzling stars.

Solomon's self-respect returned and he stood fulfilled, for life and all the meaningful days to come. God had given him the strength to rise above the sadness.

Slowly he headed toward the corroded ladder. He shut his eyes and breathed in the fresh air. He was free as the stars above.

As he approached the ladder he listened to the wind's emotional breath. The trees were prattling, which seemed to soothe his spirit. Soon his foot touched the rigid ground. He reached down and grabbed a handful of the dirt, rubbing it between his fingers. He shouted, "I'm still here! Thank you, Jesus!"

The faster he walked, the faster his heart raced. He wanted only to get home. He was slightly tense when he arrived. His jittery hands slowly pushed open the front door. He walked in and gently shut it, not looking back. The nightmare was finally over.

Solomon grabbed hold of a photograph of his family. He held it tight. He realized that this was not a dream. It was real. As real as his mother's pink dress hanging on the clothes line, and as real as the gloomy night that had nearly seized his soul.

CHAPTER 22

Sunrise revealed itself hours later. The yellow shriveled curtains on the bedroom window flapped soundlessly in the slight breeze.

Solomon's iron bed squeaked ever so softly when he turned his tired body to the side. The cotton that spilled out of the torn pillow-shaped mattress stroked his face. When he wiped his face, the tingling sensation caused him to sneeze. Then he sniffled and wiped his face again.

Soon his eyes were wide open, staring at the naked wall. He turned toward Lily and Nathaniel's bed and smiled. He got up and walked over to the window.

"What was I thinking?" he said to himself as he poked his head out of the window and stared at his mother's garden, forcing himself to breathe in the crisp air.

He glanced up at the sky. This time it was a rich silvery shade and released a wonderfully scented layer of air. Soon freshness drifted around him and the spirit of life absorbed all of him.

His head rolled back as he leaned forward. He stretched his neck from side to side, inhaling nature's completeness and exhaling as the sweet breeze cooled his face. The trees continued their mild debate. Solomon smiled.

The moisture from the sweet air touched his face. He slid his tongue across his full dark lips and sampled the dampness. The sensation was appeasing.

It was only a few hours since the world seemed so overwhelming he had tried to end his life. Now the morning seemed bright and promising. He was changed—convinced a chosen future awaited him.

He pushed the shutters away, letting more of nature's refreshing aura seep in. His body sizzled with pleasure and goose bumps ripened. Solomon cherished mornings like this—always wishing they'd never end.

"It's going to be a good day," he said.

He reached over the dusty bureau and grabbed his torn dungarees resting on top. His energy level heightened by the time he slid in one leg. He wanted to take a stroll, wandering through the countryside, eyeing the beautiful sprouting flowers, tiny homes, frayed farms, and Lake Hope.

He quietly tiptoed out of the tiny bedroom section. His right leg knocked over a pile of Lily's books and some of the girl's toys that covered the floor. He reached down and put them back in order with care. He didn't want to wake anyone but he soon realized that he was alone.

Barefoot and confident, Solomon walked toward the partition and slid it across halfway. He walked through the kitchen and browsed over the table. His stomach churned when his eyes rested on a bulky slice of Miss Parker's mouth-watering butter pound cake. He snatched the last piece and devoured it.

Before long Solomon was drifting on the dirt road. He had always been the early bird in the family, forever rising with the sun. He was happy. His flesh soaked up every ounce of energy around him. He felt powerful—as if he could have taken on the world. He only wished he'd had that energy the evening before.

"Why am I so happy this morning?" he said to himself. He shook his head and grinned. "Because," he mumbled, "Just because."

Solomon was convinced it was because of the honey-tasting breeze and the irresistible smell of the flowers that made his spirit rise. It was the rich red dirt he walked on and the battered shack he lived in that made him appreciate life. It was the brilliant sapphire color of Lake Hope and the spotless clothes hanging on his mother's clothesline that had freed his mind. It was also the books and toys he knocked over that morning and the instant gratification he felt putting them back in order that brought him joy.

He understood that he'd always experienced but never succumbed to pain or sorrow because his family provided the strength he needed to survive. They were a reason to persevere. They were the foundation that upheld him, helping him to do what was right and learn from what was wrong.

Afterward he walked behind Hope Baptist Church and headed toward Lake Hope. The church had once been a pearly white shade, but soil and severe rain stained it over the years. It was now a dull ivory color and had settled unbalanced on a bit of land.

He walked over to the edge of the lake and listened to its rhythm. He was intrigued by its peaceful style. He kneeled over and dipped his hands into the cool water, splashing a handful onto his face.

On Sunday afternoons, after church service, Solomon, his father, and friends would race to the lake sometimes fully clothed and dive straight into the warm water.

His father could swim across the lake and back. Solomon thought he was immortal. His entire family was baptized in Lake Hope. Solomon believed that shared factor kept them together as a family. Lake Hope represented faith and strength. It also symbolized their existence.

Although his father lost his life in the lake, Solomon continued to visit. The scene was breathtaking and he appreciated its comfort.

His mother, on the other hand, found it difficult to even look at the lake. After church she'd rush down the unpainted steps and head straight toward the dirt road, avoiding it. Even its smell made her sick. She'd hold a handkerchief to her nose while listening to Reverend Dean's sermon.

Ivory stopped attending baptisms after his father's death. It was Solomon who escorted the girls to the lake for their baptisms. His father's death had devastated her. She didn't blame anyone, not even God. She only blamed Lake Hope for taking him away from her.

Solomon could never blame the lake because things happen in life, just as his father had explained to him a hundred times. "Nobody has control of their time, Junior. When the Lord is ready for you, it's just your time."

This was difficult to express to his mother. It was his father's time and the Lord took him home.

One summer day Solomon and his mother argued for hours when she learned he'd taken the kids there to swim. It was important that the children learn how to swim, and it was especially important that they experience Lake Hope's gentleness. Lake Hope released a type of energy that made you stronger. It made you laugh and feel affectionate.

Yet in spite of his mother's belief that Lake Hope was evil, which was untrue, Solomon taught the kids how to swim anyway.

It was those memorable moments with his father that made Lake Hope very special to him. Solomon had become a man there.

His father would say, "Junior, you're nothing if you don't have any common sense. Remember that, son."

It was crucial that he learn all that he could. And in his father's honor, he passed down that wisdom to the other children, including the girls.

Solomon grabbed a handful of rocks and one by one tossed them into the lake. As each one fell, the splashing sound roared across the lake. It excited him. He extended his head to see how fast the rocks went down.

"Did it go down?" he said. "It must have. They surely couldn't have stayed up!"

Suddenly a hand brushed against his shoulder. He jumped. His body began to shiver. Too frightened to turn around to see who it was, he just stared straight across the lake.

"Who is it?" he said.

Solomon closed his eyes and painfully swallowed his saliva.

He was trembling. His left foot plunged into the dirt and his right leg shook. He was ready to run.

Then slowly he began to turn around. No one was there. Suddenly his entire body cramped. BOOM! He fell hard on his knees, hitting the ground. His hands and knees scraped against the earth. The skin on his knees had torn and blood trickled down. Solomon snatched a handkerchief from his pocket and wiped the red smudge off his ashy knee.

Words leaked from his mouth as if it were the first time he had ever spoken, "So . . . lo . . . mon . . . calm . . . down. E . . . ver . . . ry . . . thing . . . will . . . be . . . all right."

He ran to the edge of the lake again and dipped his shaking hands into the cold water. He splashed another handful onto his face and repeated this a few more times.

He sat there trembling, looking directly ahead. Then he saw it—a luminous reflection. It had emerged in the middle of the lake. At first he simply couldn't grasp what it was, but then he knew. It was his father's spirit.

The fiery sun beamed over him, sedating him. He glanced up at the hot fireball, then down, and back at the reflection again, but it disappeared.

"I know you're here, Daddy," he said. "I love you."

Solomon stayed at Lake Hope a little while longer, thinking about what had happened. He shook his head in wonder. He wanted the reflection to return and when it didn't, he slowly backed away, not taking his eyes off of the lake.

Solomon knew his father was there watching over him. He also knew his trials and tribulations had ended.

During the journey back home, Solomon giggled when he noticed that he'd urinated on his pants during his incredible encounter at Lake Hope.

He needed to clear his mind and decided he would gather some flowers for his mother. She adored the sight of a fresh bouquet. The bright colors and unique fragrance tickled her, making her laugh richly. Flowers forever rescued her from life's pain and sadness. The hospital's atmosphere was gloomy and he knew this would lift her spirits. There were so many to choose from. So he grabbed an assortment of colors.

He located a Coca-Cola bottle near the side of the road and put a handful of wildflowers together. He arranged them the way his mother liked, all the bright shades blended in beautifully.

Solomon wanted to visit Miss Parker before returning home. One had to walk the length of ten city blocks and down another long dirt road to get to it. And once you walked down the remote road, there the yellow dwelling stood in front of many trees and scrubs, small yet unique looking. She kept the inside as well as the grounds spotless.

Miss Parker was active. She stayed busy by babysitting the girls, cooking, and gardening. She made an effort to walk up the isolated road everyday to get the mail that was located in a makeshift wood box she had made herself. There was nothing inside most times. Even if there were letters waiting, she couldn't read them because she was illiterate. Solomon or Lily would read the letters to her when they visited. Walking made good exercise and it kept her vibrant.

Miss Parker didn't have any surviving children. She'd given birth to twin boys thirty-five years ago. One died as an infant and the other accidentally shot himself in the head with her shotgun when he was ten years old. They were born the same year as Ivory.

Miss Parker's home was a safe haven for Solomon. She'd often lend an ear to his problems and was also a wonderful advisor. She was good company as well. Her conversations were meaningful and, at times, amusing. "Being silly, sometime good medicine, Solomin," she often said.

Solomon never walked away from her home without appreciating something. She had a way of making you feel good about yourself. She made you think.

He could feel the strength of her home as he forged ahead. He smiled once he caught sight of the lemon-colored house. He ran up the steps and stood at the door for a moment before knocking on the door.

"Hey, Solomin," she said.

"Morning, Miss Parker."

"You up bright and early this morning."

"Yes, ma'am. It was just so beautiful outside," he said, looking around and then up at the sunlight. "I decided to take a walk."

"Nothing wrong with that. Come on in, baby. You came just in time 'cause I cooks some bacon and grits. You hungry?"

"Yes, ma'am," he said with a smile. Solomon's mouth watered as she spoke.

He walked in the house and followed her into the kitchen. The savory smell of buttered grits and greasy bacon simmering on the stove made his stomach chatter.

His eyes nearly spilled out of their sockets when she put a plate of hot grits, thick slices of smoked bacon, and fluffy scrambled eggs in front of him.

It was a learning experience for Solomon watching Miss Parker's disfigured hands slice fruits, vegetables, and meats, combining the ingredients for sweet cornbread, cakes, and pies.

Many times Solomon sat in that same kitchen chair mastering her techniques, taking notes, and sampling the finished products. "Umm . . . Umm . . . This is good, Miss Parker!" he said.

She laughed as he sloshed the biscuit around his plate, soaking up the grits and eggs. He ate every crumb and looked every bit fulfilled.

Once finished Solomon washed the dishes in a large pale washbasin. He gave Miss Parker a hug and kiss. "Thank you so much, Miss Parker. That was just what I needed."

She patted him on the side, smiled, and said, "Oh, just stop it now! You know you welcome anytime."

Solomon had to return home because it was getting late. He wanted to see how Lily and Nathaniel were doing before heading to work.

Tossing the washcloth on the chair, he said, "I'm going to have to chat with you later, Miss Parker. I'm sure Lily and Nathaniel are waiting for me by now."

"Okay, Solomin. You go on yo way. I see you in church on Sunday."

He looked down at his shoes and then in the opposite direction, feeling a bit uneasy. She knew he hadn't attended church service since his father's death. Nevertheless, it was Miss Parker who reminded him that the Heavenly Father's home was not in Solomon's house but in the good Lord's house. She believed it was her job to keep him grounded. So she continued to push him toward God's door.

He started to pick up the jar of flowers on the table when he walked toward her front door. He said, "Uh, I can't promise you, Miss Parker, but I'll try to be there on Sunday."

Pushing the jar back toward the center of the table, she shouted, "Don't promise me nothin'."

Solomon rolled his eyes. He had heard this lecture before. She pointed her finger at him and remarked, "You better promise the good Mighty Lord, Solomin. He the one you have to talk to in the end."

She was angry, nearly tipping over the chair. Solomon scurried to her rescue.

"Leave me lone!" she yelled, waving her hand at him. "I'll be fine."

Her warm hand reached over his and she held it still for a second. She said, "You use to go all the time, Solomin. What happen?"

His body trembled. "I don't know, ma'am. Ever . . . ever . . . since Daddy died and Bill . . ."

He started to speak again but she cut in. "That's mo of a reason to go!"

He lowered his head feeling ashamed. She took her finger, placed it under his chin, and raised his chin up. "Go talk to Him, baby."

"But . . . I do, Miss Parker. I talk to God all the time."

"No, you don't. You talk to yo Daddy all the time, not the Lord."

Her curled hand covered the side of his face. "God waiting for you, baby, and I knows you need Him."

All he could do was shake his head. He grabbed hold of the jar and headed for the door. Then he opened it and said, "Okay, Miss Parker, I'll try to go."

"Okay, Solomin," she said smiling. "It would be nice to see you at service on Sunday."

He hugged and kissed her. "You have a good day, Miss Parker. I'll see you soon."

"Don't forget to tell Ivry hey!"

"I won't. Bye now!"

"Bye."

Miss Parker stood on the porch and watched him walk down the road. He turned around and saw her waving. To this he smiled and waved back.

CHAPTER 23

Ivory fought hard for life. Solomon didn't think she was going to live but she did. She beat the deadly disease and passed the test of God.

When she was discharged from the hospital, Solomon, Lily, Nathaniel, and Miss Parker greeted her with open arms. They were happy that she was well and able to return home.

Solomon was so lively and wore the biggest smile. The nurses saw his silly grin a mile a way. He'd waited so long for this day to come. The day his family would be complete again. It was the best day of his life.

Lily brought Ivory a fresh bouquet of flowers from her garden and Nathaniel sketched a welcome home card. Though still weak, her condition had improved since her initial radiation treatment. Her mind was sound and she had gained more weight.

When they got home, Lily and Nathaniel helped her into bed. They were careful with her delicate body and tried not to cause her any more discomfort. She lay in her bed and looked around. Everything was the same: *just right.*

She inhaled the sugary scent of peach preserves and biscuits Miss Parker made for her that were on a small table next to her bed. She looked over by the three-legged chair that leaned against the wall and saw a pair of jeans that belonged to the girls. She grabbed the denims and held them to her nose. She took in a powerful sniff and slowly exhaled. She looked at Solomon and smiled. Then she said, "Junior, please go get my babies."

* * *

Solomon would have liked to think when he left his house that afternoon to get his sisters, that things would be the same. He couldn't have imagined that his life would change that day and that he would be forever scarred.

He needed normalcy back in his life. The girls' homecoming would have made him feel human again, made him feel like his hard work had some real meaning. Their arrival would have put his mind in one piece again and made his life complete.

That evening after breaking his mother's heart with the horrible news, he sat on the steps outside the house and read the bible. He skimmed through the pages and began reading Psalm 142 aloud while Lily and Nathaniel sat on the ground listening.

Solomon moved closer toward the kerosene lamp that was resting on the staircase ledge. He looked into Lily's eyes and recited, "I cried unto the Lord with my voice; with my voice unto the Lord did I make my supplication."

"I poured out my complaint before him; I shewed before him my trouble. When my spirit was overwhelmed within me, then thou knewest my path. In the way wherein I walked have they privily laid a snare for me."

Lily smiled and held Nathaniel's hand. Solomon continued, "I looked on my right hand, and beheld, but there was no man that would know me: refuge failed me: no man cared for my soul."

Tears fell. Solomon paused for a minute, but then wiped his face and went on. "I cried unto thee, O Lord: I said, Thou art my refuge and my portion in the land of the living. Attend unto my cry; for I am brought very low: deliver me from my persecutors; for they are stronger than I."

He cried out, "Bring my soul out of prison, that I may praise thy name: the righteous shall compass me about: for thou shalt deal bountifully with me."

Solomon and his family were heartbroken by this nightmare. He wanted to rid his mind of the destructive forces surrounding him—his father's unsolved death, Bill's abrupt departure, their struggle with poverty, his mother's illness, his suicide attempt, and the girls' abduction.

That evening Solomon put his trust in God and would wait for His help.

CHAPTER 24

Fannie Mae and Carter moved north to Paterson, New Jersey at the end of the year. Fannie Mae's eldest sister had lived there for years. She insisted there were plenty of jobs there that paid well.

Fannie Mae wrote all the time, reporting the vast opportunities in the north. She begged Ivory to visit. They were like sisters and she missed her.

Fannie Mae said the white folks were not as one-sided in New Jersey. She bragged about the money she and Carter were earning and how black folks not only worked at good-paying jobs but also owned their own homes. She and Carter had purchased one. They were finally homeowners after fifteen years of marriage. They bought a house on 18th Avenue and had plenty of rooms to spare.

She assured Ivory that she would enjoy the new and welcome atmosphere. The offer was too good to resist. Ultimately Ivory and the children visited Fannie Mae and Carter in early summer.

Paterson was drastically different than Mission. There were more cars parked on the streets than people. Factories, apartment buildings, and stores lined every avenue. Hundreds of people walked the busy streets, hustling and bustling, talking jive, singing, dancing, and just having fun.

Ivory's only complaint was that the air was dirty, but she was captivated by this contemporary, exciting, strange, flavorful city.

When they arrived at Penn Station in Newark, Solomon grinned and laughed. "Yes, this is where we belong!"

During their two-week visit they went to New York City. The East Coast's summer weather was a lot like Georgia's—hot and humid. It was a blazing afternoon when they crossed the George Washington Bridge. Lily and Nathaniel were scared straight because they had never seen such an immense bridge before, nor had they ever witnessed so many tall buildings and ethnically diverse people. The buildings were larger than life and the people were phenomenal. They must have overheard at least a hundred different languages spoken.

There was much to do back east. They visited many carnivals and amusement parks, beaches and most of the historic sites in Paterson and New York. Ivory grew tired of the constant traveling and sightseeing but the children were thrilled to experience such a vibrant way of life.

The kids that lived on Fannie Mae's block often teased their southern pitch. They would say, "You talk country."

Nevertheless, they were friendly. Fannie Mae promised she would get Ivory a job working at the candy factory with her. After much thought, Ivory agreed to move to New Jersey. Fannie Mae and Carter sent for them in December.

Lily, Nathaniel, and Solomon were overjoyed. They burst opened several bottles of soda and toasted, "To New Jersey— Paterson, New Jersey." Smiling and raising the bottles, they said, "To the good life—here we come!" Their bottles clinked together. "Yes, to the good life," Solomon said. He took another sip of drink. It was the best soda he had ever tasted.

They were excited to escape the pain in Mission. Too many sad memories adhered to everything: the house, the farm, Lake Hope, the school. Those memories dampened their spirits. They needed a picker-upper and New Jersey was the perfect answer.

The laughter and joy that once filled their home was gone. They all agreed it was a great idea. It was time to move on even though they would certainly long for Miss Parker's keen advice and tender loving care, Mr. and Mrs. Williams' uncommon friendship, and the fun they had with their neighbors, who were like an extended family.

One night, as Solomon packed his belongings, he heard Rose's voice. "Junior, where you going? Are you leaving me? You coming back?"

The sound of her voice brought him to his knees. He felt the brush of her soft hand caressing his face. He looked around the room and envisioned her standing before him. She smiled as he held up her hand to kiss it. Then suddenly she disappeared.

He broke down and sobbed. He asked God to give him the strength to hold on to life, and vowed that one day he would find his sisters.

The family said their good-byes that Saturday afternoon at the train station. They promised to write and visit often. Ivory hinted to Miss Parker that she come with them, but she flatly refused.

"I ain't never leaving Mission. This here my home," Miss Parker said, beating her walking cane on the ground.

They boarded the train. Nathaniel and Lily raced up the short flight of stairs and proudly took their seats. Ivory and Solomon waited behind for a few minutes. It would be her final moments with the people she loved.

Her eyes began to well and her hands shook as she held onto the handrail. She slowly glanced back at Miss Parker, then at Mr. and Mrs. Williams. Soon tears began to overflow and it was difficult for her to stop sobbing once the train had pulled away.

* * *

They settled in with Fannie Mae and Carter for a few months. When the children stepped out of Penn Station, fluffy white snow filled the skies, fascinating them. It was the first time they had seen such heavy snowfall.

The snow was knee deep. The beautiful sight had them spellbound. Ivory couldn't believe she had left Mission for this freezing weather. Fannie Mae dashed over to the Myers Brothers department store and bought some winter coats and boots for them.

It was blissful standing there on the cement ground watching the snowfall, letting it graze their faces. It looked like thick white rain, the kind Solomon always dreamed about. The feeling reminded him of those peaceful spring mornings he cherished—mornings he wished would never end.

The children glanced at each other and giggled. They were thinking about the girls. How they would have loved this joyous occasion. They would have been playing in the streets, making snowmen, and having snowball fights.

They continued smiling rather than expose their thoughts. They kept their reflections to themselves. That was their private moment.

Lily shouted, "It's just like the movies, isn't it?"

"Yep, but it's real this time and it feels so good," said Nathaniel.

"Hope it's like this every day," Lily said as she grabbed a handful of snow.

Nathaniel somberly remarked, "Lily, not every day. I couldn't imagine it being like this every day."

She made a snowball and threw it at him.

"Ouch!" he yelled. "Then again, maybe I could," he laughed, throwing a fist full of snow back at her.

They laughed and enjoyed that wonderful day. Lily fell on her knees into the deep snow. "I would really enjoy having weather like this on Christmas day," she said.

Christmas, Solomon thought. *The day the girls were born: Jesus' birthday and our favorite day of the year. The time of year we all looked forward to.*

He pondered some more. *Maybe the move and excitement of living in New Jersey will cover up the bad things we've been through. By next Christmas, maybe we will have forgotten it all.*

For years Ivory vowed every day she would return to Mission. It was difficult for her to tolerate the brutal weather and the fast pace of the city. Everything was in close proximity and she couldn't keep up with anyone. She could not understand how Fannie Mae and Carter loved it.

However, Solomon knew one thing for sure: his father would have loved Paterson. He and Carter always talked about moving north but the timing was never right so it simply didn't transpire. Now they were here fulfilling his dream, living it for him. Solomon knew his father would have been happy for them.

The only thing Ivory did enjoy was her job at the candy factory. She brought home candy every day. She said her coworkers treated her well and she enjoyed bringing home a good and steady paycheck. Ivory anticipated paying rent and buying food and other necessities. It gave her a sense of responsibility.

Ivory lost that when she met Bill. He made her feel careless and unreliable. She blamed herself when she couldn't feed her children. Yet it was Bill who took everything. Ivory lost her self-esteem and was embarrassed because she could not take care of her family without asking someone for help. It was a blessing to have a handle on life again. After she'd saved some money, she rented a three-bedroom apartment on Jackson Street.

Something was always going on at their place. Solomon found city life fascinating. He adored the diversity, the people, the ample opportunities available, and the gorgeous women. And boy, were they plentiful—a dime a dozen. It seemed there were fifteen women for every man, and he was really into that. They seemed to take a liking to him, being the new cat in town: the good-looking dark-skinned country boy. Of course, he took in all the admiration that came his way.

Solomon soon began dating a young woman he nicknamed BeeBee. He liked her because she enjoyed school and she was not so grown-up. By this time, he had begun attending high school and worked part-time with Carter at a meat shop.

BeeBee was a few years younger than he was. They spent considerable time together. But Ivory didn't approve of their relationship.

One morning while standing over the kitchen sank washing dishes, she said to him rolling her eyes, "Junior, that's all you need to do is knock some girl up! You never gonna finish school then. What you know about being a daddy?"

Her words hurt him. He abruptly stood and walked straight toward her. He was so furious that he snatched the plate she was washing out of her hands and yelled, "What do I know about being a daddy? Hell, I damn near raised five kids!"

Ivory began to sob. Solomon knew he had said the wrong thing. He apologized and she did the same.

That evening he visited Fannie Mae. While slicing a piece of sweet potato pie for him, she said, "You know you your Mama's first child, Junior." Sitting on her comfortable cushioned kitchen chair, she slowly sipped some lemonade. "She'll always be hard on you. She's gonna always expect you to do right."

Solomon understood. He was no longer angry with his mother. She didn't mean to be critical; she was only concerned. The girl's abduction had taken a toll on her. She was under a lot of stress.

Solomon told Fannie Mae that he did not regret his experiences raising the kids. He was their role model and proud of it. He knew that he was what he was because of his mother and father. And he had tried to instill those qualities in the kids. He could only be grateful for that.

Despite his mother's concerns, Solomon and BeeBee continued seeing one another. It was a good thing too—really good. Ivory knew him to be responsible and she knew what his goals were.

* * *

On Christmas day it snowed just like Lily had hoped. Solomon glanced out of the window, where he saw everything was white, bright, and serene. Children were playing in the streets. Lily and Nathaniel were thrilled. They eagerly opened their presents while Ivory and Solomon ate breakfast.

That evening they went over to Fannie Mae and Carter's home for dinner. Fannie Mae prepared a feast: turkey and dressing, collard greens and cornbread, macaroni and cheese, chopped barbecue, chitterlings, baked ham, potato salad, sweet potato pies, egg pies, and a red velvet cake—most of Solomon's favorite foods.

They sat in the dining room content and ready to celebrate. Ivory smiled as she glanced around at her children. She softly muttered, "You all know we've come this far by faith."

Solomon knew the phrase well.

Fannie Mae said, "Amen to that."

They all smiled. No one mentioned the girls' or even recalled that delightful Sunday back in 1960. They knew what the day meant to them. This was the day the girls were born—the happiest day of their lives. It was a day they celebrated with love and praise.

One Christmas day God extended the Walker family. And on that day they grew closer to Him, having so much strength and hope. God instilled in them a power that was overwhelming—a power that remained embedded in their hearts.

They blessed the food and thanked God for their health and for guiding them to Paterson. They asked Him to protect them and to take care of their friends and family in Georgia.

Everyone remained quiet after the prayer. And no one mentioned the girls. Solomon knew their thoughts and feelings would forever be silent. He believed that God would come through for them one day. He knew He would never forget them.

Their prayers for the girls were personal. They were unspoken.

PART TWO

THIS PLACE IN MY HEART

This place in my heart I searched to find
A place I journey
To maintain strength, peace and solitude
To find myself, to be with myself
I become stronger

I learn from my mistakes
I focus on me
Myself
My being
My knowledge
My purpose in life

I know what I want
This place in my heart I searched to find
I go there often and I stay long
I absorb all that's around me
The positive
The negative
The unthinkable
The thinkable
I ask questions
I think
I learn
I know
I cure my soul

CHAPTER 25

September 2002

Frustration set into the mind of a slender, curvaceous, coffee-complexioned woman who stopped walking up the endless flight of stairs. She wanted her husband's attention and he wasn't listening.

Her neck extended up and then turned sideways toward their bedroom. She frowned at the sound of running water coming from the bathroom. He was in the shower and she was furious. She hated when he ignored her.

The woman was quiet and stood halfway up the staircase. She took in a short breath and released it. She rested her tired body on the elegant banister when she reached the head of the stairs. It had been a long day. She'd left the house at 5:00 that morning and headed to New York City to put in an eleven-hour workday. She was worn out.

She called out his name in a low-pitched voice, "Anthony."

There was no answer. Then she screamed his name: "Anthony!"

Still there was no answer. She shouted again, "Anthony! Anthony! I know you hear me!"

Suddenly the bedroom door creaked open. A heavy current of mist filled the hallway. In the center of the haze stood a tall, chocolate, fine-looking man.

He took his time and strolled toward the railing. He leaned over it, water dripping down his hard body. He stood firm and spread his legs with not a care in the world.

He grinned slyly and calmly said, "I heard you, woman. What's wrong with you?"

He quietly laughed again as he wiped his wet face with a towel. "You act like you're dying or something."

She walked up to him slowly. She was inches away from him when she looked down and examined his genitals.

"No, I'm not dying," she said. She rolled her eyes. "If I was, I guess I would be dead by now, huh."

Anthony's large fruit moved when he stepped back. He said showing all teeth, "Now, come on baby, you know I was taking a shower. Why didn't you join me?"

"Please, I don't have time for this, Anthony. You always act like you're deaf." She chuckled. "Playing with yourself again, huh?"

His big brown eyes were fixed on hers. He giggled and slid his hand, which was large enough to palm two basketballs, up and down his muscular abdomen. He stared at her as he grazed his pubic hair and grabbed his flesh. She turned her head to the side and made a silly laugh like a young girl who had never seen it before.

Anthony yanked her dress and grabbed hold of her firmly. When she took a step back, he looked into her eyes and tried to entice her. He sank his head into her voluptuous breasts then softly kissed her lips.

She tried to pull away from him but he held her tight. He studied how the low-cut blue dress she wore outlined her sexy physique. His eyes were glued to her erect nipples. He shook his head, inhaled, and enjoyed the moment.

He coaxed his penis into moving by flexing his muscles there while holding her. She placed her hand over her mouth and laughed. "You're so silly, Anthony. You're something else," she said.

She knew what he wanted but she was not in the mood. A thousand thoughts were going through her head and she knew she wasn't ready to make love. It wouldn't be fair to him.

She walked down the flight of stairs and said in a mild tone, "Honey, I'm heading out to meet Linda. I'll be back in a couple of hours." She waved her hand. "I'll see you then."

"Hurry back, you know what night it is."

"What did you say?" she said.

He naively laughed at her.

"I didn't hear you," she said as she opened the front door.

"I said, hurry back! Tonight is the night. Remember!"

"Oh, it is!"

"Yes, it is!"

"Oh, well . . . I guess I've just been so absent-minded all day, I've completely forgotten," she said, shaking her head. "I . . . I . . . I don't know what's come over me."

Her husband's face dropped. He was disappointed. "Absent-minded," he whispered. "Come on now, you've got to be kidding me. It's been three weeks, baby."

She placed her hand to her chest and said, "Just three weeks, Anthony. And you're still horny."

"You damn right! Three weeks is a long time, baby." He leaned over the banister and pleaded, "I'm hurting, baby—can't you see. I really need you."

She started down the stairs to exit the front door. He raced after her and yelled, "Wait a minute!"

Then she spun around, gritted her teeth, and charged at him, "Please, don't pressure me, Anthony."

Gasping, he held his hands in the air and gave in. "Okay. Okay." Then he stroked her face and said, "What's troubling you, woman?"

"Nothing. Just be patient with me."

"I'm sorry. You know I would never pressure you."

She immediately changed the subject. "What do you want for dinner—Italian? I'll stop by Nino's and get something."

He nodded, "Nah, don't skip the subject." He pulled her body close to his and kissed her forehead. "We had that on Wednesday."

She was relieved he didn't pursue the issue. She smiled. "Chinese then—"

"No, I had that for lunch today." He paused and then said, "Look baby, don't worry about dinner. I'll cook. I see you have a lot on your mind." He rubbed his nose against her face. "I'll stop by the fish market and pick up some shrimp. How's that?"

"Umm, Shrimp. Shrimp scampi sounds great."

"It'll be ready when you get back." He kissed her lips and then grabbed her butt. "I guess I'll see you in a couple of hours."

"In a couple of hours," she said, giggling.

His hands covered her flawless face. When she closed her eyes for a moment, his lips grazed her forehead again, then her cheeks, then her lips.

He couldn't take his eyes off of her. "Hurry home. I'll be waiting," he said.

She hugged him and kissed his cheek. She moved her hands up his back but then quickly forced him away from her. She whispered, "Anthony, I have to go."

Reluctantly, he freed her. "Magnolia, please don't stay all night. You know how it is when you and Linda get together. You two—"

She covered his mouth with her manicured fingers, the nails painted a marshmallow color. "Don't worry, baby. Linda has an early flight tomorrow. We just need to go over a few details for the meeting on Monday, that's all."

He kissed her again. "Okay. I can live with that. Drive carefully."

"I will."

Magnolia headed toward her car. Anthony stood by the door and watched her drive off. After she pulled out of the driveway, he closed the door and sniffled. Then he stretched his neck back and to the sides. He threw up his athletic arms and tossed the bath towel over his broad back and slowly walked back up the stairs.

Magnolia parked her white onyx colored convertible Jaguar in the upper-level garage of a black sky-rise. She turned off the ignition and relaxed in the comfortable seat. Suddenly she inserted the key back into the ignition but pulled it out again. She wanted to turn around and head back home, to be with the man she loved. She didn't want to be in this cheerless place that always brought bad feelings, feelings she preferred to suppress. She reached over the passenger seat and clutched a cold bottle of iced tea that she purchased at the 7-Eleven two blocks away. She gulped down half the bottle and then sucked in an intense breath.

Magnolia reclined the oatmeal colored leather seat and began to consider her existence—her purpose in life.

Magnolia lied to Anthony. She wasn't going over to Linda's. She was sitting in a dark, isolated parking garage thinking. Ten stories above her in the modernistic office building was the office of her psychologist.

Linda thought these visits were pointless. She thought Magnolia put herself through unnecessary stress. "You're wasting your time, energy, and money, girlfriend. Believe me, you are," she insisted.

When Magnolia revealed her secret to her, Linda remarked, "Girl, we all have dreams like that. There's absolutely nothing wrong with you. You worry too much."

But Magnolia knew something was wrong. Why else would she have started having such awful dreams after she and Anthony moved into their second home in Alpine?

Magnolia wanted to believe that the source of the dreams was the stress of relocating and possibly the fact that she and Anthony had been trying to have a child for ten years.

Matters worsened when Magnolia's mother died four months after they moved into their lovely, new home. Loneliness became her constant companion.

Magnolia never knew her father. Her mother said he died when she was four. There had been so much strife in her life—so much so that she often asked God why her. Why had she been handed all of this turmoil?

The dream was always the same. It's their wedding day and Anthony and Magnolia are at the altar. They begin to recite their vows to each other. Then suddenly Magnolia turns to glance at her mother for a final approval and everyone in the church fades away. They are both stunned as they look back at each other. She is in a state of confusion and finds herself running through a massive maze searching for her friends and family. She journeys to a place she has been before, but for the life of her she cannot remember the place. Finally she awakes from her daze and when they both glance back at the crowd, the guests reappear.

The details surrounding the dream are beyond her understanding. It is as though her life vanishes for a moment. Where are her family and friends? She has asked herself that question a thousand times. Dr. Jean-Pierre Bellamy, her psychologist, has taken her back to the dream through hypnotism, but to no avail.

He is an attractive, well-dressed, stocky French man. Magnolia met him at a book party three years ago. For months they both had made a tireless effort to try and solve the puzzle. Yet the search for her family remained hopeless. It was as though her mind traveled through this mass of confusion trying to decipher the familiar.

While hypnotized, Magnolia can see several children playing on a farm. She wonders if the children are hers. They are laughing and waving at an elderly man and woman.

Magnolia reached for the half-emptied bottle of iced tea and took another sip. Feeling rested, she raised her body forward and opened the car door. This would be her last session.

She walked down the corridor and through the lobby, all the while thinking about her dilemma. Everyone had dreams. But she was fairly sure hers were unusual—dreams of knowing but not really knowing.

She theorized her dreams and the events that take place in them might be about an actual place she'd forgotten.

"It's a dream of recognition—" that is what she told Linda.

Many times she rationalized them, concluding that her family and friends fled to another place in time. Her family ran off so that she and Anthony could find themselves and unearth their real selves. Maybe they needed to reconsider their marriage. But why would they do that? They were in love and would gladly die for each other. Soon Magnolia dismissed the idea, realizing that her family and friends, including her spiteful mother, understood her relationship with Anthony.

For weeks she carried this heavy load, and it had grown frustrating. She wanted to be strong, to move on. She was embarrassed to confide in Anthony. He knew she and her mother had a distant relationship and that her mother hated him for no apparent reason, yet he always sided with her mother. It was probably because he loved his mother so dearly and treasured her. Anthony embraced the idea that mothers were always right.

He knew Magnolia's mother had some problems, but in his mind, they weren't big problems. He felt Magnolia entangled herself in situations of little concern. He thought he understood her mother, but he didn't.

Magnolia's mother had problems she couldn't overcome and she held Magnolia responsible. Her mother took her anger out on her. The anguish was embedded so deep, Magnolia could not understand why her mother was so troubled and angry with her.

At a very early age, growing up in a middle class neighborhood in New Jersey, Magnolia sensed her mother didn't like herself. She despised the fact that Magnolia had nothing in common with her. She liked to sew; her mother bought clothes at fancy stores. She liked to cook; her mother dined at restaurants. She liked to garden; her mother bought fake flowers from K-Mart.

Her mother was a nurse, constantly surrounded by people who needed her attention. Giving that to strangers wasn't a problem, but bringing that affection home was very difficult. Magnolia never knew why her mother hated her. She assumed it had something to do with her father.

Her mother had very few friends. She was private, highly pessimistic, and trusted no one, not even Magnolia.

Magnolia's mother wanted her to attend a college near home, so Magnolia attended Rutgers University. That is where she met Anthony.

Magnolia thought for sure her mother was changing, willing to establish a bond between the two of them. But she was wrong, dead wrong. Her mother didn't change at all. She simply feared being alone. Magnolia was her only child and she had no extended family, other than a sister and a few cousins.

Although Magnolia attended an in-state college, she tended to stay on campus. Her mother lived in Hackensack whereas Magnolia lived in New Brunswick—forty minutes away.

Magnolia spent most of her time with Anthony and his family. It was useless spending vacations with her mother. There were always confrontations. Her mother hated the fact that people quickly accepted Magnolia and that she could maintain long-lasting friendships with schoolmates.

Linda couldn't understand why Magnolia's mother was so unhappy and resentful of her own child. She too wondered what had happened.

Magnolia tried not to focus on her mother and the problems that came along because it made her very uneasy, often resulting in severe headaches. So she shifted her energies to someone positive and overlooked the friction and tension: she fell in love with Anthony Lewis. They truly loved and appreciated each other and would develop a wonderful relationship.

Anthony was from Los Angeles. Magnolia spent every summer there while in college, and it was there she met one of her closest friends. Anthony's mother was a social worker at a hospital in the San Fernando Valley. She had told Magnolia about a young woman, not too much younger than she, who resembled her. This young woman was a phlebotomist.

They were introduced in Magnolia's junior year. Billie Holiday Hartley was a freshman and pre-med major at UCLA. Everyone wanted to be a doctor back then, but not Magnolia. Medicine didn't interest her in the least.

Billie was two years younger than Magnolia. They did share some features but Magnolia didn't think they favored each other at all, despite what Anthony and his mother thought.

Billie was on the heavy side. Her father had named her after Billy Holiday. Magnolia thought being named after a famous singer was cute. Billie and Magnolia became best friends soon after their introduction. Several times during spring breaks, Billie visited Magnolia in New Jersey.

Billie's parents lived in Encino. Billie was nothing like her father. She had a bubbly personality whereas her father was very quiet. Yet they were very close. She was an only child like Magnolia, except, unlike Magnolia, she was a spoiled brat. Her mother and father owned a jewelry store and a popular restaurant in Woodland Hills. Her father was an expert at repairing jewelry, often restoring Magnolia's jewelry.

Billie's mother's family was affluent. Magnolia didn't know until she'd actually met Billie's mother that Billie was half-white. Magnolia thought her father must have strong genes because Billie didn't appear to be interracial. She was light complexioned and had the kinkiest hair. Billie would go on to become a well-known pediatrician in Los Angeles.

Linda Webb was Magnolia's other best friend, and they had known each other since grade school. Linda had seen Magnolia through all of her trials and tribulations. She was Magnolia's maid of honor and Billie was her bride's maid.

* * *

This was Magnolia's final visit with Dr. Bellamy. She felt strong enough to find the place in her heart she'd been searching for. He insisted that she continue visiting him, but Magnolia insisted there be a closure to all the pain.

Magnolia had finally concluded that she hadn't let go of her mother's passing. That was why she disappeared in the dreams. Still, Dr. Bellamy insisted that she continue coming to see him.

Resting on the cushioned sofa in Dr. Bellamy's homey office, Magnolia described her relationship with her mother. She told him that her mother didn't have strong family ties like Anthony and his family. She told him that her mother was gone and she had to accept that. Sure, she regretted not telling her mother that she loved her as often as she should have; not being able to hug, kiss, or hold her hand, especially when she was on her death bed. But she wouldn't forget her and didn't hate her. She needed to let go so she could finally have peace.

After all of Dr. Bellamy's ideas and plans, Magnolia believed this was the right thing to do. Despite Dr. Bellamy's call for more therapy, Magnolia thanked him for his assistance and direction. She promised him that if the dreams persisted and interfered with her life, she would contact him.

She left his office relieved, fulfilled, and grateful that it was all over. It was time to get on with her life. She and Anthony had a great deal to accomplish.

She walked out of Dr. Bellamy's office and closed the door behind her. She looked down at her cobalt blue shoes and clicked her heels. She made a wish like Dorothy. She wanted to go back home, back to the place that made her happy.

After clicking her heels, she looked down at her shoes again and laughed. They weren't red like in the fairy tale but they were still brilliant. She grabbed her keys out of her purse and headed toward the elevators at the end of the hallway.

Tonight she would start anew.

CHAPTER 26

Magnolia drove onto the elongated driveway that stretched the length of her upscale house. She was excited that her visits with Dr. Bellamy were over. She hated digging up the past and coming clean with the intricate details of her life with her mother—especially, the bad part, the part that made her sad.

She raced to the front door and inserted the key into the doorknob. She opened the door halfway and poked her head inside. "Baby, I'm home!"

There was no answer. Her eyes widened as they searched for her soul mate. She pushed open the door and walked inside. Anthony heard the clicking sound of her high heels and hid in a large walk-in closet in the kitchen.

Magnolia smiled when she turned her head toward the kitchen. The flavorful aroma of shrimp scampi filled the house. Her mouth began to water at the scent of the melted butter, garlic, cayenne pepper, and chives.

She walked into the kitchen and saw the scampi simmering on the stove. She grabbed a fork and dipped it into the skillet, skewered with a jumbo shrimp. She bit into the scrumptious meat, patting her mouth because it was sizzling. "Ooh, this is too good," she said as she chewed.

The large closet door slowly opened. Anthony stepped out and moved quietly as a snake. He approached her from behind.

His eyes inspected her shapely body. Then he gently tapped her shoulder. Magnolia jumped and screamed, dropping the half-eaten shrimp on the floor. When she turned around, she hit her forehead against Anthony's and said, laughing, "Anthony, I could kill you!"

Giggling, he held her by the waistline and stared into her eyes. His lips touched hers. Magnolia wrapped her arms around his neck, giving him the biggest hug. She passionately kissed him. Her fingernails moved up his chest and she deliberately dug deep. "I love you, Anthony," she said.

He kissed her cheek, "I love you back." His hand covered the back of her head and he gently yanked her hair. Then he pulled her head forward and kissed her more, this time trailing kisses down her neck. "Leah, I want to make love to you tonight," he said as he continued to kiss her. "It's been way too long. I need you."

Words began to seep out of her mouth when the telephone rang. Magnolia reached over to pick it up and Anthony tried to stop her.

"Anthony, it could be Linda."

He rolled his eyes and sucked his teeth. Magnolia caressed his chin and smiled. She shook her head and said, "Remember, our meeting."

Anthony shrugged his shoulders and walked toward the stove, putting a lid over the pot.

"Hello. Oh, hey, Carl. How are you? I'm fine." She turned toward Anthony and scrunched up her eyes. They both smiled.

"Doing pretty well, actually. How is Brenda? What? That's wonderful. What color is it? Oh, baby blue, my favorite color."

She tugged on Anthony's shirt.

"What year is it? A 2003 coupe. I bet it's beautiful," she said. "Tell her congratulations and I can't wait to see it."

Magnolia placed her hand over the mouthpiece and whispered to Anthony, "Carl bought Brenda a new Mercedes."

Anthony didn't look at her—he just half-smiled.

"Hey, Carl, what gourmet meal did you cook up this evening?"

She laughed. "I know you." Then she looked at Anthony and grinned. "I knew it!"

She turned to Anthony and said, "You see Anthony, we should have gone over to Carl's. He made chicken lasagna, a Caesar salad, and a cheesecake."

Anthony chuckled. He knew what she was up to. "You mean to tell me I spent hours slaving over this stove and we could have gone over there instead? Tell him he better save us a slice of that cheesecake."

"You hear that, Carl?" She turned to Anthony and winked her eye. "He said he would."

Magnolia kicked Anthony in the butt and smiled. "Here's Anthony, okay. Talk to you later. Goodbye."

Anthony grabbed the telephone. "Hey, what's up, Carl?"

Anthony listened for a minute and then he made a straight face. "Are you serious?" he said. "When do they want to meet?" He began to grin. "Hey, you know that's not a problem. I can always fit that into my schedule."

Anthony started to bang his fist on the stove. Then he began to jump up and down. "Man, if this falls through," he said, laughing. "This is just what we need, Carl. Great leg work, man."

Magnolia tugged on his shirt. Anthony slid his finger across her lips. She knew she would have to wait.

"Look, let's get together tomorrow. Do you want to meet at the office or here? Okay, I'll be there at ten. Goodnight, man."

Anthony kept banging his hand on the stove excitedly.

"What was that all about?" Magnolia said, standing in front of him with her hands on his buttocks.

He kissed her and hoisted her body. Her legs wrapped around his waist.

"I can't believe it, baby."

"Believe what, Anthony?"

"Remember that contract I told you about? The one we've been trying to get for a year now?"

"Yeah, the Simon General contract."

"Yes, exactly! We'll, they're ready to do business, Leah. I'm flying down to Miami Beach next week—most likely on Thursday. Carl can't make it. He's working on the Chicago deal."

Magnolia wrapped her hands around his neck and said, "This is wonderful, baby!"

"Magnolia, if this falls through. I'm talking a hundred-million-dollar deal, baby. Got damn, I'm happy."

"Oh, now you're happy. Just a few minutes ago you were ready to fuck."

"Hey, watch your mouth," he said chuckling. "Well, I was happy then too." He laughed. "Anyway, why have you been so hard on me lately? So distant." He glanced down at his flesh.

"Please, don't give me any of that shit again, Anthony. Let's eat. I'm starving."

At the dining table, Magnolia twirled the pasta around on her plate. Then she slowly inserted some into her mouth. Sauce dripped down her chin. Anthony immediately reached over the table and gently brushed the side of her mouth with a napkin. He would play her little game.

He wanted to grab her and force her on top of the table, shoving everything on it aside, stroking her harvest and loving her like he never had. But he knew she was still tense. *Should he or shouldn't he?* He smiled and watched her perform for him.

Magnolia returned a smile. Even though she was agitated, she felt it had been a long time too. So she continued to arouse him. Something she was good at. She moved her upper body to the side and stared into his eyes. Magnolia knew that Anthony couldn't live one day without sex. God forbid she ever went away on a business trip—he would lose his mind.

Anthony was born to love—to make good love, which was what she told her best friends Linda and Billie. Magnolia decided to go ahead with her plan. She took one last sip of the red wine. "Anthony," she said softly, "do you know why I married you?"

"No," he said, feigning ignorance. "Why?"

"Because you're an excellent cook."

"Is that so?"

She smiled. "Yes, baby. You make sure your woman is satisfied. You take great care of me. Did you know that?"

He chuckled. "Of course I knew that." Rubbing the wine glass, he took a sip. "But, I thought you married me because of my good looks, my sex appeal."

She burst into laughter. "No, no, baby, I'm sorry to disappoint you. Did you really think that? Those qualities were at the bottom of the list."

His facial muscles tightened. "And what qualities were at the top of this list?" he said.

"Your smile."

He started laughing hysterically. "My smile! You've got to be kidding me."

"No, I'm not. And you also take good care of your teeth. I like that in a man."

Anthony slammed his hand on the table. "This is it! I've had enough! I don't want to hear any more of your phony bull shit."

Instantly he stood and ran toward her, just as she knew he would. Magnolia dashed toward the stairwell and he rushed over, trapping her. He lifted her forcefully into his arms and walked up the stairs, heading toward their bedroom. He softly kissed her breasts and neck as he walked up the stairs.

He whispered, "Those qualities will soon move to the top of the list once we get into the bedroom."

Magnolia lay in his arms and took in his smell. The scent was purely sensual. So good, she began to taste him. He reached the top of the stairs, still kissing her. Soon her tongue intertwined with his. He kicked open the bedroom door and lay her on the bed.

"I want you, Leah. More than ever." He slid his hands up her dress, gently pulling off her pantyhose. He felt her wetness and squeezed shut his eyes. His fingers caressed all of her. She flamed like a raging fire out of control. His hands meticulously moved between her thighs.

Unbuttoning her dress, his tongue lingered on her nipples. Then his head dropped and he left a wet trail of saliva across her belly. Ever so slowly his head moved up and down as he kissed her entire body and skillfully fondled her voluptuous breasts.

"Anthony . . . Anthony . . . baby . . . don't stop."

Her hands fell back against the bedpost and he turned her to the side, kissing and caressing her backside. She held onto a pillow and moaned, "Anthony . . . Anthony."

"Let me love you," he said.

"Don't stop, Anthony," she screamed, clutching the pillow. He turned her onto her back, and this time he thrust hard, penetrating deeper and deeper.

"Oh baby . . . Oh baby . . ." she screamed out. Her nails dug into the taut muscles of his back.

They continued to kiss passionately. Then Anthony held her close, protecting her. She wrapped her legs around his thighs.

He stared into her eyes and whispered, "I love you, Magnolia."

He sighed, releasing a soothing breath. He glanced at her again and they both smiled.

They lay cuddled together in bed. This moment had been long overdue. They both needed the lovemaking.

Magnolia's back touched his front upper body and he stroked her gently. "How are you feeling, baby? Are you relaxed now?"

She smiled and said, "I feel safe. That's just what I needed." She pecked his lips. "Yes, I'm relaxed now."

"You've been so uptight lately. What's wrong?" he said, caressing her face. "Did I do something to you?"

"No, you haven't done anything. I'm just a little stressed, that's all. There's so much going on at work." She chuckled softly. "Everything took off so fast. I never thought business would be this good when Linda and I decided to become literary agents. We have thirty-five clients now. And twenty book deals this year with major publishers."

"That's great, baby!" he said, stroking the contour of her body.

"Yes, it is. But—"

"But what?"

She turned around. "Well, there's just one prospective client who's been very difficult to work with."

"There's no need to get stressed out because of one client." His body ascended and he reached over her and grabbed her firmly. "Is this client that great?" he said. "Maybe it's a good idea to let someone else deal with him or even considering letting him go."

"It's a she and her work is excellent, Anthony," she said. "It's just that . . . she hasn't agreed to any of our terms. Can you believe that? A first-time writer." She sighed. "But I don't want to lose her; that's how good her work is. Her name is Mackenzie Gary. She lives in Toronto. She is a very sincere person but extremely stubborn. Linda wants to let her go. She refuses to work with a first-time writer who is inflexible."

Touching Anthony's face, she said, "Baby, there is this strange connection between she and I. Although we've never met, I relate to her in a curious way. Maybe because we're both so persistent and strong-willed."

Anthony laughed. "Persistent, strong-willed. That's an understatement, baby."

Magnolia slapped his chest. "That's not funny, Anthony!" She rolled her eyes. "Be that as it may, I've only communicated with her via the telephone but there's something there." She looked in his eyes. "I can't figure it out yet. I don't want to give up on her, Anthony. I really want to represent her."

"Leah, you have to take it one day at a time. If this person is that difficult, I don't care how good her work is, you may have to let her go."

"You know me, Anthony. I tend to pursue things to the very end."

He kissed her forehead. "I don't remember you ever compromising your health. Promise me you won't let this make you sick."

"I promise."

Holding her body against his, he said, "It's okay to pursue things, but you also have to know when to let go, especially when you have no control over the situation."

He tapped her forehead. "You have too many things going on

up here. Sometimes, you have to be strong enough to know when to let go, Leah. Remember that. You're only human."

"I know. I know. I also know that things are going well for the two of us. We're blessed, Anthony. We've both worked so hard. And I'm very happy for you and Carl. When the two of you started the company, it seemed like a lifetime ago, but it was risky and it paid off."

"Yes, it definitely paid off. The two of us make a great team."

Magnolia slipped her fingers through his hair. "Carl's been like an older brother to you, hasn't he?"

"Yeah, I have so much respect for him. He's taught me everything I know. I learn more from him everyday. But you know what?"

Magnolia rolled her eyes at him. She knew what he was going to say. "What?"

"He loves you more than me."

"Stop it, Anthony. Carl and I get along very well. And that goes the same for Brenda and I. He's like an older brother."

"Leah, Carl's crazy about you. There is no denying that. Sometimes I have to wonder about my best friend."

She hit his chest again. "Wonder about what, Anthony?"

Magnolia got up and moved over to the edge of the bed and held her hands up. "That maybe he cares for me in that way? Carl's just a protector."

She reached over to the bureau, grabbed a water glass, and took a sip. "You of all people should know that. He's very protective of you and I. He just wants us to do well, that's all." She took another sip. "Anyway, how's his mother doing?"

Anthony snatched the glass from her hand and drank. "Don't skip the subject, Leah."

"I'm not skipping the subject. Anthony, Carl would never disrespect you or me and I know for sure he loves Brenda to death. What is your problem? He's never given me any indication that he wants me."

"Well, he's given me plenty."

She blew out a deep breath and tossed the pillow at him.

"Anthony!"

He stood up and walked to the window. Glancing out he said, "I've never told you this before and maybe I shouldn't now."

Magnolia sat upright. Her heart was racing. "Please, tell me."

"Remember our fourteenth-year anniversary?"

"Of course I remember."

"Well, I wanted so desperately to make you happy and to do something special for you." He paused, then briefly tightened his fists and stared out into the dark night. "At that particular time, money was really tight, and we were in the process of buying this house."

He wiped his hand across his mouth. "Well, I went to Tiffany's and saw this spectacular diamond ring that I knew you love."

Magnolia smiled, looking at the ring on her right hand. "I remember, Anthony. It's resting so lovely on this finger."

"Leah, it cost $75,000."

"Anthony! You didn't have to tell me that," she said.

"Leah, I wanted to buy it that day, but I couldn't afford it." He shook his head. "I told Carl about it the next day. I needed an outlet because for the first time, I couldn't afford to buy something as simple as jewelry for you."

Magnolia's expression turned solemn as she stared at Anthony.

"Baby, it was too much," he said. "I told Carl how much I loved you and wanted you to have everything you deserved."

"And . . ." she said, her hands up the air.

Anthony did not respond.

"And . . ." she repeated.

He looked at her and said, "And . . . three days later, the saleswoman from Tiffany's contacted me at the office and informed me that the ring was ready for pickup."

"What?"

"I was baffled too, baby. I told the saleswoman that there must have been some kind of mistake."

Anthony took another sip of water and swallowed hard. "But then she said Carl had purchased the ring."

He blew out a forceful breath. "Later that day, I confronted

Carl and he said he knew how much this meant to me. He told me I could repay him later."

Magnolia shut her eyes and dropped her head. She locked her hands as if in prayer. She couldn't believe it. "I didn't know . . ." she whispered.

"I shouldn't have told you this. But . . . it's just that . . . I'm a man and I know when a man feels for a woman. I never felt right after that," he said. "It's as though Carl gave you that ring, not me!"

Magnolia jumped out of the bed and strolled toward him. Her arms covered him and her head fell forward. "Anthony, look at me."

He looked up at her. Tears flowed down her face. "Trust me, baby, Carl is not in love with me."

He shook his head in disagreement.

"Anthony, I'm not saying that you're imagining things, but I'm certain he's not. You have to believe me. I'm absolutely positive."

Anthony wiped away her tears. "I know this must be painful, baby," she said. "You think your best friend is in love with your wife. But baby," she said, lifting his chin, "remember, how you always told me that I never understood my mother? Well, now the tables are turned. I don't think you understand Carl. You don't understand his way of expressing his generosity and love for the two of us. You've never experienced that type of affection, at least not with another man."

Anthony downed the last of the water. "Okay . . . Okay . . . I hear you. I just hate—"

Magnolia pointed her finger at his chest. "You hate the fact that someone else cares for me. You want to be the only one. This conversation would have never taken place if Carl were a female. Would it?"

Chuckling, he agreed. "You know, you're absolutely right, baby." Hoisting his arms in the air, he said, "I'm jealous. Okay, okay: I admit it."

The night's calm air circulated in the room, absorbing their fears and frustrations as they embraced. They grew rejuvenated standing by the window. They remembered what they were here for: to love, honor, and respect each other.

Anthony softly nibbled her chin. "Anyway, his mom is doing better. He thought it might be something serious, but it's just a touch of sugar."

"Well, that's pretty serious."

"Yeah, it is, but she's watching what she eats and she's exercising. As a matter of fact, she's going to see a dietitian on Monday. She's on insulin and that's going a long ways."

"When you see her, tell her I said hello."

"I sure will," he said. Then he began to laugh. "Speaking of his mother—"

"Oh, please, Anthony! I know what you're going to say."

He grinned. "She is. She's crazy about you too. I can't figure it out, Leah."

She bit down on his chest. "Can't figure out that everyone loves me because I'm a beautiful person? Sweetheart, I'm really sorry that it took you twenty years to figure that one out."

"Oops, I keep forgetting."

A can of shaving cream sat on the dresser and Magnolia grabbed it.

"No!" Anthony screamed.

Firmly clutching it, Magnolia sprayed him thoroughly.

"No! Leah, stop that!"

He tried to run out of the room but stumbled and fell. She jumped on top of him and covered his face with the white cream. All he could do was cover his eyes.

CHAPTER 27

The songs of birds, the warmth of the radiant sun comforting her skin, and the smell of a fresh breeze were clear signs for starting anew.

It was the day after Labor Day and Magnolia was ecstatic about life. Everything was falling into place. She and Anthony had a wonderful weekend. Finally life seemed promising.

All Anthony could think about was the promising new deal. He danced in the shower for an hour, singing *I feel good*. Magnolia was happy for him. She peacefully lay in bed, her body wrapped in silky evergreen sheets. She looked at her husband through the glass shower doors and smiled. She couldn't have been more proud.

Anthony stepped out of the shower and slowly walked over to the bed, his penis was hard. Magnolia giggled and displayed that infamous bashful expression.

"Anthony, not this morning. I have to be on time today. Remember, Linda's not at the office."

Ignoring her plea, he climbed on top of her, ripped off her gown, and pulled her body down, kissing her nipples.

She resisted. "Anthony, I don't want to fight you."

"Then don't," he said lustfully.

"Anthony—"

Climbing off of her, he said, "Okay, go get ready for work."

She stayed in bed for a few minutes and watched him get

dressed. While he buttoned his shirt, zipped his cuffed pants, and meticulously knotted his tie, she smiled and thought about his willpower.

Anthony had worked his ass off to get to this point in his career. Everything had escalated at the right time. From the moment she met him, she'd wanted to spend the rest of her life with the man.

It was the beginning of her freshman year at Rutgers. She majored in journalism, and Anthony was a senior and a premed major at Cook College. Linda also went to Cook College. She too was a senior and a pre-med major.

Linda and Magnolia were inseparable. Magnolia's mother always thought Linda was much too old for her, but Magnolia latched on anyway. Maybe it was because she never had any sisters, but she was comfortable around Linda. She felt safe. Linda understood her and she learned from Linda. She knew Linda would always be by her side and she knew Linda loved her.

One afternoon Magnolia met Linda for lunch in the cafeteria. Linda ordered her food and was gossiping as usual with a group of students, including the most handsome African-American man Magnolia had ever seen on campus. Linda and Anthony were working on a project for genetics class. They frequently spent afternoons reviewing and planning their course work.

At first Magnolia assumed they were dating. Why wouldn't they be? Linda's weakness was attractive men. She'd just about kill for them, especially the athletic types.

One day while sitting in the park, Magnolia couldn't resist the subject. Linda calmly said, looking straight at the pond, "No, we're not dating. What made you think that?"

Linda seemed surprised by the question. Yet she knew had it not been for Anthony's Caucasian girlfriend, she already would have tried to screw him.

His girlfriend, Hillary, attended William Paterson College. Magnolia was shocked that this handsome black man, who was surrounded by hundreds of beautiful, educated black women, would be with a white woman.

Of course, Linda didn't help matters when she said, "Girl . . . and he's from Los Angeles too. What you'd expect?" she said chewing on a bagel. "That's all the brothers date out there."

She ended the conversation on a slightly positive note by saying, "Things aren't working out between them though."

Magnolia's head rolled up as she listened carefully.

"They're having serious problems," Linda said. "You know what I mean, girl? Her family doesn't like him at all."

Linda stuck her finger in the cream cheese and then put it in her mouth. "Girl, I can't figure white folks out. The brother is going to be a physician one day and these simple folks will still think of him as a nigger."

Damn! Magnolia thought. She was available. If only he knew. Linda read her mind like a true sister.

"Oh, he did mention something about knowing she's wasn't wife material and that he is ready for a commitment," Linda said, dipping her finger into the cream cheese again.

Then she added, "He's ready to settle down. He's looking for someone he can trust." She winked. "Someone that will love him for him." She chuckled. "Would you like me to introduce you two?"

"He met me already."

"So what? He really doesn't know you."

Magnolia looked around, making sure no one was listening. "Why haven't you fucked him, Linda? I know you too well." She looked around and then back at Linda. "He's fine, has a body like I don't know what, and educated!"

Linda inhaled and exhaled. "First thing, girlfriend, Gerald is my one and only."

"Yeah, right," Magnolia said. "You love no one but yourself."

"I'm serious. He puts me on a pedestal and I'm not leaving him for no one." She giggled. "You know what I mean, girlfriend. And second . . ."

Linda took another bite of bagel and chewed quickly. "Anthony is going back to L.A. There's no ifs or buts about that. He's going back. He hates New Jersey." She sat poised and said, "It's too cold out here for him. And, besides, California is not for me, girl. All those earthquakes and mud slides—please!"

Magnolia ruminated on this.

Linda pointed at Magnolia. "Third—"

"Oh, now there are three reasons," Magnolia said, laughing.

"Yep. And third, Anthony and I would just bump heads. I'm too stubborn for him and he doesn't like that in a woman."

"Oh, really!"

"Yes, really!" Linda answered.

"Umm, then this man is definitely rare."

Linda nodded. "If that's what you want to call it," she said. They both laughed.

Several weeks passed before Linda formally introduced them. Anthony and Magnolia immediately hit it off. They spent all of their time together, which upset Linda. At first she was uncomfortable with their relationship because she in fact was attracted to Anthony, but knew the feeling wasn't mutual. Soon her resentment tapered off because Gerald, a tall light-skinned brother with curly hair who practiced law in Edison, filled her every need. He gave her plenty of sex and showered her with expensive gifts and money.

Within weeks, Magnolia fell in love with Anthony. He was everything she wanted in a man. He was faithful, honest, understanding, and a friend. Most importantly, he respected her.

She knew his affection was genuine when he asked her to come home with him during the Christmas holiday break. Her mother didn't think it was a good idea, but at the time Magnolia could not have cared less what her mother thought.

They traveled to Los Angeles hand in hand. Magnolia even saved the airline tickets. She would keep them for more than twenty years.

It was her first trip to Los Angeles, and she was nervous and excited. His family was wonderful. She felt loved for the first time in her life.

Anthony's mother and Magnolia developed a special relationship. They traveled throughout southern California. She gave

Magnolia the world. They communicated like real mothers and daughters do.

Magnolia was a virgin when she met Anthony. She knew before she left New Jersey that she wouldn't be one for long. Anthony's constant sexual overtures during the past weeks were a clear indication that it was time. Most importantly, she was ready too.

Anthony's older brother, Marcus, a vascular surgeon, lived in Malibu. During the holidays, Marcus and his family vacationed in Europe and Anthony house-sat for them.

Anthony never pressured Magnolia into having sex with him, but his desires were perfectly evident. At the airport, Magnolia could feel his heartbeat quicken when she rested her head against his muscular chest. The way he held and touched her excited her. Her body became saturated with goose bumps. His sensual scent and heavy breath aroused her. She knew he wanted her. She wanted him too, but didn't know quite how to go through with it.

Anthony sat silent at the dining table at his parent's house in Santa Monica. He remained composed all night, his eyes locked onto her. As he gazed, his eyes widened and he stroked his tongue over his full lips.

Magnolia prayed he would not do anything out of the ordinary. She turned to his mother, hoping a conversation would distract his thoughts. But Anthony continued to stare at her body.

When his mother stood and walked into the kitchen. Magnolia muttered to herself, "Magnolia, stop acting like you're a little girl!"

They drove up Pacific Coast Highway to Malibu. While driving, Anthony kept glancing at her. He couldn't resist keeping his hands off of her any longer and the temptation was too high. He slid his hand up her thigh to find her warm and moist. Magnolia wanted to say, "Anthony, I thought you weren't going to pressure me."

But instead, she looked at the limitless gray sky and thought, *Magnolia just let it happen*. She knew what was lacking in their relationship was sexual intimacy.

They approached the front door of his brother's mansion that overlooked the ocean and looked like something out of a magazine. And as soon as he inserted the key, he turned to her and began tenderly kissing her neck.

Immediately, their clothes were off, both were excessively sweating, she was screaming and crying, he was moaning, and he was wishing she would relax.

* * *

Anthony and Linda graduated from Rutgers. Linda decided to put medical school on the back burner and explore the world. For four years, she traveled Europe. She did some sight-seeing, plenty of shopping, and a lot of lovemaking, including surviving two marriages.

Meanwhile Anthony was accepted to Howard University College of Medicine and UCLA School of Medicine. He decided to attend Howard and be near Magnolia.

He proposed that summer. It was important to Magnolia that she remain in New Jersey. Her mother would have had a nervous breakdown if she'd relocated out of state.

The two of them vacationed in Cancun before he attended medical school. Relaxing on the bronze sand, Magnolia caressed his thick afro. The sky was bright blue and the scene was languorous.

Anthony spun around and faced her, his eyes sad. He told her he'd always wanted to be like his older brother—the perfect child. All his life he followed in his brother's footsteps, and wasn't sure if he should attend medical school and become a physician or do something entirely different. He asked Magnolia for her advice and she told him to follow his heart.

So he went ahead with medical school, becoming Dr. Anthony Lewis. He completed his residency in internal medicine and worked in the ER at a hospital in New Brunswick. Soon afterward, he attended Princeton and earned a MBA. That is where he met Carl.

Carl was vice president of a computer software corporation in Princeton. Anthony introduced himself when Carl was a guest speaker in one of his classes speaking on his company's role in the computer software industry.

Anthony's initial impression was very positive. Carl felt likewise and he offered Anthony a managerial position at his company. Their working relationship proved to be very productive. It was just a matter of time before they became business partners.

With Anthony's science, medical, and business background, and Carl's extensive engineering and managerial experience as well as his business savvy, they created a high-tech computer software company that developed medical software for hospitals and pharmaceutical companies. They named the company C&A Medical Dimensions.

After graduating, Magnolia assisted them in running the company. She typed correspondence and presentations, handled the accounting, purchased office supplies, and made coffee for clients.

Initially their business flourished. There wasn't much competition although they did encounter race-based obstacles. It was tough and occasionally damn near impossible, but they survived.

Now, more than ten years later, Magnolia lay on her king-size bed, staring at her husband, someone who was about to embark on the path to millionaire stardom because he never gave in to hopelessness. He and Carl simply refused to fail.

CHAPTER 28

"Magnolia," Mya Jones said. She was Magnolia's young assistant, who recently graduated from college.

"Yes, Mya."

"I have Mackenzie Gary on line three. Linda specifically informed me that you're to talk to her."

"Can you put her on hold, please?"

Praying that Mackenzie Gary didn't change her mind about signing on with her agency, Magnolia flipped through the business-card holder to find Linda's cell phone number. She tapped her fingernails on the cream-colored desk while waiting for Linda to pick up. Magnolia thought, *Please, I don't need any problems. Let's both agree.*

Linda finally answered. "Hello, this is Linda."

"Good morning, Linda. This is Magnolia, how are you?"

"Fine. I'm on my way to the meeting. How's everything there?"

"Mackenzie Gary is holding. So, what's the deal here? What should I say to her?"

Magnolia shut her eyes. She coiled with the telephone cord and waited for a response. Then she picked up her wedding picture and positioned it straight on the desk.

Linda slammed hard on the squeaky breaks at the traffic light. *How could Magnolia ask her such a ridiculous question?* she thought. *Magnolia knows my feelings about Mackenzie Gary. Her work is good* but she's not worth taking on as a client. What's Magnolia's problem? Maybe she and Anthony are having problems. Maybe she's needs a damn vacation.

It was Linda's understanding that they were supposed to be devoted to their clients and that they would give 110% support, but that didn't apply to someone who acted like she didn't want to be represented.

Mackenzie Gary is running the show, Linda thought. *She's telling us what to do. She is playing games, and I'm too old for games.*

Magnolia had a pretty good idea what was going to come out of Linda's mouth. She hoped she'd changed her mind. Magnolia was compelled to speak first. "Are you there, Linda? Linda, before you say anything, you know how much I want to sign her on."

Linda released a savage breath. Magnolia was wasting her time.

Magnolia imagined Linda's facial expression—her head jolting, eyes rolled, lips stuck up, and nose in the air. She was probably inserting a Luther Vandross CD in the player and ignoring her all together. Magnolia knew Linda only too well.

Her depiction wasn't accurate, though: Linda had in fact popped in a Carl Thomas CD.

Desperately wanting to resolve this no win situation and proceed to her meeting, Linda said, "Magnolia, you know what we have to do. I've given her our terms. If she agrees, everything is final. If she doesn't, tell her to go straight to hell. As a matter of fact, tell her to kiss my black ass! We're not making any other concessions. Okay? Let her find some other agent. I'm tired of her."

"Fine! Don't you think it's a little early in the morning for that kind of language?"

"I apologize. But—"

"But . . . I don't want to hear your mouth when some other agent signs her."

"Trust me, no one else will put up with that egotistical, inexperienced attitude!"

"Goodbye, Linda!" Magnolia slammed the phone down on the console.

"Damn it," she said. Magnolia didn't agree with her decision. They agreed 99% of the time, but it was that other 1% that surfaced every now and again. Magnolia was feeling stress and she didn't like it. She knew stress could be healthy, but she liked to stay focused, be positive and relaxed. On the other hand, Linda was infatuated with stress. It was her nature to challenge people. Her motto: everyone's life will be as difficult as mine. She made things exhausting, so much so that people said bad things about her—people like Anthony. He would say, "She needs a good ass whipping."

"Mackenzie Gary, you had better say yes," Magnolia whispered.

Then she considered calling Linda back. Sweet talk her, remind her of all the things Mackenzie Gary's success could do for them. She would talk about the money they would receive and the future book deals. But she decided not to. She too had had enough of Mackenzie Gary's funky attitude.

She was reluctant to pick up the phone, but she did. Somewhat nervously, Magnolia clutched it and pressed down on line three. "Good morning, Mackenzie. How are you? I'm glad to hear you're doing well. Have you made a decision?"

Suddenly Magnolia threw up her hands like a marathon runner advancing through the winning tape. She beamed. "So you agree with everything? That's the best news I've heard this morning. I'll have my assistant mail you the contract."

She paused for a moment and leaned back in the beige chair. "Oh . . . you'll be in New York later this month. Okay . . . I can work with that. I'll inform Linda. I'll keep in touch with you soon. Thank you, Mackenzie. Have a good day."

Magnolia couldn't believe it—Mackenzie had agreed to their terms. She knew they had a bestseller on their hands. Then she said, "Magnolia, don't get too excited. Nothing is finalized until she signs the papers. Oh, what the hell, I know she will."

Magnolia was so thrilled she called Anthony and gave him the good news. "Anthony."

"Hey."

"Baby, guess what? She said yes."

"Who said yes?"

"Mackenzie Gary! The writer from Toronto."

"Oh! Okay, now I remember who you're talking about."

"She'll be here the end of September."

"That's wonderful, baby. I knew you could do it. I have some good news too."

"Oh, Anthony, I'm sorry. I totally forgot about the Simon General deal. So what's your plan?"

"I'm flying to Miami Beach on Thursday like I said."

"So soon!"

"Yeah, the meeting is scheduled for Thursday. This is it, baby! The big one! Carl and I are preparing for this meeting as we speak."

"Well, I'll let you go. Tell me more about it when you get home tonight."

"I may be a little late. Better not wait up for me."

"You know I'll wait up for you. I love you."

"I love you too, baby."

When Magnolia arrived home, she headed straight to the bedroom. She started packing for Anthony because she knew that as soon as he arrived home, he'd be on the telephone with Carl discussing more details. Anthony was a last minute man and she wanted him to appear sharp for his meeting.

She packed his clothes and thought about how things were turning out with her life. Everything was going so well. She had a wonderful husband and a fantastic career. She just wished she had children. She longed to have someone to love and protect. She knew Anthony was patient. She knew he wanted kids too. But he understood. They had endured so many tests. At times it was embarrassing. But according to the fertility specialists, there was nothing wrong with either of them. It was purely odd that they weren't conceiving. Magnolia believed children would make their lives complete. She had always desired a family, and family also meant a lot to Anthony.

She heard Anthony unlock the door. "Leah, I'm home."

"I'm upstairs in the bedroom."

He walked into the bedroom wearing a huge smile. "You don't have to do this, baby."

"I know you have a lot to do tonight and—"

The telephone rang, interrupting their conversation. Anthony picked it up, "Hello. Hey, Carl, I just walked in."

Magnolia drifted toward the bedroom door. It was just like she imagined. She sure knew her man. She turned to Anthony and grinned. He blew her a kiss and she shut the door behind her.

* * *

It was Thursday morning on a warm September day. Magnolia lived for days like this. She simply loved autumn.

She got up from the bed and looked at Anthony, who was reading some documents. "Isn't the weather just wonderful?"

"I bet it's even better in Miami Beach," said Anthony.

"Yes, it probably is. What do you plan to do over the weekend?"

"Paperwork, baby. Paperwork."

"Yeah right, Anthony!"

He turned to her. "Magnolia, this is a very important contract."

"Oh, thanks for reminding me."

"There's work to be done, baby," he said in a mock serious tone. "Next time I'm down there vacationing, I'll do some sightseeing."

Magnolia couldn't help but laugh. Who was he fooling? But she loved him to death and that's all that mattered. She knew he wasn't going to be stuck up in some hotel room in gorgeous Miami Beach doing paperwork. What she did know was that he had a secretary and she usually took care of the tedious details and the other nonsense called paperwork. But Anthony was excessively hardworking, dedicated, and loyal and would probably lock himself in his hotel room completing the necessary documents.

At the kitchen table, Magnolia fed Anthony a fork full of blueberry pancakes. His head fell back as he chewed it and begged for more. Then the doorbell rang. She walked to the front door. A very handsome young brother in a navy uniform greeted her. "Good morning, my name is Muhammad and I'm with Star Shuttle. I'm here to pick up a Mr. Lewis."

"Umm, good morning, Muhammad. I'll get my husband."

Muhammad inspected Magnolia's silk robe. Pleased with what he saw, he paced forward, trying to get a whiff of her perfume. Magnolia smiled and admired his boldness.

"Anthony, the airport shuttle is here," she yelled.

"Okay, baby, one second. I'll be right there."

Anthony mentally skimmed over his itinerary, making sure he had everything. He finally put all the papers into his briefcase and walked to the front door, where he saw the young man eyeballing his wife.

Anthony came close to Magnolia, smoothed back her long hair, and intimately kissed her. She could taste the sweet maple syrup on his lips.

Muhammad stepped back a few paces and jerked his head back and said in a low voice, "Damn!"

"Good luck, baby. Call me when it's over," she said.

Anthony winked his eye at Muhammad, giggled, and said, "I'll call you the second it's over."

Anthony set out for Miami Beach to seize the fortune that was his due. It was a day that would forever change their lives.

CHAPTER 29

A blonde haired, blue eyed petite white woman pushing a beverage cart on the airplane approached Anthony. "Good morning, sir. How are you today?"

"Just fine. And yourself?"

"Wonderful, thank you," she said. "What would you like to have for breakfast—a vegetable omelet or bran cereal?"

"I'll just have orange juice. Thank you."

The woman reached over the cart and grabbed the carton. She poured the juice into an ice-filled cup and handed it to Anthony. "Here you go, sir."

"Thank you."

As she pushed the cart back to the end of the plane, Anthony thought about Hillary. The woman resembled her. He recalled the strife, the pain, and the hurt. He remembered her family and their hatred toward him. He didn't want to get mad thinking about it, so he flipped open a magazine and enjoyed the juice.

Anthony mentally prepared himself for the meeting. He kept examining his presentation. "Damn! I should have included exhibit M in the summary," he whispered. "Oh, what am I doing? Carl and I have gone over this a thousand times. Everything I need is here. Just calm down—you know what to do and you know what to say."

His presentation should be a piece of cake because he had

done it so many times before. But never had the dollar figure been so high. He would pull this one off too, no doubt—it was just a matter of time.

He gave Carl one last call from the plane. His secretary, Naomi, informed him that Carl was out of the office.

Anthony was breathing hard and Naomi sensed he was a bit nervous. So she went over the accommodation and car rental details with him again.

"You're not nervous, Anthony, are you?"

"No . . . No . . . I'm not."

"You've done this alone many times before. I know you can pull this one off."

"Thank you, Naomi."

"You're welcome. Shall I have Carl call you at the hotel?"

"No, Naomi. Everything is fine."

"Are you sure, Anthony?"

"Yes, I'm sure."

"Well, if you need anything, please call me. I'll fax it right over."

"I'll do that, Naomi."

"Have a productive meeting, Anthony. Good luck and I'll talk to you soon."

"Thank you. And you have a nice day. Goodbye."

An announcement came over the intercom as Anthony read through his presentation. "Good morning, ladies and gentlemen. My name is Captain Lansing. We will reach Miami International Airport in twenty minutes. Please return to your seats and fasten your seat belts. Currently, the weather is eighty-five degrees in Miami Beach."

As Anthony exited the plane, the blonde flight attendant lightly touched his hand, smiled, and winked her eye. He returned a smile and hurriedly walked away. He said softly to himself, "I had enough of y'all shit to last two life times. Sorry, but not interested."

In the airport, Anthony registered with a rental car service and then anxiously drove to the hotel. He arrived at the Grand Palace Hotel downtown and checked in.

At the registration counter, Anthony hissed, "Damn, I should have eaten that vegetable omelet. I'm hungry."

He glanced at his watch. "The meeting isn't until two o'clock. I got to get some real food. I'll order food service. Nah, I'll have lunch on the patio."

A brunette, medium built waitress approached his table. Her face glowed when she saw Anthony. She had just one thing on her mind and that was sex. She wiggled her upper body, highlighting her big breasts. She held the pad and pen in her hand and said, "Good afternoon, sir. Are you ready to order?"

Anthony read right through her body movement. His face fell in his hands. "Not again!" he whispered. "Damn, aren't there any sisters in Miami Beach?"

"Sir?"

"Oh, yes, I'll have the chicken breast with baked potato. And . . . I'll have a green salad with oil and vinegar dressing, please."

The strap on her dress slid off her shoulders and she slowly pulled it up while her eyes were glued to his.

"What would you like to have to drink, sir?" she said.

"I'll have an iced-tea. Thank you."

"Are you with the BIM group?"

"No, I'm not. Why do you ask?"

"Oh, I saw you reading some manuals and I just thought you might be with them. There's a slew of them here today."

"Oh, really? Are they occupying the ballroom on the first floor?"

"Yes, they are. So, you've seen them."

"Yes, I did. I'm not with them with though."

"Oh, well, your food will be ready shortly. In the meantime, can I get you an appetizer?"

"No, thank you."

Anthony eyes scanned the dining hall and patio area, which showcased elegant paintings. He loved art. He and Magnolia had decorated their home with beautiful African art.

His eyes continued to survey the room. He turned to the left and noticed someone familiar—too familiar.

"My God! I know that's not . . . No . . . it couldn't be. Why would she? I can't believe her."

There was a couple sitting in front of his table blocking his view. So he strained to get a closer view. When he recognized the person, he was absolutely shocked.

"For heaven's sakes, it's Leah," he said. "What in God's name is she doing here?"

Anthony marched over to the table in the middle of the patio area where two women and a man were eating. He began to speak to the younger woman but his words stammered, "Lee . . . Leah . . . What . . . what are you doing here? You . . . you know this meeting is—"

"Excuse me, sir," the young woman said. "You must be mistaken. My name is not Leah."

Nervously chuckling he said, "Come on, Leah. This is not a joke. This isn't the time, baby. You know this meeting is very important to me. Why are you here? And what's up with the wig?"

The woman patted down her hair, feeling insecure.

"This is my hair," she yelled. "And what's up with you, sir?"

Anthony firmly slammed his fists on the table, ignoring the woman. "Magnolia, when did you get here? Were you on the same flight as me? I can't believe you!"

The woman wiped her mouth with the ornamented napkin and got up, still chewing. "Sir, I'm very sorry but you must be mistaken. You have the wrong person. My name is not Magnolia. Who are you anyway?"

Anthony's eyes grew wide. His breathing increased and he paced back. He was dumbfounded when he realized the woman wasn't Magnolia. She was a bit larger, her hair was shorter, and she had a massive creamy circular birthmark on her forehead.

"I'm sorry. I'm so sorry, Miss. I thought you were someone else. I thought you were my wife."

The man sitting at the table stood and said, "You know, every time we're out somewhere people think she's someone else."

The jittery young woman looked up at him. Anthony chuckled nervously.

The other man added, "I tell her she's a twin, separated at birth. You know what they say, we all have a twin somewhere in the world."

Grinning, Anthony said, "Yes, that's what folks say all right." He paused and looked at her again. "I apologize. I didn't mean to frighten you but . . . you look just like my wife. Do you have any sisters?"

"Yes. I have one but she's much younger than I am."

He reached for his wallet and took out a photograph of Magnolia. "Let me show you a picture of my wife."

The man at the table snatched the picture and shouted, "My God, Hyacinth! She looks exactly like you!"

The woman walked over to the man. "Give me that picture! You're joking, right?" She grabbed the photo and stared at it without blinking. She tossed the picture down on the table and told Anthony, "I don't believe this. This can't be. No way!"

The man at the table signaled for Anthony to take a seat. "Do you think they're twins, man?"

Trembling, Anthony replied, "I don't know."

Hyacinth was shaken and severely distressed. "No! We're not twins. I don't have a twin. My parents have three children. You know that, Gregory. How could you suggest such a thing? And besides, she doesn't look exactly like me."

"Well, I think she looks exactly you. Precisely!" Gregory said.

Hyacinth rushed to the restroom. The older woman at the table angrily stared at the two men. "You see what the two of you have done? She's upset now. I'll go after her."

She followed Hyacinth into the restroom.

Minutes past and Anthony and Gregory chatted. "Man, people always told her they've seen her twin," Gregory joked.

"Really?"

"She's been told this many times. Even relatives have said so."

Hyacinth and the older woman returned to the table. "I apologize for leaving but I was a little disturbed by all of this. It's just that . . . I can't believe it. That woman . . . your wife . . . she does look a lot like me," Hyacinth said.

She reached for the picture again and stared at it. "Maybe we are related in some way." She nodded. "She couldn't be my sister. There's no way. I only have one and she's twenty years old. My parents have three children and I'm the eldest."

Anthony glanced at his watch. He had a meeting in an hour. "Look, I have a very important meeting to attend. Can I get your number? I'm staying in room 85. I'll be here until Saturday afternoon."

He tried to clear the frog in his throat. "By the way, my name is Anthony Lewis."

Gregory extended his right hand. "My name is Gregory Clark and this is my fiancée, Hyacinth Johnson. This is my mother Marjorie Clark."

"Pleased to meet you all. This has been one hell of a day. For a minute there, I thought you were my wife playing a joke on me. I'm totally baffled. We have to talk more. This is unbelievable." He laughed and said, "Wait until Magnolia finds out she has a twin."

Angry, Hyacinth said, "Wait a minute! Your wife looks like me but that doesn't mean she's my twin."

She glanced at Gregory, then his mother, assuring herself. "How could she be? There's no way in hell she could be my twin. It's impossible!"

Gregory said, "Anthony, I'm the hotel manager here. Go to your meeting. We'll definitely keep in touch. Ask for me at the front desk."

"Okay, Gregory. I'll do that. You all have a great day. Again, I apologize for the—"

"Listen man, don't worry about it. If your wife is related to Hyacinth, we definitely want to know."

* * *

Still thinking about the confrontation at the hotel, Anthony distributed materials to the conferees in a large burgundy and black conference room at Simon General's headquarters. Stephen Simon, president, his son Stanford, vice president, and his attorney, Michael Webster, were seated and conversing.

Stephen Simon raised his lips as he inspected the materials. "Anthony, your presentation was outstanding. Simon General definitely wants to do business with C&A Medical Dimensions. We look forward to a productive relationship with your firm. Michael has read over the contract and finds it acceptable. All we need is my signature and the deal is final."

"Thank you, Stephen. Carl and I are delighted to manage this project. Our services and products that we provide your company are superior to any other medical software corporation in the industry."

Anthony extended his hand.

Stephen Simon shook his hand and said, "I'm looking forward to a great future with C&A Medical Dimensions." Then he glanced at his watch. "Well, it's that time of the day. Shall we go to dinner?"

"Uh, thank you for the offer, but I'm going back to the hotel, there's a considerable amount of work to be done. The sooner we get things started the better!"

"Okay then. Well, you have a good evening, Anthony. I hope you have a pleasant stay in Miami Beach."

"I certainly will. Thank you again, Stephen. You will be hearing from us soon."

The three gentlemen exited the room. Elated, Anthony extended both arms toward the ceiling and shouted, "Yes! We did it! We got the big one!"

He sat in a black modern-looking chair and stared out the window. He saw a dazzling water fountain with a large sculpture of swans inside the elegant solid white pool.

Anthony was drained physically and mentally. He had labored

for nearly a year to do business with this company and his hard work finally had paid off. The past week he'd spent preparing for this meeting seemed like the equivalent.

He fell forward and rested his upper body on the table. He locked his hands together and said, "This has been the most exhausting, exciting day of my life. I've snatched the biggest deal in the industry and I think I may have discovered my wife's twin. My God, what a day! I don't know who to call first, Carl or Magnolia."

He smiled as he sipped his club soda. He picked up the black telephone next to him and began dialing. He looked out of the window again and shook his head and grinned. Carl's voice came on the other end. "Hey, Carl. It's Anthony. Yes . . . Yes . . . it's finalized. We got it! Everything went as planned. He's expecting a call from us soon. We did it, man!"

Carl carried the telephone over to his office window. He leaned his head against the glass and said, "Were they satisfied with everything?"

"Yes. There were no inconsistencies. We gave them what we promised and Stephen anxiously signed," Anthony said after taking another sip of club soda.

"Great! I'll finish the additional paper work on this end. So, how's everything else down there?"

"You're not going to believe this, Carl, but . . . this afternoon, I saw a woman at the hotel and . . . she looked . . . uh . . . exactly like Magnolia."

Carl dropped the telephone.

"Carl, are you there?"

Carl quickly reached down and picked the handset up and nervously said, "Yes, I'm here."

Carl wiped his forehead with the back of his hand and said, "You're kidding me, right?"

"No, man. I'm not. This woman could be Magnolia's twin. I'm going back to the hotel and talk more with her. Her name is Hyacinth Johnson. She lives here in Miami Beach."

Carl sluggishly turned away from the window. He grabbed a hold of the chair, turned it around, and sat down.

"Carl, are you there?"

Carl sucked in his breath and said, "I'm here. What was it you said again?"

"I said her name is Hyacinth Johnson."

"And who is she?"

"The woman I saw at the hotel this afternoon—the woman that looks like Magnolia. Man . . . are you okay?"

"I'm just overwhelmed by this deal, that's all." He stopped twisting the chair around as he sat. "Uh, what did this woman say to you?"

"I approached her at the restaurant. She was having lunch with her fiancé and his mother. She was a bit puzzled and a little upset after I showed her Magnolia's photo. I think we all were."

"And who else was there?"

"Her fiancé and his mother," Anthony said again. "I shouldn't have mentioned anything. I know this is just too much to handle, but I'm telling you, Carl, Magnolia has an identical twin. I know it."

Carl spoke with mild doubt. "Are you sure, Anthony?"

"Yes, I am. I'm positive she's Magnolia's twin. Well, not exactly positive. But . . . but she looks so much like Magnolia."

Naomi escorted Brenda into the office. Carl had arranged dinner at his office that evening. He gestured with his right hand, signaling for her to eavesdrop. She squatted down while he held the telephone close to her ear as they listened to Anthony's conversation. Carl scribbled Hyacinth's name on a notepad. Brenda's mouth opened wide and she stared at him in shock.

"So she was there with her fiancé and mother-in-law and her fiancé manages the hotel?"

"Yes, that's right."

"Is she from Florida?" said Carl.

"I didn't ask her that, Carl. I believe she is. I don't know if she's from Florida or not. She said she lived here."

"How old is she? Is she the same age as Magnolia?"

"I didn't ask that either, Carl."

"So how do you know she's Magnolia's identical twin? Does

she look exactly like Magnolia? Are you absolutely positive, Anthony?"

"I'm positive, man!"

Jerking Carl's shirt, Brenda quickly jotted down something on the notepad and gave it to him.

"So, what are you going to do now?" said Carl.

"I'm going back to the hotel. They're waiting for me," Anthony said scratching his head. "Well, he is."

"Who's he?"

"Gregory Clark, her fiancé, is the hotel manager. I'm going back to talk to him. Look Carl, I don't mean to rush but I have to go. I promised him I would meet him this evening. I'll talk to you tonight, okay?"

"Please call me back."

"I'll try."

"You just said you promised."

"Look here, if I don't call you back tonight, I'll talk to you when I get back on Saturday. Okay?"

"Nah, man. Call me back tonight!"

"What if she's not Magnolia's twin?"

"Okay. Okay, I understand. Saturday's fine. I can't believe this, Anthony."

"Neither can I."

"Are you really sure about this?"

Anthony knew how much Carl loved Magnolia. "Carl, I really feel . . . I'm one hundred percent certain. There's no doubt in my mind that this woman is Magnolia's twin. If she isn't Magnolia's twin, she's definitely related to her in some way. Some way."

Anthony glanced at his watch. "I have to get back to the hotel. I'll talk with you on Saturday. Goodbye, Carl."

"Goodbye."

CHAPTER 30

Swerving down Miami Beach's busy streets, Anthony slammed on the brakes when the door of a silver Bentley swung open. A good-looking, tall, muscular black male stepped out. *He looks familiar*, Anthony thought. *He's probably a famous athlete.*

Anthony realized he was driving recklessly, so he pulled over. He needed to collect himself. It was extremely important that he appear calm and alert, at least for Magnolia's sake.

He leaned forward and shifted into drive. He wanted to speed but it wouldn't be safe. He followed the scent of the King James Steak House, which was located several blocks from the hotel. When he made a left turn onto Hotel Plaza Drive, he drove past more expensive hotels, hot clubs, and fancy restaurants.

"Magnolia will never forgive me if I get back to the hotel and he's gone," he muttered.

Suddenly his eyes grew wide. "Oh my God! Magnolia! I haven't called her," he yelled. He slammed his hand on the driving wheel. "Damn it!"

But then he thought, *First, let me talk to him. I need to get more information before I startle her. This may all be nonsense.*

Anthony knew he was near the hotel when he noticed the enormous white statue of a nude man and woman in the front. He drove up to the valet attendant standing next to the work of art and handed him the keys. He dashed into the front lobby. It was as though he was a wild animal searching for prey. He ran so fast, he whacked down an elderly man who was reading a magazine.

His heart pounded. *Slow down, man. The last thing you need to do is kill someone. Just slow down and everything will be fine. Gregory will be there.*

Out of breath, Anthony frantically approached the desk clerk. "Greg . . . Gregory Clark, please."

The stocky man cheerfully responded, "Mr. Clark is in a staff meeting at the moment. You must be Mr. Lewis."

"Yes. Yes, I am," said Anthony, breathing wildly.

"He's been expecting you. He apologized for the delay but an emergency meeting was called. He instructed me to tell you that he'll stop by your room in an hour or so. Will that be okay, Mr. Lewis?"

"Yes, that will be fine. Thank you."

"And thank you too, Mr. Lewis."

Anthony returned to his room. This time he walked slowly like a robot. He was very hungry and his body was weak from fatigue. When he got to his room, he sat on the firm bed and rolled his body back. Then he sat up and snatched the telephone handset off of the console on the end table. He quickly placed it back on the table.

"I need to wait," he mumbled. "Magnolia will kill me for sure if I tell her something that may not be true."

He shook his head, trying to stay awake. He walked over to the bathroom area, slumped over, and turned the faucet on. He filled both hands with cold water and splashed his face.

He wiped his face with a soft white towel that had the hotel's emblem on it and smelled like fabric softener and said, "It's hard to believe she's grown up all of these years without any siblings and may have had one all along."

He rubbed the towel against his face. "That's why her mother was so troubled. She carried this guilt trip around and took it out on Magnolia."

He watched himself in the mirror, examining his bloodshot eyes. "Why would she give up a child, though?"

He dipped his dark hands back into the running water and gave himself another splash.

He mumbled, "What are you doing, Anthony? Creating these crazy scenarios."

There was a knock at the door. Anthony quickly walked over and looked in the peephole before swinging it open.

"Good evening, Gregory," he said in a slightly tense tone.

"Good evening," Gregory said, rubbing his chin. "I'm sorry I took so long but I had to attend an emergency meeting."

"Oh, yes, the receptionist told me," Anthony said. He took a deep breath. "How is your fiancée, Hyacinth?"

Gregory stared at Anthony for a moment. "Can I come inside?"

Stepping to the side, Anthony said, "Of course. Please come in and have a seat."

Gregory sat down on the small armchair and appeared sad. His eyes were dull. "She's not taking this very well, as you can imagine. As a matter of fact, no one is taking this too well. I'm completely puzzled myself."

"Where is she?"

"She's home with her family, asking plenty of questions."

Anthony stepped toward the circular table and reached for a piece of paper. It was important that he jot down the details. But Gregory suddenly stretched out his hand to stop him. "Look Anthony, there's something I need to tell you."

Anthony's heartbeat slowed as he looked up at Gregory and freed his hands. "What is it, Gregory?"

"Um, Hyacinth called me this evening."

"And?"

"And . . . she told me—"

"She told you what, man?"

Breathing heavily, Gregory continued, "Uh . . . we need to go over to Hyacinth's house now."

"What's the problem, Gregory?"

"You really don't want to know, Anthony. Not now. Not here."

"Yes, I need to know now."

"Look, let's go over there. I can't tell you anything. You need to hear it from them. Her family."

Anthony blew out a gust of cool air and left the hotel room with Gregory. When they arrived at Hyacinth's house, a young woman greeted them at the door. There were five people present, including Hyacinth and the young woman. Seated in the living room were an elderly couple and a younger man.

Anthony stood at the doorway. His eyes cautiously scanned the room, scrutinizing everyone. The tension was so thick you could cut it with a knife. Everyone seemed mad, uncomfortable, and depressed.

The older woman sat at the end of the sofa. She was distraught and crying, while the older man wrapped his arms around her and tried to calm her.

"Hello, Anthony," the young woman softly said. Her eyes were soaked. She extended her hand. "I'm May-Lynne, Hyacinth's sister."

He shook her hand. "Hello, May-Lynne. How are you?"

"Not too good," she said wiping tears from her face. "Please come inside. We're anxious to meet you."

Anthony and Gregory approached the people. Then Gregory announced, "Everyone, this is Anthony Lewis."

Turning to Anthony, Gregory rubbed his nose. "He's the gentleman we met earlier today."

The only person to speak was the young man. He approached Anthony and shook his hand. "Good evening, Anthony. It's a pleasure to meet you. My name is Lawrence. I'm Hyacinth's brother."

Shaking his hand, Anthony said, "It's a pleasure to meet you, Lawrence."

Hyacinth came close. She pointed her finger at the elderly couple and faintly said, "Anthony, these are my parents, Sam and Patricia Johnson."

Patricia's spongy eyes were glued to his. Anthony's hand trembled as he raised it to her. He stood there motionless. She scared him in a way no else had ever done before. She wasn't evil; she just made him uneasy.

He said, "Hello."

Neither Patricia nor Sam uttered a word. To break the tension, Hyacinth spoke first. "Anthony, my mother told me—"

Gregory cut in, placing his arms around her. "Take it easy, honey. You don't have to..."

Her head sank in his chest. "No, I have to," she said. She wiped the wetness on her nose with a tissue. "Anthony, I've just been told that... that..."

She began to sob again. Her tears soaked Gregory's black suit. "There's no rush," said Anthony. "I understand."

"It's important that you know."

"Know what Hyacinth?" he said.

"Your wife... she is my sister."

"Oh my, God. Are you sure?" The staggering news forced him to step back.

"I... I... I believe she is."

May-Lynne handed Hyacinth another facial tissue but Hyacinth was too distressed and had not the strength to take it. So May-Lynne gently wiped her face for her.

Hyacinth said, "To my surprise today, I learned that I do have other family. Your wife very well may be my sister."

Anthony said, "How could this be?"

Patricia moved closer to Hyacinth and hugged her. She started to intervene but then looked down at Anthony's polished Italian shoes and paused. She calmly said, "My husband and I adopted Hyacinth when she was four years old." Sniffling, she went on. "At that time, we thought we couldn't have children."

Tears flowed down Patricia's cheeks. She reached for a tissue and tried to dry her face but it was no use. "We were told that Hyacinth was a triplet."

"A triplet!"

Ignoring Anthony's remark, Patricia continued calmly. "Yes, she was one of three sisters who were given up for adoption."

Then Patricia turned to Sam, who nodded his reassurance. She proceeded. "If your wife is Hyacinth's sister, then there is one more out there."

Lawrence held his mother's unstable hand. "It's okay, Ma," he said.

"Sam and I desperately wanted children and we couldn't conceive back then." She shook her head in disgust. "We definitely couldn't afford three children at once, so we asked for one, and they sent us Hyacinth."

Her mature hands grabbed Hyacinth's arm. Ashamed of what her mother had said, Hyacinth turned away.

Gregory said, "My God!"

Anthony said, frantically, "Who sent Hyacinth?"

"The adoption agency," Patricia said.

Puzzled, he mumbled, "Adoption agency. What adoption agency?"

"I don't know! It was a long time ago. I can't possibly remember every detail," Patricia cried out.

Anthony approached Patricia. "Where did the other two go?"

Infuriated, Sam stood up from the spacious cushioned chair and threw a box of facial tissue at Anthony.

"Listen, young man, my wife said she doesn't know! So if she doesn't know, why are you asking her these foolish questions?"

Sam had a bad habit of not thinking before acting. He wasn't rational and Patricia knew what he was capable of.

She grabbed his hand and placed it up to her chest. Partially composed, she said, "We never asked. Hyacinth's birth mother was from Georgia. That's all we know."

She closed her eyes. "The other two girls—her sisters—were named Maggie and Rose. I think. That's all we know."

Anthony sat down on the sofa trying to comprehend it all. The name Maggie was too similar to Magnolia. He glanced at Patricia. He knew now there was some hope to Magnolia's horrible life story. Now Magnolia might be truly happy. She had family, blood family, family that could love her. Magnolia would no longer have to live life confused.

His eyes watered as he calmly said, "My wife's name is Magnolia."

Fed up with Anthony's harassment, Sam broke a pencil in

half. Fearful of what was going to happen next, Patricia looked over to Sam. He knew she didn't want him to do anything stupid.

"Her name could have been Magnolia, but I'm not certain of it. It was a very long time ago."

"I understand, but it's important that I ask you more questions."

"I can't answer them," she said crying.

The past few hours had worn down Patricia. She wanted to crawl into bed and escape the dark secret she had kept from everyone all of these years, but she realized it was time to confess, lay it all on the table and heal the wound in her heart. After all, it was important for Hyacinth to know too.

Waving her hand in the air, Patricia said, "Fine then, go ahead and ask all you want."

Anthony walked over to Patricia and gently touched her arm. "I do apologize for any uneasiness but I need to know. My wife needs to know."

Breathing heavily, he questioned her again. "Were they all given up for adoption?"

"Yes."

Firmly grabbing her arm, he said, "Patricia, do you know why they were adopted?"

Tears began to flow again. "No. I'm sorry, but I don't know why," she said. She lowered her head and thought for a second. "Wait . . . wait a minute! I was told their birth mother was terminally ill."

She smiled for remembering. "Yes, I believed she died shortly after we adopted Hyacinth."

Anthony was relieved. The more questions he asked, the more she remembered. "Can you can tell me the name of this adoption agency? That would be so helpful."

Patricia stared at Sam. His face filled with rage. He shook his head and yelled, "No, we don't know the name of the adoption agency."

"You must have the adoption papers," Anthony said.

"No, I don't have them," Patricia said.

Anthony looked at Hyacinth and then at Patricia. He was extremely puzzled. "You don't have them?"

Sam angrily interrupted again. "Look young man, it is obvious that my wife is very upset. My family is upset. Damn it, leave us alone!" Sweat drizzled down his face. "For God sakes, please leave us alone!"

Anthony relented.

Sam aimed his jittery finger at Anthony and yelled, "Why did you come here anyway?"

Stepping forward, Patricia shoved Sam's arm down and away from Anthony. "There were no papers, Anthony!"

Perplexed, Anthony said, "No papers. I don't understand."

"That's right. None." Tears streamed down her face. Then she stared at Sam again. "We . . . we paid . . ."

Sam rushed toward Anthony like a raging bull. Gregory and Lawrence secured him. Suddenly he freed his arms from them and tried to choke Anthony. Anthony jumped back.

Sam yelled, "Stop it! Stop right there, Patricia. Don't say another word."

Sam fell to his knees and sobbed. When his short, stocky body collapsed on the floor, he held onto the sofa for support. But his weight was too much. Lawrence dashed over to his father and gripped his arm so that he wouldn't tip the sofa over.

Distraught, Hyacinth grabbed her mother and shook her. "What do you mean we paid? You bought me, Mommy?"

Patricia hands wove through Hyacinth's flawless short bob.

"Is that what you were going to say? You bought me?"

Hyacinth raised her hands to the ceiling and cried out, "I can't believe it. My parents bought me!" Her eyes were swollen and red.

Patricia burst into tears. "Yes, baby. We did. I'm so sorry, baby."

Patricia extended her hand to Hyacinth, wanting to comfort her eldest child, but Hyacinth turned away and ran into Gregory's arms. She was ashamed of what her parents had done. Her life was a total lie.

"Oh my God!" May-Lynne screamed. "Tell me this isn't true!

Tell me this isn't happening! Please, somebody tell me this is a dream!"

Lawrence held her and together they sobbed.

Sam moved closer to Patricia and put his arms around her. He held her tight. "It's okay," he whispered.

"She hates me," Patricia muttered.

"No, she doesn't. She's upset right now," said Sam.

Hyacinth slowly released herself from Gregory and glanced into Patricia's eyes. "What price did you pay for me, Mommy? Huh? How much was I worth? A few dollars?" she cried. "Why did you do it?"

When Patricia looked up, she was unhappy. Her face filled with embarrassment and sadness. She stood motionless and stared at Hyacinth while her hands trembled. She needed forgiveness. This wasn't supposed to happen.

"The truth will set us free," she mumbled.

"What? What did you say, Mommy?" said Hyacinth.

"Because I loved you, baby," said Patricia. "I loved you and wanted you. That's why I paid for you."

Sam stormed out of the living room and into the kitchen. Lawrence immediately followed him.

Patricia turned and extended her hands to Hyacinth once more. "Please forgive your father and I, baby."

Hyacinth placed her hand on her forehead and nodded. Then she stretched her arms to her mother. Patricia rushed to her daughter and they embraced.

Patricia whispered into her ear, "I never meant to hurt you. Your father and I just wanted to love you."

Anthony didn't understand their grief. He thought of Magnolia and her pain of growing up with a bitter mother. Hyacinth lived a great life. There wasn't any conflict between her families until now. He grew irritable and wanted his questions answered immediately. He wished someone could explain Magnolia's unstable and strained life.

Trying to contain himself, he slipped his hands into his pants pockets and calmly said, "Patricia, I don't want to upset you more, but there are so many questions. Where . . . was this adoption agency?"

Ambling to her, he gently held her arm. "Where did the other two girls go?"

Patricia's eyes were fixed on Hyacinth and silence controlled her. Finally Anthony pulled her arm firmly. "Do you know the birth mother's name?" he said.

Patricia was speechless. Her heartbeat accelerated and she wanted to run and hide. She was shamed.

Anthony became frustrated and sternly said, "Where exactly was Hyacinth born? What town?"

Sensing that Anthony was unsympathetic to his wife's emotions, Sam abruptly broke in. "Look, young man . . ." He aimed his pudgy finger at Anthony again. "Enough is enough!"

Gregory jumped up. "Sam, he has every right to ask and every right to know!" Wiping the sweat from his face with a handkerchief, he said, "You're talking about his wife's livelihood here. Remember that!"

Patricia said, "Anthony, this happened thirty-eight years ago. I can't possibly remember everything and I can't possibly answer all of your questions."

She nodded. "Not now, at least." She glanced at Hyacinth. "I wish I could. I never expected this to come out. Never!"

Sam conceded and tried to explain their actions. "We . . . we didn't do anything wrong, Hyacinth. You must believe us. Your . . . birth mother was dying and she . . . couldn't care for you. Please, Hyacinth . . . please . . . you must believe us."

Mucus dripped from his nose as he continued. "Your mother and I couldn't afford three children. We love you, Hyacinth. We did it for love."

The room was quiet. Sound was as dead as the fly on the windowpane. Hours passed and everyone was uncomfortable. Who was to blame? Who should Hyacinth trust? She felt as though she was in an operating room watching the surgeon analyze her existence—searching for and trying to fix the affliction. And in the end, the doctor simply hoped that once she awoke from the anesthetic she wouldn't remember the pain.

They all stood around spooked and staring at each other. So much was disclosed that evening and yet they knew so little.

Finally Gregory shattered the utter stillness. "I think we all need to take a break and calm down."

"Yeah, that sounds like a good idea. I'll go in the kitchen and get something to drink," Lawrence said.

Several minutes later, he returned with a serving tray filled with mugs of coffee. He gave everyone a mug. Patricia blew into the simmering liquid. The rumbling waves of the hot water soothed her strained mind. Then she took a sip. For the first time that evening, she seemed calm. She tapped Anthony's hand and said, "Anthony, what's Magnolia like?"

Anthony jumped, shocked by her inquiry. A moment ago, she cared only for her daughter's feelings. He half-giggled at the notion of being insensitive and selfish himself.

"She's beautiful, Patricia. She's the love of my life."

He paused, remembering he and Magnolia's first encounter. It was on a Friday and his class had ended at noon. Anthony was starving and rushed to the café on campus. He saw Magnolia having lunch with Linda. Assuming she was like Linda, and that she too had a pessimistic attitude, he ignored her.

But who could have overlooked those mahogany bedroom eyes and her blazing smile and gentle laugh. The sight of her excited him. And she wore his favorite color, blue.

"I call her Leah," he said. "She's a good person, Patricia. She loves people."

He reached into his pocket and pulled out his leather wallet. He flipped it open and handed Magnolia's photograph to her. Patricia looked speechlessly at Magnolia's picture and couldn't keep her eyes off of the photo.

Anthony said, "Leah . . . thought she was born in New Jersey. Hackensack, New Jersey. It's on her birth certificate. She's the only child. She and her mother had a very difficult relationship. It was very strange. They did not get along at all." Sniffling, he added,

"Leah comes from a small family. Her mother only had one sister and a few other relatives."

Hyacinth glanced up and smiled as Anthony talked. He walked over to the couch and sat. "She's a literary agent and works in Manhattan. I met her in college."

Gregory tapped his shoulder. "Man . . . you okay."

Anthony shook his head. "Yeah, I'm okay." He sucked in the cool air and said, "We both attended Rutgers. We've been married for sixteen years now. We don't have any children."

Anthony clutched the mug and lowered his head. "We've been trying so hard. We both cherish our family and friends—they are really important to us."

Anthony looked at every person in the room. "You'll really like her, Patricia. All of you will. She's a wonderful person." Anthony smiled. "I haven't met anyone who has respected, trusted, supported, and loved me the way she has. No one!"

Nervously giggling, Hyacinth said, "She sounds a lot like me. I want to meet her, Anthony."

Her hands trembled and her eyes lit up when he said, "Oh, you will."

"It's . . . it's . . . so unfortunate she grew up without any siblings. I have no idea what it's like to be without family. It must have been very lonely," said Hyacinth.

She turned to Sam and Patricia. She loved her parents more than anyone on earth. She raised her hands to her chest, exhaled, and in a mild tone said, "Mommy and Daddy, I don't hate you for what you did, I only wished you had told me about it sooner. I know this is something you don't disclose to anyone, but . . . I deserved to know. Lawrence and May-Lynne deserved to know."

She held Gregory's hand and said, "When I was seventeen and had knee surgery—what would have happened had I needed blood? Would you have told me then? What if I'd never met Anthony—would I have known now?"

Sitting on the sofa, Patricia leaned closer to Sam and squeezed his shoulder. They wondered themselves. What would they have done if she needed blood? Patricia could only think of Magnolia and how lonesome life was for her. Then she thought of Rose and wondered if life had treated her kindly?

Hyacinth glanced over at her parents and smiled. She refused to let resentment and hate into her heart. Not now. "I know we have a lot to discuss. We have time," she said.

Patricia turned to Anthony. "Anthony, have you called your wife?"

"No, I haven't." Embarrassed, he shook his head. "I feel so guilty, but I didn't know how she would take this. I wanted to be certain. I'll call her when I get back to the hotel," he said.

"I hope she handles this better than I did," Hyacinth confessed. "I really would like to meet her if that's at all possible."

Slowly Hyacinth walked over to Anthony. When she gently rubbed his broad shoulders, his large frame softened.

"I'm sure that won't be a problem," he said. "Leah would love to meet you and your family. I know she will."

Then he smiled. "Initially, yes, she'll be stunned, but then she will be thrilled to learn that she has family."

Glancing at his watch, he said, "Look, it's late and I know you all have more details to discuss. I don't want to keep you up. I assure you, I will be in touch with you before I leave."

Anthony reached into his shirt pocket and grabbed a pen and business card. He began writing on the back of the card. "Hyacinth, here is my hotel number. I'm staying there until Saturday. I hope we can talk more before I leave."

Hyacinth took the business card and smiled. "You can count on it," she said as she hugged him. "Anthony, thanks for coming. I really appreciated it."

"You're welcome, Hyacinth."

She hugged him again, this time firmly. "I truly mean it, Anthony. Thank you for coming to Florida. I would have never known."

He returned a hug and whispered into her ear, "Thank you for being at the right place at the right time."

Giggling, she said, "Oh, I have lunch there every Thursday."

She tugged on his shirt. "God was looking out for us because I was going to cancel."

"You were!"

"Yes, I'm trying to cut down, you know." She pressed her hands down against her dress. "See? I've been gaining too much weight. And I know it's because of those weekly visits to the restaurant. I'll need to fit into a wedding gown soon."

"There's nothing wrong with you," Anthony joked.

"Yeah, that's what Gregory says. But . . . all that matters is that I was there today and so were you."

They laughed.

"Anthony, I hope your meeting went well," she said.

"It did. Extremely well. I'll tell you about it some time." He patted her on the back. "You need to get some rest."

She winked. "I will." Then her voice began to crackle when she placed her hand on her chest. "But really, Anthony, I thank you from the bottom of my heart."

Grabbing her hands, he said, "You are welcome, Hyacinth. Truly welcome."

Hyacinth rushed to get her purse from the coffee table and pulled out her business card. She handed it to Anthony. "Here, take this and have a safe ride back to the hotel." She tugged on his jacket. "If you get lost, my number is on the card."

"Thank you and goodnight."

Anthony waved to them and left the house. He sat in his car for a few minutes before turning on the ignition.

For years he had known Magnolia's pain. She thought he didn't understand her anguish but he did. It was intensely difficult for him to reach out to her during those hard times because he was unable to give her what she needed: a mother who genuinely loved and appreciated her.

CHAPTER 31

Entering the lobby, Anthony recognized the hotel clerk standing behind the counter. "You're still here, huh?"

The receptionist was reading a novel. He put a bookmark between the pages and closed the book, which had a picture of a woman carrying a young child on the front cover.

He looked up at Anthony and smiled. "Yes, I'm still here. "The person working the night shift called out sick."

"You're a dedicated worker."

The clerk smiled again. "Why, thank you, Mr. Lewis."

Anthony walked through the lobby and headed toward the elevators still suffering from hunger pangs. He stepped inside and pushed number eight. *This has been one hell of a day*, he thought. *Miami Beach, I'll never forget you.*

Anthony got off the elevator and dragged himself to his room, himself feeling like something of a horse-drawn carriage. As he unlocked the door, the telephone rang within. He quickly opened the door and picked up the handset, but was met with a dial tone.

He slammed the phone down. "Damn! I'm sure that was Magnolia," he shouted. "I should have called her earlier."

When he grabbed the phone again, he inspected the soft, light carpet that looked good enough to eat. He wasn't sure whether or not he should call her back. He shook his head. *What should I say? How am I going to say it?*

He dialed his home number without a firm plan of attack and Magnolia answered. "Hello."

"Hey, baby."

"Anthony, where were you?"

"I'm sorry I didn't call you earlier." His eyes rolled as he wondered how was he going to explain all that had just transpired. "Everything went as planned," he said. "We got the deal, baby!"

Wearing a long pink nightgown, Magnolia lay in bed and stretched her neck. She placed the book she was reading on the small glass table. "I wasn't worried," she lied. "I figured you were busy working out the details with Carl and the people at Simon General."

Anthony was relieved she wasn't upset. "Everything worked out great, but—"

He paused and fiddled with the telephone cord. "I've also been . . . Uh . . . Leah . . ." He quickly untangled the cord.

Magnolia held the telephone close and heard his heavy breathing. "Anthony, you sound troubled." She cradled the telephone closer. "No . . . nervous. Are you okay, baby?"

"I'm fine, Leah. But—"

"What is it, Anthony?"

"Leah . . . something incredible happened today," he said, still fidgeting with the telephone cord. "What are you doing?"

She sat up straight. "I'm in bed. Anthony, are you okay?"

"I'm okay." His eyes filled with tears. "Leah, I love you. I love you with all my heart."

Magnolia covered her mouth and prayed her worst nightmare had not come true—that he had had an affair. "I love you too, baby."

"I know . . . that we've been through . . . a great deal." He caught his breath and went on without stammering. "Especially with the problems you've had with your mother. And the two of us trying so hard to conceive, but that's okay. All that matters is that I love you and that we have each other. Life goes on, you know. We can adopt children. I need you to understand that."

"I understand, Anthony. You've never pressured me and you've never blamed me for anything. And yes, what's really important is that we have each other."

Magnolia rubbed her knees and legs hard—a sure sign of her nervousness. "Anthony, you're my best friend and I love you."

Anthony paced, holding the telephone console in one hand and the earphone with his head and shoulder. "You mean the world to me, Leah. It kills me to see you so distressed. When you hurt, I hurt, baby. I've seen you in pain for so many years and I don't ever want to contribute to any of that. Ever!"

"I know, Anthony. I know you will never hurt me."

Anthony sucked his teeth. "Leah, something happened today and . . ."

She held the pillow to her breasts—so tight, her hands quivered and her head sunk into it. "Anthony, please God, tell me you didn't have an affair."

"No, baby! Never! Leah, listen to me—I love you."

She began to cry. "I'm listening to you, Anthony. But . . . I sense you have something else you want to say."

"I do. Baby, I do."

He sat on the bed. His head fell back and struck the headboard. The room seemed dim, closed in, and the atmosphere was suffocating. He mumbled, "I saw . . . I saw your twin today."

"My twin! Anthony, I'm the only child."

"No, Leah. You're not. You have more family, baby."

"Have you been drinking?"

"No."

Now her shock turned to anger. "Well . . . it sounds like you have. That's impossible, Anthony." She stood with her hand on her hip.

With the receiver locked to his ear and the telephone console in his hand, Anthony strode over to the mirror and stared at himself. His shirt was drenched and his hands trembled and his eyes were large and dark. He softly giggled at his unknotted tie and wrinkled shirt; he looked like he was drunk.

He continued to stare at himself and wished he were in their bedroom, lying next to her warm body, touching her face, sliding his fingers through her hair and holding her—keeping her safe.

"Leah, you know I haven't had a drink in years," he said.

Magnolia's body stiffened. She shook her head in disbelief that her husband was tormenting her.

"Then what's all of this shit you're telling me, Anthony? You know, this isn't funny. Don't play with my emotions, Anthony. Please, not tonight. I'm not in the mood."

Still before the mirror, Anthony knew a response would only ignite her rage, so he stayed quiet. "Anthony, this is the most ridiculous bullshit I've ever heard out of you! I can't believe it! You score a deal of a lifetime and now you're Mr. Comedian! Well, fuck you, Anthony!"

She stood and paced the room. She lifted her long fingernails and began to scratch her scalp. Her eyes rapidly blinked. She could strangle him. Then she flung the pillow in front of her, leveling the perfume bottles that were on the dresser.

"Tonight isn't the night for games, Anthony!"

Anthony's chest moved up and down. He put the telephone on the dresser. "Listen to me, Leah. It may sound crazy but it isn't. Trust me."

His eyes rolled back. "Leah, how long have you known me? I don't play games. I'm too old for that shit. The only games I've ever played with you were in the bedroom and you know that!" His face dripped of sweat. "You must believe me, Leah. How I wish you were here with me, right now."

He squeezed shut his eyes. "Leah, before the meeting today, I had lunch here at the hotel. And I saw this woman . . . she looked exactly like you. At first I thought she was you, but then . . ."

Magnolia nodded her head as she listened to her husband tell her something that couldn't be true.

"So . . . I approached her. She was having lunch at the hotel with her fiancé and his mother. Her fiancé runs this hotel. Leah, are you listening?"

"Yes, I heard you, Anthony," she said. "I'm listening."

"I thought she was you so I asked her why was she at the

restaurant."

Clutching another pillow, Magnolia lowered her chin to it and wiped the tears off her face.

Anthony knew she was crying. Shaking his head, he said, "Oh man . . . I knew I should have waited until I got home."

"No . . . no . . . please go on," she said.

Anthony had no choice but to continue. She deserved the truth. "To make a long story short," he said, "her name is Hyacinth Johnson and she lives in Miami Beach with her parents, sister, and brother."

"Anthony—"

"No, baby—wait! Let me finish first. Leah, she's the same age as you."

Magnolia let go of the pillow and collected her thoughts. "Anthony . . . it just so happens that you saw a woman who looked like me and now you are telling me she's my twin."

"Believe me, Leah, she's identical to you."

"I don't believe you. I'll never believe this shit until I see her face to face. You're talking like your mother, Anthony. Remember, she said Billie looks exactly like me."

"Billie looks a lot like you but this woman, Leah, she is your identical triplet."

Magnolia was beyond confused.

"Forget it, Leah. I'm not saying another word. We'll talk on Saturday."

"The hell we will. A triplet, Anthony! Oh, now she's my triplet! For God sakes, Anthony, I don't know what the hell you've gotten a hold of but you'd better get your black ass back on the plane now! That meeting put you on a real fucking high, didn't it? You son of a bitch. How can you be so cruel?"

She started to laugh quietly. "Baby, you really made me mad this time. You better hope I'll get over this insane shit real soon. Before your ass comes back home."

"Magnolia, please calm down. Please, baby. Listen to me. She was just as shocked as I was. Then I finally showed her your photograph. She was beside herself and damn near passed out. I went on to my meeting but later got in touch with her fiancé who asked me to come to her home. Baby, when I arrived at her home, she told me that she was adopted and that she just discovered she is a triplet."

His body shivered. He snatched the glass of water on the desk and poured it on his face. "Magnolia, she's originally from Georgia. Her adopted mother said that the other two were girls as well. Their names were Maggie and Rose."

Magnolia dropped the telephone. "No! It can't be!"

"Magnolia! Magnolia! Baby, pick up the telephone," Anthony shouted.

Magnolia fell over the bed and tried to grab the telephone. Her shaky hands clutched onto it and she said, "I'm here, Anthony. Come home. Please, come home now."

"I will. I will. Take a deep breath and lie down. Relax, baby. Just relax."

Sobbing, she said, "Anthony, this is a dream, right? Tell me this is a dream."

"Baby, I wish it was. God, I wish it was."

Her eyes glanced around the bedroom; she felt defenseless, alone, and scared.

Scratching her face, she said, "Anthony, what else did this woman say?"

"Her adopted mother said the birth mother was sick. She may have died."

Magnolia was now sitting on her bed pressing her fingers against her temples. "Anthony, tell me exactly what this woman looks like. I mean, you know how many men I see that look like you, baby. Resemble you, maybe. Does she resemble me or does she look exactly like me? Like the woman you've spent the past twenty-four years with."

He tasted the water that leaked from his face. "She looks precisely like you, baby. She's about fifteen pounds heavier, though, her hairstyle is short, and she has a light birthmark on her forehead. But, she really looks like you. I'm certain of it. I wouldn't lie to you and I wouldn't call you up this late at night and tell you this if I wasn't convinced."

"Maggie—it's so similar to my name."

"I know. Hyacinth's mother really couldn't remember. Maybe she meant to say Magnolia."

"I can't believe it, Anthony. If what you're saying is true, then I've been living a lie my entire life." She began to cry.

"Don't cry. This happened for a reason. I know it happened for a reason."

"You think so?"

"Yes."

"Now I know why mother suffered all her life. She suffered from guilt. She was living a little white lie."

Magnolia threw the pillow across the room, knocking over the lamp. She screamed, "Mother, no wonder you couldn't love me. I wasn't yours!"

"Leah . . . Hey . . ."

"I'm okay."

"She wants to meet you."

Magnolia swallowed hard and climbed out of the bed. "Who does?"

"Hyacinth."

Magnolia was silent. She closed her eyes and envisioned her last therapy session with Dr. Bellamy. She thought about the fights she had with her mother. She thought about the dreams—her wedding day and the children waving on the farm. She remembered concentrating on closure to all of her pain. She wanted the curtain to come down and she never wanted to dream about her past again. But now, it's all come back.

"Leah, are you still there?"

She didn't respond. Anthony was nervous and screamed her name again. "Magnolia!"

"I'm here, Anthony. When was she born?"

"Baby, I think it's best that I come home and tell you the other specifics to your face. This is overwhelming and I need to be with you."

"No, baby. I can handle it. Tell me, when was she born?"

"Leah, she was born on December 25, 1960. The same day

and year you were born."

Magnolia squatted on the edge of the bed, composed. She wanted to know more. "See? I can handle this. Now, tell me what state is on her birth certificate?"

"Florida. But she has a fraudulent birth certificate. I'm sure you have one, too."

Magnolia's small frame staggered forward. Her hands crammed against her abdomen and she wanted to vomit. Anthony could hear something crackling in the background. Magnolia took her bedroom slippers and pressed down on the glass from the broken perfume bottles that was on the floor. It kept her from daydreaming and made her focus. Then she swept the broken glass to the side and crawled back into bed, pulling the covers over her. "Anthony, I'm feeling weak."

"Baby, just relax. Take a deep breath for me. I'm going to call Carl and Brenda. I'll have them come over."

"No, don't. I'll . . . be fine."

"No, I'm going to call them!"

"Anthony, I'll be fine. Please believe me. Oh, baby, I wish you were here."

"Baby, I love you. I wish I was there holding you. Leah, I didn't mean to upset you. I really didn't."

"I'm not upset because you told me. You know I needed to know this. It's just this seems like a bad dream. But I won't believe it until I see this Hyacinth face to face."

"You will. Trust me, you will. Leah, promise me you'll call Carl and Brenda if you're not feeling well."

"I promise, I'll call them."

"I love you, Magnolia Lewis."

She smiled and held the phone next to her chest. "I know what that means. It's time to go, huh? Some of mother's old papers are in the attic. I think I'm going to look through them and see if I can find something."

"Baby, it's late. Wait until I get home."

"No, I need to know."

"But you said you were feeling weak."

"I'm fine now, Anthony. Call me first thing in the morning."
"First thing, I promise. I love you. Goodnight, baby."
"I love you too, sweetheart."

She began to hang up the telephone when Anthony yelled, "Leah, promise me that if you're not—"

She broke in: "Anthony, I promise. If I'm not feeling well, I'll call Carl and Brenda. I tell you what—I'll call Linda and have her come over."

"Good. I feel much better knowing that."

"You worry too much. I'm going to give her a call as soon as I hang up with you. We'll talk tomorrow."

"Goodnight, Leah. I love you with all my heart."

"Me too."

After he hung up with her, Anthony continued to pace the room. He glanced out of the window and saw that the streets were crowded with pedestrians, lights were on in buildings, and the traffic was flowing.

Suddenly his stomach grumbled and he realized he had eaten nothing all day except for the pancakes. He had practically overlooked lunch and totally skipped dinner. He skimmed through the yellow pages and located a pizzeria nearby that was open late. He ordered a large pepperoni with extra cheese, an antipasto salad, and a large bottle of soda.

The deliveryman knocked thirty minutes later. Anthony raced toward the door and tripped over his luggage. When he finally reached the door, the smell of the hot pizza gave him goose bumps. He tipped the young man and immediately devoured a slice.

"Damn," he said as he munched. "I tell you, there's no place like New Jersey and New York when it comes to some good pizza. This shit is for the birds." Taking another bite, he said, "Thank God I'm dying of hunger or else this would really taste bad."

An hour later, he grabbed the telephone and called Magnolia back.

"Hi, Anthony," she said.

"How did you know it was me?"

"I had a pretty good idea it was you."

"Sounds like you're eating?"

"Pizza. Believe me, it's not good. How are you feeling?"

"I'm feeling better. Linda is here."

"Tell her I said hello and thanks for coming over."

"I told her about Hyacinth and guess what?"

"What?"

"She's just as amazed as I was. She doesn't believe you. We both think this is a joke. We know you, Anthony. Unfortunately, we won't believe it until we see her."

Anthony grinned. "Magnolia you will see her, believe me."

Looking at Linda and grinning, she said, "I trust you, Anthony. I know my husband."

Sitting on the bed, Anthony crumbled the pizza box and flung it into the garbage container. "What are you guys doing?"

"We're talking about my twin," she said, placing her hand to her mouth. "Oops, my triplet, remember?"

Anthony appeared stoic. "Yes, I remember. This is not a joke, Leah. I would never lie to you about something like this. I can hear Linda laughing in the background. Magnolia, this is not funny!"

Magnolia stopped laughing. "You are serious, huh? I can hear it in your voice."

"You'll see. You both will see. What's Linda saying?"

"She's saying you're a trip. She can't believe you're getting me all shook up about this."

"Listen, tell Linda to shut the fuck up. She talks too much anyway. She thinks she knows every fucking thing."

Magnolia turned to Linda, who was standing on the balcony. "Linda, Anthony said—"

"No, baby, don't tell her. I did not mean it. Look, I am really tired, Leah. I just ate and now I am going to bed. I hate that feeling. I'm exhausted too and I can't keep my eye's open."

"Go to sleep and call me in the morning. I pray this isn't a joke. I know you wouldn't do that to me. We both need some rest. Don't forget to call me in the morning, okay?"

"I will."

"Goodnight, Anthony."

"Goodnight."

Anthony heard Magnolia's voice right before he put the handset down. "Anthony."

"Yes, what is it?"

"When you talk to Hyacinth tomorrow, can you ask her if she remembers a farm?"

Anthony looked confused. "What about a farm?"

"Anthony, just do me that favor, okay? Please ask her."

"Okay, I'll ask her."

"Bye, Anthony."

"Bye."

CHAPTER 32

Anthony tossed and turned all night, unable to get Magnolia off of his mind. And he couldn't stop thinking about how he'd looked at Hyacinth and seen Magnolia's spirit glowing through her warm smile.

Hours later he awoke to find his body soaked in perspiration. It was eight in the morning and rays of sunlight lit up his face. The drapery rod had fallen off its frame. He pulled the sheets up to cover his face. Gradually he rose and walked to the window. He started to put the rod back on its frame when the phone rang. Startled, Anthony dropped the pole and the long curtains and ran to the telephone. "Leah!"

"No. Good morning, Anthony. It's Hyacinth."

"Oh, good morning, Hyacinth. How are you?"

"I'm okay. Feeling a little better, I guess. How about yourself?"

He sat on the firm bed. "Still in shock." Then he kicked a shoe across the room. "I talked to Magnolia last night."

"Did you tell her?"

"Yes, I told her."

Twisting her hair in locks, Hyacinth got up from the kitchen and walked toward the back porch to get some fresh air. "How is she?"

"She was shocked, too. She thinks I'm pulling her leg. She won't believe any of this until she sees you."

"I can imagine how she feels, Anthony." Hyacinth's breath became heavy. "I'm sure she's pretty confused right about now. I know I am."

"She is. I should have waited until I got back home before I said anything. I'm worried about her. Really worried." He fiddled with the floral bedspread. "I pray I didn't hurt her. She can be very sensitive."

"I hope she's all right. This whole thing is crazy," she said, half-giggling. "I meet my fiancé for lunch, something I've been doing for the past year and a half, only to discover that there's a missing chapter in my life. I should say chapters." She began to laugh again. "Hey, didn't you say Magnolia is a literary agent?"

"Yes, I did."

"Well, this sounds like a bestseller, wouldn't you agree?"

"I agree. She'll be fine and I'm sure she's recruited a writer by now."

They chuckled.

"Her best friend is staying with her now," said Anthony. "But I have to get back home as soon as possible. I need to be with her."

"Anthony, Gregory and I were talking. We would very much like to go back to New Jersey with you." She turned and glanced at Gregory. "Of course, if that's okay with you and Magnolia."

"Uh . . . Uh . . . that's great, Hyacinth! Magnolia is looking forward to meeting you. She has to meet you. I didn't want to upset or worry her then I turned around and did exactly that. But she—"

"I'm so sorry, Anthony."

"Oh, please, don't apologize, it's not your fault. Anyone would have taken the news the same way, I'm sure. This is like something you see in the movies. This is truly unbelievable. But everything will be fine once we all go to Jersey."

Hyacinth came back into the kitchen and stood near the stove and fiddled with the gas handles. She moved a griddle pan from the fire. "Anthony."

"Yes."

"We've been up the entire night talking. There was so much to discuss." She hesitated. "I've learned more since last evening."

"You have!"

"Yes, so much more. Mother remembered more details. Important details. She also wanted to apologize to you. She really did forget."

"I understand. I'm the one to apologize. I can't imagine being in her shoes right now. I know she and your father did what was best."

Gripping the handset, she said, "They did. Looking back, they would have done things differently. I'm sure of it. The outcome is absolutely heartbreaking. I believe they would have taken all six of us had they known how many lives eventually would be affected by it."

Anthony was confused. He scratched the back of his head and said, "Hyacinth, did I hear you correctly? All six of you?"

She laughed. "Yes, you did. That's what I had to tell you. Mommy told me that my biological mother had six children."

"What?"

"Yes, we were the youngest. You know, the triplets. She said our mother was single and raised us all alone."

"What? I can't . . . I can't believe this. So you have—"

"That's right. A total of five siblings somewhere." She smiled as she flipped a pancake. "There are four more out there, Anthony. I have two older brothers and a sister."

Pouring more cooking oil in the pan, she said, "Anthony, there's a lot of work to be done. Magnolia and I must meet. We have a lot of research to do. Gregory's already contacted his brother's ex-wife, who is a reporter and producer with the show *Separations* in New York."

"I've watched that show!"

"Yes, it's the program that—"

"Yes. Yes, I know what it is. I've watched it many times before. But—"

"I know she can help. And I know they're out there. Somewhere. They have to be."

Anthony pounded his hand on the shiny wine-red bureau.

"Hyacinth, we will find them. Trust me. We'll find them!"
"Anthony, what are you doing this afternoon?"
"Nothing, but I was going to call the airlines to get an early flight home."
"Why don't you wait a few more hours and come over here and have lunch with us?"
"Thanks, but are you sure your family is up to it?"
"Yes."
"Okay, I'll come over this afternoon."
"All right, we'll be expecting you. Do you remember how to get here?"
"Yes, I remembered the route Gregory took."
"Fine, then I guess we'll see you at noon."
"Noontime it is."
"Take care, Anthony."
Before he hung up the phone, he remembered something. "Wait, Hyacinth."
"Yes, I'm still here."
"Um, one last thing," he said. His hands were trembling and he sat on the edge of the bed. "Magnolia wanted me to ask you something."
She turned off the gas, pushed the pot to the back of the stove, and held the phone close to her ear. "Yes?"
"She wanted me to ask you if you remember a farm."
Hyacinth touched her chin and thought. Then suddenly she screamed, "Yes! Yes! I remember a farm." Ecstatic, she jumped up and down. "She is my sister, Anthony!" She leaped onto Gregory, tugged on his shirt. "Magnolia is my sister! Magnolia is my sister!"
Grinning, Gregory grabbed her arm and lifted her off the floor and jumped with her.
Then she placed the receiver back to her ear. "Of course, I remember a farm. Huh, so Magnolia does too?"
"I suspect she does. She's never mentioned it to me before."
"Anthony, do you remember the picture hanging in my parents' living room?"
"Yes, I do. That beautiful picture of—"

"Yes, a farm. I painted it in college."

"I can't believe it."

"I always had dreams of a farm, Anthony. I took a couple of art classes in college and for some reason that farm came to mind when I was completing my class project. I received an A+ for it too!"

"Is that right?"

"Yep."

"Do you remember anything else in your dreams?"

She paused and pressed her fingers against her chin. "Wait a minute. I remember a middle-aged couple and some children playing on a farm. Oh . . . wait . . . I remember a truck too. It was a shabby black truck with fruits and vegetables in the back of it. But that's pretty much all I remember."

She was quiet.

"Hyacinth, are you there?" Anthony said.

"Wait . . . Wait . . . the children . . . Hey . . . there were six of them, Anthony. Oh my, God!" She was so caught up in the moment, she gagged on the words. Gregory slapped her hard on the back and she coughed. Saliva dribbled down the side of her mouth. She grabbed a napkin and wiped her lips and said, "Anthony . . . Oh my, God!"

"Take your time, Hyacinth. Please, take your time."

"There were three little girls, an older girl and two older boys. My God!"

"How old, Hyacinth? How old were the boys and older girl?"

"Shoo, one of the boys could have been a teenager but I'm really not certain."

"And how about—"

"The younger boy was probably seven or eight. My God! I dreamed about my family all of those years and never knew it."

"Look, Hyacinth, noon can't get here soon enough. Can I come over now?"

"Yes, please do!"

"Okay then, I'll see you in about an hour."

With the receiver to his ear, Anthony stooped and picked up

his suitcase and flung it on the bed. He opened it and pulled out a pair of slacks. "Hyacinth, please stay calm."

"Stay calm? How can I? I've discovered the best news of my life. I'm so happy I could cry. Anthony, thanks for inquiring about the farm."

Patricia quietly approached her from behind, held her by the waist, and leaned her head on Hyacinth's shoulder. They wept.

"Hyacinth, are you all right?" said Anthony.

"I'm fine. I feel like the luckiest person on earth right now. Really, I'm fine."

"Are you sure?"

"Yes."

"Well then, I'll see you soon. Goodbye, Hyacinth."

"Goodbye, Anthony."

With a wide smile plastered on his face, Anthony quickly placed the handset on the console and dialed Magnolia's number. He needed to share the good news. "Hello, Leah."

"Hi, honey."

"Good morning, baby. Are you feeling better?"

"Yes, I'm much better. Linda and I are eating breakfast now. She made a mean cheese omelet."

"That's great, baby. I'm glad to hear you're better."

Anthony couldn't care less about Linda's cooking. The thought of her made his organs twirl. But whatever made Magnolia happy pleased him. He was simply grateful that Linda was by her side during this difficult time.

Magnolia seemed the only person in the world who saw a few good traits in Linda. She often lavished Magnolia with expensive gifts and trips for birthdays and holidays to compensate for her suffering.

Although Linda was a good listener and helped Magnolia deal with her mother's agony and years of pain, she was still unbearable. Everything she did annoyed Anthony.

He found Linda's demeanor usually inappropriate and her expectations and standards of others high and extreme. Those ignorant habits of hers made everyone want to kill her. She constantly interrupted people in conversation, contributing her two cents, which most of the time made absolutely no sense.

It was all about class and money for Linda. She would degrade men, especially African-American men, and only dated well-off men, only to leave them after breaking them financially and mentally.

Her infidelity and lies irritated Anthony because, somehow, Magnolia would ultimately get involved in the center of her crazy and ruthless life.

Linda had a skillful way of manipulating Magnolia to misinform people when she found herself in trouble. Once she failed to attend an important meeting with one of their new clients, Sue Young, a fresh young writer who signed a three-book contract with a major publisher, because she was in Connecticut screwing a well-known singer who happened to be married. Magnolia was accustomed to defending her whereabouts.

Anthony despised Linda for using Magnolia. She could be scandalous at times and often thought she should have the last word. Most of the time, her opinions were discourteous and her beliefs were absurd.

Yet despite Linda's trivial manners, Magnolia thought Anthony was overly critical of her.

Maybe he had been somewhat judgmental of her, expecting her to be like him: honest, loyal, and well thought of. Maybe he was a bit harsh. And maybe she wasn't so bad after all, but when he thought about their initial encounter those negative images would resurface all over again.

Even Carl disagreed with Anthony and thought he was unkind to Linda. He wanted Anthony to admit that beneath those intolerant feelings was a teeny bit of sincerity and perhaps even love. But Anthony knew that wasn't true. He also knew Linda wanted him the first time she set eyes on him, but the attraction was not mutual.

She was uncompromising and thought too highly of herself, repeatedly putting herself on a pedestal no man could ever reach. She considered herself to be exceptionally attractive, intelligent, and alluring, and all of those qualities turned Anthony and majority of the men away. The sad part is that Linda's personality was unchangeable. Black men in particular realized that attempting to shape or change Linda's basic nature was pointless. She was stubborn like a dreadful toothache, endlessly reappearing with the same persistent dull pain over and over again.

"So that omelet must be really good, huh? Your munching is so heavy, I can almost taste the damn thing," he said.

Magnolia laughed.

He paused and muttered to himself, "At least she's doing something positive this morning. Cooking omelets in my house—can you believe that shit!"

"Hey, there Mr. Lewis, I heard that," Magnolia whispered. "That wasn't a nice thing to say." She chewed some more. "Did you ask her?"

"Yes, I did and she remembers a farm. Leah, you've never mentioned this before."

"I didn't think it was important, that's why. So what did she say about it?"

"I'll tell you about it when I come home."

"I can't wait that long."

"Baby, I really think I should wait until I get home. Okay?"

"Got damn you, Anthony. Okay, I'll wait."

"I'm on my way to her house now. Her parents remembered more details about the adoption."

"Anthony, as soon as you find out more information, please give me a call. The suspense is killing me."

"Okay, baby, but I still think it's best if this all waits until Saturday. I don't want to get you upset again."

She rolled her eyes. "Fine, I'll wait."

"Enjoy your breakfast and have a wonderful day. Why don't you two go shopping or something?"

"Anthony! It's Friday. We still have another work day."

"Oh, I forget. Just relax then. Take it easy today and don't overdo it."

"I promise I'll take it easy.

"Talk with you later. I love you."

"I love you, too. Goodbye, baby."

CHAPTER 33

Anthony arrived at Hyacinth's home on time. When May-Lynne opened the door, she seemed thrilled to see him. For the first time she realized how handsome he was.

"Good morning, Anthony," she said beaming.

"Good morning, May-Lynne."

She turned around and looked at Gregory, who was talking on the telephone in the dining room. "Gregory is making flight reservations."

"Tell him to call Fly Right Airlines. I'm flying on flight 1967."

She shouted to Gregory, who was sitting at the dining room table writing down information in a notebook. "Gregory, did you hear that?"

"Yeah, I did. I have them on the line right now. Guess what, Anthony?" he said grinning.

Anthony smiled. He had a pretty good idea what Gregory was going to say.

"They have available seats on your flight," said Gregory.

"Great! How many available seats?"

"Seventeen . . . and I reserved six."

"Six!" Hyacinth shouted. She was beside herself.

"Honey, we're all going to Jersey!"

"Gregory, you can't possibly be serious! Are you?"

Ignoring Hyacinth's reaction, he glanced at Anthony and said,

"I hope that's okay with you, Anthony."

"That's fine. It's just that—"

"Is something wrong, Anthony?"

"No . . . No . . . There's nothing wrong."

Hyacinth squeezed Anthony's arm to persuade him to tell Gregory that it wasn't okay. But Anthony didn't respond to her tight grip.

"Anthony, if there's something you want to say, please go ahead and say it. Whatever's on your mind, please let us know. Gregory can be relentless at times," Hyacinth said with her hand still on his arm.

"No . . . No . . . It's nothing."

Tugging on his shirt again, she said, "Don't worry, we understand."

"Hyacinth, everything is fine with me. Really," Anthony said, squeezing her hand back.

"Are you sure?" she repeated, staring into his eyes.

Anthony winked at her and smiled. "Yes, I'm sure."

"Seriously, Gregory, what are you doing? We can't all go," said Hyacinth.

"Magnolia will appreciate this, Hyacinth. We all need to meet her," Gregory said while looking around at everyone in the room. "I know we all want to meet her. Right," he said, encouraging them. "We all need to talk. Don't you all agree?"

"That's true, but I think we're going to overwhelm her," said Hyacinth.

"I don't think she'll be overwhelmed," said Anthony. "I think she'll really enjoy this."

"Are you sure, Anthony?" Hyacinth said. "I don't want to overburden her." She glanced at her mother. "And I don't want to frighten her either."

"Everything will be okay. Trust me."

Anthony looked at Patricia. "How are you doing, Mrs. Johnson?"

Wiping tears away, she lowered her head and softly spoke. "I'm feeling a little ashamed."

"Oh, Mommy, don't say that. You did what was best. You really did," said Hyacinth.

"But, look what I've done. I'm the cause of this tragedy—all of it. I separated a family and destroyed many lives in the process."

Angrily, Sam stood and shouted, "We did the best that we could, Pat! There's no reason to feel guilty! No reason at all!"

Patricia walked over to her husband and stood so close, the moisture from her face grazed his lips. "No, we didn't, Sam. We could have done better and you know it."

She leaned forward and caressed his face and then gently kissed his wet lips, their faces soaked by each other's grief. "We could have tried harder. We didn't have to do what we did. I have every right to blame myself because what I did was immoral."

"Pat, please stop!"

She pulled her hands away from his face and raised them in the air. She had heard enough excuses and knew it was time to tear down that wall of denial she and Sam had created over so many years. It was time to put an end to the denial. Crumpling her hand, she said to Hyacinth, "Last evening, I did a lot of thinking, Hyacinth, and it's only right that you know."

"Know what, Ma?"

Everyone was still and all eyes were fixed on Patricia. Hyacinth stepped back and her mouth hung open. *What is she going to tell me now?*

Patricia shut her eyes. "I did meet your mother. I . . . I met her a year before we adopted you." She inhaled and released a long-anticipated breath—the truth was finally on the table.

Hyacinth gently kissed her mother's forehead. "You'll always be my mother. I love you with all my heart, Ma."

Patricia cuddled Hyacinth—she did not want to release her because she knew what she was about to say would hurt her more than everything else. But she was bound to tell the truth.

"I know, baby. But . . . she was your mother—your biological mother. It's important that you know this."

Staring into Hyacinth's eyes, she said, "As I was saying, I did meet her briefly."

"Who, Ma?" said Hyacinth.

"Your birth mother."

Lawrence handed Patricia a handkerchief and she wiped her tears. Sniffling, she whispered, "I promise, these are the last tears that will fall from my eyes today. There will be no more crying. I want to be free of the pain. No more pain. No more."

Gregory gently tapped her shoulder and uttered, "Please continue, Patricia. Please."

She paused for a moment, staring at the damp handkerchief. "The woman who helped organized the adoption . . . she was the person who introduced us to your mother."

Lawrence pulled a chair from the table and pushed it toward his mother and she slowly sat down. She sobbed and said, "Your mother was very religious. Boy . . . did she love her children."

She blew her nose, took a deep breath and whispered, "I promised myself there would be no more tears, didn't I?"

May-Lynne and Hyacinth began crying. They held each other. "It's okay, Ma," May-Lynne said.

"No, it's not okay," Patricia yelled back, waving her hands at her. "Everyone in this room knows damn well what your father and I did was wrong!"

Patricia's interludes were paining Anthony and he grew impatient. "When did you meet Hyacinth's mother, Mrs. Johnson?"

"I met her at a church in Mission, Georgia. That's where you were born, Hyacinth."

Stunned, Hyacinth said, "Mission—so you always knew where I was born."

"Yes, I did. You were born at home."

Anthony stretched his athletic body over the table and gently held Patricia's hand. "So you do remember, Mrs. Johnson? You remember everything, huh?"

Her eyes reddened and she quietly sobbed. "Of course I do. The woman who introduced us was a schoolteacher like myself and taught school there. Your older brother and sister were her students. She befriended their mother."

Then Patricia stared at Hyacinth. "Your real mother, Hyacinth."

"How long had she known them?" Anthony said.

"Not long. Maybe two years." Patricia rubbed her nose and then pondered for a few seconds. "You know, the teacher is from Florida too and still lives here."

"Here?" Lawrence said pointing to the floor. "She lives in Miami Beach?"

"Yes."

"Who is she?" Hyacinth said.

"What's her name?" Lawrence demanded.

"Your—" Patricia said sobbing. "She's . . . She's . . . Henrietta Smith."

The sound of crashing glass was heard. Lawrence jumped and grabbed Hyacinth, who had dropped her coffee mug. "It's okay, sis. It's okay." He escorted her to a chair. "Take it easy."

Hyacinth cried, "Aunt Henrietta!"

"Yes, baby. Your father's sister."

May-Lynne fell to her knees and put her hands over her ears. She didn't want to hear that her favorite aunt was involved too. "No! I don't believe what I'm hearing! This can't be true!"

Tears rushed down Lawrence's face and he turned to his father. "Oh man, how could you two do something like this? Why?"

Sam remained still. His eyes were slightly red and his face moist from sweat. He turned away, avoiding his children's pain, and stared out the window. In the end, he was still in denial. He stayed composed and firm—he didn't utter a word, refusing to share the blame.

"Did you hear me, Daddy? Why?" Lawrence said. "Your sister, of all people! She's behind all of this mess. I can't believe this."

Lawrence approached Sam and shouted, "I know what we need to do. We need to go over there right now and talk to her. But—oh—I'm sure you've talked to her already. Haven't you, Daddy?"

Sam turned slowly to Lawrence and attempted to raise his unsteady hands to him but failed—weakness controlled his short frame. He stared at his only son, appearing insecure and shaken. He softly said, "No, she doesn't know about Anthony. She doesn't know that Hyacinth knows she's adopted either. Lawrence, your Aunt Henrietta is sick and that's all she knows."

"I don't care how sick see is. She knows something, Daddy," Lawrence said.

Anthony stepped in and tried to calm the hostile scene. "Listen," he said, shaking his head to confirm that he wasn't affected by the news and that he was unperturbed. "Look . . . what happened, happened. We can't do anything about it now. Lawrence, your parents did what anyone else would have done at that time. Please, don't be angry with them. This all happened for a reason and I believe God is the only one who knows why. He allowed it to happen."

"Yeah, well, I guess He allowed a lot of other things to happen, huh?" said Lawrence.

Lawrence nervously placed a cigarette in his mouth and began to light it but his hands continued to tremble and he dropped the matchbox. He sobbed just as he did when his grandmother passed away five years ago. He had refused to accept her death. He thought she would live forever and couldn't fathom why God let her die.

Then he realized he had to forgive his parents' actions. Lawrence walked over to his father and did the unexpected: he gave his father a hug. "I love you, man," he said weeping.

Sobbing, Sam said, "I love you too, son. But you know my sister isn't well. She has a heart condition and the last thing we need to do is go over there and upset her. She'll have a heart attack for sure."

"You're right," said Anthony.

"But we need to talk to her. She knows more, Sam," said Patricia.

"I don't know about this," said Sam, rubbing his forehead. "Okay, okay. But—"

"No, buts—we're leaving on Saturday, Sam," Gregory said. "It must be today."

"Okay. I'll give her a call right now."

Sam grabbed the telephone from the oak table, appearing sad as he dialed cautiously. He felt remorse. Then he glanced at Patricia.

"Hello, Henrietta. Yes, this is Sam. How are you? Oh, I'm fine. Yes, Pat and the kids are fine too."

He paused for a moment and turned toward his family. "Henrietta, what are you doing right now? Oh! Well, that's good because . . ."

Sam procrastinated as his eyes filled with tears. "We're coming over there. Yeah, that's right—Pat, myself, and the kids. We have something to tell you. No . . . no . . . everything is fine, don't worry."

Clutching an ornament he picked up on the table, Sam said, "We're on our way, okay? See you in a few."

CHAPTER 34

They all jumped into a gold-colored van and drove to the nursing home, which was located on a towering hill. The street was lined with large palm trees and, from afar, the residence looked like a mansion Anthony had seen in Beverly Hills.

The Johnson family was nervous when they arrived. They wished they were somewhere else far, far away. They knew that from this day on, there would be no more lying and justification for the past. Their true destiny, particularly Hyacinth's, would surface, and they were prepared to face it.

Man, I hate nursing homes, thought Anthony as he got out of the car. *I'll never forget the time Leah's mom was in one of these. How depressing.*

Hyacinth sensed his uneasiness and whispered into his ear, "It's not what you think. The people here are very much alive and well. Most of them are alone and have no families. That's why they are here."

Anthony smiled. "You must have read my mind. Magnolia does that often."

Hyacinth smiled back. Once outside the nursing home they saw it had all the makings of a luxury hotel. There were three massive white columns lined in front, wide French doors, handcrafted glass windows, and elegant architecture.

The morning air was cool and beautiful palm trees danced

gracefully in the surging breeze. They walked past a rich, green, manicured lawn and noticed exquisite flowers flourishing in the front and on every side.

Anthony stood in awe once he stepped inside. He knew the occupants paid generously to live here. There were sparkling chandeliers, elaborate miniature sculptures, blooming towering plants, large striped cream-colored wallpaper, stone glass tables, decorated centerpieces, fancy paintings, arched doorways, marble floors, plush sofas, and heavy oak furniture in every bedroom. The doors and trimmings were snow white and every non-bedroom was named after someone famous.

They headed to a recreational suite that was located down a wide corridor and toward the right. It was Henrietta's favorite area.

They saw her sitting with four elderly women at a square card table playing poker. A gray haired Caucasian woman quickly glanced up and said, "Oh, look, Henry, it's Sam."

The other women excitedly spoke to him at once. "Hi, Sam!"

"Hello," he said.

An elderly, well-proportioned, light-complexioned African-American woman who sat in a wheelchair chirped, "And look, there's Pat too."

She waved her hand at Patricia and noticed there were others. "Oh, and they brought the kids."

Sam mumbled to himself, "I can't believe she forgot. I just called her thirty minutes ago and told her we were all coming."

Henrietta looked concerned when the rest of them started to approach the table. "I hope everything is all right, Sam."

She frowned and touched her chin. "This is unusual. I mean, all of you visiting me at the same time."

May-Lynne spoke first. "Hello, Auntie."

"Good morning, May-Lynne. Glad to see you here."

Then Hyacinth and Lawrence said, "Hey, Aunt Henrietta."

"Hey, there. How are you today?"

Hyacinth and Lawrence were speechless. They didn't know what to say to the aunt they loved so dearly.

Then Patricia spoke. "Hello, Henrietta."

She smiled and said, "Hi, Pat."

"How are you feeling today?"

"Things couldn't be better. I'm winning," said Henrietta grinning. "I'm so glad you all came to visit." But then her curiosity got the better of her. "Are you sure everything is okay?"

Sam signaled for everyone to leave the room. Then he whispered into Henrietta's ear, "Henrietta, can we talk in private?"

"Oh, sure we can, Sam," she whispered back. She turned to the other women. "Ladies, Sam and I have to talk. Please continue without me. Sorry to break up the game but I'll be back later."

The gray haired woman yelled, "Oh, don't worry, Henry, we'll wait until you get back."

"Okay, it shouldn't take long," she said glancing at Sam. "Right, Sam."

Sam didn't respond at first. When Henrietta didn't take her eyes off him and waited for a response, he nodded and said, "Right, it shouldn't take long, Henrietta."

He pushed the wheelchair down the corridor and to her room. Along the way, Henrietta noticed May-Lynne and Anthony chatting by a water fountain. "Oh, May-Lynne, is this your friend?"

"No, Auntie. This is not my friend."

Anthony seemed puzzled and May-Lynne laughed. "He's not my boyfriend if that's what you mean, Auntie. He's a friend of the family."

"Oh, is he! He's so handsome. I've never met him before, have I?"

"No, you haven't, Auntie."

Henrietta put her hands above her mouth. "Well then, is anyone going to introduce us?"

Then Sam announced, "Henrietta, this young man's name is Anthony Lewis and he's visiting here. He's from New Jersey. He's married to—"

He was interrupted by a deliberate cough. "Let's . . . Umm . . . Umm . . . Hmm . . . let's just go inside your room and I'll tell you who is he later."

Sam quickly pushed the wheelchair into the room and closed

the door. Jittery, Henrietta looked back at him. "You did say everything was all right, Sam. Who was that young man? Do I know him? He looks familiar."

"Henrietta, that young man is married to Hyacinth's sister."

Henrietta was startled. "What? What are you talking about, Sam? When did May-Lynne get married?"

Agitated, Sam yelled, "May-Lynne isn't married. I'm talking about Hyacinth's other sister. Remember!"

"No, I don't remember. May-Lynne is Hyacinth's other sister!"

"Henrietta, please, just stop it."

Appearing confused, she said, "But Sam—"

"But Sam, my ass!" Wiping sweat from his forehead, he said, "Henrietta, that man is married to Hyacinth's sister Magnolia. Remember Magnolia?"

She placed her hands to her ear as if she hadn't heard him. "Who?"

Bending down, Sam shouted into her ear, "Magnolia!"

"I don't know who or what you're talking about, Sam. Get out of here and go home!"

Aiming her finger toward the door, she yelled, "Please, leave me alone!"

He shook the wheelchair and screamed, "Henrietta, I know you remember! It wasn't that long ago! Your mind is still sharp—that I do know!"

"No . . . No . . . I don't remember."

Then she placed her quivering hands to her heart. "I'm sick, Sam," she said. "I'm—"

"Henrietta, calm down. You're all right. I know you're not feeling well but you're not that sick. Just take it easy."

"Sam, what's your problem, huh? You come here and try to intimidate me."

"Henrietta, I'm not trying to scare you. The truth is out. Okay? I'm referring to Hyacinth, Magnolia, and Rose."

His undersized frame jolted and he quickly grabbed her hand

and held it firmly. His body's vibration embraced hers and soon, both of their hands shivered.

"Three sisters! Triplets!" screamed Sam. "Pat and I adopted Hyacinth thirty-eight years ago."

He was so mad, he slapped his other hand against his thigh. "So-called adopted her." Then he tugged on her shirt. "Anthony is married to Magnolia and we need to know where Rose and the other children are."

Suddenly Patricia, Hyacinth, May-Lynne, Lawrence, and Anthony entered the room.

May-Lynne begged, "Auntie, please tell us. We need to know. We're not here to criticize or blame you. We just need to know where they are."

Henrietta lifted her sad wrinkled face up and softly said, "Know what, baby? I don't know anything about a Magnolia or Rose or any triplets."

"Henrietta, yes you do," said Patricia.

"No, I don't!" shouted Henrietta, who pointed to the door. "Please go away! Leave me alone! Please!"

Sam pleaded with them to leave. He grabbed his sister's hand again and gently brushed her silver hair with the back of his hand. Then he carefully stroked her chin. "Henrietta, look at me." Soaked in tears, she turned to him. "Hyacinth knows everything. They all know."

"How, Sam?" she said crying. "Why? Why did you tell her?"

"Because, Henrietta, it was time. Besides, she would have found out sooner or later."

"No, you're wrong. She wouldn't have known."

"Yes, she would have," said Sam as he placed his shaky hands in his pockets. "Sooner or later, Henrietta."

She screamed, "Sam, it's been thirty-eight years! You never said one word. Why now?"

"She had to know, Henrietta!"

"Had to know what, Sam? I didn't do anything wrong," she said aiming her finger at him. "Not one damn thing!"

Nodding his head, he said, "I know. But—"

"But nothing," she snapped. "Their mother was dying and you know that."

"Yes, she was, Henrietta."

"I did what was right. We all did what was right."

Rolling his eyes, he pretended to agree with her. "Yes, we did what was right, Henrietta. We all thought we did the right thing. Even though we felt it was wrong."

Sam strolled over to the window and stared out for a moment. "I'm going to ask you one last time. Where did they go, Henrietta?"

"You think I remember that, Sam? Like I said before, it's been thirty-eight years."

"I know you remember. You can't possibly forget something like that. You can never forget."

"So, what're you saying, Sam?"

"I'm not saying anything unkind about you. I'm just saying that I believe you know the whereabouts of the other children."

"Oh, I'm the bad person now. Hyacinth hates me. Doesn't she? And May-Lynne and Larry too, huh?"

Clutching her hand, he calmly said, "No, Henry, they don't hate you. They want to know the truth, that's all. It's very important to them that they know."

Suddenly she pushed the wheelchair in front of the bureau and stared at herself in the mirror. "You, know Sam, I always knew God would punish me for what I did."

"Henrietta, God is not going to punish you."

"Oh yes, He already did," she said looking down at her dismembered legs. "And when it's time for me to go home, he's going to send me down to the dungeons."

She began to sob again. "Send me down where it's cold and dark. And no one will be down there but me and the got damn snakes."

"Henrietta, stop talking like that."

"You know it's true, Sam. But . . . but . . . I'm not going alone, Sam."

Sam's head slowly turned and he faced her. She went on: "You and Pat and those others are going too! Yeah, that's right, you all are going down with me."

"Henrietta, stop it!" screamed Sam. "Just stop it!"

She clutched a holy cross she had grabbed from the bureau and wept like a baby. "We've been living in sin and . . . I've tried to repent but . . . God didn't want to hear any of it. That's why I've been alone my entire life, Sam. That's why I don't have any children either."

"Please, stop it, Henrietta. Things happen. Every now and again we make bad choices."

"No, Sam. We do have control over those choices. We were educated adults. We knew what we did was wrong but we did it anyway. That's why I'm in this wheelchair."

Vigorously shaking her head, she said, "Yes, that's why. He certainly made sure I would never do this again."

"Henrietta, that was an accident."

"It was Him. I know it was. It was the work of God. Yes it was. He crushed my legs for a reason, Sam."

"Henrietta, you were in an automobile accident and there were other people in the car, too."

"Yeah, Sam, but those other people are well now except for me. They've all since recovered but I didn't walk away from it. No, not me."

"Henrietta, we can't blame anyone for what we've done. And we can't blame anyone for what has happened to our lives."

"Why not, Sam?"

Lifting the window curtains to the side, he shouted, "Because, damn it! That's why!"

"Well, I'm not blaming anyone, Sam. I'm just saying that I paid the ultimate price for what I did. I lost my freedom."

She was quiet for a few seconds and then slowly pointed to a closet door across the room. "It's all in the closet."

"What's in the closet, Henrietta?"

"The information you came here for."

Sam hastily walked to the closet and opened the door. He looked inside and saw an old brown box on a shelf. Then he came out, grabbed a chair, and stood on it to reach the box. He lifted the box off of the shelf and carried it to her bed. Slowly he raised the lid and fingered through a pile of papers.

"The papers are clipped together. You'll see it," said Henrietta.

"Yes, I see it," said Sam.

After reading a few pages, he fell on the floor with the papers in his hand and began to sob. The past was now staring him in the eye—the part of his life he had chosen to forget and vowed never to recall. The denial was over.

"I should have never agreed to any of this, Henrietta," he said crying.

"It's too late for that, Sam."

"Yeah, too late, huh. So many people were hurt in the process." He fiddled with the papers. "Look at this mess. We didn't adopt these children. We stole them. We went about this as if they weren't human beings."

"Like I said, Sam, it's too late for sad stories. It's too late to dwell on it. You should have thought about that before. Remember, you and Pat couldn't have children and you wanted to please her. You wanted to have the perfect family."

Teardrops fell on her hands. She lowered her head. "You did nothing wrong. I was the one who left out the important details. I wasn't truthful about everything. I was wrong and I apologize. But there's nothing we can do now, Sam. Absolutely nothing."

"Well . . . there's . . . a substantial amount of work I have to do, Henrietta." He began to stutter. "You . . . you may feel that way but . . . but . . . I don't. We'll find them. Don't worry, we will. Even if I have to pursue this until the day I die, I'll find them."

She quickly threw the cross she was holding at him. "Good. I hope you do find them!"

Sam stared at her. His eyes did not move. He overlooked her sarcastic comment and said, "I mean it, Henrietta. Mark my words!"

"I know you mean it, Sam. It's just that . . . I've . . . I've been living in sin."

His hands fell to his sides. "What are you talking about,

Henrietta? We've talked about this before. I told you, no one person is to blame for this mess. We all brought this predicament on ourselves. We were all responsible adults and we all knew exactly what we were getting into."

"I don't care what you say, you're the lucky one. You weren't cursed."

"Oh, Henrietta, not again. Lord please, not again."

"You and Pat got the chance to raise a family. I've been miserable my entire life. And I know it's because of this. I need some comfort, Sam."

She grabbed his arm. "You're right, they must be together again. That's all I want to know is that they're together again."

She lowered her head and began to pray. "Dear Lord, save me. I'm so sorry, Solomon. Please forgive me for what I have done."

Henrietta stayed in that position for five minutes until Sam nudged her arm. When she quickly bounced back up, he said, "Henrietta, what did you say?"

"Oh, never mind me!" yelled Henrietta, waving her hand at him.

"Who is Solomon?"

"You'll find out when you read the rest of the papers." She hesitated for a moment before adding, "Sam?"

"What is it, Henrietta?"

"When you find them, I mean all of them, please tell Solomon that I am genuinely sorry. Tell him that I wasn't a happy person then. I was envious of his family." Her frail body tightened. "I resented the closeness they shared. They had each other and I had no one."

She steered her wheelchair over to the window and solemnly glanced out. "There wasn't a soul I could love or to love me back. Tell him I've paid for my wrongdoing."

She held onto the window ledge and then turned her head to Sam. "Promise me you'll tell him that, Sam."

"I promise, Henrietta."

"He must know this. He has to know. I know he's not bitter—that wasn't his nature."

She giggled, then whispered, "Knowing, Solomon, huh . . . he's probably found them already."

She laughed. "Hell, I'm sure he's one step ahead of you, Sam. He loved those girls. Shucks, he loved all of those children."

Sam watched his sister thinking she had gone insane. "I promise I will tell him, Henrietta."

She laughed again, clearly thankful for his response. She opened the bible that was on a shelf next to the window and began to softly mutter. "If we confess our sins a contrite heart wilt not despise."

Sam rubbed her shoulder to draw her attention and whispered into her ear, "Henrietta, I have to go. Will you be okay?"

Henrietta seemed comatose. Sam firmly brushed her shoulder again. "I'm not going to leave you here alone if you're not."

She waved her hand. "I'm fine, Sam. I'm glad I got it out of my system. It's been a long time," she said laughing. "Huh, it was time to let it all go. Don't worry about me. Just find them."

He embraced her. "Everything will be fine. Trust me."

He walked toward the door and then turned back to her and raised his right thumb in the air. He smiled.

"I trust you, Sam," she said smiling. "I know you will do the right thing."

CHAPTER 35

Sam proceeded to the reception desk. After placing his pager number and Anthony's home number on the desk, he said, "Please, call me if you need me."

The receptionist smiled. "Of course, Mr. Johnson. I will certainly do that."

Sam walked over to the lobby area and met the rest of them. They quickly rushed toward him. Hyacinth noticed the brown box he carried. "Daddy, what is that? Did you find out anything?"

"Yes, I did." He was panting and his eyes scanned the papers sticking out of the box. "I have the adoption papers and additional information. She kept them all of these years. Can you believe that?"

"Did you look at them?" Hyacinth said.

"No, not thoroughly. There's a ton to read."

He carefully spread the papers on the coffee table. They each grabbed several sheets of paper and began to read quietly.

Astonished, Hyacinth said, "Look, it says here that Magnolia was adopted by a Freddie Cooper and she lived in Hackensack, New Jersey."

"Yes, that's right. She's Magnolia's mom," said Anthony.

"Freddie was the sister of Alice Cooper," replied Hyacinth.

"Yeah, and what does she have to do with this?" Anthony said.

Gregory said, holding the sheet in his hand, "It says here that

Alice Cooper was the secretary who worked for Lincoln Moore."

"And who the hell is he?" said Lawrence.

"He's the attorney who put this whole thing together," Patricia said.

Shaking his head in disgust, Gregory said, "Huh, and all for money. That's a damn shame!"

Sam interrupted: "He befriended Henrietta and she fell in love with him. She knew he was married. He didn't love her. As a matter of fact, he couldn't care less about her. He used her and he knew Henrietta would do anything for him. He was selfish and she was so damn naïve!"

Furious, Anthony said, "What kind of person could do something like that? He was a low-down dirty crook. A thief. Yeah, that's what he was. Is that son-of-a-bitch still alive?"

The thought of his wife being stolen from her family and the thought of his children not knowing where they came from made his blood boil.

But he soon regretted his comment. "I'm sorry," he said to Sam and Patricia. "I'm just so damn angry. This man didn't care whom this would affect just as long as he got paid. Damn him!"

Patricia began to shiver. "It's cold in here," she said.

Lawrence reached over the pink sofa that had elegant lacework on it and put the blanket positioned on the arm across his mother's back.

Patricia looked at Anthony and said, "Don't apologize, Anthony. You meant every word and there's nothing wrong with what you said. You're right. He was a criminal. There's no doubt about that. He got paid very well too. Sam and I gave him our life's savings and I'm sure the others did as well."

"Hey," Gregory said, "it says here that Rose was taken to upstate New York—to Buffalo. She was adopted by a Mr. and Mrs. Earl Field."

Hyacinth approached Anthony and grabbed hold of the papers. "Can I look at it?" she said.

He handed over the papers and the tears swelled. "It also states that Rose had a disability," said Hyacinth.

May-Lynne stood next to her and softly read along. "She severely injured her right leg at age two and developed an irregular gait," they said.

Hyacinth glanced up and hissed, "I wonder if she still has that handicap."

"Probably so. I believed she fell into a hole in the back of her house," Patricia said. "I don't think they could have afforded surgery to correct that type of injury."

Stepping toward her mother, Hyacinth said, "Is that the reason you didn't take her, Mommy?"

Patricia's hands fell heavily to her side, and for a moment, it seemed she'd stopped breathing. Taking in a drawn-out nervous breath and then powerfully exhaling, she said, "Oh . . . no, baby."

The muscles in Patricia's mouth began to shift and soon, she continued: "The three of you were identical and her handicap had nothing to do with your father and I not adopting her. We only had funds for one child and, besides, by the time Henrietta and Lincoln discussed the final details with us, Earl Field decided he wanted Rose. You see, baby, he was a physician and that's why he took Rose. He was able to give her the necessary care."

Hyacinth shook her head. She was embarrassed about her insensitive comment. Gently she held Patricia's hand. "Forgive me, Ma. That was a cruel thing to say."

"No, baby," said Patricia, jerking Hyacinth's hand. "Every now and again you're going to have questions. And at times, they may be harsh. I can't blame you for that. You have every right to inquire and even get angry."

Anthony stood back and observed. He knew history was in the making. Yet he only wished Magnolia were there; maybe she could ask more concrete questions without offending Patricia. Her words never harmed anyone. She was very effective bringing things to light. Moreover, perhaps she and Hyacinth would have been able to comfort each other during this difficult time.

Gregory glanced at his watch. "It's getting late. We all need to get back home and pack."

"Anthony, I'm sure you want to call Magnolia. I know you're

anxious to get back to New Jersey," said Patricia.

"I'll call her as soon as I get back to the hotel. I miss her."

Hyacinth smiled and said with a slight giggle, "I can't wait to meet her. You know, I miss her too and I haven't met her yet."

May-Lynne said, "Gregory, when are we returning?"

Gregory slowly turned to Hyacinth and stuttered, "Uh . . . Uh . . . it's . . . in . . . indefinite."

"What?" they all said in unison.

"What do you mean it's indefinite?" May-Lynne said.

"I didn't book any return flights," said Gregory.

Turning to him, May-Lynne said, "How come?"

"Is there a problem, May-Lynne?" said Gregory defensively.

"No . . . No . . . I just thought—"

Hyacinth flapped some papers at him. "Gregory, we all have jobs, you know. Anyway, I'm sure Magnolia doesn't want us there indefinitely. What were you thinking?"

Wiping his damp mouth, Gregory said, "Well, you never know. Why are you all complaining anyway? Mr. and Mrs. Johnson, you don't have a job to go to. Larry's off this semester. May-Lynne, you call the shots at the beauty salon. And Hyacinth, if I recall correctly you work at home. You don't report to anyone!"

"Oh, and what about yourself?" Anthony said.

"Well . . . I . . . I . . . I can make some arrangements," said Gregory.

They all laughed.

"Oh, you can, huh! It's that easy," said Hyacinth.

Gregory shrugged. "Sure, it's that easy. Hey, let's get out of here." He grabbed his jacket and headed toward the door. Then he winked and said, "I have to go and make those arrangements."

Hyacinth and May-Lynne shook their heads and laughed again.

"Wait. Before we leave, let's say goodbye to Auntie," said May-Lynne.

They walked back into Henrietta's room. When Sam's big hand knocked on the door, utter stillness surrounded them. They all waited, assured that Henrietta would answer, but she didn't. He slowly twisted the doorknob and opened the door. He peeked in.

Her back faced him. She sat in the wheelchair with her eyes closed. She was slightly slumped over in front of the mirror. Sam thought she was mumbling some words from the Bible, but she wasn't; she was praying.

"Auntie," said May-Lynne.

Henrietta slowly opened her eyes and spun her wheelchair around. Her eyes were dark. She looked tired. "So, you didn't leave, baby. I thought you left without saying goodbye to me."

May-Lynne walked toward the wheelchair and grabbed the handle. "No, we're still here. I would never leave without saying goodbye."

"Are you going to New Jersey too, May-Lynne?"

"Yes, Auntie, I am."

"That's good. I hope it all goes well."

"It will, Auntie," she said, softly kissing her forehead. "I love you."

"I love you too, baby."

"Goodnight, Aunt Henrietta," said Hyacinth and Lawrence.

They hugged her and then left the room. Sam and Patricia remained.

"Well Henrietta, we're leaving tomorrow. We're taking an early flight," said Patricia. Then she stroked her back. "Henrietta, I hold no grudges. I'm not angry with anyone. Life goes on. We learn from our mistakes, no matter how old we get." Looking at Sam, Patricia said, "Sam and I understand that now. God always forgives. We'll always be here for you—always."

Henrietta looked up at them. "I know, Pat." She smiled. "You better go now."

"Goodnight, Henrietta."

"Goodnight and have a safe trip," she said.

Sam and Patricia glanced back at her once again, and then cautiously closed the door.

They had unveiled their wrongdoing. Now it was time to mend the spirit of a family they damaged nearly thirty-eight years ago. They were prepared to face the consequences and whatever else that would unfold.

CHAPTER 36

On the road, they skimmed through the pile of yellowing adoption papers, trying to determine the whereabouts of the other children.

Once at his hotel room, Anthony stuffed his clothes into the stylish black suitcase Magnolia had given him on his birthday.

After packing, he called her. "Hello, Linda," he said, securing the overnight bag fastener. "Hey, this is Anthony. Is Magnolia there?"

Linda snapped her fingers to get Magnolia's attention. "Yes, she is. Hold on for just a moment, Anthony. I'll get her."

Magnolia rushed to the telephone. She had anticipated his call earlier but knew that he was most likely caught up getting more details from Hyacinth and her family.

"Hello!" she said.

"Hey, baby. How's everything up there?"

She crumpled her bathrobe. "Everything's good. How's everything down there?"

"I'll be in Newark late afternoon tomorrow. And . . . they're coming with me."

Magnolia was quiet. Her fingers suddenly went numb and she quit fidgeting with her robe. "Hyacinth's coming," she said.

"Yes. Is that okay with you?"

She had to think about it. If they were coming, then all of this was real. Anthony wasn't pulling her leg after all.

She smiled and said, "Yes, of course. That's wonderful, Anthony. What time are you arriving?"

"We'll be in Newark at three."

"Okay, then. Linda and I will be there. I can't wait to see you again, and I can't wait to meet her too."

"Magnolia."

"Yes?"

"Everyone else is coming too."

Her eyes widened. "Everyone? Like who?"

"Her entire family."

Magnolia's mouth dropped. "Are you serious, Anthony?"

"Yeah. I'm serious. If it's going to be too much to handle, I'll tell them not to come, but . . . they're very eager to meet you."

Linda, who was eavesdropping in the guest bedroom, broke in: "Her entire family! Anthony, you have a lot of nerve. You're going to give your wife a fucking nervous breakdown. Black men, I swear . . . they don't have any common sense whatsoever."

She shook her head. "Anthony, how many degrees do you have, huh? And still, you haven't learned a got damn thing."

Anthony eyes bulged, his front teeth lunged into his lower lip, and his spine tingled as he scrunched his fingers into a tight fist. "Linda, I know that's not you."

"If it's not me, then who the hell do you think it is?"

"Get the fuck off my telephone, Linda!"

"I'm not going anywhere. And why should I get off the phone? That's your fucking problem, Anthony. Magnolia lets you get away with too much shit. You're going to listen to me for once, brother man!"

Anthony pushed his suitcase off of the bed and clutched the handset tight. "I'm warning you, Linda. Get off or else," he said breathing heavily. "You know what? If you don't get off the fucking phone . . ."

He hesitated. "Better yet, get the fuck out of my house now. How dare you listen to my conversation with my wife and me? Who do you think you are? Got damn bitch!"

Magnolia had had enough. "Stop it! Please! The two of you, just shut up! This isn't necessary. I don't need this mess right now."

Anthony muttered, "The nerve of her eavesdropping on our conversation."

Twisting open a small bottle of red nail polish, Linda yelled, "That's right, Anthony! I'm eavesdropping. Your wife is extremely upset about this entire situation. Triplet sisters and all that stupid shit. And I really think you're making all of this up. I never knew you wanted to get into the entertainment business, Anthony. Huh, and I can't believe your black ass is still in Florida lollygagging and having a hell of a grand time. Who do you think you are—Magnum P.I.?"

Anthony's nostrils flared and his hands began to tremble. He knew that arguing would only upset Magnolia.

"Look, Linda, I'm still here because I'm trying to find out some important information. And, hey, you better watch your mouth. You can talk that way to your little boyfriends but you don't talk to me like that."

"I'll talk to your black ass any way I want, shit!" she said, poorly stroking the polish on her nails and blowing to dry them.

"If it was so important, why didn't you fly Magnolia down there?" she said. "You're probably screwing around and doing something you ain't got no business doing. Yeah, I knew you weren't no boy wonder!"

"You know what, Linda?"

Again, Magnolia intervened, "Stop it. Please! Linda, please hang up!"

Reluctantly, Linda slammed the telephone down and rushed outside to the balcony, where she lit a cigarette.

"She was eavesdropping. Was that the first time?" Anthony said. "Huh, the nerve of that fat ass bitch. I should have known better. Linda will never change."

There was silence. Magnolia had listened to this conversation many times before and she knew that neither Anthony nor Linda would ever conform—they would always be at each other's throat.

"I apologize, Leah. I shouldn't have said those things. Are you okay?" he said.

"I guess I'm fine. You and Linda really know how to communicate with one another," she said, nodding. "I'm fine. It's just that . . . the suspense is killing me, that's all. I can't wait until tomorrow. I've been trying to keep busy around the house."

She sat on the bed, crossed her legs, and began playing with her toenails. "I've been doing some house cleaning, cooking, and baking. Linda and I have been going crazy waiting."

"I'm sorry I didn't get back to you earlier. We visited a family member who had more information about the adoption."

"You did! Who was this person?"

"An aunt of Hyacinth's—her father's sister. She assisted with the illegal adoption and, apparently, she knew your birth mother very well."

Magnolia's heart raced.

"We have some important papers that may help us locate your other sister," said Anthony.

"Anthony, I also went through mother's things in the attic. The only thing I found was my birth certificate. I guess she really kept it a secret."

"Yeah, I guess so. How could she risk letting something like this leak out? Especially you, Miss CNN. She knew you would find it if you set your mind to it."

Magnolia giggled but realized what he said really wasn't amusing. She noticed the time on the clock. "It's getting late, baby. Get some rest and I'll see you tomorrow."

"I will. You get some rest too, okay."

"Oh, Anthony, you said you were going to tell me about the farm."

He snapped his fingers. "Oh, damn, I can't believe I forgot to tell you. That simpleminded Linda, she pissed me off and I totally forgot. So much has happened since we last talked. I feel like I'm a part of this entire thing. I feel like I'm one of the children."

He deeply breathed in and out. "I won't go into any more details, but I will only tell you this."

"Please, Anthony. I need to know."

"But, I'd rather wait until tomorrow."

"No, tell me now!"

"I'm afraid it will upset you," he said. Then he giggled. "Now, Linda would really want to kick my ass if I leave you in suspense, huh."

"I can handle it. Trust me, I can."

"All right then. Yes, baby, she had dreams about a farm ever since she was a child. She dreamt of children playing on a farm."

He hesitated. "Leah, have you had these dreams too."

"Yes."

"Why didn't you tell me?"

"I didn't think it was important. I thought it was my imagination . . . and besides, I thought the dreams had to do with my difficulties with mother and I know how you feel about that. You were so protective of her."

"Ah, baby. I wasn't siding with her. Promise me you'll never keep anything from me again."

Comforted by his words, she said, "I promise."

"Were there children present in your dreams?"

"Yes. Several, I think."

"There were six in her dreams."

Magnolia nearly choked. "Six children! You mean to tell me that—"

"Yes, you have five siblings."

"You're kidding me, right?"

"Nope. Your biological mother had six children—a set of triplets, which of course, included you, Hyacinth, and Rose. And you have two older brothers and an older sister."

Magnolia was silent again.

"Baby, are you there?" Anthony said.

"Yes, yes. Please, continue."

"I'm just making sure you're all right."

"I'm fine."

"Anyway, at the time you were taken away, your brothers were probably fourteen and eight. And your sister was around twelve.

Solomon was the oldest. We don't have the names of your other brother and sister. Hyacinth's aunt only mentioned Solomon."

"Solomon, huh? A biblical name," she muttered.

"Yeah."

She grabbed the telephone cord and squeezed it tight. "I have two older brothers. Solomon's the eldest."

"He would be about fifty-two today."

"Huh, fifty-two you say? Can you imagine that, baby?"

She pondered. "Got damn, Anthony. Shit! I have five brothers and sisters." She shut her eyes briefly, inhaled, and released a long gratifying breath. "Thank you, Lord," she whispered.

"All of this information was in the papers that Hyacinth's aunt gave to her father," Anthony said. "And guess what, baby? Your Aunt Alice—"

"And what about her? That old witch. I don't know who treated me worse—she or mother."

"Well, get ready for this."

Magnolia became weak at the knees.

"She was the secretary to the attorney who arranged this so-called adoption."

Magnolia's mouth lay agape in disbelief. Her hands trembled so, that she unwittingly peeled her fingernail away from her flesh. She felt no pain. It vanished every time her heart beat.

"What?" she said faintly. Suddenly she glanced down and noticed the torn fingernail on her lap. The oozing blood from her wounded finger soaked her bathrobe. She got up and ran into the bathroom, opened the medicine cabinet, and grabbed a Band-Aid and put it on her bleeding finger.

"That evil bitch," she said as tears fell. "It's no wonder I always disliked her."

"I'm so sorry, baby. Now you see why I wanted to wait until tomorrow. I'll show you the papers when I get home. Leah, please don't worry, everything will be fine. And I know you'll like her."

Wiping away the tears, she said, "Believe me, I'm not worried and I'm not mad. I'm a little nervous and confused, but the past is the past and I have to put it behind me and focus on my future. I can't wait to meet her. Anthony, my life is just beginning. I've waited a long time for this, haven't I? I deserve this. My family's coming home!" She tossed the wrapper in the air.

Anthony laughed with her. "Yes, baby! They're coming home!"

"I don't know what I'm going to say to her," she softly said. "Once I meet her—I'll know what to say."

"You will, baby. You will. Just take it easy." Then he said. "Baby, did Carl call?"

"Yes, he did. He and Brenda were by earlier this morning, asking me a million questions. I told them I didn't know much. They're really concerned. I told him that I was holding up pretty good. I said you were still in Florida getting more information. I'll call him tonight and let him know Hyacinth and her family will be accompanying you here tomorrow afternoon."

"Maybe they can come with you to the airport," said Anthony.

"I'd asked them to, but Carl thought it would be best if I met you alone. He thought I might need some privacy. You know Carl, he's so sweet and considerate. Anyway, Linda will be with me, so I will be fine."

"Yeah, that sounds just like my man Carl. Always looking out for you."

"Hey! He's always looking out for the two of us, remember that."

"Yeah, if you say so."

"Oh, he said his family will be here for the holidays, and he invited us over but he didn't know how everything would be at that time. I told him we'll just have to wait and see."

"That sounds great. I'm sure we'll be able to attend by then."

"I hope so. I haven't seen his family in a while."

"Hey, guess what?"

"What's that?"

"I talked to Billie and she's going crazy too. She's been calling on the hour. See what you've done? It's total chaos here."

Anthony laughed. "It'll all be settled tomorrow." He glanced at his watch. "Look, baby, I'm going to let you go. I love you, Magnolia."

"I love you too, sweetheart. Anthony, you miss me?"

"You know I do. I can hardly walk, it hurts that bad."

Chuckling, she said, "You're so full of it, Anthony. You crack me up sometimes. Goodnight, baby."

"Goodnight, my love."

CHAPTER 37

The Johnson's were expecting Gregory when he knocked hard on their front door at 10:00 a.m. sharp.

Enthusiastic yet restless, Gregory and Lawrence loaded the luggage into the van and soon were en route to the hotel.

The morning was calm, accentuated by a mere whisper of a breeze. Anthony sat on the edge of the water fountain out front nervously awaiting their arrival. The trickling water that wet his skin comforted him.

When the van pulled up, Gregory jumped out and quickly approached Anthony, helping him load his belongings into the vehicle.

At the airport, Anthony, along with the Johnsons and Gregory, stood in front of the check-in desk. He thought about Magnolia and what had occurred over the last few days. Their relationship suddenly flashed in front of him in sequence. Whenever he was down and out or consumed with emotions, thinking of Magnolia always smoothed things out within him.

He remembered the summers they spent at Carl and Brenda's summer home in Virginia. Magnolia loved the spacious countryside home. The vast green land stretched so far it appeared it met with the sky at some distant point. They always had a good time: horseback riding, boating on the lake, barbecuing, playing football games, talking politics, going on shopping sprees, and of course, watching Carl and Anthony's cooking competitions.

The times they vacationed with Carl, Brenda, Billie, and Linda in Europe were just as memorable. The volleyball games and bonfires on the beach, the picnics and traveling, were simply wonderful. Anthony treasured those times and even longed for them.

While he stood and the rest of the group sat, a tall thin woman bumped into Anthony. "Oh, I'm sorry."

"No problem," Anthony said.

Then the head airline attendant standing by a podium announced over the intercom, "May I have your attention please. Passengers seated in rows twenty-two and above may now board the aircraft."

"I guess this is it, guys," said Gregory.

"Yeah, I guess so," said Hyacinth, who nervously jerked her purse.

They all retrieved their airline tickets. Hyacinth glanced at her parents and smiled.

They boarded flight 1967, preparing themselves for an unforgettable yet unpredictable journey.

"What are you reading?" Anthony said looking at Hyacinth's novel.

Raising the book and passing it to Anthony, she said, "It's a mystery."

"Do you like mysteries?"

"Yes, I do," she said smiling. "I've always been fascinated with secrets and the unknown—books that are really deep. You know what I mean?"

Anthony nodded. "Yeah, I know what you mean. Deep, huh."

She giggled and said, "Yeah, books that make you think. Hey, how long has Magnolia been a literary agent?"

"Three years. She was a writer for the New York Sector. Before that, she wrote for a woman's magazine and was chief editor there for a number of years. Writing and reading tons of books has always been her love."

"Really."

"Yes. She wrote poetry for a while in college. I always loved her but her poetry made me love her even more. It had a simple way of making you feel good about yourself. Writing was an escape for Magnolia. I think it camouflaged the troubles she endured in life. It was her safe haven and took her to places she wanted to go," Anthony said. "And she did."

"That's wonderful. You know, Magnolia and I share similar interests. I like to write too, but I thought I wasn't all that great. So instead, I painted. It was my way of expressing myself. It was my escape."

Anthony smiled a peculiar smile.

"Anthony, don't get me wrong," she said. "My family is wonderful, but no family is perfect. I never felt abandoned or considered myself an outsider, but you know what, Anthony?" she said, rubbing his hand. "I always felt special. And those dreams of mine supported my way of thinking."

Anthony leaned forward trying to make out her words.

"And it seemed as though something was missing from my life," she said. "Like a hole that was never closed. You see, those feelings lingered inside me until now." She closed the book. "Huh, isn't that something?"

"Yes, life is strange indeed. When you think about it, we always search for a new perspective in life, especially when we're not content or when life throws us a curve ball. We challenge ourselves to find another approach, believing somehow that it would be better the second time around."

"You're absolutely right, Anthony. We spend a great deal of time wondering why things aren't right or why things don't go as planned. We devote too much attention to the future and how we want things to be, instead of being thankful for our experiences and accomplishments, scant though they may be. Many times, we don't find the answer and that drives us mad. Life was meant to be the way it is. You can't change it, you can only strengthen it."

"Exactly."

Hyacinth mediated for a moment. "I wonder what Rose does for a living."

They laughed nervously.

"Hey, maybe she's a writer too."

They laughed again.

"Really, I'm sure she's just as creative as you and Magnolia," said Anthony.

"Oh, I'm sure she is," Hyacinth said. Then she tugged on his sleeve. "Hey, what time is it?"

"It's two o'clock."

"Umm, one more hour," she said as she placed the book into her purse.

"Are you nervous?" Anthony said.

"Extremely. My heart is about to lunge out of my chest."

"Don't worry," Anthony said as he hugged her. "Your family is here. Imagine how Magnolia's feeling right about now?"

He nodded. "To tell you the truth, I'm a basket case myself. But you know what? I bet . . ." he said, giggling, "I bet . . . Linda has the network stations waiting for us at Newark."

"The networks! As in television networks!"

"Yeah, she probably called the major ones too. She has quite a few contacts there."

"Oh, no! I hope not!"

He held her hand, moving it back and forth. "I'm just kidding, Hyacinth."

"Anthony, don't kid like that!"

"I'm sorry," he said.

Then he leaned over and covered her with his husky upper torso. "It will all be cool. Don't worry." He glanced at her again and said, "Although, it wouldn't surprise me if she did contact someone."

He winked his eye. "Believe me, Linda is something else. You'll see!"

"She's the total opposite of Magnolia, isn't she?"

"You got that right," he said, rolling his eyes. "The total opposite."

"Just like Gregory and I. We're total opposites. But I love him to death. She's just looking out for Magnolia."

She patted his large thigh. "Trust me, she is."

"I know she is. It's just that . . . sometimes she handles things carelessly and can be deceitful too. She trifles with people's feelings. She's very selfish and, at times, immature. I believed her behavior stems from her many disastrous relationships with men. They really did a number on her," said Anthony with his finger pressed against his temple.

Just the thought of Linda brought on a headache. "They screwed up her head to the point where she's uncompromising, extremely defensive, and just plain evil. You know, I've never told anyone this, not even Leah."

Hyacinth's eyes bulged, her palms began to sweat, and her heart raced. "Please, you don't have to confess, not now," she said half-jokingly.

"Oh, I trust you."

Hyacinth's eyes stayed fixed on his as he began to divulge his opinion of Linda. He slowly wiped his mouth. "When we were in college, Linda dated this football star. She knew he had a girlfriend but she thought she was so fine that he would eventually leave her. Well, he didn't, and he used her like any man would have done in that situation. If you act like a whore, people will treat you like one."

Anthony took a sip of his soft drink. "Well, the guy screwed her brains out, day in and day out, like a nail in the wall. A few months later he grew tired of her but didn't have the nerve to end their so-called sexual relationship. So he asked me to break the news to her and I flatly refused. He got himself into this mess and he needed to get himself out of it."

Hyacinth nodded her head in agreement. "Ultimately he stopped calling her, but because I befriended him she continually inquired about him. I wouldn't give her any information on the guy. It was none of her business. Then one day Magnolia approached me after class and she was extremely upset about something. She said that Linda told her that I was cheating on her."

Hyacinth covered her mouth with her napkin. She couldn't believe what she was hearing. Anthony chuckled. "At first, I didn't understand why Linda would lie, but then I realized the guy must have really broken it off with her and somehow my name got caught up in the mess. When I confronted Linda, she denied everything."

Hyacinth's eyes swelled again. She wanted him to continue, but at the same time she wanted him to stop.

"I went to her dorm to talk to her. I approached her, not to lecture, curse, or embarrass her, but to let it be known that she needed psychological help. She really did."

Hyacinth laughed. "I also went there to say two things. I told her never to interfere with our relationship again and that this was the first and last time she would ever take her personal life out on Magnolia and myself. And if she did it again, I would break her neck."

When Hyacinth slowly reached for her purse, Anthony said bitterly, "I didn't go there to explain or defend myself. I went there to make those two things clear."

"Oh, no. What happened next?" said Hyacinth as she inserted a butterscotch candy into her mouth.

"Well, this girl really thought I was kidding and she really thought she was a tough cookie because when I turned around, she pulled out a pocket knife and jabbed it into my upper back."

"Oh, my God!" said Hyacinth. She shook her head in disbelief.

Anthony patted her hand. "Wait, listen to what happened next. It wasn't a harmful cut but it was bad enough. The blade didn't go through my flesh. But, I tell you Hyacinth, it was like I lost my mind. I threw that bitch on the floor and whipped the shit out of her."

He sort of chuckled again. "Hyacinth, it was as though I was beating another man. The more she hollered, the more I punched and choked her. I definitely wanted to do bodily harm. I beat her so bad she couldn't talk or walk. I remember her coughing and crying, struggling to breathe. Hyacinth, I tell you, I really lost it."

"Wow, that's deep, Anthony. What was she thinking?" said Hyacinth.

"I don't know. Never have I laid my hands on a woman. Never!

And you know what?"

"What?"

"She never said a word to Leah about that incident and neither did I. And she's never meddled with our relationship like that again. You see, that's the kind of person she is."

"She's really something else, huh."

"A downright bitch, that's all I can say. I think she was born that way. I try to keep my emotions within when it comes to Linda because I know how much Leah loves her. The sad part is she's a big influence on Leah. Boy, do I wish you had come into her life sooner."

Hyacinth smiled. "Do you and Magnolia have serious disagreements?" she said.

"Rarely. I have no doubt that Leah keeps our personal life from Linda, if you know what I mean. Sure, there are some things she discloses, but as far as the important stuff goes, she keeps it to herself. At least I hope she does. If she didn't we wouldn't be together today. She knows what and what not to communicate to Linda."

"I wished you hadn't told me that."

"Why not?"

She shrugged. "Because now I'm a little biased. You're such a lovable and kind person. It's hard to imagine anyone doing that to you."

She touched his shoulder. "Do you have a scar?"

He smiled and pointed toward the exact location of the wound. "Yeah, but it isn't extensive. Leah thinks I cut myself playing basketball. I told her I fell and scraped my back against some broken glass."

Hyacinth giggled. "Excellent cover up!"

He laughed along with her.

"It takes a while to get used to Linda," he said. "Sometimes you never do. At least I haven't. Leah believes she can be sweet but I couldn't disagree with her more."

CHAPTER 38

Magnolia frantically paced the living room, inspecting the furniture, the pictures on the wall, even the carpet, making sure everything was spotless. She wanted her guests to be comfortable when they arrived.

When she entered the kitchen, she ambled over to the stove and slowly turned on the oven and inserted a large cranberry baking dish inside. Then she opened the refrigerator door and studied the contents. Suddenly she ran into the bathroom near the den and nodded. Everything looked wonderful. Her home was beautifully decorated and she was ready to receive the sister who had been deliberately omitted from her life.

She felt fortunate but was still somewhat jittery.

"Hey, woman. Are you ready?" said Linda, who was leaning on the bathroom door.

"Yep, I'm ready." Then she brazed her teal-colored pants suit and said. "How do I look?"

"You look fine, girl. Let's get out of here before we hit traffic," Linda said.

"Okay."

Linda reconsidered her wording. "Leah, you look fantastic. That suit just brings out the best in you, girl. I really love that color."

Magnolia placed her hands on her hips. "Well, why didn't you say that when I asked you?"

Linda shrugged.

Magnolia's chin fell to her chest and she tugged on her blouse again, trying to arrange her outfit. *I wonder if she's wearing the same color*, she thought. Then she stood in front of the gold rectangular mirror and began to tease her hair some more. *I wonder if her hairstyle is the same as mine. Hmm, probably not—Anthony said her hair was shorter.*

Linda stomp her foot. "Woman, you're going to have a nervous breakdown before you get to the airport."

Magnolia cleared her throat. "Well, aren't you thinking about her?"

Linda frowned.

Playing with her loose curls, Magnolia said, "You know, like what she's wearing today. How does she talk? How tall is she? What—"

Linda stepped in front of Magnolia and gently stroked her fingers through her hair. "Yes, I'm somewhat curious. I guess I could think of a million things about her, but I need to see her face to face. I have to see her first before I can speculate."

She elbowed Magnolia. "Hey, and by the way, I want Bernard Brooks to write the book."

Magnolia grabbed Linda's arm and angrily said, "Linda, you didn't tell anyone, right?"

Linda giggled.

"Who did you call? I know you didn't call Bernard Brooks or Jamie at Channel 16." Squeezing Linda's arm firmly, she pressed her again. "Did you?"

"No, I didn't."

"Linda!" Magnolia said. She tossed the hair comb on the basin's counter and angrily marched into the kitchen and lowered the oven's temperature.

Linda quickly followed her. "Look, Leah, you know I wouldn't do that to you. I know how you get."

Bending over the counter, she turned to face Magnolia. "Trust me. I wouldn't do that to you, girl." She hugged Magnolia and kissed her. Then she moved her head to the window and whispered, "I wanted to, though. And . . . I was really tempted."

All Magnolia could do was huff and stare at her with anger.

"But . . . I knew you had asked me not too," said Linda.

"I can't believe you, Linda," Magnolia said, taking a quick look into the oven.

Linda reached into the refrigerator and grabbed a slice of cucumber out of the salad bowl. "Don't you want this documented?" she said, munching on the vegetable. "This is a special occasion."

Magnolia rolled her eyes.

Steadily chewing, Linda carried on. "This is very rare, you know. There are not too many people in the world who get a chance to meet their missing sibling. The world should know, Leah." She aimed her finger at Magnolia. "Now . . . you see . . . if I were you—"

"It's not you, okay?" said Magnolia, slamming the oven door.

"Okay, okay! I'm sorry."

Magnolia nodded as she walked toward the front door.

Then Linda opened the refrigerator door again and grabbed another slice of cucumber. Biting into it she yelled, "Okay, let's get on the road."

She tapped Magnolia's shoulder. "By the way, did you call Billie?"

Standing at the front door, Magnolia said, "Yes. She's going to try to fly out here soon. But if she's unable to, she will definitely be here for Christmas. She really wants to meet Hyacinth and her family."

"Will Carl and Brenda meet us at the airport?" said Linda.

Slightly frustrated, Magnolia said, "No, they won't be there. They thought it was best for me emotionally if they weren't around."

Linda hopped into the passenger's side of the Expedition and immediately lowered the window. She flapped down the sun visor, stared into the mirror, and wiped her face with a tissue. "That doesn't make any sense to me. But, Carl is a little strange anyway—with his fine ass."

Magnolia moved her hand to the side of the car and angled

the side view mirror upward. "Linda, can you please move your mirror up some more—so I can see?"

"That brother knows he's stacked liked that. Damn, and has a juicy ass," said Linda.

Then she frowned. "But he's a little too intellectual for me."

Magnolia nodded her head and cranked up the car. "Yeah, I always knew you had a crush on him."

As Magnolia began to drive the car, Linda flipped the sun visor up and laughed. "A crush! Girl, I had more than that, and besides, I wasn't the only one who had a crush."

"What? I know I didn't hear you correctly."

"Yes, you did, girlfriend," said Linda pressing down on her clothes.

Waving her hand, Magnolia said, "Linda, please, don't come into my car talking that stupid nonsense."

Linda shrugged and turned, glancing at the stores that lined Route 4. "Okay, I won't."

Then she turned back to Magnolia and sneered. "Like you didn't know."

Magnolia pounded her hand on the steering wheel, causing the horn to blow. "Shut up, Linda!" Suddenly she swerved the vehicle onto the shoulder of the highway and stopped in front of Kohl's. "Listen, before we go any further, I just want to say one thing." She aimed her finger at Linda. "Just one thing, Linda."

Linda rolled her eyes. "And what's that, Magnolia?"

Magnolia's breathing was heavy and it seemed as though the blood in her body suddenly rushed to her head. She wanted to gag but instead she inhaled and swallowed hard, regaining her composure.

Then she turned toward Linda and gazed into her eyes and as quietly as possible, said, "Look, Linda—I love Carl and Brenda. I love you, too. As a matter of fact, I respect all of you. I really do. And, I know how you can be at times, Linda. Especially with men."

Linda lowered her head and stretched her arm toward the radio control knobs and callously turned on the radio. Her head bopped back and forth to the sound of Whitney Houston's soft voice.

Magnolia immediately turned the volume down and yelled, "Look at me, Linda! I know you better than you know yourself. But please, not Carl. Okay?"

Magnolia waved her hand. "You can have any man in this world, but not Carl. You're a better person than that, Linda." She hit her hand on the steering wheel again. "Are you listening to me?"

Linda faced Magnolia. "I hear you."

"Well, I hope you're listening because . . . men will be men. And—I know—women will be women. I know that and you know that. I'm not a child. Yeah—you're right—I have eyes too."

Explaining herself, she grew very animated. "Sure, we all look, we all have desires, and we all dream of being with someone we've fantasized about or someone we've seen in the movies or someone we work with. No one is perfect, Linda. Not even me. It's a weakness I think we all possess, especially when things aren't going the way we want them to."

Her eyes never left Linda. "But that doesn't mean we cross the line, Linda!" Magnolia was motionless. "I know he wouldn't do it and I pray to God you have better sense to do likewise."

"Are you finished?"

"Yes!" said Magnolia, who slowly edged the vehicle back onto the highway.

Linda said softly, "You know, Nordstrom's and Lord & Taylor are having a big sale starting today."

Giggling, Magnolia said, "Yeah, I saw the ads in the paper on Wednesday. I could use a pair of red boots, but with everything that's going on, I don't think I'll get the chance to stop by. I'll try to sneak over there sometime this week. I would like to get some Christmas shopping out of the way too."

"Yeah, that's what I'm going to do. The sale is going on through Wednesday," Linda said.

Magnolia suddenly jumped up. "Ooh, turn the volume up."

She snapped her fingers. "Oh, yeah, this is my part. Yeah, *you give good love...*"

A wide smile overtook Linda's face as she increased the volume. They sang together. "*So good... take this heart of mine into your hands... baby, you give good love...*"

* * *

"Remember turn off at exit 8B," Linda said as Magnolia drove through Newark.

"No, it's exit 8A. I've been driving this route for years," snapped Magnolia.

Linda rolled her eyes. "Okay, whatever you say. You're always right."

Magnolia second-guessed herself and followed Linda's advice. She began to turn off on exit 8B. Then she realized she made a mistake.

"Oops! You were right," said Linda.

"You see? We missed the exit because of you. Damn it! Now I'm going to have to circle around again. I hate that shit. Why did I listen to you, Linda? Why?"

Refusing to circle around again, Magnolia reversed the vehicle and backed up to exit 8A, ignoring the sound of blaring horns.

Linda patted Magnolia's leg. "Boy! You are nervous. Calm down sister, we'll get there on time."

Magnolia began to laugh. "This is what happens when I don't pay attention."

"It's not your fault. I sure thought it was exit 8B. See, that's why I hate coming here, it's so confusing."

At Newark International Airport they parked in Lot C.

Glancing at her watch, Linda said, "See, we're on time. Shoo, we're even half an hour early."

For a moment there was silence as the two of them stood in the parking lot. Magnolia stared at a young mother putting her infant into a car seat. She smiled ever so softly and then grabbed Linda's hand. "Let's pray."

They lowered their heads. "Heavenly Father," said Magnolia. "I ask you for strength this afternoon because I really need it right now. I pray that you guide my sister and I in the right direction, Lord. I pray that nothing but good will come out of this situation. I am blessed to be here, this special time. And I am especially thankful."

Linda peeked opened her left eye, taking a glimpse of Magnolia and hoping that no one else was looking at them.

"I have a beautiful husband and wonderful friends. Lord, I thank you for sending Anthony, Linda, and Billie to me. For many years, they've been by my side every step of the way. You gave me a family, Lord. And now more is on the way. Thank you, Lord. Lord, if the rest of my family is somewhere in the world, please let them know that I will never lose hope or give up my efforts to find them. Let them know that they are in my thoughts and prayers and that I love them. Protect them, Lord. Amen."

"Amen," said an embarrassed Linda.

CHAPTER 39

They entered the airport at a leisurely pace. Magnolia was so nervous her hands began to sweat. Linda reached inside her purse and pulled out a tissue and handed it to Magnolia, who gently wiped her hands.

After walking past security and through the sliding doors heading toward concourse, Linda pointed to the restroom near an ATM machine. "Leah, look over there, by the ladies restroom. It's Billie!"

Magnolia strained her eyes and noticed a woman wearing a gray dress marked with beige streaks. "Oh my God, it is her! She did come and I don't believe it!" she screamed.

They waved their hands and yelled across the wide open space. "Hey, Billie! Over here!"

Briskly, they walked over. Billie hugged the two of them.

"I can't believe you're here!" shouted Magnolia.

Billie took a deep breath. "I changed my schedule, just for you, babe! I couldn't miss this for the world!"

Then Billie turned to Linda. "Hello, Ms. Linda. Long time no see, girlfriend."

"Hey, girl. Give me a hug."

Caressing Magnolia's shoulders, Billie said, "So, how are you feeling, sweetie?"

Trembling, Magnolia said, "Can't you feel me? I'm shaking like an earthquake."

Billie smiled. "Who wouldn't be under these circumstances?" She rubbed Magnolia's shoulders again. "Just take a deep breath and relax."

Clutching Magnolia's hand, Billie said, "You see, everything will be fine." She looked around the concourse, staring at the people. "Hey, where's Carl and Brenda?"

"Oh, they couldn't make it," Magnolia said.

Linda turned her head away and rolled her eyes.

"Never mind Linda, Billie. They didn't want to overwhelm me," said Magnolia. "You know Carl and Brenda. They thought it would be better for me if they weren't here."

Reaching out to Magnolia, Billie blurted out, "I understand. Hey, we're here and that's all that matters."

"You're absolutely right. So, how are your mom and dad?" said Magnolia, evasively.

"Dad's doing better. He has bad days and he has good days. Mostly bad, though. I don't know how much more time he has left. The last stroke really took a toll on him. His body is extremely weak." She pointed to Magnolia. "But, I told them about Hyacinth and they were extremely excited. They wanted me to tell you hello and that they love you and miss you dearly."

"Oh, I miss them too."

"Billie, what time is it?" said Linda.

"It's two-forty."

"I'm going over to the coffee shop. What would you guys like to drink?"

"I'll have a cup of the hazelnut coffee. No sugar, just crème," said Billie.

"I'll have a regular coffee. Light and sweet, please," said Magnolia.

Magnolia and Billie sat down on the semi cushion seats. They faced the door that opened to the walkway that connected to the aircraft.

Billie laughed. "So, this is it, huh? I'm surprised Linda didn't call Montel or Oprah."

Feeling panicky, Magnolia said, "Oh please, let's not go there.

She was tempted to call someone, believe me she was."

Billie roared. "That's Linda for you."

Magnolia smiled. "Yeah, that's Linda, all right." She paused. "You know Billie, life's really been good to me. Even after all I've gone through with mother. Sometimes I was angry but I never complained because I had you, Linda, and Anthony. That's what kept me focused. You guys encouraged me and so I believed."

Billie turned to Magnolia. "In what?"

"I believed in myself. I believed that there was a brighter future for me. I believed that I would overcome the pain. I knew I could get through the bad times."

Billie pinched her cheek. "You are the most determined and positive person I've ever met." She waved her hands. "You may disagree with me but in spite of all the anguish, you were always in control, and you were always so damn calm, cool, and collected. I wish I possessed those qualities."

Magnolia patted her on the leg. "Oh, come on."

"It's true."

They laughed.

"Did you talk to Anthony?" said Billie.

"Yes, he called last night. He's not going to believe you're here."

"How is he doing?"

"As good as can be expected. Initially he was shocked too. Now he's so intrigued with it all, he has been busy finding out more information about my adoption and my other siblings. I really miss him. I know we both can't wait until this day is over with. It's all been so overwhelming."

Billie stared at Magnolia strangely.

"Don't get me wrong," Magnolia said. "It's the waiting and anticipation that's killing me. This day has to pass, or else I'll have a nervous breakdown."

Billie held her hand. "It will. But this day is so special. Let it take its course and go with the flow. Enjoy the moment because you really don't know what it's like to be alone."

Startled, Magnolia said, "Billie, are you talking to me? Oh, yes . . . I know what it's like."

Billie shook her head. "I keep forgetting you were an only child too." She rubbed her bulky leather purse. "At least you had Linda in your life. She was there ever since you two were kids."

Billie patted her chest. "I had no one. Mom and Dad were good to me but that wasn't enough. They sheltered me from the rest of the world. I don't know why but they did. I always wondered if it was because of Mom's family and their hatred of Dad or from the pressure they received from society. I haven't a clue. They sheltered me and immersed themselves in their many businesses."

She clutched Magnolia's hand. "I really thank God we met, Magnolia. I love you."

They embraced. "I love you, too."

Linda returned, struggling with three large cups of coffee. She handed them to Billie and Magnolia.

Sniffing the coffee, Billie said, "Mmm, this smells so good. Thanks, Linda."

Sipping her light, sweet prize, Magnolia said, "It tastes good, too."

"You're welcome," Linda said grinning. She knew a simmering cup of tasty coffee would make their afternoon and cut through the thick tension.

Billie took a sip. "You know, when I told Dad about Hyacinth, he said something really strange."

Magnolia rested her cup on a metal table not far from her. "Oh really, what did he say?"

"He said he was happy for you and that—" She looked down at the young child who was staring at her. "Oh, I'll tell you later."

"Okay."

Billie tossed her hands in the air. "Look, their plane has arrived."

Slowly they stood and held hands, terrified. The sound of their heartbeats was powerful. Magnolia was edgy and she nearly fell back into the chair. Her hands began to shake vigorously. Soon there was wetness under her arms and on her face and neck. She felt dizzy and began to gasp for air. "I can do this," she muttered.

"Yes, you can," Billie said softly. "We are here for you. Just breathe in and out. Relax."

Feeling her chest, Magnolia said, "I'm scared."

Linda hugged her. "I'm scared too but it will be fine. Just fine."

Linda's eyes scanned the terminal expectantly.

"What or who are you looking for, Linda?" Magnolia irately said.

"No one."

Magnolia dropped her hands to her hips. "Are you sure?"

Linda laughed.

"I'm serious, Linda. I hope you didn't contact anyone."

"I didn't contact anyone." Then Linda looked through her bag. "Oh, shoo, I forgot my camera."

Billie passed over her large purse to Linda. "Don't worry, I have my camcorder inside. Here, take it—you're good at this stuff."

"I can't believe you guys," Magnolia said smiling.

"Because we love you, that's why we're doing this," said Linda.

CHAPTER 40

In the plane . . .

Anthony stared at Hyacinth as he unbuckled his seat belt. "Well, we're here. Are you ready?"

"Um hmm," she mumbled, slowly releasing her seatbelt.

Gregory frowned and massaged his tired shoulder with his left hand. He stood and reached for his duffel bag in the baggage compartment above. "This was a long flight—too long."

"Gregory, you've been out here before. This isn't anything new for you," Hyacinth said.

He leaned over and kissed her. "Yeah, I know. I say the same thing every time. But, my back and legs are aching, baby. And they sure don't feed you good either. I'm starving."

Fed up with his complaints, Hyacinth smacked his back and yelled, "You're complaining about comfort at a time like this. Can't you see I'm going crazy here?"

"I'm sorry, honey." He hugged and kissed her again. "I can't believe I'm thinking about myself at a time like this."

He hurled the bag over his shoulder and grabbed her hand. "Come on, let's go meet your sister."

Once the aircraft's door opened, a wall of hot air burst in. They turned their heads away from the door as they moved forward, trying to escape the uncomfortable layer of air.

One by one, the passengers slowly exited the plane. Meanwhile, Magnolia, Billie, and Linda tiptoed closer to the door to get a glimpse of the disembarking people. But Anthony and Hyacinth could not be seen.

Then they observed a group of three tall men dressed in athletic apparel approaching the doorway. Billie and Linda stretched their necks, hoping to catch a glimpse of Anthony and Hyacinth, but the view was blocked by the three big men who casually walked in front of them.

Linda, the tallest of the three women, muscled her way forward and shouted, "Oh my, God!" She aimed her finger toward the three men. "Here they come!"

"Where?" Billie said. "I can't see them."

Pointing to the three men again, Linda yelled, "See? There they are. Behind the men."

Pulling Linda's arm, Magnolia said, "Do you see her? Is it really them?"

"Yes, Yes, I see them," Linda exclaimed. She ecstatically jumped up. "Oh my God! Oh my God! Magnolia, she does look like you. It's her. Oh my God!"

Furious, Billie waved her hand at Linda. "Of course she does, Linda! They are identical."

Suddenly all of the people waiting for relatives and friends turned toward the three of them and stared. Then they looked at the people exiting the plane. They continued doing this until their eyes located Hyacinth. Their mouths hung wide in disbelief and they whispered amongst themselves.

Straining her neck, Billie said, "I don't see anyone that resembles Magnolia. Oh wait . . . wait . . . there's Anthony." Slowly she clamped her hand to her chest and screamed, "Oh, Jesus!"

Jittery, Magnolia said, "What? What? Please tell me."

They stood motionless. Magnolia's breathing and heartbeat slowed down. She firmly clutched Billie and Linda's hands.

Suddenly a petite, muscular Latino woman who sported a short pageboy hairstyle raced toward the three men. When one of the men, an athletically-looking Caucasian man with a polished beard, leaned forward to greet her, Hyacinth's face appeared.

"It's her!" screamed Magnolia. "It's her!"

"Ooh," said Linda quivering. She quickly pulled out the camcorder. "I got 'em! I got 'em all! Don't worry, I got 'em!" she screamed, nearly dropping the device.

Magnolia placed her hands to her mouth and goose bumps covered her body. She cried, "My sister. I don't believe it, I have a sister."

The crowd of spectators slowly withdrew, allowing Hyacinth, Anthony, and Gregory to pass. Hyacinth's legs trembled while Anthony and Gregory held her by the arms.

She immediately recognized Magnolia but stood shock-still. The noiseless room terrified her and she fell. Anthony and Gregory quickly picked her up. As they assisted her, she mumbled, "Mag . . . Mag . . . Magnolia."

Magnolia rushed to her. Hyacinth's hands spread out for her sister. Magnolia grabbed her and they both sobbed, glued to each other for minutes. Then Magnolia freed herself from Hyacinth and began to softly kiss her face. Then she touched it, feeling her beauty, her essence.

Hyacinth studied Magnolia and smiled. She whispered into Magnolia's ear, "I have another sister."

Weeping, Magnolia said, "Yes, you do." She looked up and said, "Thank you, Lord."

Magnolia held onto Hyacinth again and rocked her slowly. The connection felt familiar, just like the bond she shared with Linda and Billie. She held her tight. Magnolia's mouth started to move but she was tongue-tied. Suddenly she muttered, "I'll never let you go. You hear me? Never."

After recognizing Billie, Anthony said, "I'm so glad you're here, Billie. It's so good to see you."

She hugged him. "Good to see you too, Anthony."

Magnolia began to smooth out Hyacinth's hair. "I told Anthony I wouldn't believe it until I'd met you."

Hyacinth laughed. "Well, do you believe him now?"

"Yes!" she shouted. "Yes!"

All eyes were on the two of them. Passersby continued to gather around them and whisper. One elderly woman with a striking pink trench coat said, "Oh my, twins!"

Another gentleman said, "Yeah, looks like a reunion of some sort. You know, the lost and found kind."

Smiling, the elderly woman's husband said, "That's so wonderful. I remember when Arnold Stance met his brother and sister for the first time after fifty years."

"Oh, yes, I remember," said the woman. "And, it was on that show."

"Yes, that's right," said her husband.

Grabbing her arm, Hyacinth pulled Magnolia toward her family and said while wiping away tears, "Magnolia, I want you to meet my mother and father, Sam and Patricia Johnson."

Magnolia's throbbing eyes blinked a few times before she could respond. She sniffled and said, "It's a pleasure to meet you both." She extended an unsteady hand.

Patricia responded first. "So nice to meet you, Magnolia."

Then she nervously stared at Sam, who stood frozen, inspecting an exact copy of his first child. When he hesitated for a moment, Patricia jerked his arm and he promptly extended his hand. "A pleasure to meet you."

Sensing his uneasiness, Magnolia smiled and said, "Likewise, Mr. Johnson."

Walking her over to May-Lynne and Lawrence, Hyacinth said, "And this is my sister May-Lynne and brother Lawrence."

Trying to keep from breaking down and crying, Magnolia smiled again and softly said, "Hello, how are you? It's a pleasure to meet you."

Sobbing, May-Lynne mumbled, "It's so nice to—"

She stumbled and Lawrence quickly caught her. After clutching her arm, he finished what she started to say: "It's so nice to finally meet you, Magnolia."

Tears began to fall once again and Magnolia stepped forward and hugged May-Lynne.

Then Gregory assumed an awkward look. Hyacinth noticed his disappointed expression and giggled. "Oh, I'm sorry, honey. Magnolia, this is my fiancé Gregory."

"Hello, Gregory," said Magnolia.

"Hello, Magnolia. I've heard so much about you."

Still shivering, Magnolia smiled. For a second, she was speechless. To judge from her appearance she was composed, but actually she was overwhelmed and extremely nervous. She turned toward Billie and Linda. "Everyone, these are Billie and Linda, my girlfriends."

"Oh, hello. Nice to meet you," they said.

"A pleasure to meet you," said Billie and Linda.

Gregory commented while biting his lip, "Hey, for a moment there, I thought you were going to say 'sister.' Billie looks a lot like you too."

Everyone glanced at Billie again and chuckled.

"Everyone says that, including my Mom," said Anthony.

Magnolia took a deep breath and excitedly spread her hands apart. "Welcome to New Jersey!"

Laughing, they all answered, "Thank you."

"We're so excited to be here," Gregory said.

Caressing Hyacinth's back, Magnolia said, "You must be restless and hungry."

"I know I am," said Gregory. Hyacinth poked his side.

Magnolia chuckled. "Men, they're all the same. Aren't they?"

Hyacinth laughed and nodded in agreement.

"Well then, let's get the luggage into the cars and head home. I prepared a nice meal," said Magnolia.

"You didn't have to do that," said Patricia.

"Oh, I wanted too."

"Do you live near here?" Hyacinth said.

"No, we live about thirty-five minutes away."

"And that's . . . Alpine, right?"

"Yes."

They all rushed toward the baggage claim area while Magnolia and Hyacinth held each other's hands.

"We have so much to talk about," Magnolia whispered, jiggling Hyacinth's arm.

"I know. I wrote plenty down in the airplane. Didn't want to forget anything. I didn't know what to say first or how to say it."

Chuckling, Magnolia said, "Don't worry. We have plenty of time. So much time now."

Hyacinth smiled and thought, *We sure do. Given the fact that my brainy fiancé over there didn't book any return flights.* Tapping Magnolia's shoulder, Anthony said, "Do we have enough cars, baby?"

"Yes. I brought the Expedition."

"And I rented a van," announced Billie.

"Good. We definitely have enough room then," he said.

The teardrops had smudged Magnolia's makeup. She lifted a compact from her purse and began applying another coat of foundation and lipstick. Cuddling Hyacinth, she said, "I can't believe I have a sister. I really can't."

Suddenly anguish etched itself across her face and tears rolled down her cheeks. "I can't lose you again. No one or nothing will ever come between us, Hyacinth."

Hyacinth started to cry. "Nothing," she said.

Anthony strolled over to Magnolia and gently touched her shoulder. "It's okay, baby. She's not going anywhere." Rubbing her neck and back, he said, "It's okay."

Hyacinth squeezed her hand too, consoling her. "I'm glad to be here. Don't worry, Magnolia, I'll never leave you."

Gregory attempted to ease the emotional atmosphere. "Hey, you guys both have on the same colors. A coincidence or what?"

Hyacinth turned to Anthony and said, "I knew we had more than writing in common."

Magnolia's eyes widened with surprise. "Do you write?"

"Well, I like to but I'm not a great writer. Not like you. My words usually end up in a portrait."

Somewhat confused, Magnolia crossed her eyes.

"I'm a painter," added Hyacinth.

Magnolia cheerfully responded, "Oh, okay. I get it."

Anthony and Gregory burst into laughter.

At the baggage area, Linda winked at Anthony and glanced at Gregory. "Mr. Lewis, why don't you two strong men go and get the luggage and we'll get the cars."

Anthony avoided looking at Linda and said, "Fine, Linda." He pointed to the outdoor driveway. "Just pull the cars up here."

"I see they want to do some girl talk, huh," said Gregory.

"Yeah. Wait until we get home—it's going to be non-stop, especially if Linda's there."

Leaning over, Sam said, "I expected this."

Lawrence said, "I don't mind it at all. I can't believe my big sister is a triplet. And, I actually met another of the three. It's just so hard to believe."

They all nodded.

Gripping a large piece of luggage and tossing it onto the floor, Lawrence said, "You're right, Gregory, they look alike."

"Who, Magnolia and Billie?" Anthony said.

"Yeah, man," said Lawrence.

"Yeah, my mother swears by it, too. I think they've been around each for so many years that they began to favor one another."

As they talked, Anthony led the way to the curbside, where the cars were parked. Gregory, Anthony, and Lawrence loaded the luggage.

"Who's going to ride in what car?" Anthony said.

Sticking her head out of the Expedition, Linda pointed her finger. "The men will ride in Billie's van and the women will ride in here."

Disgusted with Linda's selfish attitude, Anthony shook his head and softly said, "Whatever, bitch."

"What? What was that, Anthony?" Linda said.

Grinning, Anthony said, "That sounds great, Linda." He rolled his eyes at her. "We'll all ride in Billie's van."

Linda said, "I didn't think it would be a problem." Then she turned to Billie and yelled, "Hey, girl are you ready?"

"No, go ahead. We have a few more bags to put in the van."

"Are you sure?" said Magnolia.

"We're fine. It's not like we don't know how to get to your

house."

With her eyes fixed on Lawrence's broad shoulders and well-built upper body, Linda started the ignition, waved her hand at the men, and pulled off.

Tugging on Anthony's jacket, Lawrence whispered, "Man, that Linda sure got a behind on her. I must admit, she's built."

Anthony grinned. "Yeah, she's built all right, but she's not worth the aggravation. She's a got damn pain in the ass. That woman can cause any man mental anguish."

Lawrence laughed quietly.

Anthony's eyes slowly rolled over to Lawrence while he dipped his hands into his pants pockets and pulled out a ten-dollar bill for parking. "Yeah, laugh now, cause you'll cry later if you fuck with her."

CHAPTER 41

The drive home...

Linda didn't waste any time with her inquisition. She asked Hyacinth a thousand questions. "So Hyacinth, how did you meet Anthony again? Was it at your husband's club?"

"Oh, no. It was at the hotel Gregory manages," said Hyacinth. "In the restaurant."

Observing her body movements and manners through the rearview mirror, Linda continued probing. "Oh, okay. It was at the restaurant. Your husband must make a handsome salary, huh."

"He does well," Hyacinth said, crossing her eyes at May-Lynne.

Magnolia concentrated during the ride home. She turned and looked at Hyacinth and smiled. She sat content and was grateful that a piece of her life story, thirty-eight years of it, had fallen into place. She leaned her head against the plush car seat and meditated. *See mother? God brought her back, and one by one they all will come home. He protected them. Mother, I don't hate you. No one is to blame.*

Suddenly her tears didn't feel heavy. They were now rejoicing tears, soothing tears. Soon they delicately touched her face and she was happy, holding no more resentment. Her life would begin anew.

This is a beautiful feeling, she thought. *Thirty-eight years of sepa-*

ration, thirty-eight years of yearning, and thirty-eight years of finding that place in my heart that I've been searching for. At last, I've found it.*

Ignoring Linda's prying, Hyacinth said, "The plane ride was very smooth."

But Linda was determined to get an answer. "Umm, they usually are. So, Gregory's doing pretty good then."

Hyacinth quietly snickered and gave in. "I guess you can say that."

"And what is it that you do for living?" Linda said.

"I own a medium-size employment agency specializing in clerical and accounting temporary and permanent job placement. I'm there half of the time. Most of the time I'm at home painting and creating pottery."

"Oh, really?"

Annoyed with Linda's prying, Magnolia whacked her with a pencil. "Linda, what are you trying to accomplish here? Are you going to write a book or something?" said Magnolia.

Grinning. "Maybe," she said.

"Welcome to Linda's world, Hyacinth. Get used to her," said Magnolia.

Reflecting on what Anthony had told her of Linda, Hyacinth said, "Oh, I will." Her eyes cut toward Linda's direction and she grinned. "She's just interested, that's all. I understand."

Suddenly Hyacinth drifted into a peaceful stage, thinking about the day. She glanced at Magnolia and a slight look of concern crossed her face. She thought, *Umm, all of this is surely a dream come true. I wonder what it would have been like to grow up with her, with them both?*

She rubbed her chin with her slender finger. *Huh, with all of them—all six of us—we probably drove our poor mother insane.*

She snatched a tissue from her purse and wiped her nose. *Look at me—I'm choking up,* she thought. *I guess it will be a while before I can really get used to it.*

Then she glanced at May-Lynne and thought, *I'm sorry, little sis. You know I love you, but I do wonder. Would I have been the same person I am today if I had grown up with them? So many questions, yet not enough answers.*

She grabbed May-Lynne's hand and caressed it. *Aunt Henrietta what were you thinking? Were you in your right mind? You took away my life. A life I had a right to live.*

She gazed out the window. *Okay, Hyacinth, calm down. When you're angry, you can't think. Remember, stay positive and focus on the future. In order to move ahead, you must forgive.*

She gazed at Magnolia again, closed her eyes and shook her head. *Look at her. She has the same mannerisms as me. She even talks like me.*

Suddenly she burst into laughter and May-Lynne whispered into her ear, "Hyacinth, what's so funny?"

"Oh, nothing. I'm just thinking about something that happened years ago."

May-Lynne grinned with her. "What?"

"It's nothing, really." Then she winked at May-Lynne. "There has to be a reason for all of this."

She gazed out the window at the beaming sun above.

Linda drove north on Route 4 near the Garden State Plaza Mall. Magnolia directed Hyacinth and May-Lynne's attention to the left side of the highway. "Look over to your left. That vacant lot used to be Alexander's—a large retail store that went out of business a few years ago. My mom and I shopped there when I was a kid."

"I wonder who owns the property now," said Linda.

"I don't know," Magnolia said. She pressed her hand on the remote control and lowered the window, providing a better view of the construction site.

"Oh, and there was this massive mural on the top left-hand corner of the building. I think it was a picture of the world. It's shape was odd. Different. Too bad they've torn it down."

"It sounds like it was a beautiful piece of art," said Hyacinth.

"Yeah, it was."

"Who's work was it?" said Hyacinth.

"I have no idea," Magnolia said. "You know, I've been living here all my life, driven past it probably several times a day, and never thought about the artist."

Magnolia pointed at the right side of the highway. "That's the Garden State Plaza Mall. It's a really nice mall. They remodeled it and added many new stores. One day, I'll take you all there." She laughed. "Oh, by the way, my pastime is shopping."

They all laughed.

"Gregory can't keep me away from the stores in Miami Beach," Hyacinth said.

"How far do you live from here, Magnolia?" said Hyacinth.

"Less than twenty minutes."

"Wow, this is pretty convenient."

Linda and Magnolia grinned and both said, "Very convenient."

"Where do you live, Linda?" said May-Lynne.

She turned toward May-Lynne and winked. "With Magnolia and Anthony."

They all laughed again.

"Just kidding. I live in Mahwah."

"Mahwah—where is that?" said Hyacinth.

"You don't want to know. It's quite a ways from here. Going north on Route 17," she said, pointing toward the Route 17 entrance ramp.

"So, do you stay over at Magnolia's quite often?" said Hyacinth.

"Yeah, when Anthony's away," Linda said giggling. "But, seriously, Magnolia and I own a brownstone in the city. So, our agency is there and an apartment. I stay there sometimes."

"That's pretty cool."

"Yeah, Magnolia and I refurbished it about three years ago. You have to see it."

"That would be nice. I've never been to New York before."

"Well then, Magnolia and I will have to take all of you over there and have some fun!"

"Great!" said Hyacinth.

When Linda pulled into the driveway, she noticed an unfamiliar car in front of the house. "Whose brand spanking new Mercedes is that?" Linda said.

"Carl and Brenda are here!" Magnolia said. "He bought it for Brenda recently."

"Good for Brenda," Linda said. "She's got a good man."

Magnolia shook her head at Linda and smacked her lips and began to open the car door.

"Who are they?" said Hyacinth.

"Oh, I'm sorry. Carl and Anthony are business partners and Brenda is his wife. We've been great friends for many years. I'm so glad they're here," said Magnolia. "Our housekeeper, Jean, must have let them in."

A tall slender woman pulled the draperies back to see who had arrived. Then a handsome, chestnut skin-toned man with a clean-cut goatee leaned over her and looked out. Unable to get a clear view of the passengers, they decided to go outside and meet them. They walked toward the cobblestone driveway.

Brenda held Carl's hand and whispered, "It's all right."

A numb feeling overwhelmed him. He nervously said, "I don't think I can go through with this."

"Yes, you can. I know you can. We're both going to go through it. We have to be strong for Magnolia. She needs us now," whispered Brenda.

Brenda squeezed Carl's hand again. "I'm here, don't worry."

Smiling from ear to ear, Magnolia stepped out of the car and rushed toward them. "You came! I knew you would," she said as she embraced them.

"Jean let us in. I hope that was okay," said Carl.

Patting his shoulder, Magnolia said, "Of course it was okay. You know that."

"We brought some food. We knew you were going to have your hands full this evening," said Brenda. She kept glancing at the vehicle. "We're not going to stay long because . . . you . . . you need to spend some time with your sister and her family."

Magnolia was disappointed. "Oh, no. Don't leave, stay a while. Please."

"Okay, we'll stay just a little while, sweetie," said Brenda while Carl huffed.

Then Magnolia turned toward the van and announced, "Carl and Brenda, this is Hyacinth Johnson."

Linda exited the car and approached the three of them. Her eyes carefully examined Carl's chestnut tone and athletic built. His salt and pepper hair complemented his smile and pearly white teeth.

She spoke first. "Hello, Carl." She kept eyeballing him but then looked at Brenda and said, "Oh, hello, Brenda. How are you?"

"I'm doing pretty good, Linda. It's been a long time."

"Yes, it has been a long time," she said as she faced the new Mercedes. "I just love your car."

"Thank you," Brenda said. "Carl—"

Before she could go on, a foot dangled from the van. Brenda and Carl jumped at once, their eyes were locked on the foot. Magnolia noticed their reaction and quickly walked over to the van and helped Hyacinth out. She waved her hand, signaling for them to approach. As they walked closer, Carl stumbled over his right foot, nearly knocking Brenda down. He struggled to get up and quickly grabbed his wife. Finally they reached the van. Their bodies were wet with perspiration.

Hyacinth smiled and grabbed Magnolia's hand. When her feet touched the ground, only a side view of her face was visible, but then her head slowly turned in their direction.

Carl and Brenda shivered. Brenda quickly looked at Carl when she saw her.

Oh, sweet Jesus, Carl thought. He pinched his fingers to keep them from trembling. Brenda put her hand in front of her neck to calm down. Then she grabbed onto Carl's polo shirt.

Magnolia knew they were nervous. She pulled Hyacinth's body forward and said with a big smile, "Carl and Brenda, I want you to meet my sister, Hyacinth."

Assisting Patricia and May-Lynne out of the van too, she said, "And this is her mother Patricia and sister May-Lynne."

Carl stood frozen in his tracks. He mumbled, "My God, it is

her."

Brenda jerked on his hand to get his attention again. Then she whispered to him, "Carl . . ."

Yet he stood there still as the rocks that lined the garden. The atmosphere grew absolute quiet. Unable to speak a word, Brenda and Carl just watched her in awe. Hyacinth ambled over to them and extended her hand. When her flesh touched his, his eyes began to tear. He gently shook her hand and suddenly touched her face. Hyacinth stepped back.

Finally he spoke, "I'm sorry. It's just that . . ."

"I . . . I understand," she said.

Partially grinning, he said, "It's . . . a pleasure to meet you, Hyacinth." And he hugged her.

Then Brenda hugged her and said, "I'm so glad to meet you."

Teary eyed, Carl approached and greeted Patricia and May-Lynne.

Once Brenda released Hyacinth, she whispered into her ear, "This is truly unbelievable." She started to fondle her hair and her face and said, "This is a glorious day. Welcome to New Jersey, sweetheart."

Then Carl said, "Where is Anthony?"

"He's in the van with Billie. I guess they made a wrong turn or something. We lost them at the airport. It was really backed up, especially with all that construction going on," said Magnolia.

Linda said, "Besides, Billie was driving. She drives like an old woman. You know what I mean, Carl."

They both chuckled.

"I keep forgetting that those Los Angelians can't drive," said Carl.

"You know," said Linda.

Then Magnolia whacked Carl on his chest and said, "Stop making fun of Billie. They should be here soon. Let's go inside."

Clasping onto Patricia, Magnolia said, "I'm sure you're restless. It's been a long weekend."

Patricia nodded.

They walked into the house. Hyacinth couldn't keep her eyes

off of the beautifully decorated home. "Your home is gorgeous, Magnolia!"

"Thank you. Anthony and I spent a great deal of time decorating it. In fact, we hired Brenda's sister, who is an interior decorator."

"And it's so huge!" said Patricia.

"Yes, that's what we wanted—plenty of room for family and friends."

Brenda said, "I'll take them upstairs and get them settled in, Magnolia."

Magnolia held Brenda's hand and whispered, "Thank you."

Magnolia strolled over to Hyacinth, patted her back, and said while looking toward the living room, "Go ahead and make yourself comfortable. I'll get dinner ready."

"Dinner! It's that time already."

She smiled. "Yep."

An exhausted Hyacinth walked into the living room and collapsed on the cozy sofa.

CHAPTER 42

A car horn blared somewhere nearby. Magnolia glanced out of the window and saw the rental van. "It's Billie and the rest of the gang." She stretched her neck more. "Looks like they stopped by the supermarket."

When she opened the front door, Anthony and Lawrence rushed in, struggling with large grocery bags in each arm.

She laughed and said, "We thought you guys made a wrong turn or something."

"Nah," said Anthony. "I decided to stop by the store to get some drinks." He raised his eyebrows. "You know—a little something for the men."

Magnolia grinned and shook her head. "Yeah . . . Yeah . . . I know." She waved to Billie, Gregory, and Mr. Johnson. "Come on in and have a seat."

When Anthony entered the kitchen, Carl walked out of the bathroom.

"Hey, man!" Anthony said.

"What's up!" Carl replied with a wide grin. He took hold of Anthony's hand. "Congratulations are in order."

"Thank you. We both did it."

"Sure did." Carl grabbed a shopping bag from Anthony and placed it on the counter and said, "You go to Miami Beach to make off with the big one and you come home with one of your wife's sisters."

Chuckling, Anthony said, "Can you believe it! We see this kind of stuff on television."

Resting the bags on the kitchen table, Anthony said, "Perfect timing though, huh." He nodded. "Yeah, that's what it was. Perfect timing, Carl. Now I believe there is a God."

"Yes, there is a God. My Mama always said God is good."

"God is good my, brother!" said Anthony, hugging Carl.

Brenda strode into the kitchen wearing a serene smile. When Anthony rushed to her and kissed her, she said to Carl, "Your mama always said what?"

"That God is good, baby!"

"Hmm," she said, staring at Anthony. "And how are you, Mr. Lewis?"

"Just fine, thank you."

Tugging on his shirt, she said, "You're looking mighty handsome as usual."

He smiled. "And I must say, you're looking lovely as always."

Anthony pulled the kitchen curtains to the side, took a quick look out of the window, and blinked at Brenda. "I really like that Mercedes. I know you're just loving it."

She laughed. "I sure am. I never leave home without it. We have to go for a drive sometime. I was hoping that the four of us could drive up to Massachusetts and visit Mama."

Then she glanced at Carl. "Oh, but we can do it another time."

"Leah would love that. And you're right, another time would be better."

Then Anthony yelled to the other men, "Gregory, Sam, and Lawrence, come meet our good friends, Brenda and Carl Walker."

"Hello," Brenda and Carl said.

"A pleasure to meet you," said the men.

Anthony put the beer into the refrigerator, then turned to face Brenda and Carl. "Sam is Hyacinth's dad. Lawrence is her brother and Gregory's her fiancé."

Reality soon set in and Carl and Brenda shook their heads in disbelief. Brenda leaned back on Carl's chest as her heart raced. He wrapped his arms around her.

Looking around the room, Anthony said, "Where is Hyacinth?"

"She's resting in the living room," said Gregory. "She's really worn out."

"I bet she is," said Anthony. "Everyone, please have a seat and relax. The food is ready. There's plenty to eat. Magnolia cooked and Carl and Brenda brought over some great dishes too."

Anthony glanced at Brenda and Carl. "Thanks for everything."

"You're welcome, sweetie," said Brenda.

Carl stood quiet behind her and managed to smile. Magnolia came in and eyed the pots. "Umm, they outdid me. I just made a casserole and a salad."

"What's in the oven and on the stove?" Anthony said.

"Some fried chicken, chopped barbecue, collard greens, baked ham, macaroni and cheese, lemon pound cake, and a sweet potato pie."

"Damn!" Anthony blurted as he glanced at Carl.

"We gonna eat good today."

Carl laughed. "Oh, it's just a few dishes."

"A few dishes!" said Sam. "Sounds like a feast to me!"

Carl laughed again. It felt good to alleviate the tension bunched inside him. He looked at Anthony. "Besides, the way you like to eat, man. Don't even try it!"

They all laughed.

"Carl, you make me look bad," Anthony confessed. "I don't know anyone who can cook as good as you except for Magnolia and your mother."

"Oh, really!" said Brenda.

"Oh, you too Brenda."

Brenda and Carl chuckled.

"You don't have to pretend, Anthony. I know I can't cook, but I do try."

Anthony winked at her and she jiggled her hips to his side and said, "I knew we had something in common."

Everyone retreated to the dining room except for Sam, who

was high-strung from the flight. He walked into the den, rolled his head back on the sofa, and closed his eyes.

"Are you feeling well, Sam?" said Gregory.

"I have a headache," he said, rubbing his temples.

Kneeling beside him, Magnolia placed her hand over his and said, "Would you like some pain killers?"

"Yes, can I have some?"

"Of course." Magnolia entered the bathroom on the lower level and returned with a bottle of headache medicine and a glass of water. "I hope this works. Do you usually use this brand?"

"Oh, yes, I do. It'll work. Thank you," he said, smiling.

Patricia began to stroke her husband's clean-shaven head, relieving some of the pressure and easing the pain. He stared at her and said, "I'm fine, honey. Between the flight and what has gone on the past couple of days, it's all been very exhausting. But I'm fine, don't worry."

"Why don't I take you upstairs, Mr. Johnson? Maybe you need to lie down for a while," said Magnolia.

Sam put his hand up. "No, I'll be fine. Remember, I'm hungry too, and I'm not about to pass up on the food I smell in there."

Magnolia and Patricia laughed.

"Well, I tell you what, Mr. Johnson, how about if I bring you a plate in here. That way, you can rest while you eat."

"That sounds good, sweetheart. Thank you."

"If it's okay, I'll stay in here with him," said Patricia.

"Okay, I'll bring two plates then."

"Thank you, dear," said Patricia.

Everyone sat at the dining table. They were hungry and prepared themselves to devour the succulent food that was in front of them. When Magnolia returned from the den she sat opposite of Anthony at the head of the impressive glass table.

The cream-colored place settings matched their floral draperies. Fresh pink roses stood in an exquisite vase and the silverware sparkled. Hyacinth glanced around the room and smiled. Everything looked wonderful. The aroma of the delicious food and sweet roses made a pleasant combination. She felt right at home.

Magnolia said to Hyacinth, "Would you like to bless the food?"

Hyacinth hesitated. "Umm . . ."

She wasn't religious and saying the blessing wasn't something her family did. Gregory and Lawrence turned away, hoping Magnolia wouldn't ask them.

Smiling, Magnolia said, "It's okay. I'll say it."

Everyone bowed their heads and held hands.

Magnolia spoke softly: "Heavenly Father, we thank you for this special meal we are about to eat. We pray that it sustains us and enables us to continue to be strong. Heavenly Father, we ask that you pray for those who do not have what we have. Keep them safe and show them love. Protect them and feed them your wisdom and energy. Heavenly Father, thank you for bringing Hyacinth and her family here today. It is truly a blessing. Thank you for making my life whole again. In Jesus' name, Amen."

"Amen," they all said.

The platters were quickly passed around the table. Serving himself a heaping portion of macaroni and cheese, Anthony whispered to Hyacinth, "How are you feeling?"

"Wonderful. This is so special, Anthony," she said as she glanced over at Magnolia. "I haven't felt this happy in a long time."

Linda sat across from Lawrence staring into his hazel eyes, which were slightly concealed by his thick eyebrows. She placed her hand to her face, leaned her elbow on the table, and whispered, "This is better than the movies. Isn't it?"

"Yes, it is," he said in a husky voice. "I can't wait to get back home and tell all my friends. They're not going to believe this."

Lawrence stared at her erect nipples and was captivated by her. "Everything happened so fast. I didn't have time to call anyone."

"How old are you, Lawrence?"

Taken aback by her inquiry, he said, "Twenty-six. Is that too old for you?"

Linda nearly gagged on her food. "No. No." She wiped her mouth with a napkin and smiled.

"What type of work do you do?" she said, studying his muscular physique. "Are you an artist too?"

"No, I'm not. I'm a senior in college. I'm a late starter."

She chuckled.

"I'm a pre-med major. I have one more semester to complete."

She took a sip of wine, all the while screening his every move. "Really?" she said, taking another sip. "I was a pre-med major, too."

Linda's mind was on his upper torso when she took another sip of wine. It suddenly trickled down her mouth. She quickly slid her tongue out and to the side of her mouth, stopping the wine from dripping.

"I was accepted to Columbia but I decided not to attend," she said.

When he pulled his body forward to hear her clearly, she flinched.

"Why didn't you go?" said Lawrence.

She slowly sipped the wine again, gazed into his eyes, and said, "I fell in love."

Twirling his fork around, he said, "Love can make people do crazy things."

She laughed. "It sure can. But, I don't regret it." She passed her glass to him for a refill. "So, Lawrence, what do you want to specialize in?"

Grinning, he said, "Obstetrics and Gynecology."

She choked on her food again. "Get out of here!"

He laughed. "Yes. I am especially interested in that field of study. As I youngster, I always wanted to address women's issues, and curing gynecological diseases is important to me. And of course, the thought of bringing a child into this world is absolutely beautiful and meaningful."

"Oh, that's touching," said Linda.

Linda had other things on her mind aside from Lawrence's career goals. One of her bad habits was having very little patience. She ignored Lawrence's discussion. "Do you have a girlfriend?"

Lawrence jumped back in his chair, taken aback by her boldness and inquisitiveness. "No, I don't," he said, his eyes hooked on her breasts. "Is there someone in your life?"

"No. I'm single too."

"Well, that's too bad. A beautiful young lady like yourself shouldn't be alone."

She wiped her mouth with the embroidered napkin and said, "Maybe Mr. Right will come my way soon."

He smiled and took a bite of food. "Maybe he'll come sooner than you think."

Watching the movement of his broad shoulders, she said, "That would be just fine with me."

Meanwhile Anthony was listening in on the conversation and was furious. He knew what was on her wicked mind and was irritated that she had chosen Lawrence as her next victim.

Fuming, he shook his head and turned to Linda. When she smiled, he rolled his eyes and crumpled the napkin in his hand.

She winked her eye at him and quietly whispered, "I love you too, Anthony."

When she turned toward Billie and started a conversation, Anthony leaned over to Lawrence and whispered, "What medical schools are you going to apply to?"

"I want to attend Howard but there's a couple more schools here on the East Coast that I will also apply to."

"Good. You know, I attended Howard."

"How was it?"

"It was great, man. I wouldn't have gotten a better education anywhere else. I don't want to influence you, but you've chosen a damn great school."

"Thanks, man."

"Do you really want to be a gynecologist?"

Grinning, Lawrence said, "Nah, man. I was just kidding. I want to specialize in surgical cardiology."

Anthony glanced at Linda, making sure it was safe to talk. "Watch out for her, man. I'm telling you, her head is harder than a fucking rock."

Lawrence chuckled.

"I'm serious, man," Anthony said. "Lawrence, I know she's my wife's best friend, but she's trouble. I don't trust her as far as I can see her. Mark my words!"

Lawrence quietly laughed again.

"She's got you already," Anthony said.

"What are you talking about?"

"Man, she's done pussy-whipped you and it ain't even been a whole day. Didn't even hit the bedroom yet."

"Believe me, it's not like that. She's a nice woman and—"

Anthony laughed. "And, I want to fuck the shit out of her, right?"

"Nah, you got the wrong idea."

"Yeah, I got the right idea. Anyway, that's your business. But don't say I didn't warn you."

"Like I said, Anthony, Linda's really cool people."

"What?" He lifted his hands to his ear. "What was that you said?" Anthony said.

They both laughed.

"She and Magnolia are total opposites, huh."

"Yes, total opposites. Linda has this strange way of attracting people to her, and it's not because of her friendly attitude. I guess it's that big ass of hers."

They giggled again.

"I'll have to admit, though, she's been good to Leah. Stuck by her through it all."

He bumped his shoulder against Lawrence's. "But man, watch out. The woman has been married three or four times. She's jumped the broom more than anyone I know."

He leaned closer to Lawrence. "She's always had the upper hand in her relationships. She always wants to be in control. You don't want that, man. Believe me, you don't."

CHAPTER 43

Magnolia began to place a bowl into the dishwasher but Billie snatched it from her hand. "This is your day, love. I'll take care of it. Go and enjoy your family."

Magnolia smiled. "I love you."

"I love you too." She waved her hand. "Now, go and enjoy the rest of the evening with your family."

Everyone retreated into the large living room and remained quiet, but only for a moment. Magnolia leaned her head on the sofa and stared at Hyacinth. She was still amazed that she had a sister.

Hyacinth sat on the other end of the sofa and slid closer to Magnolia. "So, here we are," she said.

"Yep." Magnolia reached for her hand and held it.

"We have so much to say but we're too worn out to say anything," Hyacinth said.

Magnolia rubbed Hyacinth's hand on her lap. "I apologize if I'm a little distant."

"Oh, I understand. These few days have seemed like a year."

"I hope you are going to stay here for a while."

"You're sure you don't mind?"

"Not at all. I would be heartbroken if you didn't."

Magnolia couldn't keep her eyes off of Hyacinth's birthmark—

an innocent blemish that stretched across her face. She wondered if her biological mother had one just like that.

Then she gently placed her hand on Hyacinth's forehead. "What was it like growing up?"

Hyacinth closed her eyes for a moment. "Let's see . . . Mommy and Daddy, including my grandparents, spoiled me, of course. They gave me everything. Sometimes I think too much."

Magnolia laughed.

"You know, for a while I was the only child but I had plenty of cousins who were my age—many of them have moved out of state. Speaking of which—we need to have a family reunion. Once we find them all."

She tapped Magnolia's leg. "Magnolia, there's so many people that I want you to meet. And so many folks on the Johnsons' side that I want you to meet as well." She paused. "Being the oldest, there were many expectations, and I had to be a role model for Lawrence and May-Lynne. I never questioned anything. Mommy and Daddy's family never said anything."

She turned to Magnolia. "How about you, Magnolia? How was it growing up in New Jerzee?"

Chuckling, Magnolia said, "It wasn't the same, that's for sure. I wasn't surrounded by family. I didn't get much love either."

Hyacinth was astonished.

"Don't get me wrong," Magnolia said. "I'm not bitter. My mother and your mom handled it differently. I guess my mother felt guilty. Maybe even ashamed."

She nodded. "Then again, she was a single mother. I'm sure it was difficult raising a child. She probably thought that eventually she would be happy."

Magnolia kicked off her shoes. "Who knows, maybe she blamed me for being alone. You know—what man wants a woman with a child?"

Hyacinth nodded in agreement.

"Look at me—I'm talking about my mother instead of myself," Magnolia said. "If it wasn't for certain individuals in my life like Linda, I guess I would have given in to loneliness or depression. I think God for my friends."

She leaned closer to Hyacinth and whispered, "Hyacinth, I always knew a better day would come. I had always hoped mother would be a part of that day. But the distance she put between us made me love her more. I believe in my heart that she loved me. She just didn't know how to show it."

She stared at Hyacinth. "When people aren't loved, they don't know how to give love." She winked. "I knew my life would be whole again someday. I had this feeling that one day I would be a part of someone's family."

Hyacinth hugged her. "And you were right. Dreams do come true. Too bad it took thirty-eight years. Can you imagine—the two of us growing up as kids or even teenagers?"

They laughed again.

Magnolia said, "Yeah, I can see us now. Spoiled brats." She patted her suit. "Were you self-conscious when you were a teenager."

"Yes, I was! I'll gain ten pounds and have a nervous breakdown!"

"Me, too!"

"And acne."

"Oh, you too!"

"It was terrible. I would say, why me God? Why me? Ma would tell me, Hyacinth, you're beautiful. And I would say, Yeah right, look at your face—it's perfect. Your hair is flawless too."

Their laugh was so intense, Magnolia slid off the couch.

"Yeah, we would have been something else back then, huh!" Magnolia said.

"It's a good thing no one took all three of us. We would have been too much to handle!"

"Too much!" Magnolia screamed. Then they stared at each other. They held hands and tears rolled down their faces.

"We'd better watch what we say next time, huh." Magnolia said.

"But it's all good. Crying won't kill us and laughing won't either."

CHAPTER 44

Sam and Patricia retired to bed. They sluggishly trekked upstairs, exhausted from what had seemed an unending flight. They were relieved there would be no more secrets and no more lies. Finally the truth had set them free. They were now able to sleep peacefully.

"It's been a long day and we're going to bed," Sam said to Magnolia.

Carl and Brenda got up. "Well, we're going to go too. We'll see you tomorrow, dear."

Anthony and Magnolia escorted them to the door. Brenda hugged and kissed Magnolia.

"Thank you for being here," Magnolia whispered.

Grabbing her hand, Brenda said, "You know we love you, baby."

Hyacinth walked toward the door and stood near Carl. He was still for a moment. Her staring made him nervous. He shook his head a few times looking teary-eyed and hugged her.

Meanwhile Linda and Lawrence slyly entered the living room after talking on the patio.

"I'm going to take Lawrence over to Manhattan."

"This time of night!" said Anthony.

Sassily blowing her breath, she said, "Anthony, please, he's grown!"

"Okay, do whatever you want," Anthony said, turning off the

light. "I'm not saying another word. You're right, he's grown."
Before they left, Hyacinth's beeper buzzed and she ran into the kitchen and grabbed the telephone.

"Is everything all right?" Magnolia said.

"Oh, yes," Hyacinth said, looking down again at the pager. "I just received a page from Gregory's ex-sister-in-law."

She dialed the number. "She's a producer for the show *Separations*."

Hyacinth turned to Magnolia. "I'm sorry, Magnolia—can I use the telephone?"

"Of course you can."

Her heart raced as she punched in the numbers. She tapped her fingers on the kitchen counter while she waited for an answer. "Hi, Zoe. Hey, this is Hyacinth. So you got my message, huh."

She paused. "Yes . . . Yes . . . isn't that something? We're all in New Jersey right now."

Hyacinth peeked through the kitchen window. "Yes, we didn't waste any time, huh." She laughed. "Oh, she's wonderful. You have to meet her. Yeah, she looks like me. Yes, exactly like me. Wait until you see her."

"Yes, everyone is here including Gregory," said Hyacinth as she stopped tapping. "Are you serious? Great, I'll tell everyone. Okay . . . okay . . . hold on and let me find out."

She slammed the telephone on the counter and shouted, "Zoe wants to know if she can come by tomorrow—in the afternoon."

"Who's Zoe?" said Anthony.

"She's a producer with the show *Separations*."

"Oh, okay. Hey, that's what we need—publicity."

Magnolia looked at Anthony and said shyly, "It's fine with me."

"She's going to bring the camera crew," yelled Hyacinth.

"Camera crew!" Magnolia said. "Oh, no!"

"Don't worry, it'll be okay. She wants to talk to all of us."

Anthony grabbed Magnolia from behind and whispered, "The sooner she airs this, the sooner you'll find Rose and the rest of your siblings."

"You're right. Tomorrow is fine."

Hyacinth picked up the receiver. "Tomorrow afternoon is great, Zoe. See you then. Good night." She hesitated. Then her speech accelerated. "Hey, Zoe, I'm glad you called. See you tomorrow." She placed the receiver back on its case.

"Wow, that was quick!" said Billie.

"Yeah, wasn't it," Hyacinth said, looking amazed. "Zoe and I have known each other for years. She worked at a local television station in Miami Beach."

Her head fell back and she turned it sideways. "It was ten years ago and she produced this art program. At the time, I started to paint again."

She poured herself a glass of water. "We became good friends. She was the one who introduced me to Gregory."

She took a sip of water and went on. "And soon after, she and Gregory's brother Jerome began having marital problems. They couldn't work things out and eventually divorced."

"Really!" said Billie.

"Yeah, but she and Jerome remain good friends now."

"Wow!"

"Um—hmm," she said, pointing her finger at Billie. "Then she got a job with this show and moved to New York. The show was a big success."

"Tell me about it," shouted Billie. "Everyone watches it."

"I tune in every chance I get," said Anthony.

"Sometimes, I can get so emotional," said Hyacinth.

Magnolia laughed. "Yeah, and never knew I would be on it."

"Funny how life is, huh. You never expect the unexpected," said Hyacinth.

Soon nighttime crept up on them. Hyacinth and Billie went on to bed. Linda and Lawrence headed to the city.

Anthony and Magnolia stayed awake, chatting in the bedroom. He turned the television on while she undressed and stepped into the shower. Afterwards she sat in bed putting lotion on her body.

"Baby, you smell so good," he said.

She giggled. "You kill me, you know that." She touched his chin and lay next to him.

He kissed her lips. "I missed you, Magnolia." He held her by the waist. "You mean the world to me, woman."

"Umm-hmm."

Kissing her again, his tongue slid down her neck. She glanced up at him. Her eyes were on his face. "Baby, make love to me."

They touched, cuddled, and loved each other that night.

* * *

Linda and Lawrence sat calmly in her BMW.

"So this is the infamous 42nd Street?" said Lawrence.

"Sure is. You've never been here before?"

"Never."

"That's crazy."

"What's crazy, Linda?"

"How people can live in a place all their lives and never leave."

He moved closer. Her body squirmed like a centipede. He stared at her and she pulled the car over to the side and put it in park.

"I didn't say I've never been out of the state of Florida. I just said I've never been to New York City. But I've been Upstate."

"Wow, what's Upstate? If you've been Upstate then why haven't you hung out in Manhattan?"

"I don't know. Manhattan isn't all that, you know."

Caressing her thighs, he said, "My best friend went to college Upstate. We were busy having fun up there. Manhattan is far away to folks up there."

"See? That's what I mean. There's more to life than Upstate. That is what's wrong with black people today. We'll never grow if we stay in the same place."

"That's how you feel, Linda." He unbuttoned her blouse and his lips brushed her ear. "Everyone doesn't think that way. You're a person who likes to travel. You had the opportunity to do that.

Everyone isn't that lucky and everyone doesn't have those opportunities. Besides—"

"Besides what?"

He kissed her neck and she giggled.

"Like I said, Manhattan isn't all that," he said.

"Oh, just be quiet."

"You are one stubborn woman." He gently pulled her hair and her head tilted back. "When things don't go your way, you throw a tantrum, don't you?"

"You've been talking too much with Anthony."

He laughed. "I'm speaking from experience."

"Don't lie to me."

He laughed. "You're a trip, Linda. Those walls are going to come crumbling down one day."

She looked at him sideways.

"Relax. Stop carrying around that hopeless attitude. Turn that negative energy into positive energy." He withdrew the key from the ignition. "Don't be so defensive all the time. It's okay to be wrong sometimes. And it's okay to be right, but don't let that be your focus."

She snatched the keys from his hand and turned the car on. He leaned over her, kissing her more. His hands pushed through her blouse and then down between her legs. He whispered, holding her face in both hands, "Just let things happen. Don't try to control everything around you. You'll go crazy. Power means nothing if you don't know how to use it."

She kissed him back, pushing her body close to his. Then his mouth topped her breast. "Is there a hotel around here?"

"Let's go to my office. I have a room there." She pulled out and drove down 42nd Street, making a left on Third Avenue. They parked in front of a brownstone. He grabbed her butt as she entered the security code. Lawrence reached down and slid his hands up her legs. The door abruptly swung open and they intimately kissed as they entered the office.

Linda tried to turn on the light but he stopped her. His hands encircled her waist and he pushed her body to the wall. He pulled down her hosiery and lightly caressed her vagina. She enjoyed it and spread her legs wider. She stopped him and walked over and opened the door to the bedroom suite.

Inside the large apartment was furnished with brown and black pieces—dark but warm. African art and sculptures were everywhere.

They plunged onto the bed and ripped away each other's cloths. She grabbed his head and kissed him wildly. His head pressed against her breasts and he could feel her heartbeat.

"Relax, Linda," he said. "Don't fight me."

His head dropped and his lips grazed her breasts. Her moans were nonstop. She grabbed his wavy hair, and when he reached her stomach, her hands fell back.

"Lawrence! Lawrence!"

He climbed upward, grabbing her thighs, penetrated her, and began to thrust hard. His breathing grew heavy. Linda clutched and squeezed his buttocks, pressing down with each thrust.

"Linda, you feel so good," he moaned.

Their bodies entwined in ecstasy like a beautifully stitched blanket.

It was five in the morning, and their night of passion had soothed them. Linda softly rubbed his arm and his eyes slowly opened. "Good morning," he said. He brushed her hair back. "How are you feeling?"

"I feel great." She kissed him and he smiled. Then she walked nude to the large frame window and looked out. He stared at her butt and sat up. She walked back to the bed, enticing him, smiling all the while. "Are you hungry?" she said.

"A little. Are you?"

"Yes. I can cook something. Would you like that? We have a kitchen here, you know."

He reached for her thigh and pulled her body close. "I want you," he said.

She laughed and leaned over, kissing his luscious lips—teasing him. Suddenly she paused and glanced at her watch. "Oh, shit!"

"What is it?"

"We have to get back. It's five o'clock."

He grabbed her breasts.

"No, really! The last thing I need is to hear Anthony's big mouth. Besides, Magnolia will kill me."

Lawrence jumped up. "I guess we should get back then. Where is the shower?"

She pointed to the door. "Behind you," she said.

When he stepped into the shower, she slipped into her camisole and strolled over to her desk. She hadn't retrieved her messages since Friday. Picking up the phone, she peeped into the bathroom, scanning Lawrence's tall lean body.

She dialed into her voicemail. She couldn't believe her ears: "Hello Linda, this is Mackenzie Gary. I wanted to let you know that I am looking forward to a productive and long-term relationship with Acirfa Literary Agency. I have to apologize for my weird behavior. I know I haven't been, well, exactly cooperative these last few weeks, but that's all behind me now. Just letting you know that I'll be in New York City in a few weeks. Feel free to call with any questions. Have a good evening."

Linda raised her hand to her head. "Can you believe that shit? The bitch is really coming. If it wasn't for Magnolia . . ."

"What's that?" Lawrence said, stepping into the room dripping wet.

"Nothing."

He eyed her. "What do you mean nothing? Come on now, don't be that way," he said as he wiped himself dry.

"It's about a future client who I really don't want to represent."

"Linda, what did we just talk about last night."

She waved her hand at him. "Oh, forget it. I guess Magnolia really wants to work with her. I don't want to be bothered with her. You know, I called around to find out if anyone else had attempted to represent her, and you know what?"

"What?"

"Three top agents are dying to represent her, yet for some reason she wants us to. I can't figure it out."

"What have the other publishers offered?" he said.

"A hefty advance and a three book deal. I'm talking a lot of money, Lawrence. We don't have the same pull as the other agents, having just started a few years ago."

"You mean she's missing out on some loot by coming to you and Magnolia?"

"Yeah."

He massaged her back. "Maybe she likes your style. I know I do."

She giggled.

"Hey, maybe she's heard about your reputation or your working relationship with other writers," he said. "Maybe she's talked to other writers you've represented."

"No, maybe not. I checked that out, too. None of our other clients know her. That's what's so strange."

Linda shrugged. "I guess we'll never know, huh."

"Never say never!"

Biting his chest, she said, "You're right, but I'm still curious. Anyway, I'm looking forward to meeting the heffa. Maybe after we sign her on and her book becomes a bestseller—"

"Stop it now!"

"No, I'm serious. Then we'll definitely be in!"

"Hey . . . Hey . . ." He slapped her buttock.

"Ouch . . . Okay . . . Okay . . ."

"Are you going to take a shower?"

"Yeah, in a second."

He slapped her butt again when she walked by. She wickedly stared at him.

"And what—now you're ready to jump on me, right!"

Aiming her finger at him, she said, "No, that's what you assumed I was going to do."

He spanked her again.

"Oh, I know you didn't do that again."

"Woman, go take a shower! I'm just messing with you!"

CHAPTER 45

Linda drove through Lincoln tunnel like a madwoman.
"Did you watch that movie?" Lawrence said.
"Yeah."
He nervously looked at her. "Can't you go any faster?"
She swerved the car to the right, then to the left.
"Linda!"
She laughed hysterically. "You're not going to die, Lawrence. I promise."
Massaging her thighs, he said, "I had a good time."
She smiled. "So did I."
She pulled into the driveway. "How are we going to get in?" said Lawrence.
"I have a spare key."
"You do?"
"Yes. And please, whatever you do, don't tell big mouth."
They tiptoed into the house and all the lights were off.
"Do you remember what room you put your suitcase in?" she said.
"Yeah."
She kissed him. "Well, I'll see you later."
He grinned. "See ya."
Lawrence went upstairs and Linda walked into the kitchen before going to her guestroom. She opened the refrigerator and

pulled out the casserole. She opened the lid, reached for a spoon, and dug out a hefty serving. She placed it on a saucer and popped it into the microwave. She sat down at the kitchen table and started to eat. Then she heard footsteps. "Lawrence, is that you?" she whispered.

Silence.

"No, it's not Lawrence," said Anthony.

"Oh, damn! It's you."

"Where the hell have you been, Linda?"

"That's none of your business. I'm not your child, Anthony."

"I know you're not," he said nodding. "I can't believe you. You don't waste any time, do you?"

She laughed.

"Everything is about you, isn't it? You know how important they all mean to Leah."

She turned away and continued to chew.

Anthony slammed his fist on the table. "Look at me!"

She jumped up.

"Linda, for God's sake. You could have gotten to know him first."

She stood up. "Anthony, it's way too early for a lecture. I've been here all night. I don't know what the hell you're talking about."

He shook his head again and started to walk away. Then he hesitated and turned back.

"Anthony, I said it's way too early for this," she repeated.

"Linda, I don't care what you do with your life and your body. Just don't put Leah in the middle of your bullshit."

He walked to the refrigerator, took out a carton of eggs and a package of bacon, and placed it on the counter. Linda walked away.

Sam entered the kitchen a few minutes later.

"Good morning, Mr. Johnson. Are you rested?" Anthony said.

"Sure am. I slept good last night." He grinned. "You know, that bed was really comfortable. Haven't slept that good in a long time."

They laughed.

"How is Mrs. Johnson?"

"She's doing better. They're upstairs now looking through some of Magnolia's photo albums."

Flipping over the bacon in the frying pan, Anthony said, "Is that right?"

"Yeah, they're talking like they've known each other all of their lives." Glancing through a magazine, Sam said, "How long has Magnolia known Billie, Anthony?"

"Oh, about as long as she's known me."

"Really!"

"Yeah." He chuckled. "I know what you're going to say. They really resemble each other."

"For a moment there, I thought she was Hyacinth. She has the same gestures, you know."

"Yeah!"

"And the same eyes too. The same smile."

"Come on now."

"Really, Anthony."

"Hey, maybe she's Rose."

Sam's thick eyebrows raised and he said, "Yeah, you never know."

"No, I'm just kidding," Anthony said. "But it's interesting how you can favor someone you're really close too. You know what they say."

"Yeah, the more you hang around someone the more you look like them."

They laughed again. Then everyone entered the kitchen.

"Good morning," Anthony said beaming.

"Good morning," they all said.

Magnolia kissed him. "What's cooking, baby?"

"Everything."

Everyone sat down at the large kitchen table and ate breakfast. Suddenly the doorbell rang. Magnolia answered the door. It was Carl and Brenda. "Hey! Look who's here, honey."

"Good morning!" Carl said.

Throwing the dishcloth on his shoulder, Anthony yelled, "Come on in."

"I smell food," said Brenda.

"Yep, and it's jamming," said Anthony. "Have a seat." They entered the spacious kitchen and said, "Good morning, everyone."

"Good morning," Sam and Patricia said.

Carl barely touched his food, so much was on his mind.

"Are you okay?" said Anthony.

"Oh, yeah. I'm fine. I'm just a little overwhelmed with everything." He leaned toward Anthony and whispered, "I sat up all night thinking about the whole thing. I still can't believe it."

Magnolia smiled and said with a mouthful of scrambled eggs, "Oh, by the way everyone, Carl and Anthony recently signed a major contract with a company in Miami Beach."

"Yes, that's true," said Anthony.

"That's right. That is why you came to Miami Beach, huh? You said you had an important meeting to attend," Gregory said.

"Yes. We finally grabbed a prospective client. We've been after this company for a very long time."

"That's wonderful," Patricia said.

Linda took a glass of orange juice and said, "Let's toast."

Anthony frowned. "No . . . No . . . that's not necessary."

"Oh, come on, Anthony! You and Carl worked so hard. You both deserve it."

Raising his glass, Sam said, "That's right. To your success."

"To your success!" they expressed.

Anthony seemed embarrassed.

"Man, she's right, you deserve it," said Gregory.

After breakfast, the men went into the den while the women washed dishes. They chatted and reminiscence about their younger days. Then the doorbell rang again.

"Who could this be?" Magnolia said as she went to the front door.

A short thin blond Caucasian woman surrounded by three men stood at the steps smiling. One man held a camera and the other two struggled with production equipment. Magnolia nervously smiled.

The woman stepped forward and hugged and kissed Magnolia on the cheek. Shaking her arms, she said, "Hello, stranger. You look great. It's been a long time!"

Magnolia was speechless.

"What's wrong? I know this has been quite an ordeal but you didn't forget me now, did you?"

"I'm not Hyacinth."

Tongue-tied, the woman placed her hand to her mouth. "Oh my gosh, I'm sorry. You must be . . . Magnolia."

"Yes, I am."

She extended her hand. "I'm Zoe. It's a pleasure to meet you."

Suddenly they laughed. Zoe stared into Magnolia's eyes and the camera crew smiled.

One cameraman said, "This is going to be very interesting."

"Please, come in," Magnolia said as she guided them into the house.

CHAPTER 46

Hyacinth stood in the background when Zoe and the camera crew entered the living room.

"Hey, you," shouted Zoe. "You tricked me!"

"No, I didn't," said Hyacinth with a laugh.

They hugged and Zoe whispered into Hyacinth's ear, "I didn't expect this, you know. She looks exactly like you."

"But, that's what I told you."

"I know, but . . . it's different hearing it than seeing it."

Magnolia interrupted: "Everyone is surprised when they see us. It's difficult when you've known someone for a very long time and suddenly confront their triplet."

"I know."

Magnolia looked concerned. "So Zoe, how long will this take?"

"A couple of hours. Maybe more."

"Why so long?"

Before she could respond, Gregory approached Zoe from behind and said, "Hello . . . sis. It's been a long time."

Zoe turned around, hitting him on the arm. "Hey, there. Yes, it's been a long time indeed." She kissed him.

He eyeballed her. "You've lost some weight, haven't you?"

"A few pounds."

"Where do you want to interview us?" Magnolia said.

"The living room is fine," Zoe said as she sucked on her teeth

345

and turned to a cameraman. "Maybe we can shoot them outside. What do you think?"

He nodded. "It's up to you, boss."

Hyacinth tugged on Zoe's blouse. "She's a little nervous." Zoe smiled. "I can see."

"Why don't you have a seat, Zoe," said Anthony.

Zoe pulled out a notepad and pen. "When Hyacinth called me I thought she was kidding. She filled me in on everything."

She glanced at Hyacinth and then at Magnolia. "This is unquestionably incredible!" Then she held Magnolia's hand. "You must be very stressed out and nervous right about now. I know this is difficult, but hopefully we can find your other sister."

Magnolia said, "And the others too."

Zoe appeared confused. "What do you mean?" she said.

"Our biological mother had six children."

"You're kidding me?"

"No," Hyacinth said. "Besides Magnolia, Rose, and myself, there are three more."

* * *

Staring straight at the camera, Hyacinth said, "Yes, we were the youngest."

"Well then, now I have additional questions to ask," Zoe said, scribbling notes on the pad. She perused them again. "I'm going to go over the questions with you now, and then we'll tape everything later. How's that?"

She squeezed Magnolia's hand again. "We have a 99 percent success rate. Since the show aired ten years ago, we've only been unsuccessful once." She pointed her finger straight up. "Only one time, Magnolia. Just once."

Magnolia smiled.

Turning the pages of her notepad, Zoe immediately began to question them. "Hyacinth, how and when did you meet Magnolia?"

"I met Magnolia's husband first—just last week, on Thursday.

Gregory, Mrs. Clark and myself were having lunch at the hotel and that's when Anthony approached me."

Zoe eyed Anthony and then Hyacinth.

"Yes, for some reason . . ." Hyacinth said. "Well, it really wasn't strange, considering what took place."

She giggled. "Anyway, Anthony thought I was Magnolia. He thought she was playing some kind of joke."

Zoe was speechless. Then she chuckled. "It's amazing." Her notepad fell off of her lap.

"Are you okay?" said Magnolia.

"Oh, yes, I'm fine. I've known Hyacinth for years and would have never believed this before." She picked up the notepad. "So when did he realize that this wasn't a joke?"

"I insisted that I wasn't who he thought I was. Then he yanked out a picture of Magnolia."

"What happened then?" Zoe said, reaching into the candy dish.

"I nearly fainted."

Untwisting the candy wrapper, Zoe queried. "Did you know you were adopted, Hyacinth?"

Patricia butted in: "No."

Teary-eyed, Magnolia broke in: "I must admit, I questioned it."

Right then, Anthony walked behind her and kissed the top of her head. "It's okay, baby, we understand."

"My mother and I had a very strange relationship. I always considered her so removed from everyone. But still, I had no evidence," Magnolia said as she pulled on Anthony's hand. "I thought she was depressed. But I never imagined, not in my wildest dreams, that she could do such a thing. Separate a family."

Tears began to fall. She wiped her face. "But life goes on, huh."

Anthony rubbed her leg. "Yes, it does, and you've found Hyacinth. It's just a matter of time before we find the rest."

"I just have one more question, Magnolia," Zoe said.

"Yes?"

"This adoption—was it legal?"

"No, it wasn't. It—"

"My sister and her lover orchestrated everything," said Sam.

Zoe stood up. "Mr. Johnson, I'm sorry, I—"

"Please sit down. Don't be sorry. Patricia and I were educated adults back then; we knew what we were doing. We also knew that it was deceitful."

"Can we not mention this on the air?" Hyacinth said. "The others might be reluctant to come forward, including Rose's adoptive parents."

"I think we can work around it. Don't you?"

They all smiled.

"There's one thing, Zoe," said Magnolia.

"Yes, what's that?"

"We don't know the other children's names. We only know the oldest name is Solomon. The only information disclosed in the documents was their ages."

"What happened to them?"

Hunching her shoulders, Magnolia said, "We don't know."

"What happened to your mother?"

"All we know is that she was very ill and may have died," Hyacinth said. "That is the reason we were separated. She couldn't take care of us."

"So you don't know if she's alive or dead?"

Brenda and Carl cuddled closer. Billie glanced at Linda and Lawrence. Patricia began to cry. They were all wondering if she was still alive.

"Right," said Magnolia.

"Umm," Zoe muttered to herself while scribbling notes, "where were the triplets taken?"

Hyacinth said, "As you can see, I ended up in Florida, Magnolia was taken to New Jersey, and Rose, she could be anywhere. Maybe upstate New York."

Zoe stood. "Our show airs internationally, remember that. Don't worry. We'll find them."

She walked over to Magnolia, knelt down, and grabbed her hand. "Magnolia, tell me why it is important that you find them."

Magnolia started to cry. "All of my pain must end. All of it." Her head sunk in her lap.

"It's okay," Zoe said, caressing her back.

Magnolia looked back up at Zoe. "But most importantly, I need to know my family. I must be with them."

Zoe got up and approached Hyacinth. "And you, Hyacinth?"

"I want to be able—" She began to cry as well. Gregory embraced her. "I just want them in my life again. There's so much to catch up on. I desperately need to know what happened and what went wrong."

"You will. Trust me," Zoe said, turning to everyone. "Okay, are you guys ready?"

She rubbed Hyacinth's arm. "Stay calm. I'm going to ask you those same questions again, okay? Stay calm. Just look into the camera."

Then she turned to Magnolia. "Are you comfortable?"

"Yes."

After what seemed like hours, the camera crew fidgeted with the equipment and finally finished setting up. The bright lights blinded Magnolia and she quickly turned away, finding protection against Anthony's chest.

Joking with her, Anthony said, "I can't believe you're nervous, Ms. Assertiveness!"

"This is different, Anthony. This is about my livelihood. I'm so afraid that—"

Stroking her skin, he said, "You will have closure to all of this, baby. Believe me. They'll be watching."

Magnolia smiled.

"Did I tell you you look beautiful today?" he said.

Her soft brown eyes shone. "Thank you."

Zoe yelled from across the room, "Anthony, I want you to remain right there by Magnolia's side, okay?"

He nodded.

Hyacinth sat next to them. They all laughed. It seemed a perfect time for laughter. There had been so much pain and bad memories that had surfaced that week. They were delighted to move forward. Finally the hole that ripped their lives apart would soon heal their hearts again. Now they had the power to close it. The end was near.

Zoe initiated the interview. The rest of them stood in the dining room and watched. They were the audience, except this time there were no cheers and no clapping. Jubilation rang in their hearts.

Carl leaned over and whispered to Billie, "I hope Rose will be watching this."

"Oh, she will be."

"You've been rather quiet. What's up?"

She tried to smile. "I have so much on my mind, Carl. I apologize for being a little withdrawn."

"Oh, don't worry about it. We've all been stressed the last couple of days."

Then she turned completely around and said, "My father is very sick."

"I'm sorry to hear that."

"Yeah, and he insisted that I come out here and be with Magnolia. You know how much he cares for her."

"Yes, I know."

"I'm trying really hard to support her but it's so hard to stop thinking about him."

Carl embraced her. "He'll be okay. Don't worry."

Linda tugged on Sam's shirt. "They look great, huh."

"They sure do," Sam whispered.

Linda smiled.

His eyes fixated on Billie. "I swear," if Billie sat in Anthony's place, she could take the place of the other."

"You mean Rose."

"Yes."

"Nah."

"She could."

"Do you know that woman gets sick and tired of people saying that." She handed him a piece of chocolate.

"Really!"

"Yeah! How would you feel?"

"Hmm, I guess you're right."

Two hours later, the interview was over. Zoe made a call to the executive producer and then yelled to Hyacinth, "Guess what?"

"What's going on?"

"This show will air Sunday night."

"No way," Hyacinth said.

"So soon?" said Magnolia.

"The sooner the better, don't you think? Zoe said.

"Everyone's gonna work on this piece."

She jumped up and down. "It will be edited and ready to air by Sunday. In the meantime, take good care of yourselves."

She tapped Magnolia on the shoulder. "Get some rest."

Magnolia glanced at Anthony and smiled.

Zoe said, "And I'll talk to you on Sunday."

Magnolia, Hyacinth, and Anthony escorted Zoe and her crew to the door.

Hyacinth embraced her. "Take care, girl." Then she whispered, "What's going on with you and Jerome?"

"Not a thing. Absolutely nothing. We're great friends."

Hyacinth chuckled.

"Really, we are. I'll always love him. We can't go back to what we had. It's over."

Hyacinth hugged her again. "Zoe, you take care."

"I'll call you on Friday and let you know how it looks."

"Okay, sweetie."

Zoe walked over to Magnolia. "Everything will be fine."

"Thanks for everything," Magnolia said.

"You're welcome. I'll do anything for Hyacinth and her family."

Hyacinth laughed. "You know, I'm still angry at you for leaving Florida."

"You knew I would eventually head up this way."

"Yeah, but I didn't think you would stay."

"I love it here." She waved her hand. "We have to do lunch or dinner before you guys leave."

"That sounds great."

Zoe stepped back. "It's been a pleasure to meet you all. Good luck."

"Thank you," they said.

Magnolia and Hyacinth hugged.

"Sunday," Hyacinth said, quietly laughing.

Magnolia grabbed Hyacinth's hand and screamed. "Yes, Sunday!"

"It's happening, sister. It's going to happen." She gave Magnolia a high five.

"We'll find the rest of them. Wait and see."

CHAPTER 47

That afternoon, Magnolia sat in a patio chair and stared at the blue sky. "Hey, want to go for a walk?" she said to Hyacinth.

"Sure. It's a beautiful day."

Magnolia yelled to the others. "Anyone care to take a walk?"

"No," they said. "You two go ahead," said Billie.

Soon she and Hyacinth left the house and headed down the street.

Meanwhile the men all sat in the den chatting.

"Your sister-in-law really has power at the show," Anthony said to Gregory.

"It seems so." He glanced down at the floor. "That's a lot of power, isn't it? You think she's—"

"She has to be," said Carl.

"Yeah, no woman could call those kinds of shots unless she was," said Sam.

"Hmm, she shoots a segment on a Sunday, then picks up the phone—next thing you know, it's airing in a week. Come on. If she isn't, then she must be one hell of a producer," Carl said.

"You're right, man," said Gregory. "I knew she had to be."

"Something like this normally takes months to air," said Lawrence.

Eating some of Linda's chocolates, Gregory said, "My brother swears—excuse my French—that she fucked her way up."

Anthony burst into laughter.

"Oh, no," roared Carl.

The women were eavesdropping and walked into the den.

"She seems like a dedicated worker," said May-Lynne. "I knew she would be successful."

"I can't believe you men," said Brenda.

"Yeah, the nerve of you," yelled Billie. "You are all jealous. Player hating."

"Why would I be jealous of Zoe?" said Carl.

"Oh, shut up!" said Brenda. She pointed her finger at him. "You know why."

The men laughed.

"Well, you know how it is in the entertainment business," said Lawrence.

Then Anthony said, "Yeah, it happens all the time."

Brenda snatched the candy from Carl's hand. "Yeah, but . . . how far will it get you?"

"Apparently it's gotten her very far," said Sam, quietly laughing.

"Sam!" yelled Patricia. "I can't believe what I'm hearing."

Billie said, "Only in rare occasions does this happens. Zoe did not come across as a person who is easy to manipulate or who would sleep around to get ahead."

Patricia said, "She sure didn't come across that way to me." She threw a toss pillow at Sam and Lawrence. "Look, she's a positive and aggressive white woman. Hey, the only one I know who understands us, if you know what I mean."

Billie grabbed her hand.

"But she's still white," said Linda.

"And . . ." May-Lynne said.

"White folks will never understand us. Please, they don't even want to get to know us."

"You know," Lawrence said, agreeing with Linda.

"But she's not snobbish at all," May-Lynne said, "She's one sharp lady who can fit in anywhere. That is what's gotten her to this position."

"That's right," said Patricia.

Gregory said, "Oh, I don't know why we brought up the issue." He cleared his throat and rolled his eyes. "I forget how close she's become to this family."

Gregory whispered to Anthony, "I'll tell you something, though."

"What's that?"

"Hyacinth knows more about my brother's marriage and the shit that went on than I do. You'd think she would tell me."

Anthony smiled.

"Hyacinth can keep a secret, especially when it concerns Zoe," Gregory said.

Anthony grinned. "That's just like Leah. She only tells me what I want to hear."

"You mean she lies to you."

"Yeah, you could say that."

They laughed. Anthony turned and looked at Linda. "Say Linda, how come you're so quiet?"

"I'm just thinking."

"About what?"

"About everything."

Anthony turned to Gregory and whispered, "I guess Lawrence tore it up last night."

Gregory howled. "You know he did."

Linda started to smile when she looked over at Lawrence. She fiddled with her long hair. Then she glanced back at Lawrence and winked.

Anthony and Gregory looked at each other and both remarked, "Yeah, he did!"

The walk . . .

"It's so quiet and peaceful here, Magnolia. You and Anthony really have a beautiful home," Hyacinth said.

"Thank you. We debated over it, believe it or not."

"Really!"

"Yes, we couldn't come to an agreement."

"Men! I tell you."

Magnolia chuckled. "He fell in love with a home in Peapack. It's near his company."

"Peapack. That sounds like a really well-to-do town."

"So people say. But there was something about this house that really felt like home."

She stared at Hyacinth. "You know what I mean?"

Hyacinth nodded. "Yes."

"The atmosphere was warm and peaceful and I wanted to raise my children here."

"So, how did you come to an agreement?"

"We compromised."

Hyacinth placed her hands on her hips. "You did what?"

"We bought this home but," Magnolia laughed, "Anthony would choose our vacation home."

"Oh, I see. And where is this?"

"We decided to wait until the children came along. We wanted it to be our special hideaway. We have a condo in Santa Monica. But that's not the same. We're looking at the Carolinas or Virginia."

"Wow! That's great, Magnolia."

They walked near a park, stopped, and sat down on a bench. "Are you having difficulty conceiving?" Hyacinth said.

"Yes, I am. The doctors say everything is perfectly fine with the two of us." She shrugged. "Maybe it's stress. Now that my business is doing well, maybe my life can go on the way it should."

Hyacinth held her hand. "Stress can kill you, sister. Never let it take control of you." She stroked her hair. "Release some of that tension."

"I'm trying really hard."

"Don't worry. It will happen. You're still young."

"You think so?"

"Shoo, yeah. Your biological clock hasn't run out yet." There are women in their sixties that have babies."

"But . . . but . . . I don't want to wait that long. I'll adopt if it doesn't happen soon."

"What do you mean? It'll happen," Hyacinth said, kicking the grass. "I feel guilty talking with you about kids. Here I am postponing it, knowing deep down that I really don't want any. And then there's women like you who really want and deserve them yet are having difficulties."

"You don't want kids."

"Am I selfish?"

"I don't think so."

"I've always wanted to travel and see the world. I wanted to experience life and do things before I settled down."

"Well, are you?"

"Yes, and I'm still doing it. It's great to be able to go when you want to and not worry about obligations or responsibilities. I mean, I have responsibilities, but . . . children are a huge responsibility." She laughed. "I must sound horrible."

Magnolia squeezed her hand. "I understand. See, that's something we don't have in common."

They laughed.

Hyacinth said, "I love children and, yes, maybe one day I would like to have one, but for now I want to concentrate on me. My career. I don't want to have any regrets. I don't want to look back and wish I should have done this or that."

She leaned her head back. "For many years, I always got involved with the wrong man. I let them use and abuse me."

Magnolia stared at Hyacinth.

"Not physically, but emotionally and financially. I never had control of my life, Magnolia. Finally I woke up. I matured and learned from my mistakes. I realized that I was important too. I needed to cater to myself. Me."

She pounded her hand on her chest. "This person right here deserved to be treated right."

Magnolia laughed. "One day, we are going to write a book about this. It's going to be one hell of a read."

"Maybe we can have it made into a movie," Hyacinth joked.

"Yes, and Zoe can produce it."

Hyacinth laughed. "Yeah!"

Then Hyacinth grew serious. "Anthony's one hell of a person, Magnolia. He reminds me of someone I used to know."

Magnolia looked at her with an odd expression. "No, this person was a good person, but I let him slip away. They always say you don't know a good thing until it's gone. I was so used to that abusive treatment, you know. But I thank God for Gregory. He's my knight—my prince. He really is. Even though he's twenty years older than me."

"What?" Magnolia said.

"Oh, you didn't know," Hyacinth said giggling.

"No, I didn't. He doesn't look it."

"I know. He looks great, doesn't he?"

"Hell, yeah! If you hadn't told me, I would have thought he was in his early forties, maybe late forties, but not—"

"I know. Don't say it."

"Does he have any children?"

"Yes, he has a thirty-year-old daughter. She lives in Seattle."

"Really."

"Umm—hmm. She's great. She comes to visit every summer and most holidays."

"Does Gregory want more children?"

"Believe it or not he does. He wants a son. His heir. Oh, yes, an heir."

"All men want a male inheritor. Well, I'm happy for you, Hyacinth. Take your time and follow your heart. Travel, explore, and treat yourself to life's riches."

Hyacinth smiled. "This was nice. We definitely have to take more of these walks."

"Yes."

They got off of the bench. "Let's head back," said Magnolia.

When they arrived home, Anthony took out some more photo albums and showed them to the rest of the gang.

Patricia looked up. "You're back."

"Did you miss us?" Hyacinth said.

"Yes, I did." Patricia said. "Your wedding pictures were beautiful, Magnolia. You looked like a princess."

"Thank you."

"Let's see," said Hyacinth. "Oh, Magnolia. You were beautiful. Your gown was gorgeous."

She gave Magnolia a curious look. "Do you still have it?"

Magnolia smiled. "Of course I do." She rubbed Hyacinth's back. "It's upstairs in the attic. I'll show you it later."

Hyacinth smiled.

Carl and Brenda cuddled in a corner, taking a moment to relax and breathe. Gregory and Lawrence sat near them. Lawrence couldn't resist asking Carl about his business.

"Say, Carl. I'm still stunned about the good news I heard earlier."

"You mean the Simon General contract?"

"You speak so lightly of it."

Carl slouched up and leaned forward. "When you've been in this business for as long as I have, a person begins to talk this way."

He stood and walked over to the counter and poured himself a glass of Chardonnay. He turned to Lawrence. "You see, Lawrence, I try not to make this an obsession. This is my career."

Carl held the glass in one hand and moved the other hand up and down. "I like what I do no matter how much money is involved. I can't put too much emphasis on the dollar sign because it would drive me crazy."

Lawrence seemed confused.

Then Carl said, "Man, the money can be here today and gone tomorrow. My goal is to continue to expand the company, do great work, and get more business."

He gulped down the wine and poured another glass. "Believe me, I don't take anything for granted. But money isn't everything to me. It never was and never will be. You know what I mean, man?"

"I do now."

"Anthony and I were always successful businessmen, regardless of the money. Our company did exceptionally well. We took it to another level." He shrugged his shoulders. "And of course, more money came into play. You understand me."

"You bet I do." Lawrence gave him a high five. "How long have you known Anthony?"

"Ever since he was in business school."

"Oh, really!"

"Yeah, I was a guess speaker at Princeton," he said grinning. "Back then, I was Vice President of Investment Product Systems at a computer software corporation. Anthony impressed me so much, I hired him on the spot."

He twirled his glass. "His medical background, expertise, and personality were outstanding. It was clear to me the two of us would make a dynamic team. A few years later, we both agreed that we needed to start our own company."

"That's great, man. Perseverance, I hear you!"

Winking, Carl said, "Anthony's a hard and dedicated worker. So is Magnolia. He'll say he's learned everything from me. But really, we learned from each other. The man is brilliant. Absolutely brilliant!"

Lawrence and Gregory chuckled.

"If you want, we can sit down and talk more about the business, medical school, and where you want to go from here," said Carl. "There's so much you can do with a medical degree aside from practicing."

"I understand. But definitely, man, I would really appreciate that talk."

They shook hands.

"Anthony's like a younger brother, huh." said Gregory.

"Yes, he is. He and Magnolia are my family. I care for them deeply."

CHAPTER 48

The women chatted in the kitchen. Magnolia wanted to know more about her birth mother. "What was my mother like, Mrs. Johnson?" she said to Patricia.

"She was very family oriented," Patricia said smiling. "Her children always came first. She worked extremely hard to take good care of you and your siblings. She even worked three jobs."

"Wow!" said Linda.

"Yes, she was a housekeeper, a seamstress, and she also worked in the cotton fields."

"My, God!" said Billie. "She sounds like an incredible woman."

"Oh, yes. Do you know how you got your name?"

Magnolia and Hyacinth glanced at each other and said, "No . . . how?"

"Your mother loved nature and she was a gifted gardener, so she named you all after flowers."

Shaking her head, Magnolia said, "You know, the significance of our names never came to mind even after meeting Hyacinth or learning about Rose."

"And, I bet the others are named after flowers too."

They all laughed.

"I'm sure," said Hyacinth.

"What did she look like?" said Hyacinth.

"She was a very attractive lady," Patricia said softly. "She had a beautiful complexion, much like yourself." She touched Magnolia's hair. "And her . . . her hair was long and thick like yours, Magnolia. She had the prettiest smile. She looked like an angel."

"Really," said Magnolia.

"Yes. You and Hyacinth are both gorgeous—exact images of your mother."

Billie said. "Did you meet the other children?"

"Only the oldest boy. He was quite a handsome young fellow."

Billie turned and stared into the den, observing the men. When Carl noticed her looking, he turned his head and wondered what was the topic of their conversation.

Slamming her hand on the kitchen table, Patricia said, "And boy did your mother brag that he was such a bright kid." She giggled. "He was a role model for the others, you know."

"Did she have a hard life—Ma?" Hyacinth said.

"Just in the end. It was extremely rough. She couldn't afford anything, not even food." There was a twisted smile on her face. "And to make matters worse, her boyfriend—your father—abandoned her and she fell ill."

Billie looked away. She felt sorry for their birth mother. She felt sorry for the person who had struggled to raise six children in the Deep South alone and against so many odds.

"That's so sad," Hyacinth said.

For a moment, everyone seemed disheartened but then Linda ended the sadness. "It's amazing the two of you had similar dreams. I wonder if Rose had them too."

"Tell me about them," Billie said. "When I received the call from Magnolia, she briefly told me the entire story, including the dreams."

Hyacinth began, "Well, I've always dreamt about a farm. There were children playing outside, and an elderly couple who always sat on the porch." She paused and giggled. "And, the man drove a black truck."

"Yes, the kids joyously played outside," Magnolia added. She pinched her chin. "What . . . what was it they were playing?"

"They were playing kick ball," said Hyacinth.

"Yeah. That was it."

Looking at Billie, Hyacinth said, "It was like we had this intuition about each other."

Billie said, "It must have been some powerful force that brought you two together."

"Powerful indeed," Brenda said, pulling out a cigarette from the worn box. She walked to the back door and opened it. She lit a cigarette and nodded her head. Then she turned her head to them. "Things like this don't happen by chance. This was meant to be."

"You think so?" Magnolia said.

She took a strong puff. "You know, this faith I have in my heart," she said patting her chest, "it came through for me and a lot of people."

With the cigarette still in hand, she pointed to Magnolia. "Magnolia, I truly believed your heartache would end and a better day would come."

Linda kicked Magnolia, then slapped Billie on the lap. She whispered to them, "Something must be wrong at home. She ain't talking right." Linda chewed on a pretzel. "No wonder Mr. Man bought her a new Mercedes."

"Shut up!" Magnolia said.

"That's right. There you go assuming again," whispered Billie.

Finally Hyacinth said, "Anyway, it turns out that the children were us and the couple could have been our parents."

"We don't know that for sure," Magnolia said.

"Oh, you'll find out soon," Brenda said.

"Do you know how many times I've heard that?"

Brenda extinguished the cigarette and put it in the ashtray and sat down. "I'm confident because I can feel it deep down here."

She placed Magnolia's hand to her chest. "Right here. Can you feel it?"

Magnolia stared at Brenda strangely and the tears began to fall. "No, I can't feel it."

Brenda immediately pressed Magnolia's hand firmly on her

chest. "Feel it, baby! It's right in there. All the love you've ever wanted is in here."

Suddenly Hyacinth began to cry.

"Keep your head up, Magnolia," Brenda said. She wrapped her arms around her. "Because one day, they'll come knocking on that door."

Hyacinth said, "And, I hope that day is soon."

Brenda winked at Hyacinth. "It may be sooner than you think."

Speechless, Carl and Anthony stood by the kitchen door and watched the women. Carl's hands began to shake. He walked over to Magnolia. "Is everything okay?"

She waved her hands. "Oh, don't pay me any mind, I'm such a baby."

They laughed but Brenda knew that, in time, happiness would come into their lives again.

Attempting to break the edgy atmosphere, Anthony said, "So Carl, when is the family coming?"

"Probably Christmas," he said. "Mama's really excited."

"I can't believe your sister moved to Chicago. As much as she loved New Jersey."

"Well, her job led her there."

"How's fat man?"

"Still fat."

They both laughed.

"Nah . . . he's great. He's cut down on junk food and lost some weight," Carl said. "We hardly ever get to see him, especially since he moved to Massachusetts."

"What's your sister's profession?" Sam said.

"She's the president of a college."

"Really!"

"Yes."

Hyacinth said, "And your brother."

"Oh, he's this big time criminal lawyer."

"That's great."

"Yeah, I'm really proud of them."

"How about your mother? Is she retired."

He stared at Brenda. "Yes, my mother retired years ago."

"And your father?"

Brenda pulled out another cigarette, placed the lighter to it, and said, "Excuse me, I'm going to have another smoke." She walked to the back door and stepped outside.

Carl's eyes followed her every move, making her tense. She looked back at him and shut the door.

"My father passed away."

"I'm sorry to hear that."

"They'll all be here for the holidays. Hopefully, you will get a chance to meet them. They're looking forward to meeting you."

"Is that so?" said Hyacinth.

"Yes. They wanted to meet you now but I thought it would be best for you all if they waited. Give you and your family time to get adjusted to Magnolia and everything that's going on."

"Well, I can't wait to meet them. I'm sure if they're anything like you it will be a pleasure."

"You know, Anthony and Magnolia are like my mom's children too."

Anthony and Magnolia smiled.

"She adores them," Carl said.

"Will they stay a while when they get here?" Anthony said.

"Yeah, they will."

"So will we," said Gregory. Hyacinth tapped his leg.

Billie said, "Are you guys planning on staying through the holidays?"

"I sure hope so," said Gregory. "I'll just take a leave of absence."

Hyacinth said, "Well, we'll have to see how everything goes."

Anthony kissed Magnolia's cheek and said, "Hopefully, everything will go your way. Sunday is the big day, huh."

Yes, Sunday, Magnolia thought.

CHAPTER 49

Sunday morning . . .

Anthony and Magnolia lay blissfully in bed protected by the silken sheets. The delicate autumn breeze scented the air. When he groped her, he could feel her body stiffen. So he held her close. "What's wrong, baby? Are you still nervous about the show?" he whispered into her ear.

"No, not at all. Actually, I've been looking forward to it. I'm just a little nervous about what's going to happen after it airs."

Anthony smiled and she rubbed her fingers across his lips.

"Will we get any calls? Will someone recognize our faces? Is Rose alive? Is the rest of my family alive?"

His weighty body leaned over hers. "Stop worrying. Of course they are all alive. We'll find them."

He kissed her. "When they call, we'll all sit in the den, just like the other night, laughing, talking, drinking, and eating—we'll have a grand time."

He kissed her again, "We'll be reminiscing, learning more, asking plenty of questions, getting to know each other."

"I wonder what mother is thinking of right now."

"She's relieved that soon it will all be over," he said, stroking her hair. "Soon you will finally unite with your family."

Magnolia inhaled and exhaled.

"Your mother was young and lonely then. The thoughtless one is Aunt Henrietta. She deceived everyone because they all believed they were doing some kind of generous deed for the children. Your mother loved you, Magnolia. She really did. She just didn't know how to show it."

Sunday afternoon . . .

Linda sat with Lawrence on the patio, exchanging stories of the good old days growing up with Magnolia and Hyacinth.

They giggled and stared at each other frequently. She smiled when the trees swayed, loosing their yellow leaves onto the ground.

The weather was so fitting, she suggested they all visit Manhattan. She would be the designated tour guide.

Their first stop was 42nd Street and Times Square. Hyacinth, May-Lynne, and Gregory stared in awe at the buildings and people.

Next stop was Brenda's sister, Wednesday's, store on Park Avenue. Wednesday had been an interior decorator for many years. Her clients were mainly celebrities and famous athletes. She was thrilled when she saw Magnolia and the rest of the group walk into her business, which proudly displayed pictures of the magnificent homes she had decorated.

Then they strolled through Central Park, stopping at The Metropolitan Museum and even the offices of Acirfa Literary Agency.

Once inside Linda showed everyone the massive balcony that encircled their office. Lawrence glanced down at the figures roaming the streets, and then smiled at Linda. He thought about their lovemaking the night before and how exciting it would have been to make love out there.

Magnolia began to lead them into the studio apartment, but when she opened the door she noticed the unmade bed and immediately closed the door. She knew Linda had been there recently. So she turned everyone's attention to the shelf that housed the books they had sold. She stared at Linda and rolled her eyes. Linda giggled. Magnolia suspected Lawrence from the start. Then she thought, *No, he wouldn't. He barely knows her.*

Linda found the situation amusing. She wasn't concerned about Magnolia's feelings. Ever since she was a young girl, she never conformed to anyone's rules. Linda did things her way even under the touchiest circumstances. She knew that one day her past would catch up to her. Living on the edge would be her undoing.

Later she took them to Harlem. Exhausted from the long walks and sightseeing, they went to a nearby restaurant for dinner. Afterwards they headed back to New Jersey.

Once back home, they nervously sat in the large den drinking sodas. Everyone remained quiet and waited in front of the enormous television screen for the show to come on.

Finally the music began to play and the title of the show scrolled up. The host of the show, a tall, slender man dressed in a brown suit, began to discuss the matter of a missing World War II veteran.

There was a commercial break, which broke the ice in the room. Carl initiated a conversation about the missing veteran and everyone tried to unravel the mystery, providing an educated guess as to where he could be.

When the show returned the host began to discuss the case of the Walker triplets. The title read, 'A Family Torn Apart—Can A Rose Bring Them Together?'

The scene of Zoe sitting in their living room introducing herself and presenting an overview of the saga appeared.

"Oh, my God!" said Magnolia, who put her hands to her mouth. "I can't believe that's me. Look at me."

"Hush!" whispered Billie.

So they silently listened. At the end of the segment, Zoe said, "Rose, if you're out there and watching, please call our 800 number."

Zoe paused and glanced at Magnolia and Hyacinth. "If anyone has any information about the Walker family, please call the number you see on your screen."

The host stared into the camera and said, "Thank you and good night."

Carl held Brenda's hand. She patted his thigh and rolled her head back on the sofa.

Magnolia released a deep breath and said to Hyacinth, "Do you think she was watching?"

"If she wasn't, someone she knows was."

Gregory said, "This will be aired again on Monday. Zoe will continue to air it until we find someone."

Suddenly the telephone rang. The sudden loud tone frightened them all. Magnolia and Hyacinth's eyes widened.

Anthony hesitated then jumped up and answered it, "Hello. Oh, hello, Zoe!"

He smiled and looked back at the rest of the group. "Yes, we all watched it. You did a terrific job. Yes, thank you. Believe me, our fingers our crossed."

He signaled for Hyacinth, who began walking toward him.

"Okay, Zoe. I'll let them know. Goodbye," he said.

"What did she say?" said Hyacinth.

"She said the show will continue to air until someone calls. She promised she wouldn't give up on this."

Hyacinth smiled. Magnolia turned to Linda and Billie and they all smiled.

Late Sunday Evening . . .

When the telephone rang again later that evening, Magnolia thought, *Who could it be this time of night?*

She picked up the telephone, and to her surprise, it was Mya.

"Good evening, Magnolia."

"Hello, Mya. What's up?"

"I watched *Separations* this evening. I didn't . . . I didn't . . ."

"Oh, I'm so sorry, Mya. That was inconsiderate of me. I should have called you. Everything happened so fast. I'm really sorry."

"I thought you weren't yourself. You had been acting very strange lately. It is amazing, Magnolia, that you are a triplet."

Magnolia laughed. "Isn't it?"

"Is Hyacinth . . ."

"Yes . . . she's here now. You'll meet her soon, don't worry."

"When I saw the two of you sitting there together, I was completely astonished. I still have goose bumps."

Magnolia laughed again. "We all do."

"I know you have your family there and I don't want to keep you on the telephone long, but I thought you should know this."

"What is it?"

"I went to the office this evening to catch up on some work." She giggled. "I must confess, I watched the show there."

"And what else is new. You love that office."

"I really do. I'm so glad we moved into it. Anyway, I had to make a thousand copies of the Roderick Stein manuscript and I knew Monday morning would be very busy. I didn't want to tie my day down making copies."

Magnolia rolled her eyes. "Okay . . . and . . ."

"There were two messages from Mackenzie Gary."

"Oh, really?" said Magnolia.

"Yes. The first one was on Saturday afternoon. She wanted to let you know that she's looking forward to you representing her. And . . . she left the second message just as I was leaving the office. She's changed her mind."

"She's changed her mind about what?"

"Oh, about coming later this month."

"Don't tell me she canceled on us again."

"No . . . No . . ."

Magnolia was silent. Then she softly said, "What then?"

"She wants to come sooner. She'll be in the city this coming Tuesday."

"Tuesday!" Magnolia screamed, virtually dropping the telephone.

"Magnolia, are you still there?"

"Yes, I'm still here."

"She said she's really excited about everything. She's anxious to get the book published. She confirmed her travel itinerary with me. I checked your calendar and that day is practically open." Mya paused. "I didn't know if I should trouble you with this, especially with all that is going on right now."

"I'm glad you did. I'm really excited that she's coming sooner."

"Would you like for me to pick her up at the airport? You know, she's not at all familiar with the city."

By now Anthony sensed something was going on because Magnolia was extremely quiet. When he walked behind her and kissed her neck, she grabbed the side of his face.

"I tell you what. I'll pick her up. There's so much to discuss— we have many details to work out," Magnolia said.

"Okay, that's fine with me."

"Thanks, Mya. By the way, you're a workaholic, you know that."

They both laughed.

"But really, thanks for all your hard work. I really appreciate it. You're terrific."

"Thank you, Magnolia. Will I see you on Monday?"

"No, I'm going to work at home next week. I'll stop in from time to time, though."

"Sounds good. Have a good evening."

"You too, Mya. Good night."

Magnolia turned to Linda and told her the good news. Linda threw her hands in the air. She shook her head and said, "Please, don't tell me any more. That's your client."

"She's our client!"

"No . . . No . . . you're going to handle her from now on. When is she coming again?"

"Tuesday."

Waving her hand at Magnolia, Linda sarcastically said, "Whatever, you deal with it, Magnolia. I'm serious. I can't believe you're going to pick her up."

"Why not? What's wrong with that?"

Linda was so angry that her complexion turned red. "You've never done it before."

"Well . . . this will be the first time."

"You're too generous, Magnolia. I bet you she's pulling our leg again, for the umpteenth time. She'll probably sign on with someone else. She's talked with Geoffrey at Blue Page Agency."

"Who cares who she talked to—I know for sure she wants our representation. Besides, Blue Page Agency doesn't have her best interests at heart. She'll read right through that."

"I bet you're wrong."

"I guess we'll just have to wait and see."

Hyacinth said, "Who are you talking about?"

Linda said, pouting, "You don't want to know, girl."

"Our client is coming in on Tuesday and—" Magnolia said.

"A prospective client."

Magnolia raised her voice. "She's coming to sign a contract with our agency. She had been a pretty difficult person to deal with the last few weeks but she's a wonderful writer nonetheless."

"Pretty difficult," said Hyacinth.

"Intolerable," said Linda.

Rolling her eyes at Linda, Magnolia said to Hyacinth, "Would you like to come with me to the airport on Tuesday."

"I would love to," said Hyacinth.

Magnolia walked toward Linda and patted her back. "How about you, Linda?"

"I'll have to think about it."

CHAPTER 50

On Monday morning, Magnolia stepped onto the balcony and heard Hyacinth and Gregory talking as they sat on the comfortable lounge chairs below.

Hyacinth glanced up at Magnolia. "Your garden is beautiful, Magnolia. Did a landscaper do this?"

"Yes and no. Someone helped me arrange it all, but I did most of the planting."

"You're really creative. I really dig the arrangement. The colors are so brilliant."

Magnolia smiled. "Thank you."

"Your home is beautifully decorated," Gregory said. "It's warm and cozy. Hyacinth and I are going to hire Wednesday to decorate our place."

Magnolia laughed. "You really like it, huh?"

"Yeah. We're in the process of looking for a home, so she'll be expecting a phone call from us soon."

She laughed again. "She would really love to help you two."

She stared down at Hyacinth. "Hyacinth, you're just as creative."

"No, not like you. You do everything so easily. Was your mother that way?"

"No, my mother wasn't that way at all. She was into antiques.

Not that our home wasn't striking—a lot of the pieces she bought were nice, a little old-fashioned."

"Umm," Hyacinth muttered.

"What time is it?" Gregory said.

"It's a quarter to ten," said Magnolia.

"We should go inside—the show is coming on again in fifteen minutes."

"I can't believe you!" said Hyacinth.

* * *

Carl and Billie sampled some fruit Anthony purchased the day before and chatted in the living room.

"I knew it was only a matter of time before you and Anthony made it big," said Billie. "You two are such great businessmen—intelligent and imaginative. I'm really happy for you."

"Thank you, Billie. We knew it was coming, but we didn't know exactly when it would happen. Now I sleep a little better at night."

"What are you talking about? You guys have always been successful."

"Well, things are really beginning to go my way—the way it's supposed to be. You know what I mean."

"Not exactly, but I think I know where you're going."

"Everything's right. My home, my family, the company."

"Ahh, I see."

"Enough about me, so how's the practice?"

"It's okay. These HMOs are really killing most physicians. I'm losing most of my patients to them. I was offered a medical director position at one of the major insurance companies."

Carl stared at her. "An HMO."

"No."

"Well, I knew managed care would eventually destroy the medical industry. So, are you going to take it?"

"I'm not sure. The way things are going, I should, huh."

"It's up to you. Why don't you come and work with Anthony

and me?"

"Are you out of your mind? Business and friends don't mix well."

"Come on! We've done it!"

"I love Anthony to death and I wouldn't want to ruin our relationship. I've seen it happen."

Putting his hands in the air, he said, "Oh, well, I tried."

"Thanks for the offer. I really appreciate it. But, I was thinking about coming out here and maybe starting my own costume jewelry business."

"I forget, you know all about that stuff, huh."

"Yeah, Dad taught me everything. I really like creating jewelry."

"I've seen what you've made for Magnolia, Linda, and Brenda. I think that's a great idea. You would really do well out here, too."

Billie smiled. "I believe I'm going to do just that. And hey, if that doesn't work out for me, then I can always get back into practicing or even teaching."

"You are something else, Billie. Every time I look at you, I see a lot of qualities that Magnolia has and I know where she gets them from."

"Please, don't start that again."

"You and I both know that when two people hang around each other for a long time, they begin to look alike. That's what people say about Anthony and me."

Billie laughed. "You and Anthony look and act nothing alike and you know that."

They both chuckled.

Suddenly Carl grabbed her arm. "Billie, I've been meaning to ask you—are you okay? You've been acting really strange the past few days."

"I'm . . . I'm fine."

"You're not the same, Billie. A little reserved, nervous maybe."

She stared into his eyes. "We've both been a little reserved this past week, wouldn't you agree? You always say I look and act like Magnolia, but you want to know the truth?"

"What's that?"

"You and I share a common quality."

"We do?"

"Yes, we do. We keep things inside—deep down inside. We're connoisseurs of keeping secrets. Aren't we?"

"What are you getting at, Billie?"

"Oh, nothing. It's just that there's a lot going on in my life, like my father's illness. My mom and I are having a hard time dealing with it."

"Hey, if there's anything Brenda and I can do, don't hesitate to call."

"Thanks."

Billie paused and quickly changed subjects. "So Carl, how is everything with you? Aside from the business life, how is everything at home?"

"Everything is perfect. Brenda and I are doing great."

"I saw that new Mercedes. I guess everything is great. But, is it really perfect, Carl?"

He shrugged and stared at her.

"I always imagined you being the father of twenty children," Billie said.

"Why would you imagine that?"

"I guess, you always seemed like someone who could be the father of twenty children. And then there's your contributions to all those children's organizations. You and Brenda were going to adopt once before. What happened?"

"We decided not to." His fingers grazed his hair. "There were things going on in our lives personally that we needed to take care of before we adopted. And before we knew it, time just passed us by. We've gotten older and things have changed."

"Did you finally take care of those things, Carl?"

"We're getting around to it."

"Well, that's good to hear."

"Besides, my sister has three and my brother has two. And hopefully, Anthony and Magnolia will start their own family soon."

Billie smiled. "Yeah, I can't wait for a little god-nephew or—

niece."

"What about you, Billie? When are you going to have some?"

She laughed. "As soon as I find a husband."

They both giggled again.

"And I know that will take forever." Carl shook his head. "Woman, your standards are way too high. You'll be eighty years old before you settle down."

"Excuse me!" She put her hand on her shoulder and rubbed it. Then she nodded. "My standards are not high at all."

"So then, what's the problem?"

"It's just that . . ."

"Um-Hmm."

"It's just that . . . for some reason . . . it's difficult to remain in a stable relationship right now."

Carl stared at her.

"Maybe I should definitely relocate out here," she said. "Black men are different out here."

"Really!"

"Yes, they are. That's who I really want to spend the rest of my life with. Besides, I've grown tired of Los Angeles. I'm looking for something fresh."

"What? More thrill?"

"No, I'm looking for stability and growth. I feel like I don't have that and I'm ready to make the move to obtain it."

"Are you serious? You're really considering leaving L.A?"

"Yes! I don't have many friends or family in Los Angeles, and I really miss Magnolia. We see less and less of each other as the years go by."

"What about your family? Where are they?"

"Dad is originally from Georgia. He has a sister and a brother in California, but dad was the only one that had a child."

"Oh, really!"

"Yeah. Mom's family cut her loose when she married him."

"Umm."

"Yes, she has three brothers and one sister. Do you know that my grandparents are still alive. Mom was the oldest. When she left home, her mother gave her some money. That kept her and Dad on their feet when they came to Los Angeles."

"Have you met them?"

"No—none of them. And I don't care to meet them."

"Why did your parents decide to live in California."

"Mom wanted to be a movie star."

"Umm."

Billie stared at him. "Very interesting, isn't it?"

"Yes."

"Mom and Dad are full of secrets." She laughed. "I guess we all keep secrets, huh. We keep them inside until we can't breathe, can't think, and can't even live anymore. We carry that heavy load throughout our lives."

She smacked his leg. "Sometimes it's time to let go of them, Carl. Let go of the pain."

"There you go talking about secrets again. Whatever it is you're trying to say, please come out and say it, because I can't read your mind."

"Carl, all I'm saying is, live and love."

He nodded.

"Life is too short to walk around with pain and bitterness. Dad taught me that. Sickness really brings the worst and best out of you."

"Hmm, I guess it does."

Their eyes locked to each other.

Then Magnolia approached. "*Separations* is on but our segment is not up yet."

"Okay, we're coming in," said Billie as she glanced at Carl. "Are you ready?"

"Yes."

She smiled and grabbed his arm and they casually walked into the den.

CHAPTER 51

Tuesday morning

September's cool inviting air circulated in the bedroom, stimulating Magnolia's high spirits. She pranced around the bedroom in her robe, humming a song about happy feelings.

Anthony stood at the bathroom door and giggled. It pleased him to see her smile.

"What time are you going to pick up Miss Mackenzie?" he said.

"For your information, it's Miss Mackenzie Gary."

Shaking his head, he said, "Excuse me!"

She laughed. "You're excused. Anyway, she's flying into Newark at one o'clock."

"Will Mya accompany you?"

"No, Hyacinth and possibly Linda will."

Magnolia plopped onto the bed. "You know, I think I'm going to take care of Mya's wedding reception."

"What?" Anthony said, putting his hand up to his ear. "Did I hear you right?"

"Yes, you did, sir. She's been great to me and I really appreciate her hard work."

"What's wrong with a gift certificate from Nordstrom's or lunch at the Hilton?"

"Yeah, I'm going to have it at Tavern on the Green."

"Are you insane! She'd better be thankful she got a job."

"You just don't appreciate exceptional employees, Anthony. But I do."

"Well, I hope the money is going to come from your earnings, not mine."

"Oh, please, Anthony. You don't have to worry about a thing."

"I won't."

After breakfast, everyone remained at the dining table and conversed. Hyacinth said, "So Linda, have you decided whether or not you're coming with us?"

"I think it's about time I meet this strange woman."

Hyacinth laughed. "You might like her."

"I don't think so. I really would like to give her a piece of my mind but—"

"But, you are a professional, right?" said Magnolia.

"Yes, I am."

Magnolia glanced at her watch. "I guess we'd better get going."

"Get going!" shouted Linda. "It's eleven o'clock. Ain't' she coming at one?"

"Ain't she," said Anthony. He turned to Carl and whispered, "You can take a person out of the ghetto but you can't take the ghetto out of the person."

Carl laughed. "You know."

"You're always rushing folks to get to the airport early, and all we do is sit and wait," Linda said.

"Come on, woman! Let's go now," shouted Magnolia.

On the way to the airport, Magnolia stopped at Toys 'R' Us and purchased something for Mackenzie's son.

"I can't believe you're doing this shit for her," barked Linda.

"You need to watch your mouth," said Magnolia.

When Linda glanced back, Hyacinth shrugged. "Can you believe this? She's kissing this woman's ass. I know one thing, she needs to be licking ours," Linda said.

Hyacinth laughed. "You two are incredible. I can't believe you work together."

They both looked at her. "Neither can we!"

After parking, Magnolia lowered her head to pray. Linda suddenly jumped out of the car. "I don't have time for this. Let's pick up the bitch, have her come in and sign the got damn contract, and drop her ass off at the hotel."

Magnolia rolled her eyes, and Linda quickly walked away from the car and headed toward the revolving doors.

Magnolia turned to Hyacinth. "I apologize for her conduct."

"Oh, don't worry. I understand Linda quite well now."

Extremely upset, Magnolia climbed out of the car. She and Hyacinth followed Linda.

Magnolia had forgotten Mackenzie Gary's agenda in the car but she remembered the name of the airline. "Shit!" she said, snapping her fingers in disappointment.

"What's wrong?" Hyacinth said.

"I left the flight information and the toy in the car. I'm pretty sure she's coming through Gate 111."

"Well, let's go back to the car. It's no big deal."

She glanced at her watch. "No, it's close to one o'clock."

"Let's find an information booth," said Hyacinth.

They headed toward the gates of Conrad Airlines once inside the airport. They began to walk the long corridor that led to the gates.

While patrolling the area, Magnolia blurted, "There's no one around here."

Linda sat in the waiting area of Gate 111 and began to read a magazine while Magnolia and Hyacinth walked further down the corridor. They could not locate an information booth.

Two airline employees, who were standing on both sides of the double doors by the gate and dressed in red and blue uniforms, slowly opened the doors.

When a herd of people rushed out of Gate 111, Hyacinth and Magnolia hurried toward the gate. Linda sat fixed in her seat, ignoring them and the busy stream of passengers.

"What does she look like?" Hyacinth said.

"I don't know. She said on my voice mail that she would be wearing a red pants suit."

"Oh, okay."

"Damn," said Magnolia, feeling disappointed. "This wasn't supposed to happen."

"Don't worry. We'll find her."

In the plane . . .

"Precious, we're here. Are you ready?"

"Yes, Mommy," said the five-year-old chubby boy.

As the ginger-complexioned woman began to pull her son out of the seat, the flight attendant said, "Ma'am, would you like some help?"

"No, I'm fine. Thank you."

"Are you sure?" the flight attendant said, looking down at the floor.

"Yes, I'm sure," the woman said smiling.

It was clear the woman was in great physical shape. She threw a garment bag and a large duffel bag on one arm and then picked her son out of the seat with the other. They walked toward the exit, which guided the procession line to the gate's door.

Magnolia and Hyacinth patiently waited. Suddenly Magnolia turned to Linda and rolled her eyes. She was disgusted by her behavior. It would have been better had she stayed home.

A custodian with a Hispanic accent approached them and cheerfully said, "Hey, I remember you two from last week. How you doing? Waiting for another sister today?"

Hyacinth and Magnolia laughed.

"No, unfortunately, not today," said Magnolia. "We're waiting for someone else this time."

He smiled. "Nice seeing you. Have a nice day."

"You too," they said.

"Can you imagine," said Hyacinth. "He remembered us."

"Yeah, we made such a scene, who would forget," Magnolia said. "The thought of him saying that just sends chills down my spine."

The custodian slowly walked away, sweeping trash into a portable bin.

Magnolia and Hyacinth continued to extend their heads above the crowd hoping to spot Mackenzie Gary.

They heard a sudden loud scream. It was the voice of the custodian worker, who was waving his hand. "Hey... Hey... she over here, at Gate 113."

Magnolia pointed to her chest, unsure if the man was speaking to her. "Is he talking to me?" she said.

"I guess so," Hyacinth said.

"Well, let's go and see," said Magnolia.

As they walked toward Gate 113, they stared ahead and noticed a woman coming toward them. The person was wearing a red pants suit and holding onto a child by the hand.

Magnolia scrunched her eyes and looked at Hyacinth. Hyacinth stretched her neck forward and placed her hand on her forehead as if the sun were beaming down on her face. She tried to get a clear view of the two people. Slowly they faced each other again in shock.

Their legs locked and they stood frozen in the middle of the corridor, staring at the figures slowly coming toward them.

As the two people came near, the little boy began to smile and pulled away from his mother, who tugged him closer toward her and walked straight ahead, callously staring at Magnolia and Hyacinth.

Magnolia swallowed hard and Hyacinth nervously pulled on her hair. They trembled with fear and stood there silent and visibly confused.

When Linda turned her head slightly, she observed them standing in the middle of the corridor looking sickly. She quickly jumped out of her seat and looked at Magnolia and Hyacinth, and then stared at the figures heading toward them.

The magazine Linda was holding slid from her hand, the pages riffling as it fell. Her hands and legs swayed as though she were intoxicated. She began to stagger toward the two people.

"The nerve... of this bitch," she mumbled. "This shit isn't funny."

Linda looked back at Magnolia and then at Hyacinth, who were absolutely speechless. Linda stopped walking, then looked up at the ceiling and breathed heavily. Suddenly she rushed toward the individuals, still breathing erratically.

The woman firmly held the young boy's hand and staggered slowly. She saw Linda rushing toward her.

The woman had a twisted smile. Her face was unfeeling. She continued to walk as fast as she could without stumbling, nearly dragging her son.

Finally Linda reached her. Beads of moisture stained her face. Her hands trembled. They stood facing each other—at attention. Linda's chest heaved up and down. Her bottom lip began to sag and then her mouth slowly opened wide. She suddenly gasped.

The woman's glassy eyes gazed into Linda's. They were filled with bitterness. She grinned and in an even tone, she said, "Hello, Linda."

Linda tried to remain balanced, but she was completely mute. The woman extended her hand to Linda and said again, "It's a pleasure meeting you, Linda."

A compelling force silenced Linda, who was usually a headstrong person full of militant words and expressions. The force broke through her hard shield, tearing down her overconfident behavior, self-serving gratification, and absolute stubbornness.

When Linda did not respond, the woman forcibly grabbed Linda's hand and shook it firmly.

Perspiration streamed down Linda's face. Her heart raced and she felt as though it was going to explode. She sucked in the sticky air and bit by bit released it. Then she closed her eyes, thinking about the moment she stormed out of Magnolia's car. Thinking about how ill-mannered she was acting and how that hurt Magnolia.

Linda's eyes opened and she stared at the woman, shivering. "Rose?"

CHAPTER 52

Hyacinth and Magnolia wailed long and loud. Everyone including the custodian crowded around them.

The custodian touched Magnolia's arm. "It's all right, lady," he said, pointing to Rose. "Go . . . go to her."

Magnolia looked up at him. Confusion and fear suffocated her. She was supposed to meet Mackenzie Gary, not her sister, Rose. Maybe this was a bad dream.

She turned around and stared at Gate 111 and mumbled, "Hyacinth . . . we . . . we better go back . . . she'll be coming soon."

"No . . . no," said the worker, pointing to Linda and the woman. "She's over there."

When Magnolia's trembling body began to slump to the floor, the custodian immediately grabbed her. She sadly looked at him and then at Rose from a distance. "Why?" cried Magnolia.

"It can't be," screamed Hyacinth, cuffing her hand over her mouth. Suddenly she began to weave her fingers through her hair.

"Why?" Magnolia said again, standing next to Hyacinth, who was unbalanced. "Why?"

As Magnolia staggered toward Linda and the woman who looked uncannily like her and Hyacinth, Hyacinth nervously followed her weeping.

For months Rose had known this moment would come. She

didn't know what the end result would be and she did not care either. She wanted her sisters to feel her pain.

Months earlier she envisioned them standing in the terminal, speaking in outbursts. But here they were speechless and unable to move. The anguish on their faces inspired a peace of mind. Rose knew they were frightened of her and afraid to come closer. She couldn't sympathize with them. *Pay back time*, was all she thought.

When Magnolia and Hyacinth finally reached her, Magnolia grabbed Linda's hand and squeezed it. There was a slight jiggle coming from Linda. Magnolia held on to her hand for life. And gradually the shaking subsided.

The three of them were dead silent and simply stared at her. Magnolia's eyes welled up, and they were painfully red and swollen. She was seething. Just the thought of knowing that this woman pretended to be someone else all of these months unnerved her. Nothing could calm her down.

What Magnolia didn't know was that this was all a plan for Rose. She knew Magnolia desperately wanted to work with her. She knew Magnolia wanted to meet her and have her in her life.

Rose knew all about Magnolia's complex life's story. She knew that Magnolia connected to her and Magnolia fell prey to her cruel scheme.

Magnolia felt violated, used, and taken for granted. She slightly raised her head and compressed her lips. Then she looked at Hyacinth and Linda. She got up the nerve and softly said, "Are you Mackenzie Gary?"

"Yes," said Rose.

Magnolia shook her head, and remarked, "Well well well, what a surprise." Her head bowed slightly. "Finally, we meet."

Rose smiled and said, "Yes, finally."

Rose's son giggled as he observed all of the commotion and the bystanders gossiping.

"Mommy, who are all these people?" he said. "Do they know us?"

She looked down at him. "Shhh."

"But Mommy, they look like you. Are they your sisters?" he

said. "The ones you always talk about."

Hyacinth burst into tears.

"Yes, Solomon. They are," she replied.

Magnolia started to sob and covered her eyes. Linda finally came to her senses and released her hand from Magnolia's. She looked around at the crowd then at Rose and said, "Look, let's get of here. It's getting too crazy."

Magnolia stared at Rose and her son, then spread out her arms to let them move forward. She and Hyacinth followed.

"Good luck," yelled the custodian worker, waving.

"Thank you," Magnolia said, waving back.

CHAPTER 53

After escaping the crowd, Linda found an empty waiting area and led them to it. Magnolia noticed that although Rose was physically fit, she struggled walking. "Let me take your bags."

"I'm okay," Rose said calmly.

When they approached the waiting area, Magnolia released an intense breath. Rose just looked at her. "It wasn't supposed to happen this way."

Hyacinth couldn't speak. She was numb.

Staring into her eyes, Magnolia said as she wiped her nose, "How was it supposed to be?"

"Not like this."

Linda looked at Rose sideways and mumbled under her breath, "Can you believe this."

"Why did you mislead me?"

"It would have been more devastating if I didn't."

"Oh, really? You really think so?" Magnolia said, sort of giggling.

"Yes, I know so."

Solomon cut in: "Mommy, I'm hungry. Can we get something to eat?"

Rose looked up at the three women and Magnolia said to him, "Do you like McDonalds?"

Solomon smiled. "Yes."

"Well, there's one on our way back home. Let's go get your bags and then we can get you a hamburger."

"Great!" Solomon said.

* * *

Driving back, Magnolia couldn't remember how they ended up in the car. She only knew that her sister Rose sat in the back, staring directly into the rearview mirror, watching her every move. Solomon was also in the back eating a hamburger and playing with Hyacinth's bracelets.

Everyone was tense except for Rose. She sat comfortably, staring at the stores and cars that traveled on the highway. Several times Linda would sneak a peek through the rearview mirror, but for the most part they all were quiet, soaking up the unfeeling atmosphere.

Magnolia felt taken advantage of and let down. But she continued driving, staring straight ahead. Hyacinth was practically comatose. She had gone through so much the last few days, it was hard to be herself.

What should I say, Magnolia thought. *I just can't sit here and say nothing. This is driving me crazy. I cannot believe this is happening to me.*

She tipped her head back on the headrest and then struck her hand against the steering wheel. *I should be thankful. Hey, we found her. It wasn't as difficult as we thought it would be. She came to us.*

Magnolia glanced into the rearview mirror and stared at Rose again. She turned away when Rose noticed her movements.

All these months we've been communicating with each other and she knew. She knew about me. She knew about Linda. She must have known about Anthony. My God, she knew about Hyacinth too. She knew they were here. Why is she doing this? Does she know about the others? Why is she so angry? She barely said two words to us—not that we've said much to her.

Magnolia glanced at her watch. *I really thought by now we would be sitting in Starlight's restaurant drinking margaritas—toasting to her success and our good fortune.*

When Magnolia looked at her again, Rose donned a deceitful grin. *I bet she knows everything, even about my problems. She's a writer. She's cunning and clever. Yeah, she knows. God damn her! How could she do this to us? How could she just get on a plane pretending to be someone else, knowing that she is the person we've been searching for? What kind of person would do this to her family? What happened to us back then?*

Shortly Magnolia's vehicle was parked in her driveway. She was so nervous she struggled to release the seatbelt. Linda turned to her and pushed down on the buckle.

"Thank you," Magnolia said and half-smiled.

Magnolia turned to Rose. "If you're not up to this, I understand. I can take you to the hotel."

Rose leaned forward and pulled on Magnolia's seat rest. "Oh, that's quite all right," she said calmly. "I don't mind meeting your family."

Magnolia nervously looked at Linda again and said to Rose, "I guess you know everyone is here."

"Everyone," Rose said, looking puzzled.

"Yes, Hyacinth's adopted parents and family are here, along with some friends of mine."

Rose turned to Hyacinth and smiled. She then stretched her arms and said, "No, I didn't know."

She pressed down on her blouse and placed her hand on the door handle. "I know no more than you do, Magnolia." She quickly opened the door and stepped out.

Anthony was looking out of the front window when he saw Rose. He couldn't believe his eyes. "What the fuck!"

"Is she with them?" May-Lynne said.

"Oh, my God," he said.

"What is it?" Billie said, looking concerned.

Breathing heavily, he mumbled, "Magnolia and Hyacinth didn't have on red pants suits this morning." He looked back at the crowd. "Did they?"

"No," said Billie.

"Y'all are not going to believe this."

"Believe what?" Carl said, quietly laughing at Anthony's odd behavior.

"Just come and see."

Billie immediately ran to the window and stared at the car. It was clear Magnolia was in the front seat and Linda was in the passenger's seat. She thought she saw Hyacinth standing by the car but her hair seemed too long.

She whispered to Anthony, "That's not Hyacinth or Magnolia."

Suddenly they looked at each other, stunned and confused.

"You mean . . . that's . . ." Anthony said.

Shrugging her shoulders, Billie said, "I don't know. What do you think?"

"What's going on, you guys?" Carl yelled.

Billie and Anthony ignored him and just stared at each other. This time they were certain.

"It is her," mumbled Billie.

Shocked, Anthony yelled, "Rose!"

Everyone jumped out of their seats and raced toward the window.

Carl's shoe caught itself on the rug and he fell over the table, knocking Sam down with him. Brenda and Gregory quickly helped them up.

Anthony pulled the curtains back while they stood by the window in utter stillness, staring at the person in the red pants suit.

Anthony placed his hands in his pockets, trying to conceal his jitters.

Billie nodded. *This is too good to be true*, she thought.

Gregory and the Johnsons stood there in awe mumbling incoherently. They didn't know what to do next.

Carl's face suddenly fell forward and was pressed against the cold glass. He closed his eyes for a moment and began to cry. Brenda leaned next to him and held him.

"It's her," cried Billie. "It's Rose."

"How could it be her?" said Patricia.

"Look at her, Ma. It's her, all right," said May-Lynne.

"Then . . . where is that Mackenzie person?" Sam said.

"You're looking at her!" Anthony said.

Suddenly Anthony went to the door, opened it, and ran outside. They all followed him.

Magnolia was still in a state of shock and couldn't get up off her seat. Linda quickly stepped out of the car and walked around to the other side. She slowly opened Magnolia's door and reached for her hand. Magnolia stared at Linda and muttered, "Thanks."

"You're welcome," Linda said.

Linda slowly assisted Magnolia out of the car. Hyacinth stepped out too and helped Solomon get down.

When Anthony reached the vehicle, he walked over to Magnolia and hugged her, all the while staring at the other woman who looked like his wife.

Magnolia felt his chest heaving and his heart pounding. Somehow the sensation heightened her tension and her body began to shake.

Anthony held her tight and whispered, "It's okay, baby. I'm here."

Her head sunk in his chest and she sobbed. "I didn't know," she cried.

"Of course you didn't," he said.

Rose carefully eyed everyone. She stared at them with a straight face, noticing their nervous behavior. She sensed their uneasiness and she enjoyed every bit of it.

Then she scornfully glanced at Linda and stepped forward. Everyone stepped back. They looked at each other and then at her.

What an extraordinary moment, Rose thought.

Solomon ran to his mother, nearly pushing May-Lynne and Patricia aside. "Excuse me," he politely said. "Mommy . . . Mommy," he yelled.

Rose smiled, leaned forward, and picked him up.

He sucked on his thumb, then pulled it out of his mouth and said, "Why is everyone so quiet, Mommy? Aren't they happy to see us?"

"Of course they are, Solomon."

Brenda and Carl's heads immediately turned to her when they heard that name.

Linda said, "Umm . . . maybe we . . . should all go inside."

"Yeah, that's a good idea," said Hyacinth.

As Rose and her son passed everyone, no one uttered a word except for Gregory, who mutely said, "Ah . . . hello there."

"Hello," she said.

Once inside, Rose let go of Solomon's hand. She said, "Umm . . . nice home."

Linda and Hyacinth looked at each other. This was the first pleasant gesture she had made. Up until then, she appeared to despise them.

Anthony's hands were clamped together at his face. He pondered for a moment and then smiled. Suddenly he looked at Rose. "So, where the hell did you come from?"

Rose chuckled.

"We came from the airport," Solomon said. "It was really big and there were a lot of people there. It was just like Mommy said it would be." He giggled while he sucked on his thumb again. He pulled it away from his mouth. "Where the hell did you come from, Mister?"

Anthony shook his head and laughed. He stooped down on his knees and grabbed Solomon's jacket. "I live here with my wife."

"Which one?" Solomon said.

Pointing to Magnolia, Anthony said, "That one."

"Oh, the one that looks like Mommy."

"Yes, the one that looks like your mommy."

Rose looked down at Anthony and then at Magnolia and Hyacinth. "My name is Mackenzie Gary. Unlike the two of you, my adopted parents changed my name. My birth name is my middle name."

Her expression began to soften as she stared at Magnolia. "Yes, I am Rose Walker, the third triplet."

Patricia and Sam nervously stepped aside and glanced at May-Lynne and Lawrence.

Rose calmly continued. "I was born in Mission, Georgia on December 25, 1960. Dr. and Mrs. Earl Field adopted me when I was four years old. I moved to Toronto after high school."

She took a deep breath and continued. "Excluding my biological brothers and sisters, I have a total of nine other siblings."

"Nine!" screamed Carl.

"Yes, nine!" she sternly said, looking at him with a straight face. "Four sisters and five brothers. I'm the fifth child."

"Wow! That's interesting," said Billie.

Rose looked at Billie, admiring her facial features. "It sure is. Ahh, let me guess: Billie."

"Yes, that's correct," said Billie, seemingly puzzled. "How did you know?"

Rose grinned and said, "I'm psychic." Then she stared at Billie cross-eyed and grinned again.

Billie glanced at Linda wide-eyed. She was speechless. Linda was enraged with the entire situation. She frowned at Rose in disgust.

"Are you married, dear?" Patricia said.

"No, I'm divorced."

"I guess she knows about all of us, huh," Gregory whispered to Lawrence.

"Yeah, it looks like it." Lawrence nodded. "How cruel, though."

"Linda looks really upset. I'm sure she must have shocked the shit out of them," Gregory said.

"Wouldn't you be shocked?"

"Yeah, I guess."

"But . . . what is she trying to accomplish here? I don't know what she's trying to prove."

"I'm going to ask her," Gregory said.

Lawrence stared at him in disbelief.

"I'm serious—I don't appreciate her doing this to my fiancée."

He shook his head. "It's not right."

Magnolia roused from the hypnotic state that restrained her the past hour. She saw Anthony fidgeting with some coins he had taken out of his pocket and Linda steaming, cracking her fingers.

She was in control now and said loudly, "Honey, why don't you go into the kitchen and get Mackenzie and Solomon something to drink."

Solomon smiled. "Yeah, I'm thirsty."

Magnolia stared at everyone. "Can you guys leave Hyacinth and I alone with Mackenzie?"

"Sure... Sure..." they hissed.

Everyone scurried nervously toward the kitchen and quickly exited the back door, which led to the patio.

Magnolia gently grabbed Rose's arm. "Please, have a seat."

Rose calmly sat and stared at Magnolia distrustfully. Magnolia began to speak in a gentle tone. "This has been an incredible day for all of us, as you can imagine."

Rose was quiet.

"I... I... know..." Magnolia looked up at the ceiling to gather her thoughts, then back down at Rose, "What I'm trying to say is... I assume you know all about us. I mean... Hyacinth and myself... and the rest of our families."

When she stared into Rose's eyes, tears began to fall. "Why? Why haven't you contacted us?"

Rose turned away. She paused for a moment, then stood and slowly walked toward the massive window. "This is a beautiful view," she said.

Hyacinth and Magnolia watched her.

"You've done well for yourself, Magnolia."

Rose turned around and she looked at them. "You too, Hyacinth."

Hyacinth shrugged and glanced at Magnolia. "Thank you," was all she could manage.

Rose smiled and calmly said, "You know, the day it happened—the day they took me away—I wasn't scared at first because I knew Junior would come for me."

Hyacinth and Magnolia were dumbfounded. "Junior," they whispered.

Rose went on. "They told me I was going on some kind of special trip. Then, when I got on this huge airplane, it looked like something in the magazines Junior used to read to us. I began to cry. I even peed in my pants."

"My father spanked me and told me I was a big girl now and that big girls didn't do that. Naturally, I quieted down. On the plane, my parents told me that my family would be waiting for me."

She moved around a picture on the wall and said, "And when the plane landed, I raced toward the door, but I didn't recognize the people. There were no cotton fields, no lake, no old house, no Mama or Junior."

She began to twist together the curtain straps. "The sky was rich blue, just like back home. But the air smelled different. When I looked straight ahead, there were four children waiting for me ranging in age from six to twelve."

Hyacinth edged toward Magnolia on the couch, and their hands slowly touched.

"I told my father they're not my family," Rose said, wiping her tears. "Where's Junior? Where's Mama? Where's Teacher? Where's Magnolia and Hyacinth?' I yelled.

She pondered for a moment and then abruptly said, "They're gone! That's what he said. And they're never coming back!"

Rose wet her lips. "Why I said. Where are they? They died, he said. All of them? I said."

She patted her chest and nervously mumbled, "Yes, all of them, my father said. You mean they went to heaven? Yes, he said with a straight face."

She made a silly laugh and went on. "But Junior would never leave me without saying goodbye."

She turned toward Magnolia and Hyacinth again and began to caress her arm. "My father grabbed me by the arm. I can still feel the pain. It was excruciating. He yelled and said, Junior is gone and that's that. We are your new family now. Never speak their names again! You hear me, child?"

She looked up at the ceiling and softly said, "All I could do was nod."

"That evening, I was so terrified, I couldn't cry aloud—I kept it inside. That sadness stuck to me my whole life."

She wrapped the curtain rope around her finger. "I became really attached to my older sisters, Clarice and Noelle. Clarice was twelve years old, and Noelle was ten. I guess they replaced Junior in a way."

She stopped twirling the rope. "My father was a very strict disciplinarian. We were all afraid of him, including our mother. I think she hated him the most. He was a physician—a family practitioner. Mom was a homemaker. Dad thought he was the most prosperous black man alive, when, in reality, he was perfectly average. People still didn't respect him, despite his medical degree."

Now facing them, she said, "As years passed, his business dwindled and he retired early, making life extremely difficult for the children who were still home."

She placed her arms over her chest. "I grew up knowing that I was different from the rest. I looked different and I talked different. My father made me feel like I was different and because of this I grew up feeling worthless. There was a void in my life. I really didn't feel close to any of them—there wasn't a connection. I grew up very bitter, and as the years passed the bitterness turned to anger and the anger eventually turned to revenge. I wanted someone to pay for what I had gone through."

Her eyes were red. "Life Upstate was hard. And one by one, as each child turned eighteen, we left my parent's home and never looked back—each telling the other where they could be found, so when it was your turn, you would have a place to go."

She grinned. "Though, when I left, I told no one where I was heading. As close as I was to my two older sisters, I could not trust them. I believed they would tell my father my whereabouts. I could not risk it. So I moved to Toronto, where I met my husband Kendall. He was earning his Ph.D. in history. We married my freshman year of college. Kendall went on to teach history at a university in Toronto. It was he who persuaded me to pursue the search for my biological family."

Hyacinth and Magnolia's hands trembled.

Rose began to pace the room. "I guess we were married about a year before I decided to do it. Of course, with my background in history and a good eye for research, it took me all of three days to locate—" She paused.

Suddenly, Hyacinth coughed hard, then cleared her throat. *Which one did she find first?* she thought. *Was it me?*

Rose looked at her and smiled. "It took me three days to locate . . ." She paused again and walked to the French doors between the living room and the hallway and looked at everyone.

Hyacinth and Magnolia's mouths hung open.

"Our mother," said Rose.

"She's alive!" screamed Magnolia.

Rose turned back around and faced them. "Alive and well," she said.

"Oh, my God!" Magnolia said. "Where is she?"

Rose stood silent for a moment. "I need to sit."

Hyacinth immediately stood and gave Rose her seat.

Rose grabbed her glass of lemon iced tea and took a swig. "This is so refreshing," she said.

Magnolia stared at her.

"I'm really sorry you had a hard life, Mackenzie," Magnolia said.

"Are you really?" Rose said.

"Yes, I am. I'm sincerely sorry. No one should have gone through what you did."

Rose smiled. "You can call me Rose, you know."

They softly laughed.

Magnolia rubbed Rose's leg. "Rose, I understand your anger. When I came to New Jersey, I was also told that I was going on a special trip. But, when I arrived, the sky wasn't so blue and the air wasn't so clear either. It rained like hell that day. I don't think I was dressed for the occasion and ended up catching a horrible cold."

Magnolia glanced at a photograph of Anthony on the end table. She adjusted it slightly. "I got here by train and was accompanied by my Aunt Alice. When I first saw my mother at Penn Station, she seemed cold and distant. She sort of smiled, then she looked me up and down and said, She's okay. I really don't remember anything after that—as far as that day is concerned."

She rubbed her finger against the picture's frame. "I soon began to think of her as my mother and began to love her as one too, but I don't think she truly loved me. I guess I answered a need in her: a child companion, if you can imagine that."

Hyacinth broke in: "When Mom and Dad came to get me, they had stuffed animals, balloons, and candy in both hands. I was so thrilled, I had completely forgotten about you guys. They did tell me that Mama was sick and that she had died. When I asked about the other kids, they said that in time they would come to Florida too, but they didn't. Instead May-Lynne and Lawrence came years later."

She giggled but felt somewhat embarrassed revealing this information. "I was spoiled. I believed Mom and Dad loved me a little too much. Soon I lost sight of everything—my true being. As time went by, I couldn't remember anymore—about the farm, about the beat-up truck, about you guys." She lowered her head and began to sob. "I had forgotten you. I'm so sorry. Please forgive me."

Magnolia reached over and hugged her. "It's not your fault."

Gazing at the wall, Rose said, "But, we really did remember. Those memories were still in your mind—you just didn't know they were there."

"Do you remember?" Hyacinth said sobbing.

Rose said, "I remember everything."

Magnolia and Hyacinth glanced at her.

"I remember Mama's long black hair and her sweet smile. I remember the hot grits and butter in the mornings. The beautiful flowers on the kitchen table. I remember playing in the back yard and on the farm. I remember going down to the lake and looking at the stars. I remember Junior. He was tall and strong. I remember there was the three of us. No one could ever take those memories from me. Not even my father."

She turned and looked at Hyacinth. "I even remember your birthmark, Hyacinth."

Hyacinth sobbed again, overwhelmed.

Rose continued: "I remembered Mrs. Williams making the finest cherry—"

Suddenly Hyacinth wiped her face and glanced at Magnolia. They both stared at Rose and began to speak her words: "cherry vanilla ice cream."

Rose beamed. "Yeah, and was it good!"

"The best!" Magnolia yelled.

Rose said, "You see, you remember. Those memories were just hidden away."

Hyacinth and Magnolia immediately stood and gathered with Rose in the center of the den. With tears streaming down their faces, they joined hands and lowered their heads. The rest of the group stood at the glass doors and watched in awe.

"Are they praying?" Billie said.

"I think so," whispered Carl.

Linda, May-Lynne, and Patricia sobbed.

"This is amazing," cried Patricia. "I'm so happy for them."

"So am I," cried May-Lynne.

Linda's glassy eyes stared at the three forceful women who swayed to a sweet melody that seemed to come from within.

Three brave women were participating in a sacred ceremony. They prayed that the others would come home soon. They prayed for some peace of mind. They prayed for kinship, love, and happiness.

Linda's body moved forward and Brenda put out her hand to hold her and said, "It's okay."

Linda looked back at her, dazed. Brenda said, "Magnolia's fine. Look at her—she's having a good time with her sisters."

Linda smiled.

Solomon glanced up at them. "You're all so silly." He giggled. "They're a team again. Just like the good old days."

"And, how would you know about that?" Sam sternly said.

"Because Mommy told me so."

"She did?" Carl said.

Biting into an overflowing ham and cheese sandwich, he cheerfully said, "Yep!"

CHAPTER 54

The week had gone by quickly and the three sisters spent the days talking, laughing, and sharing stories of their life.

It was Sunday morning and they were going to church. Magnolia glanced into the mirror and smiled. She was cheerful and was wearing her and Anthony's favorite color—blue.

It was an unusually warm September day, so she wore a simple dress with short sleeves and a squared scoop neck. Anthony commented on the dress's slim-fitting style and high base knee length.

"What are you looking at?" she said, feeling self-conscious. "It's only a little above my knee."

"A little," he said with a laugh.

"Yeah, just a little."

To compliment the dress, she wore a chic beige hat. Although the dress was plain, it made her appear unmistakably smooth and elegant.

Hyacinth wasn't as daring as Magnolia. She donned a long, bronze-color dress with an easy shape to it and an elegant effect. It flared at the bottom.

Rose wore a gray-striped skirt suit. Solomon sported a brown double-breasted pants suit. He was dressed to kill.

Everyone at church had heard about the remarkable reunion. Rumors had whipped through the church like wildfire. Though most of the congregation remained misguided about the whole story, including the unlawful adoption.

Before they arrived, the congregation sat firmly in the pews gossiping and fanning themselves with square-shaped paperboard fans with wooden handles, waiting for their arrival.

Magnolia grabbed Hyacinth and Rose's hands, leading the way up the few steps and to the two wide front doors.

Pastor Louis stood at the pulpit of Almighty Baptist Church and smiled when he saw them walk in. Everyone turned toward the door and stared in awe. Eyes widened, mouths dropped, fans ceased, children stopped crying, and the Deacons stopped talking. For the first time in its history, Almighty Baptist Church was at a standstill, but only for a moment.

Magnolia inhaled, then smiled at everyone. They slowly walked down the aisle. Pastor Louis held his arms out and pointed toward the front row. They ambled forward, shaking hands and thanking everyone who said, "God bless you sisters . . . We've been praying for you all week . . . Hallelujah . . ."

Deacon Samuel immediately stood and yelled, "God is good!"

Everyone clapped and shouted, "Amen!"

Magnolia, Hyacinth, and Rose sat in the front row. They listened to Pastor Louis's sermon about mistakes, love, family, and forgiveness.

They held hands and often glanced at each other, nervously smiling. Magnolia and Hyacinth thought about what Rose said to them the day she arrived—how she found the rest of their family. Magnolia needed time to prepare herself for what would eventually come to light. But after listening to Pastor Louis's sermon, she felt courageous, motivated, and self-assured. She would ask Rose after the morning service to tell her the whole story. She wanted to know everything.

After church service ended, Pastor Louis stood outside the door acknowledging everyone who passed by. "Magnolia, I'm so glad to see you and Anthony here this Sunday morning. I didn't think you would be here so soon. Especially with everything that's gone on," Pastor Louis said smiling, looking at everyone.

"Thank you, Pastor Louis. I know Anthony called you and told you most of what has happened." Pulling Hyacinth and Rose closer to her, she said, "These are my sisters."

Pastor Louis beamed as he stared at them.

"This is Hyacinth and Rose."

"Hello there. It's so nice to meet you," he said.

"Hello. Nice to meet you too," they mumbled.

"It's so hard to believe you are all here, but God works in mysterious ways," he said, nodding. "God bless you, sisters."

"Thank you," said Hyacinth and Rose, who stared at each other. They did not know what else to say.

"Pastor Louis, there's so much to tell you. Why don't you and Mrs. Louis come and have dinner with us this evening? And I'll introduce you to everyone," Magnolia said.

"That's sounds like a good idea. Just let me tell Deacon Samuel."

Magnolia and Anthony waited for Pastor Louis to come out of the church. Afterward they headed home.

Billie kicked off her shoes the minute she stepped into the house. "Shoo, my feet are killing me," she said.

"Tell me about it, girl," said Linda, settling on the couch.

Carl and Brenda, who did not attend church, were in the kitchen preparing dinner. Suddenly Carl walked into the living room with a rag hanging on his shoulder. "So, you guys finally made it home."

"It was a very long service," moaned Gregory.

Hyacinth pinched him.

"Ooch, baby!"

"It wasn't that bad," she whispered.

"It was very long."

"Too long," said Sam.

"Look at the two grumpy old men complaining," whispered May-Lynne.

Patricia and Rose laughed.

During dinner, Magnolia and Hyacinth did most of the explaining to Pastor Louis. Rose sat still and listened while she pampered Solomon.

Finally Billie said, "Rose, did you know that Magnolia was your sister when you contacted her for representation?"

Rose hesitated to answer at first, then she slightly grinned. "Yes."

Deep down inside, Billie was hoping she would say no. "All this time you knew!"

Calmly, Rose said, "Yes."

Solomon giggled—this was all too amusing. He knew the whole story, or at least most of it. He was tickled to death to see it unfold.

"You mean, you led her on?" Pastor Louis said, cleaning his glasses with the napkin.

"Yes . . . well . . . no," she said, shaking her head. "It's a long story."

"A very long story," Solomon said, chuckling.

Carl grinned and said, "Boy, you are something else!"

"That's what my Mommy always says."

Everyone laughed.

Suddenly Rose stood. "Excuse me, please." She dropped her napkin on the table and discreetly walked toward the sliding glass doors. Slowly she opened the doors and glanced back at everyone—her eyes gradually met Carl's. She inhaled and stepped onto the short path that led to the enormous backyard.

Hyacinth shrugged her shoulders and eyed Magnolia, who was speechless—both of them wondering what to do next.

"Did I say something wrong?" Pastor Louis said.

"No, Pastor Louis. It's been pretty hard on all of us," said Magnolia.

Magnolia glanced at Anthony. When he smiled, she abruptly stood and also excused herself. She followed Rose out back. Hyacinth immediately pursued them.

Rose was sitting in the gazebo when Magnolia and Hyacinth approached her. When they entered, Magnolia stopped and collected her thoughts. Then she headed over toward Rose, who stared at her.

Magnolia caressed her shoulder and said, "You know, I always told Anthony there was this connection between you and I."

Rose smiled but remained quiet.

"It's true," Magnolia said, "I felt this incredible bond—this unusual sense of attachment that kept me hanging on to you." She giggled. "Despite Linda's reservations."

Rose nodded. "I can only imagine Linda's thoughts. She's one tough cookie." She softly laughed. "Actually, we're alike in some ways. I see why the two of you are so close."

Magnolia smiled. "You know, I couldn't sleep at all last night. I couldn't help but think about what you told us."

Rose glanced at them.

Magnolia began to cry. "About your life. Rose, I feel your pain and I'm here." She stared at Hyacinth and then at Rose. "We're both here for you. We can't change the past but we can make the future right. We can, Rose."

Grabbing Rose's hand, Magnolia said, "Let's start anew. Let's be a family again. We need you, Rose."

With tears streaming down their faces, they closed in and wrapped themselves into a shield.

"I want that too," cried Rose.

Carl and Anthony stood in the kitchen, peering out of the window.

Meanwhile Solomon jumped on Brenda's lap, eating a piece of cake. "Where did you get that beautiful name?" she said.

He shrugged. "I think my mommy really liked it."

"Oh really!"

"Um-hmm. It was her brother's name."

Linda whispered to Billie, "That boy know he can eat."

"He sure can," Billie said.

"I'm going to be strong like him. You know—Junior."

"Junior," Billie and Linda said.

"Um-hmm." he said smiling. "Mommy's older brother." Looking into Brenda's eyes, he said, "The one that's lost."

Linda and Billie looked at the men, who seemed just as confused.

"Did she tell you about Junior?" Sam said.

"Yep! She really loved him."

"Oh," said Patricia.

"Mommy said he was built—in good shape."

"Oh, yeah?" Anthony said.

"Just like Michael Jordan."

"She didn't say that," said Linda.

"Yes, she did! Mommy said he was tall and strong like Mike. And I want to be just like him too."

They all howled.

"She'll tell you," Solomon said. "Just wait. Be patient for God's sake."

"Excuse me!" Billie said.

Solomon giggled. "You all are just too nosy."

"I tell you, this boy is something else," said Gregory, laughing.

After gazing at Magnolia's beautiful garden, Hyacinth said, "I didn't get any sleep either." Nervously flaking a piece of wood off of the gazebo, she said, "I know you told us that we should give it more time, but I just can't wait any longer. I need to know now. When we were at church this morning, I was about to explode with sadness."

Rose exhaled and smiled. "You're right. You should know."

Hyacinth hadn't expected that statement. Her body quickly shifted and she got up from the bench and looked at Rose and said, "You're going to—"

"Yes. I'm ready, are you?"

Hyacinth softly said, "Yes."

Rose stared at Magnolia, who put her hands out and blurted, "You know I've been ready."

They nervously laughed.

"Well, where should I begin?" Rose said.

"With our mother. You said she did not die," said Magnolia.

"Yes, that's right, Mama," Rose said. She stared at the bluish sky and grinned. "You know, before I came here I was so angry. I knew you all had done well with your lives. I made myself believe that because my life was hard, you all were to blame—especially our older brother. When I finally located you and discovered how well you were doing, I felt cheated. It wasn't fair. I became convinced that because of my shortcomings, you would suffer too."

She glanced at them, then said, "Now I know I was wrong. I followed your lives for years, especially yours, Magnolia."

Magnolia was intent.

"And I decided to write a book and have you represent me," Rose said. "Yes, I planned some of this, but not all of it. I didn't plan on my defenses breaking down. I didn't plan on this being so easy. Me telling you the story without you two begging and pleading."

She put her hand up to her chest. "My heart stopped bleeding the moment I saw you two standing at the airport. It was like I was looking into a mirror."

"Although it was the first time you ever saw me in person, I've seen you Magnolia and Linda. The two of you appeared in *Marvelous Writers' Magazine*."

Rose looked at Hyacinth. "I read about Carl and Anthony in *The New Jersey Gazette* and I also saw them on a television program."

"Where was I—in another world?" Hyacinth said. "I know I've read those magazines before."

"Obviously, you didn't read those particular editions," said Magnolia.

"I guess you're right," she said, shaking her head.

Rose slowly circled the gazebo many times before she revealed the details. "Mama had breast cancer," she said.

Magnolia's body jerked and a cold chill enveloped her.

"Are you okay?" Rose said.

"I'm fine. Please go on."

"Are you sure?"

"Yes. Please, continue."

"Where was I?" Rose said.

"She was diagnosed with breast cancer," Hyacinth reminded her.

"Oh yes," Rose said. "She even underwent surgery and had radiation. She stayed in the hospital for a very long time. Since she was hospitalized, Junior could barely pay the bills and maintain our family needs. So, Miss Smith volunteered her help."

Confused, Magnolia said, "Who was she?"

"She's my aunt—Aunt Henrietta," said Hyacinth.

"Yes, she was also Junior's schoolteacher and supposedly a good friend of the family."

"What did she do?" Magnolia said.

"She convinced Mama and Junior to let us stay with her friends until Mama got well. That's what she did."

Rose stared at them and sarcastically said, "To stay with your mothers."

Magnolia nodded and lowered her head.

Then Rose said, "Mama believed this was a good idea but Junior flatly refused to do it." Pounding her hand on the wall, she went on. "He would never abandon his family and send them off to strangers. Especially us! We were like his own children. He practically raised us."

"After some persuasion by Mama, Junior let us go. But of course, Miss Smith had other plans. Cruel intentions. She sold us. She used us like animals."

She looked up at them and smiled. "But you see, Mama didn't die," she said, shaking her head. "It was a long battle, but she won."

Rose stared at them with tears rolling down her face. "They looked for us, you know. But by that time, we were long gone. I was taken to New York. Magnolia, you were taken to New Jersey, and Hyacinth, you went to Florida."

"What were they to do? They had very little money and no transportation. Eventually they lost hope of ever finding us," she said.

Magnolia leaned her head back on the pole. She and Hyacinth began to cry. Then they began to think about Mama. *Where was she?*

"A year later the rest of the family relocated to Paterson, New Jersey," Rose said. "Yes, they took advantage of the opportunities up north. Mama even went back to school and improved her reading, writing, and verbal communication skills. And Junior, Lily, and Nathaniel eventually went to college."

Instantly Magnolia grabbed her stomach and fell off the bench, landing on her knees. She grabbed a nearby garbage can. She'd recognized those names.

Anthony saw what had happened and ran out of the house. Carl remained in the kitchen. He was paralyzed.

Magnolia vomited. Hyacinth rushed to her side, then looked at Rose. "What's wrong?"

Rose, who always had a sly tone and disposition, turned to Anthony, who was running toward them, and back at Magnolia. "Why don't you ask her?"

When Anthony reached the gazebo and stepped inside, he stared at Rose angrily. "What did you do to her?" he said.

Rose was silent. She turned and gazed at Carl, who remained frozen by the window.

"Damn it! What did you do to her?" Anthony said.

"Nothing! I did absolutely nothing!" she replied.

As Anthony leaned forward to hold Magnolia, she glanced at Rose with total anguish. Now she truly understood her pain. Magnolia held onto Anthony and moaned, "Ahhh . . ."

Solomon raced toward the window. "I guess they know now, huh?" he said to Carl.

Carl was still standing by the window, frozen. He peered out, the entire time feeling sad.

The noise of the doorbell scared Carl and he jumped up in excitement. Solomon's eyebrows lifted. "I wonder who could that be?" he said.

Carl and Solomon quickly withdrew from the window to answer the door.

CHAPTER 55

"What's wrong, baby?" Anthony said as he held Magnolia. "Please tell me."

"Carl..." Magnolia cried, gripping him.

Leaning closer to her, Anthony pressed his face against hers. "What about him, baby?"

Sobbing, she said, "He's... he's..."

Stroking her hair, he said, "Baby, what is it? Please, tell me."

"He's... he's... my... my... brother."

Anthony watched the movement of her lips, carefully interpreting every word.

"He's my brother," she repeated.

Stunned Anthony slowly turned toward the window to look at Carl, who had disappeared. Carl slipped away into a time and place Anthony wished he had been for that moment. He was flabbergasted.

Anthony's worries about his best friend were over. Now he understood Carl's relationship with his wife and the need to protect her. He stood there holding Magnolia and finally appreciating Carl's love for her.

Now Anthony knew why Carl thought he was not complete, despite the distinguished life, successful company, beautiful wife, and magnificent home. Carl had told him that something tragic happened to him when he was fourteen years old. But he never revealed the details, simply blaming himself for his family's bad luck. He always seemed haunted by guilt and torn inside.

And after witnessing the pain in his best friend's eyes that day, Anthony didn't have the guts to ask what had happened. He assumed Carl would talk when he was good and ready. Although Carl never did, Anthony often wondered what happened to him. What was so awful that it made him carry around this burden of guilt and failure for many years?

At the door...

"I'll get it!" shouted Solomon. He opened the door, and standing outside were three imposing individuals—two women and a man. Solomon looked up at the visitors and said, "Hi."

"Hello there," said the elderly woman.

"I'm Solomon."

"Solomon," the woman remarked as she raised her eyebrows at the other two. "Well, I must say, that is a beautiful name."

She leaned forward and extended her hand to him. "It's so nice to meet you, Solomon. My name is Mrs. Walker. I'm Carl's mother."

Solomon looked at Carl, then at Mrs. Walker, and smiled. "I figured that." He shook her hand and placed his hand on his face as if he was thinking. "You're Mama, right?"

Mrs. Walker was amazed. Carl had told her several nights before that he was a bright kid, just like he had been as a child, but she had to see it for herself.

"You're absolutely right, young man," she said. "As a matter of fact, I'm your grandmother."

"I know," he giggled.

"Come give me a hug," she said smiling.

He stepped up front and hugged her.

Lily moved forward and leaned down. "Do you know who I am?" she said.

"I think so—you're Teacher, right?" Then he pointed to Nathaniel. "And, you are Nate."

Lily rubbed her hand on his head, feeling his delicate hair. "That's right."

Nathaniel smiled and casually nodded.

Mrs. Walker glanced up and saw Brenda, Billie, Linda, and the rest of the crew staring at them.

Brenda half-smiled. For weeks she had been extremely high-strung.

Linda clinched Billie's sleeve and whispered, "I can not believe what I'm hearing." She shook her head in disbelief. "Mrs. Walker . . . Carl . . . They're Magnolia's . . ."

Billie stared straight ahead. She gazed past them and into the sunlight, letting it soothe her. The warm feeling was an atonement.

Billie looked at Mrs. Walker. She stared into the eyes of the woman she knew as courageous, the woman who had raised six children alone, braving poverty and bigotry in the Deep South, the woman who tried to love a shiftless and thoughtless man, and the woman who did not have an easygoing life but who had made it through complete. She stared at a mother who braved cancer and fought to live because of an uncommon willpower that few possess, a mother who loved her children, a mother who could not hate the people who stole them because of her unwavering faith.

Mrs. Walker stroked Billie's hand and smiled. "Hello, Billie."

"Hello," Billie muttered.

She walked up to her and kissed her. "It's good to see you, dear."

Billie hugged her. "It's so good to see you too, Mrs. Walker."

Lily smiled and hugged Billie and Linda.

"Come on in, Ma," said Brenda.

When they stepped inside, Patricia quickly held her hand to her chest and sighed. "My God."

She never thought she would live to see this day.

"It's been a long time, Patricia," Mrs. Walker said.

"Yes, it has," replied Patricia nervously. "I'm . . . I'm . . . terribly sorry, Ivory."

"Please don't—it's all in the past," she said as she looked at

Carl. "Today we have to be there for them. They're going to need us." She smiled. "You took good care of Hyacinth and I—"

Mrs. Walker looked at Carl again and then at Lily and Nathaniel. "We thank you for that."

Lily apprehensively said, "I'm not quite sure I'm ready for this."

"It's out—we have no other choice," said Carl.

"Where are they?" Nathaniel said.

"They're outside," said Carl.

Ivory looked at Patricia and then at Sam. She turned toward Carl and smiled again. "Take me to them."

He held her hand and led her toward the back of the house. Everyone turned and followed but did not leave the house.

Some gazed out the large kitchen window and the others stood by the patio doors.

Anthony steadily rocked Magnolia in his arms. They were both in tears. As he rocked her, he looked to the side and saw Carl escorting his mother toward the gazebo. He slowly stopped rocking her. Magnolia looked up and saw them too. Hyacinth and Rose slowly turned around.

Their hearts raced. Rose had waited for this moment for years—the moment of truth. Though she never knew it would change her spirit. Never in her wildest dreams did she know it would make her cry and make her love them again. She was level headed as she waited for her mother to enter the gazebo.

CHAPTER 56

Mrs. Walker wore a rose-colored dress. Tiny pink and ivory flowers bejeweled it. Her hair was a brilliant salt-and-pepper color. Many soft, and light curls were perched all over her head. Her hair was still long and thick—just the way Rose remembered it. Her smile was as rich as it was thirty-eight years ago and her hands were still smooth and refined.

The three of them stared at her, examining her mild disposition and the relaxed rhythm in her walk. Rose remembered her medium frame and beautiful face. She would never forget that lovely smile.

Mrs. Walker was a bit nervous herself. They watched her come closer, all the while staring at her daughters.

She could barely recognize their faces from a distance but she knew they were there waiting for her. She knew she would identify each of them, once she was face to face with them.

Their hearts continued to race. As the adrenaline kicked in Magnolia wasn't sure she could contain herself. They all stood as Carl and Mrs. Walker came closer.

Carl firmly clutched his mother's hand as they moved forward. He held it for luck and for love. Foremost he held it for forgiveness. He knew he would need it from Magnolia.

Will she hate me for this? he thought.

Carl too had known about Magnolia for years. It was during

her senior year at Rutgers that an intern named Chad Harrison had guided him to her.

Chad was a nerd and a complete smart-ass. He thought he knew it all—everything except kindness and respect for other racial groups. He was white and grew up in upper middle class suburbia and never lived around anyone except people who looked like him. He had a serious problem with people of color. He didn't know how to talk to them or interact with them. He was a moron and he lacked common sense.

Chad would regularly badmouth a fellow student who was African-American and the editor of the college newspaper.

One day while having lunch in the cafeteria, Chad said to a fellow intern with a sarcastic grin, "I don't know why she's the editor. All she writes about is them. You know what I mean."

A few other white interns agreed by shaking their heads but most of them turned away from him, embarrassed by his ignorance and narrow-mindedness.

Chad ignored the fact that Carl and other people of color were in the cafeteria. And he didn't care that Carl was a big cheese in the company.

Chad never quite understood why he was not asked to stay on with the company after he graduated, but Carl knew why.

One day Chad brought in the newspaper to show his fellow interns, most of who attended Princeton University, what an idiot the editor was. He slammed the newspaper on the table and said with rage, "Look at this trash. She's talking about a holiday for Martin Luther. All the things in the world to write about, and she's writing about him. What has he ever done for me?"

A female intern named Melissa, who from a first glance appeared to be Caucasian, but was actually Puerto Rican, calmly said, "You mean, Dr. Martin Luther King, Jr."

Stuffing a pickle in his mouth, Chad waved his hand and mockingly said, "Yeah . . . yeah . . . whatever . . ."

"What's wrong with honoring him on his birthday?" she said. "I mean, after all that he's done, not only for African-Americans but for—"

Suddenly another Caucasian intern named Del broke in, "Yeah, that's right." His chest heaved as he spoke. "During the fifties and early sixties, Dr. King was the person who set off non-violent protests, and that resulted in the integration of public schools, facilities, and department stores."

An African-American engineer named Roy, joined in. "Tens of thousands of protesters, many of them blacks, man, were beaten and jailed. Some of them lost their homes and jobs. Thousands lost their lives."

Del said, "White people also died because of evil and ignorant people like yourself, Chad." He stood and stared at Chad. "Dr. King believed in freedom and so did my grandparents, who came here fifty years ago from Poland!"

Melissa said, "Years of sacrifice brought into existence the Civil Rights Act, mister know-it-all." She slammed her textbook on the table. "If it wasn't for people like Dr. King, I probably wouldn't be allowed to attend Princeton University today!"

Roy said, "Chad, remember man: freedom has a price." He looked around the room at everyone. "And, everybody in this room is ready to fight and even die for it today!"

Roy paused for a moment, then gazed out the window and back at Chad again. He gently smiled, remembering the experiences of his ancestors. "Listen to these words, Chad. Teach them to your children."

"Excuse me," Chad said in a snooty tone.

"I said listen," Roy said. "Let freedom ring from Stone Mountain of Georgia. Let freedom ring from Lookout Mountain of Tennessee. Let freedom ring from every hill and molehill of Mississippi, from every mountainside, let freedom ring!"

Vladimir Stanislav, an elderly handyman from Czechoslovakia, and known to everyone in the company as Mr. Stan, walked slowly over to the table as if his feet were dragging. As he approached the table, he made baby steps and took quick short breaths. Once he reached the table, he placed his trembling hands on it and then clutched Chad's arm. They both were trembling, but Stan suddenly let go of him. He knew that if he held onto to Chad much longer, he'd probably hurt him.

His eyes began to tear up as he stared at Chad. "And ven dis happens," Stan swallowed hard and then aimed his index finger at Chad, "ven we allow freedom to ring, ven we let it ring from every tenement . . . and every hamlet . . ." He paused. "From every state . . . and every city, ve will be able to speed up dat day . . ."

Mr. Stan crumpled into a chair and began to sob. He tried to speak but couldn't. He looked up at Chad, his face possessed by pain and suffering. He thought about the days when his parents had struggled to feed him and his seven brothers and sisters after they arrived in America. His neighbors weren't kind to them because they looked and talked different. His father lost many jobs because people found his heavy Czechoslovakian accent hard to understand and his ragged facial appearance unpleasing to look at.

Roy patted his back. "Let me help you, Mr. Stan." He looked at Chad scornfully.

But then Roy smiled again and said, "When all of God's children, black men and white men, Jews and Gentiles, Protestants and Catholics, will be able to join hands . . ."

Roy's tone elevated, "And sing in the words of the old Negro spiritual . . ."

Everyone could see the rage in Chad's face. He felt cornered. Then most of the interns, including Mr. Stan, stood and faced Chad. They waved their hands in triumph and shouted, "Free at last! Free at last! Thank God Almighty, we are free at last!"

This incredible force of humanity took Carl aback. *These are all God's children*, he thought. He turned toward his co-worker and shouted, "Damn!"

"You damn right!" his colleague said.

Before long Chad was outnumbered. For the first time in his life, he realized that all white people didn't share his racist beliefs. He grabbed his lunch and stormed out the room. "I don't have to take this shit," he shouted.

As he passed the garbage bin, he quickly tossed the newspaper into it. "Fuck her and fuck them," he said.

After lunch Carl walked over to the garbage receptacle, intending to throw away his trash, but as he began to empty the tray into the large container, he took a quick look down and saw a photograph of the editor.

It was a picture of Magnolia and it covered the front page. He would never forget her face or smile. She looked like a younger version of his mother.

Magnolia Cooper had written an article about several states that did not support the King holiday.

He couldn't believe his eyes. Finally he had found one of his sisters. He could hardly contain himself that afternoon and immediately hired a private investigator. The investigator informed him that Magnolia was suffering from an emotional ailment. He often wondered if it was depression—the same illness that stifled him many years before.

Carl discussed this information with a psychologist friend who thought it was best not to approach Magnolia until she was better able to handle the news.

During this time he also discovered that she was engaged to Anthony, a third-year medical student. He kept track of their relationship and marriage.

And once he learned that Anthony had applied to Princeton's business school, he immediately became a frequent speaker and soon introduced himself to Anthony. That is how he entered into her life.

Carl and Brenda instantly became great friends with them—sharing an extraordinary relationship. Magnolia soon thought of them as the older brother and sister she never had. Carl made it known that Magnolia was special to him and this made Anthony jealous of their relationship.

Despite their close family ties, Carl still did not have the courage to tell Magnolia the truth, especially after Anthony told him that Magnolia felt she had been unloved for many years. That sense of rejection gave rise to low self-esteem.

Now a few feet away from his younger sisters, the time had come to reveal the truth. Carl walked hand in hand with his mother down the spacious trail, hoping that Magnolia would forgive him and praying that this revelation would not cause her more pain.

CHAPTER 57

When Carl and his mother stood at the entrance of the belvedere, it was as though Rose, Hyacinth, and Magnolia were gazing upon a superstar.

Mrs. Walker's posture was erect and she was impeccably dressed and poised. She carefully glanced at everyone and smiled bashfully. Carl finally released his mother's hand.

She looked at her girls again, this time in detail. Hyacinth's birthmark was the first distinct trait to stand out.

With all eyes cautiously watching her every move, she slowly walked over to Hyacinth. When she reached her, she let out a sigh of relief. Mrs. Walker raised her hands in a delicate manner to Hyacinth's face. Gradually she lifted up her chin, stared into her eyes, and touched the mark. Her hand trembled as it brushed Hyacinth's forehead. Hyacinth bit down on her lip. She was on the brink of collapsing.

Mrs. Walker kissed her lips and smiled again, which brought a sense of acceptance to Hyacinth's heart. The ordeal was over. Before her stood her mother, the woman in her dreams, the woman who symbolized strength and courage, the woman who brought life to her and who had loved her dearly so many years before.

Hyacinth collected herself and wrapped her arms around her mother, holding her tight. When she released her, she closed her eyes briefly and said, "Thank you, Jesus."

Magnolia was clinging onto Anthony when Mrs. Walker casually strolled over. She placed her hand on the back of Magnolia's head, smoothing her hair.

As soon as Mrs. Walker said, "It's all right, child," Magnolia began to sob. She held Magnolia and kissed her cheek. Magnolia tried to speak but there were no words. The word "Mama" was on the tip of her tongue.

Suddenly Magnolia began to feel her mother's salt and pepper hair, then her face, and her lips. She softly touched her as though she didn't want to hurt her. She moved closer and kissed her. Then her lips touched her mother's lips again.

Mrs. Walker giggled as the wetness covered her mouth and face. She placed both of her hands on the sides of Magnolia's face and stared into her eyes. "My Magnolia," she whispered. "My baby."

Magnolia had known this woman for years. She grew close to her and loved her in a very special way. She had always wished Mrs. Walker to be her birth mother.

Magnolia leaned her head forward onto Mrs. Walker's face and cried, "I finally found that place in my heart that I've been searching for." She chuckled. "I found my mother."

"Yes, you've found me. I was always watching over you, child," Mrs. Walker said glancing at Carl. "We knew about your problems and—"

She paused. "We didn't want to cause you any more pain." She sort of giggled and whispered, "We figured, at least we found her. At least we're in her life. Let's just love and support her."

"Thank you," Magnolia said. "Thank you for being there."

Magnolia looked at Anthony and said, "I probably could not have handled this twenty years ago. My pain was so strong." She stared at the floor, then kicked her foot forward, lagging for a moment. "But, I know now and that's quite all right."

Mrs. Walker and Carl beamed. "It sure is," Carl said in a hushed tone.

Then Mrs. Walker walked over to Rose and grabbed hold of

her hand. She firmly held it and then lifted it to her cheek, sliding it across the side of her face, all the while kissing it. Rose cried.

Looking around, Mrs. Walker softly said, "I missed you all." Rose secured Mrs. Walker's hand, holding it tight. Tears suddenly rushed down Mrs. Walker's face.

"I missed you too," Rose moaned.

Still holding Rose's hand, she said, "I never forgot about you."

Magnolia and Hyacinth came closer to them.

"I never lost hope," she said, crying. "I loved you the day you were all born and I love you the same now."

Mrs. Walker extended her arms to her daughters and they all took shelter in her love and warmth. She held them, compressing them like sardines. *I'm never gonna let them go. Not this time.*

"Mama," they all cried. "Oh . . . Mama."

Slowly Carl walked up behind Magnolia and began to caress her shoulders, rubbing down all the pain. She leaned her head back on his chest and he wrapped his arms around her waist. She held him for life.

"I love you," she cried.

Anthony glanced up and for the first time he was not jealous—he was at ease. His wife finally had family to love.

"I love you with all my heart," Carl said.

After saying that he glanced at Rose, who watched him with such sadness in her eyes. It was Carl who, at fourteen years old, said he would never leave her. *Never,* she thought.

He released Magnolia and approached Rose. Mrs. Walker knew they needed time alone, so she took Hyacinth and Magnolia by the hand and slowly guided them back to the house.

Carl and Rose stood short of trembling to death and were both in tears. His hands dropped in such a way that it appeared he was surrendering—resigning to fault and shame.

"I don't know what to say," he said. He shrugged and then turned away, embarrassed.

Then he turned to her again. "I am sorry, Rose. I never meant to hurt you," he cried. "I didn't know she was going to take you away from me. Honestly, I didn't know."

Rose looked at him, carefully examining his face and body. She'd avoided looking at him in depth when she arrived because she had been so bitter. "I know you didn't."

Before she could continue, he grabbed her and hugged her. "I always loved you, Rose. I never stopped."

"I believe you," she said, crying on his shoulders. "I'm not mad anymore. I just want my family back. I want to be happy again."

Holding onto him, she mumbled, "I . . . I . . . never knew your name was Carl."

He giggled. "It's my middle name."

"I know that," she whispered. "I mean, I didn't know back then that your middle name was Carl."

"That's because everyone called me Junior or Solomon."

"That I remember," she laughed.

He yanked a handkerchief out of his pocket and carefully wiped away her tears. She held both of his muscular arms and stared into his eyes. She smiled, glanced at his face again, and gave him a peck on the lips.

"You don't know how much I've longed to do that again," she said. Then she released him and extended her arms wide. "I love you this much!" she said laughing.

He beamed with complete satisfaction—the satisfaction of being free. They were both free—free to live life without bitterness; free to live life without blame; and free to love all people again. Free to forgive.

Rose said, "Is it okay if I call you Junior?"

Carl smiled. "That's my name."

* * *

Walking back toward the house, Magnolia said, "I'm so used to calling you Mrs. Walker."

She laughed.

Magnolia faced Mrs. Walker. "And is it okay if I call you Mama?"

Mrs. Walker quietly laughed. "Yes, Mama sounds good, child.

Real good."

The rest of the gang anxiously waited for them to come back into the house. Sam and Patricia were especially nervous. After all, they were partly responsible for the family's breakup. They didn't know how they would ever repay Hyacinth and her family, but they knew they would make amends soon.

Lily and Nathaniel were outside the door. When Magnolia moved ahead, Lily cried and hugged her. "Magnolia, my sweet baby sister."

Magnolia sobbed. "Lily," she whispered.

Nathaniel stepped forward. "Hey, you," he said. "Come over here and give me a hug."

She hugged him. Then Hyacinth came closer. Lily fell to the floor when she took one look at her. Nathaniel and Gregory came to her rescue. She stared at her hard. It had been thirty-eight years since she last saw all of them together—teaching them spelling and arithmetic.

She placed her arms around her. They stood in that position for a few moments. "My girls are—" she cried. "I told Solomon not to let you go," she said. "I told him that it didn't seem right."

Nathaniel came up and slowly pried her arms away from her. "Lily, they are home now. They're not going away again. I promise."

"You promise," she sobbed.

"I promise."

She willingly let go of Hyacinth, feeling assured. Nathaniel nodded and then hugged and kissed Hyacinth.

Lawrence held the door open. One by one, they walked inside. When Hyacinth passed him, he gave his sister a big hug and kissed her on the cheek.

Linda, Billie, and Brenda were unsure of what to say. But then Linda shook her head as Magnolia approached her and laughed. "Yep, Bernard Brooks will write this book!"

Billie and Brenda laughed.

"Come here," Linda said, hugging Magnolia. "I love you."

"I love you too," Magnolia said.

Billie hugged her and so did Brenda.

"My baby sister," Brenda said.

Pointing her finger at Brenda, Magnolia said, "I knew there was something peculiar about you and your husband." She laughed. "Just couldn't figure it out."

Brenda kissed her. "Now you know, huh?"

They laughed again.

When Carl entered the house, he stared at Brenda. She was relieved and happy that he finally had found peace with himself. For years she too had lived with the heartache. At times the pressure and constant worrying had nearly destroyed their marriage—pushing her to drink and smoke heavily. But they held on for love. They held on for hope. She promised him she would stick by him through it all and she had.

"Come here, baby," she whispered.

"I love you," he said. "I know . . . I haven't been . . ."

She pressed her fingers against his lips, and said, "The bad is behind us. It's over. Let's enjoy life again."

"You bet!" he said as he held her in his arms.

Magnolia turned toward Anthony. "Anthony, you better call Zoe and tell her everything. She's going to be absolutely shocked."

"Shocked—that's an understatement," Gregory said. "I called her while you all were outside."

"What did she say?" Anthony said.

"Well, she paused for about a five minutes and then screamed, Oh, my heavens!"

Anthony laughed. "Really?"

"I'm not kidding you," Gregory said as he turned toward Hyacinth. "She wants to do a special soon."

Magnolia glanced up. "That will be great," she said, smiling.

Gregory's tone lowered. "She thought Christmas time would be nice." He paused and stared at everyone, who remained silent. "She thought it would be perfect."

Magnolia, Hyacinth, and Rose beamed. "Perfect," they softly said.

CHAPTER 58

Christmas Day . . .

After the film crew wrapped up, Zoe walked over to Mrs. Walker and said, "I've heard so many good things about you, Mrs. Walker."

Mrs. Walker smiled. "Why, thank you, dear."

"You know, this has got to be the most spectacular . . . the most intriguing . . ."

Zoe placed her hand to her chest. "Oh, the most satisfying show I have ever produced."

Mrs. Walker smiled again. "I'm so glad you were here to help." Then she looked at Carl, blinked her eyes and smiled.

Zoe glanced around the room. "I wish you all good luck. God bless you."

"Thank you," they said with joy.

"Please, stay for dinner," Anthony said. Come on, you guys don't have to rush back."

Smelling the tantalizing food in the kitchen, the crew looked around at each other. "No . . . we . . . don't."

Zoe smiled. "All right," she said. "We'll stay."

"Girl, sit down and enjoy, because you about to eat some serious . . . down home . . . good ol' soul food," said Linda. "Carl's cooking in the house!"

They all laughed except for Anthony. *When will she ever learn,* he thought.

At the dining table, Anthony and Magnolia giggled like children. Everyone wanted to know what was up, especially Linda and Billie.

Suddenly Carl and Gregory burst through the dining room door. Carl held a huge, beautifully decorated chocolate birthday cake and Gregory held a container of cherry vanilla ice cream. They placed the incredible dessert spread on the table.

Magnolia, Hyacinth, and Rose were shocked. Hyacinth put her hand to her mouth. "This is so nice."

Gregory grinned.

"Cherry vanilla ice cream!" Rose screamed. "You guys shouldn't have, Carl . . . Jun—"

"Either is fine," Carl said.

"Why not?" said Magnolia. "After all, it's our birthday!"

"That's right," said Mrs. Johnson.

Hyacinth stood. "Yeah, and it's been thirty-eight years since we've—"

She glanced over to Mrs. Walker and Patricia, who were sitting together and amicably chatting. When they looked up, she began to cry. "Since . . . we've celebrated it together."

Gregory patted her back.

"It sure has," said Billie.

Solomon laughed and dabbed his finger into the smooth, sweet-tasting frosting. "Umm-hmm . . . this is good," he said licking his finger.

Rose tapped his buttock. "Solomon."

"But . . ."

"It's okay, dear," said Mrs. Walker. "Let him have some if he wants."

Rose smiled.

Later Magnolia, Hyacinth, and Rose stood at the head of the table in front of the cake as everyone sang happy birthday. They held each other by the waist side, lowered their heads, and suddenly blew out all forty-two candles except for two.

Mrs. Walker got up and walked over to them. "Let's all blow out these," she said. "If it's okay with you."

"That's a great idea," Magnolia said.

"Yeah, let's do this," said Rose.

Mrs. Walker held Solomon next to her and pointed her finger at the two candles. "You see here," she said to him. "These two candles here stand for love and hope."

Solomon smiled and gazed into Mrs. Walker's eyes. "Grandma," he said.

Her hands flew to her bosom at the sound of the word.

"Because we love each other, right?" he said. "And because we . . ."

He was at a loss.

Then Carl interrupted: "Because . . . we always had faith."

"Yes, that's it," said Mrs. Walker.

Everyone nodded and smiled, then gathered around the women.

"On the count of three," Carl said.

Solomon shouted from the top of his lungs with the rest of the gang, "One . . . two . . . three!"

And they blew out the last two candles.

Magnolia sighed. *That was beautiful,* she thought. *Mother, I wish you were here to see this.*

Carl and Brenda sliced and served the cake. As everyone sat eating, Anthony and Magnolia said, "We would like to make an announcement."

Linda's eyes crossed over to Billie, who looked at Brenda, who then looked at Carl.

"Everyone," Anthony said. "Magnolia and I are expecting."

"What?" Brenda and Billie shouted.

"Yes—I'm pregnant," Magnolia said proudly.

Linda jumped up and hugged her. "I'm so happy for the two of you!"

"When is your due date?" said May-Lynne.

Gently feeling her belly, Magnolia said, "June."

For the first time they all sat around the dining table as one big happy family, enjoying each other's company. They celebrated a special birthday—the birth of triplets who were born forty-two years ago to a family that wanted and loved them.

Sam rose and strolled over to the head of the table holding a glass of wine. "Let's toast to the expectant parents."

"Hold on," Linda said. She quickly ran into the kitchen and came out holding a glass of milk. She handed it to Magnolia. Everyone raised their glasses and toasted. "To Anthony and Magnolia!" they cheered.

"I . . . I . . . have . . . something to say," Sam mumbled.

"Dad . . . don't," Lawrence begged.

Sam ignored him and waved his hand. "But I have to." He took a deep breath and stared at the chandelier. Then he looked at Mrs. Walker and Carl. Soon his eyes met those of Magnolia, Hyacinth, and Rose.

"Patricia and I . . ." He inhaled and then exhaled. "Patricia and I did a terrible thing thirty-eight years ago," he said trembling. "There's no need to go into details because we all know what happened."

He nervously eyed Mrs. Walker again. "Ivory, I know words cannot express our regret. I can only imagine what you have gone through all of these years."

He swallowed some wine. "A day hasn't gone by that I didn't think about you and the rest of your children."

Lily and Nathaniel stared at each other. They were looking forward to more of this overdue speech.

"My wife and I are truly sorry," Sam said. "I can't ask for your forgiveness—that would be letting us off too easily." He suddenly broke down in tears.

"I forgive you, Sam," Mrs. Walker softly said. She turned toward Patricia. "And, I forgive you too, Patricia."

Sam looked at her in utter surprise.

"If God can forgive you, so can I," she said.

Sam sobbed like a baby. He looked at Carl and mumbled, "She's sorry, Solomon."

Puzzled, Solomon looked up and whispered to his mother,

"Sorry for what?"

Rose shrugged.

Sam slightly chuckled at Solomon's comment. "Carl, Miss Smith, my sister, Henrietta, wanted me to tell you . . ."

Carl jerked forward at the mention of that name. He was all ears. "She's sorry for the pain she caused you and your family."

Carl sat still while Brenda consoled him. He thought about that dreadful day he went to get his sisters. The last day he ever laid eyes on Miss. Smith. He wanted to inquire about her but he didn't have the strength. "Sam, when you see her again . . ."

Sam wiped his tear-stained eyes and looked up.

"Tell her that I too forgive her. I hold no grudges. Not anymore," Carl said, shaking his head.

He sighed heavily. "You tell her . . . that I'm not anxious anymore. No . . . sir. I'm not anxious for what is to come."

He grinned and everyone looked at each other, "Tell her . . . that I do thank God for today because tomorrow is never certain. And that is why it's so important to appreciate life and to make every moment count."

He paused and looked at his mother and siblings. "You know . . . a family that prays together stays together."

He placed his hand to his chest. "Even if we're apart, we'll always be together up here." He began to cry.

"That's right," said Mrs. Walker.

"Yes, a family that prays together stays together," whispered Nathaniel.

Sam smiled.

A while later Carl slipped away while everyone munched on the delicious cake and ice cream. He walked outside, sat down on the rocking chair, and stared up. He looked past the brilliant stars and could see his paradise. His troubles were now over. God had guided him in the right direction.

He sat on the bench and took in the crisp wintry air, truly appreciating Christmas time.

Rose was hiding behind a bare bush tree. He quickly glanced up when he heard a rattling sound. Once he saw her, he smiled and extended his hand for her to sit. She sat down beside him and held his hand. They swayed back and forth together in the rocking chair—just like old times.

The years of separation, of not knowing, of wondering, of reasoning, ended that Christmas day. Suddenly he could hear the words of his father clearly: *God will always come through for you, Junior. He always does.*

Carl looked at Rose and hugged her. Then he stared back at the stars again and whispered, "Yes, He truly does."

Printed in the United States
1178700002B/18-36